CAT CRIMES
THROUGH TIME

CAT CRIMES
THROUGH TIME

Edited by
ED GORMAN,
MARTIN H. GREENBERG,
and LARRY SEGRIFF

CARROLL & GRAF PUBLISHERS, INC.
NEW YORK

Copyright © 1999 by Tekno-Books, Ed Gorman, Martin H. Greenberg, and Larry Segriff

First Carroll & Graf edition 1999

Carroll & Graf Publishers, Inc.
19 West 21st Street
New York, NY 10010

Library of Congress Cataloging-in-Publication Data is available

ISBN 0-7867-0555-8

CONTENTS

Introduction   *xi*

Tinkler Tam and the Body Snatchers •
    Elizabeth Ann Scarborough   1

What the Cat Dragged In • *Janet Dawson*   13

Stitches in Time • *Debbie De Louise*   29

The Cat and the Kinetophone • *Jon L. Breen*   42

Tinseltown Follies of 1948 • *Bill Crider*   56

The Death Cat of Hester Street • *Carol Gorman*   66

St. Margaret's Kitten • *Doug Allyn*   83

Slightly Guilty • *Morris Hershman*   110

Of Persephone, Poe, and the Whisperer •
    Tom Piccirilli   120

A Warm Nest • *Shirley Kennett*   133

Fur Bearing • *Brett Hudgins*   148

A Roman of No Importance • *Elizabeth Foxwell*   158

Connie • *Bentley Little*   172

Living the Lie • *Marc Bilgrey*   189

Mail-Order Annie • *Gary A. Braunbeck*   197

Carry's Cat • *Barbara Collins*   225

Byron • *Jack Albert*   241

Cloud Stalking Mice • *Bruce Holland Rogers*   249

Cat O'Nine Lives • *Jan Grape*   268

Cat on an Old School Roof • *Peter Crowther*   288

The Mummy Case • *Carole Nelson Douglas*   319

AUTHOR NOTES

Jack Albert's story "Byron" takes place during the 1958 civil war in Lebanon, and is about the adventures of a mysterious Englishwoman and her desperate search for her missing husband. Whether using a historical backdrop, or a more recognizable urban setting, Jack Albert's touch is always flawless.

Doug Allyn is an accomplished author whose short fiction regularly graces "year's best" collections. His work has appeared in *Once Upon a Crime* and *The Year's 25 Finest Crime and Mystery Stories*, volumes three and four. His latest novel is *A Dance in Deep Water*. He lives in Montrose, Michigan.

Marc Bilgrey has written for televison, magazines, and comedians. His short stories have appeared in numerous anthologies including *Phantoms of the Night* and *First Contact*.

Gary A. Braunbeck writes poetically, dark suspense and horror fiction, rich in detail and scope. Recent stories have appeared in *Robert Bloch's Psychos*, *Once Upon a Crime*, and *The Conspiracy Files*. His occasional foray into the mystery genre is no less accomplished, having appeared in anthologies such as *Danger in D.C.* and *Cat Crimes Takes a Vacation*. His recent short story collection, *Things Left Behind*, received critical acclaim. He lives in Columbus, Ohio.

Jon L. Breen has written six mystery novels; most recently *Hot Air*, and over seventy short stories; contributes review columns to *Ellery Queen's Mystery Magazine* and *The Armchair Detective*; was shortlisted for the Dagger awards for his novel *Touch of the Past*; and has won two Edgars, two Anthonys, a Macavity, and an American Mystery Award for his critical writings.

Barbara Collins has made appearances in numerous anthologies, including *Feline and Famous*, *The Year's 25 Finest Crime and Mystery Stories*, and *Celebrity Vampires*. She lives in Muscatine, Iowa, with her husband, author Max Allan Collins, and their son, Nathan.

Bill Crider won the Anthony award for his first novel in the "Sheriff Dan Rhodes" series. His first novel in the "Truman Smith" series was nominated for a Shamus award, and a third series features college English professor Carl Burns. His short stories have appeared in numerous anthologies, including past *Cat Crimes II* and *III*, *Celebrity Vampires*, and *Werewolves*.

Peter Crowther is the editor or co-editor of nine anthologies and the co-author (with James Lovegrove) of the novel *Escardy Gap*. Since the early 1990s, he has sold some seventy short stories and poems to a wide variety of magazines and anthologies on both sides of the Atlantic. He has also recently added two chapbooks, *Forest Plains* and *Fugue on a G-String*, to his credits. His review columns and critical essays on the fields of fantasy, horror, and science fiction appear regularly in *Interzone* and the *Hellnotes* internet magazine. He was appointed to the Board of Trustees of the Horror Writer's Association. He lives in Harrogate, England, with his wife and two sons.

Janet Dawson's first novel, featuring Oakland California sleuth Jeri Howard, entitled *Kindred Crimes*, won the St. Martin's Press Private Eye of America First Private Eye Novel Contest and was nominated for the Anthony, Shamus, and Macavity awards. She has since written seven more books in the series, the latest being *Where the Bodies Are Buried*. Her short fiction appears in *Once Upon a Crime* and *First Ladies*. She lives in Alameda, California.

Debbie De Louise is a reference librarian at the Hicksville Public Library on Long Island. She is a member of the Cat Writer's Association and writes nonfiction articles for *Cats* magazine. This is her first published fiction. She is currently working on a mystery novel featuring cats and time travel. She and her husband Anthony live in Hicksville, New York, with their two pampered felines, Floppy and Holly.

Carole Nelson Douglas is the author of over thirty novels, covering such diverse genres as mainstream, historical, mystery and science fiction. Her rise in the mystery field began with her quartet of historical mysteries featuring Irene Adler, the female counterpoint to Sherlock Holmes, and the only character to outwit him. Recently, her novel series involving the detective Midnight Louie has been occupying her time, but not enough to prevent another cat detective, perhaps a distant relative, from making an appearance here.

Elizabeth Foxwell is the editor in chief of *The Armchair Detective* and co-editor of the *Malice Domestic* and *Murder, They Wrote* anthology series. The resourceful "invalid" Bunbury and imperturbable Slade made their debut in an earlier story, "The Importance of Being Useless."

Carol Gorman is the author of many books for young readers, including *Chelsey and the Green-Haired Kid*, an ALA recommended Book for the Reluctant Reader and winner of the Ethical Culture Book Award; *Jennifer the Jerk Is Missing, Die for Me*, an IRA/CBC Children's Choice winner. Forthcoming books include *Lizard Flanagan, Supermodel??*, and *Dork and Disguise*. She lives in Iowa with her husband, author Ed Gorman.

Jan Grape has sixteen short stories in anthologies ranging from *Deadly Allies 1* and *2, Lethal Ladies 1* and *2, Feline and Famous, Cat Crimes Takes a Vacation*, to the recently released *Vengeance Is Hers*. Her non-fiction articles are in *The Mystery Writers Sourcebook, The Fine Art of Murder*, and *How to Write a Private Eye Novel*. A regular columnist for *Mystery Scene* magazine, she also writes for the British publication *A Shot in the Dark*. She edits the Private Eye Writers of America newsletter, as well as being the vice president of that organization. Along with her husband, she owns the Mysteries & More bookstore in Austin, Texas.

Morris Hershman lives in New York City and has published a wide variety of fiction in several genres. Other work by him appears in *Murder Most Irish, Santa Clues*, and *Crimes of Passion*.

Brett Hudgins is a native of British Columbia and says his first attempt at a cat crime story was inspired by his own cat Cleopatra. "Fur Bearing," his second sale, draws on a historical interest which began in high school social studies. He enjoys writing in several genres and is currently working on his fourth novel while trying to sell his first.

Shirley Kennett is the author of the P.J. Gray novels, which bring the latest computer technology to crime solving. She has an innate talent for combining the high-tech with the down-to-earth. "A Warm Nest" is her first published short story. She lives in St. Louis, Missouri, with her husband and son. They are outnumbered by their cats, two to one.

Bentley Little won the Stoker award for best first novel in 1991 for *The Mailman*. Expert at revealing the terror that lurks in small towns, his other novels include *The Summoning*, *Dominion*, and *The Store*. His short fiction has appeared in *Borderlands*, *Cemetery Dance*, and *The Horror Show*. He lives in Fullerton, California.

Tom Piccirilli is the author of *Dark Father*, *Hexes*, *Shards*, and *The Dead Past*. He is the assistant editor of *Pirate Writings* magazine and reviews books for *Mystery Scene* and *Mystery News*. His short fiction has sold to *Hot Blood 6* and *7*, *100 Wicked Little Witches*, *365 Scary Stories*, *Deathrealm*, *Hardboiled*, *Terminal Fright*, and others. A collection of five intertwined stories entitled *Pentacle* was recently published by Pirate Writings Press. All of the stories therein have made the Honorable Mention list of Datlow and Windling's *Year's Best Fantasy and Horror*.

Bruce Holland Rogers is not a stranger to anthologies, having appeared in *Feline and Famous* and *Cat Crimes Takes a Vacation*. When he is not plotting feline felonies, he's writing excellent fantasy stories for such collections as *Enchanted Forests*, *The Fortune Teller*, and *Monster Brigade 3000*. Winner of the Nebula award for best short science fiction story, his fiction is at once evocative and unforgettable.

Elizabeth Ann Scarborough won a Nebula award in 1989 for her novel *The Healer's War*, based on her experiences as an Army nurse in Vietnam. She has collaborated on four books with Anne McCaffrey, three novels and one anthology, *Space Opera*. Her most recent novel is *The Godmother's Web*, which uses Native American folklore as a backdrop. She lives in Washington with two cats, Trixie and Treat.

INTRODUCTION

Throughout history, cats have been venerated as living symbols of intelligence and wisdom, and were often raised to exalted positions in ancient cultures. If one were to ask the cats their opinion on this, they would probably say it was simply the most fitting thing to do, and wonder why it doesn't happen nearly so much nowadays. After all, they haven't changed for thousands of years, so why should anyone else?

Regardless, from the famous cats buried with their Egyptian pharaohs, to the kitten Edgar Allan Poe would set on his shoulder while writing, to Socks in the White House, felines have appeared in various roles throughout the ages. While most were usually content to remain behind the scenes, every so often one would step into the spotlight and take its place among the other famous animals of history.

In the following stories, we've collected cats from just about every historical period, from ancient Egypt to the Wild West to 1940s Hollywood. Of course, this being an anthology of cat mysteries, it wouldn't be complete without including an assortment of nefarious crimes for these furry detectives to solve. So sit back in your comfortable, modern-day recliner (after making sure your cat is also resting contentedly as well) and prepare to travel back into the past with *Cat Crimes Through Time*.

CAT CRIMES
THROUGH TIME

TINKLER TAM AND THE BODY SNATCHERS

Elizabeth Ann Scarborough

THE GINGER LADDIE known to his paramours, other ad-
mirers, and enemies as Tinkler Tam Chattan was a juggler by
trade. No one could flip a mouse in the air and catch it in his
mouth with such dexterity, and it was said he could nab three
birds on the wing in a single pounce. Of course, that wasn't
why Tam was called a juggler. Juggler was just a common Scots
way of saying the much grander and older term *"jongleur."* It
was originally confined to tossin' balls in the air and such. A
French word, which was fitting since Tam's real name (all tin-
klers had a called name and a real name so's not to give the
gorgios power over them by the calling of their real names)
was Jaques LeChat and he was of noble French ancestry. His
noble great great grandpere had been a *jongleur* too—not just a
tosser and catcher but an acrobat, poet comedian and musician
as well, whose antics had pleased the likes of French kings and
queens from way back. On his mither's side, Tam's people had
taken tae the road durin' the terrible times in the Middle Ages
when there were the witch hunts and, with them, the mass
murdering of all cats the stupid peasants took to be agents of
the devil. Only the quickest of wit and foot survived to follow
the life of the rover.

On Tam's fither's side, so his mither tauld him, though his

fither had lang since taken flight, his lineage came straight down from the favored chat *jongleur* of Queen Marie Antoinette. Queen MA, as his kind called her in cat cant, the gypsy cat's secret language, may have had her faults, like not realizing that people who didn't have bread wouldn't have any cake either, but that came from her abnormally sheltered upbringing and the fact that she could barely read. On the cat issue, she was rock solid. She loved cats and had a great collection of all sorts. His grandfather had been among her favorites, mum said, but he had declined to be shipped ahead to America when the others in the collection were sent and instead had taken to the road. He'd been watching from a rooftop when his former patroness lost her head, and it was said he was never quite right after that. But neither was he wrong enough to forget to squire several litters of kittens, hence, Jaques (Tam) LeChat (Chattan).

Even though he was so well bred and all, Tinkler Tam wasna one to gie himself airs, not a bit of it. He was common as the old shoe he had used as a bed when a mere kit, and he was a well-known figure to all sorts of Edinburgh folk. The kitchens of the pubs and restaurants were his favorite haunts, of course, and he was gey fond of cooks and chefs of all sorts, be they French or be they Scots or even Irish, like so many had come ower of late. But he also favored the students, many of whom were lonely for their craturs from the country, and for a bit of a purr and an ankle twine from himself could be counted on for a crumb or two or at least a kind word and a cuddle.

Homeless he might be but friendless he was not. Indeed, he considered the whole of Edinburgh his home, though never in his life would he think of himself as a settled cat. He was a cat about town, a supervisor of life, and knew beggars and nobles, lawyers and ladies of the night, doctors and dowried daughters of great families, soldiers, sailors and street urchins. He made his rounds as it pleased him, but made sure to put in an appearance at his best haunts at least two or three times a week, so's they wouldn't forget him, nor start givin' his bits to some other enterprising feline.

Natural enough then, for such a friendly cat about town, that he heard things, as a fellow will. Your flies on the wall, your wee mousies in their holes, well, all them was naethin' comparit tae Tinkler Tam when he chose tae play the cat in the corner. He'd be lyin' ever sae quiet, tail wrappit roond his wee pink nosie, but them tufty ginger ears would be prickit and pointy with listenin'. And fluffy as his tail was, it could nae keep him from peekin' ower it tae see who was talkin'. See, the thing was, if he listened close, he often heard things to his advantage. Like when deliveries was bein' made and what different ones who come in the pubs was havin' for their supper, that sort o' thing. He also listened for news that someone had grief—death or illness in the family or best of all, a Lost Love.

Tam was a great one for Lost Love. Like most males of his kind, he considered himself a great lover. And while perhaps he wisnae aware o' the finer romantic point of human courtship, he could feel a broken heart from three streets away and if there was a way to reach its owner and offer consolation—always providin', that is, that the brokenhearted individual could abide cats—why there he was, purrin' and rubbin' or simply sitting close up, offerin' of his warmth and the softness of his coat to be stroked, as if soothin' his fur might help the lovelorn to soothe away their ane misery.

He was very good with the young ones, was Tam, and knew whichuns were mean and that he should keep awa'. But mony of them were good enough folk, in frae the country and by theirsel's and the losin' of a lass was as if onybody who counted tae them at a' had turnt against them.

That was how it had been wi' the young medical student who was one o' Tam's latest patrons—a good hairted lad he was, the student, by the name of Cameron Cameron. Normally, Tam didna haud wi' the medical students. The infirmary where they studied smelt bad, o' chemicals that burnt Tam's nose and also of things ower deid for e'en a moggy tae fancy them. Things that cam' and went at night frae the doctor's classroom, brought in wheelbarrows by rough men and smellin' o' graveyard dirt. Weel, it wisnae the bodies theirsel's sae much as pu' Tam aff as the rough men who fetchit them. Sometimes, the bodies didnae smell a' that deid. They smelt o' fresh bluid and violent death. These were the bodies o' ither human bein's, and the students cut 'em up and lookit inside 'em and it was a fact that they used ony puir cratures that was handy tae study as weel. Even cats. Deid ones, true, but the human bodies were a' deid by the time they reached the infirmary. The doctors wouldna be sae picky where a cat was concerned.

But the students didnae live at the infirmary. They had lodgin's o' their ane and Cameron Cameron lived on Niddry's Wynd, near the infirmary, but no' sae near that Tam could smell the wicked place, but could tend tae Cameron Cameron's woes wi' a clear head and heart.

For Cameron Cameron, the puir sod, had the ill luck to fall for one Chantal la Chanteuse, late of Paris, France. Chanteuse wasna her real name and even a country lad like Cameron Cameron could see that she was brought up a lady, but she was a lady nae mair. She was a woman of aisy virtue and no fixed abode, and it was said of her that she was a French aristo whose family were a' deid, victims o' the guillotine. Had their heids cut off, like, for bein' richer than ither folk. Anely the darlin' dochter o' the family escapet, and the cruel captain o' the ship that brought her not anely took her passage money, but stole the family siller and jewels she carried in her clathes and then stole her woman's treasure as well, so that she arrived in Edinburgh broke in purse and spirit.

That was the story on the street and Tam had heard it often, as had Cameron Cameron, who like mony a tender-hairted laddie, didna look for a lass with as muckle wealth and lovin' family as had he himsel', but for some puir wounded bird he could tend. His tender hairt was why Cameron Cameron was sae set on bein' a doctor. His family had anely a little money and he had worked hard daein' extra wark for neighbors tae earn his chance tae medical school, and here he was. But books and studies didna satisfy the laddie, nor did carin' for sorry patients who cam' tae the infirmary. He needed tae care and cosset someone. The cats and dugs aroond toon benifited frae his needin' o' this for a while, and Cameron Cameron had been a favorite o' Tam's lang before the laddie lost his hairt. But when Cameron Cameron heard the sweet voice o' Chantal la Chanteuse singin' her wee sang and when he learned her tragical story—though no' frae her, as she never did tell it—maybe she tauld ane o' the ither girls an' they put it aboot—as soon as he saw her sweet heart-shaped face wi' its wan cheeks and its big broon een and the wee froon on its pretty curvit lips, nane wud suit him but hersel'. And she wouldna have him. Even when he saved his siller tae buy an hoor wi' her, nivver tae tak' advantage o' her, just tae talk like, she wouldna tak' his money. It was as if it were nae guid tae her.

Cameron Cameron had gone over and over it to Tam, how he had tried to force the money on her onyway, and she wouldna tak' it. How he had taken her gifts of food and she wouldna touch it till he left. "And she's no well, Tam. She grows aye thinner every day. I see it as she's shamed before me. I would marry her today if she'd bide wi' me, but instead she stays on the streets and soon she'll catch some awfy bad disease and die—or pass it on tae the mon she does accept. I know me parents wud care for her as I do." And on and on like that.

And whereas in the ordinary way o'things Tam woulda tauld him, "Move alang then, laddie. Find yersel' anither queen, ane canny enough tae care for a fine braw lad sich as yersel'," in the case of Chantal la Chanteuse he couldna think like that.

The truth was, see, that if his favorite lad tae beg a crumb from in a' the city was Cameron Cameron, his favorite lassie tae offer his comfort when she cried intae his saft gingery fur, as she did mony's the night, it was Chantal la Chanteuse. He himsel' brought her mice and birds, but she used them nae mair than she used the gifts o' Cameron Cameron. Truth was, she'd toss them aside and share Cameron's latest offerin' wi' Tam.

She did fair enough in the summertime but when winter cam', oh, but she was cauld and the winter cut through her raggedy dress and the rags she'd bound roond her bare feet.

Cameron Cameron took the blanket off his ane bed and foond her and lay it ower her in the doorway where she slept. Tam kenned this because he saw it aw' wi' his ane green een. But he saw too that ane o' the girls who didna like Chantal, Baubie the Beak, for her great nose, was watchin', and mockin', and when Cameron left, the poxy tart stole the blanket for hersel'. Tam hissed at her and would hae clawed her leg but he'd run afoul o' her before and she'd near kilt him, so he slunk awa' intae the shadows and then snuck after her tae see if he might find a way tae steal the blanket back again. He couldna though. Baubie the Beak had her a bed inside a proper building and the truth was, she didna need Cameron Cameron's blanket at all, she just didna want Chantal la Chanteuse tae have it.

The puir mite was freezin' and it was late and everythin' was closed. She didna move from her place in the door, even to warm hersel'. She was too cauld or too sad or too sick or maybe too afraid, Tam didnae ken. She kept her een closed as though she still slept but she petted him right enough. And the ony thing he could do that night was to lie doon beside her and gie her what little warmth he could. He figured she'd be deid by daylight.

Seems like he wisna the only body figured she'd die. An hoor passed, maybe twa, and two rough-lookin' men come oot o' the lodgin's where Baubie the Beak was.

Tam didnae like the look o' them at all and he scooted oot from beside Chantal and skittered roond the corner sae they wouldna spot him. He'd seen these anes before, wi' a wheelbarrow fu' o' graveyard prey between 'em, on their way doon tae the infirmary. And he'd heard 'em in his least favorite pub, where the grub was guid and the cook was kindly but the master was a hard, hard man and his clients e'en harder. Tam nivver stayed there lang, no' in sight onyway. This was less a pub than a den o' wolvesheads, murderin', thievin', angry men wha' drank harder and meaner than most and wisna a kind word or a bit o' charity tae a puir moggy in the lot o' 'em. The cook hersel' tauld Tam tae hide when men cam' in the kitchen. "Itherwise ye'll end up a spessymin for the medical students tae study," she tauld him. "Tha' means they'll cut ye op and they willna be careful aboot if ye're dead yet, me fine fellow."

These men was in a foul mood the night Tam saw them. "Wouldna pay up," one of them said. "Tauld us they already had a' the bits o' bone they needed. We warkit aw' the nicht diggin' on that grave, did we no', Bobby?"

"Aye, Davie, we did. 'Tis the ingratitude o' them tha' gits tae me . . ."

The landlord had merely grunted, "Aye, ingratitude gits tae us aw', lads, and like yersel's, I dinna care tae gie my services nor my goods wi'oot gratitude," and he'd rubbed his thumb and forefingers together for money.

"I tauld ye, he wouldna pay us," Bobby said.

There was the sound of glass smashing. "Then ye'd best gae find him somethin' fresher if ye want a drap o' wha's mine to sell. Awa' wi' ye."

Since that time, the men looked to have grown prosperous, though no more kindly.

Bobby's belly, which aince curved in, now curved oot. Davie sported a new hat and boots and wore gloves with nae hauls in the fingers.

"Lookit her, ain't she a picture?" Bobby asked, lookin' doon at Chantal.

"Aye. Puir wee lassie. We seen when Baubie took awa' the blanket that fellow gie ye, dearie. Ye maun be terrible cauld. We coom tae tak' ye inside oor new lodgin' hoose wha' Bobby an' me bought. Ye can warm up there, inside, as lang as ye like."

His words were mockin' though, and carried in them nae goodness at aw'. Chantal struggled a wee bit between them but the puir thing was aw' in frae the cauld and the hopelessness she'd brung wi' her frae France. She hadnae sung in a lang time, and noo anely coughed and that she began tae do as she nearly hung betwixt the twa great oafs, who pretended tae escort her up inta the close where their place was.

Straightway Tam was at the windas, first ane and then the ither, tryin' tae see wha' they was doin'. And there was Baubie the Beak, gi'en orders like a queen. "Thraw her doon the cellar steps wi' the rest o' the corpses," Baubie says. "Tak' anither ane doon tae the doctors t'nicht and leave her there for the cauld tae finish."

"She cudda dan' that ootside," Davie complained.

"The she'd hae been onybody's, and she's mine. Her bonnie wee face and daft sang she sings cost me a pretty penny in wark lost and noo she'll mak' it up tae me."

A hateful wooman, Baubie the Beak.

The men took her doon the stairs and when they cam' back up again, they had some puir body slung between 'em, which they threw inta a barrow beside the door. Tam jumped doon jist in time tae no' be seen by 'em as they wheeled awa' doon the lane, but Baubie, she cam' oot wi' a saucer o' milk. "Here, kitty kitty," she ca'ed, sweet as onythin'. "Here, pussy, come gie some nice milk."

Weel, he'd nae mair gae tae that auld slag than he'd turn inta a dug, so he sat on his haunches, back in the shaddas, and stared at her, his green een tryin' their best tae catch her on fire.

She threw the milk onta the cobbles and snarled, "Aye, I see ye there, ye mangy sly thing. An' I'll catch ye for the doctors tae cut aboot an' hae mittens mad' o' yer fur, ye see if I don't."

Noo, it was bad enough, her tryin' tae freeze ane o' Tinkler Tam's friends and patrons tae death, no' tae mention the love o' Cameron Cameron's life. But noo she were gettin' pairsonal like, and it were more than a body cud bear.

Tam took off doon the wynd, shot across the Canongate and doon the back lane, past the Lawnmarket and the Grassmarket and doon Niddry's Lane tae the students' quarters.

Not that he had any idea what he was going tae do exactly, aince he got there. He cud howl and scratch and carry on until Cameron Cameron saw him, but then what? Have the man tae follow him ower tae where the body snatchers was makin' their delivery? And wha' would that prove onyway? This was no' Chantal's body they was bringin.' And he had nae wish tae wait until it would be Chantal in the barrow for then she'd be past savin' and what would be the point?

When he cam' tae Cameron Cameron's rooms, however, it was much aisier than he would hae guessed tae rouse the man. Puir Cameron Cameron hae'in' gie awa' his anely blanket tae his freezin' cauld true love was now freezin' cauld himsel', as he couldna afford the coal for the fire on a regular basis. He was sittin' up in a chair freezin' his arse off, despite the lateness of the hoor. He heard Tam's scritchin's right awa' and cam' oot o' the hoose like a shot.

Furthermore, and this was a great help tae Tam, the man was nae sae thick as most of mankind. Since Tam had never cam' tae call at sich a late hoor before, Cameron Cameron said immediately, "Wha's the matter then, Tam? Is it Chantal? Has she ta'en a turn for the worse?"

But he said it while he was movin', like.

Tam didna bother wi' gae'in tae the infirmary where the body snatchers was. He had a time keepin' up wi' young Cameron as it was, stridin' up the hill tae where Chantal usually plied her trade.

The puir boy looked confused when he didna see Chantal, but Tam, by layin' claws tae pant-leg, led him ower tae Baubie the Beak's place and scratched at the door aince, tae gie him the idea.

As luck would hae it, aboot then the twa laddies wi' the wheelbarrow between them cam' toolin' doon the lane again, their barrow empty noo.

Back inside, Baubie had a lamp lit for them. Cameron sat ootside the winda wi' Tam and listened while she tauld them that the next day they could tak' Chantal, who'd be frozen tae death by then.

Cameron could hae gan chargin' in there, but he wisnae thick, as Tam had noted before. He took himsel' off tae the polis and returned with twa constables.

Baubie, when she answered the door, you'd think she'd been woke up frae a guid nicht's sleep. She was rubbin' her een an' yawnin' and aw' that.

The constables looked hard at Cameron Cameron, but as soon as Baubie opened the door, in streaked Tam and began flyin' at the cellar door.

"What hae ye got in yer basement, Baubie?" Cameron Cameron asked her.

"Nane o' yer business. A deid cat if ye don't tak' him awa'," she said, trying to catch Tam, who somersaulted over her head to land back by the door again. He was yowlin' his head off for aw' he was worth, too, and before you know it, somebody else was yowlin' too—poor Chantal from doon below started yellin', all hoarse, and coughin', and yellin' again tae let her oot o' there.

Cameron and the constables did, and Baubie and her buddies went off tae gaol. Chantal had to go to the infirmary.

It waren't as if Tam were gie'in' proper credit for his wark that nicht. He didnae see Chantal on the streets onymair at all. While she was in the infirmary, she watched Cameron Cameron at wark and fell in loo' wi' him as the daft cow shoulhae done tae begin wi' and saved them aw' the trouble. And she foond she was a dab hand at nursin' the sick hersel'. Cameron Cameron it was that tauld Tam this, while gie'in him a pettin' that was aw' too rare these days, wi' Cameron spendin' sae much mair time at the infirmary.

"I dinna ken wha' we'd hae done wi'oot yer help, Tam," Cameron said. "Well, I do, and that is that Chantal would be deid noo and I would hae seen her again on the dissection table."

That evenin' it was snowin' and Tam sat inside Cameron's winda sill. Cameron's brother had brought a nice salmon tae him frae the country, and Cameron was sharin' it wi' Tam, which was as big a thank you as a simple *jongleur* cat could handle.

"When Chantal and I are married, we plan tae gae back tae the country. Would you fancy bein' a farm cat, Tam?"

But Tam fancied nae sich of a thing, for if he went tae the country, then who would look after the toon folk and tak' care o' the mice an' rats, who would listen tae folk's problems and offer his fur tae be stroked?

He gave Cameron Cameron a last long rub and a throaty purr and accepted aye, anither bit o' fish, and then he was doon frae the sill and up the lane, ready tae mak' the roond o' the pub kitchens and listen for sad news where he might be able tae help oot, and gain a bit o' a handout in the bargain.

It wisna verra mony days until he was lyin' quiet on the kitchen floor o' his favorite pub and he heard a gentleman say tae anither, "There'll be a hangin' tamarra. Seems a couple o' fellas wanted tae sell bodies tae the doctors, but wisnae findin' fresh, so they killed folk tae sell. Unfortunate for them that ane o' the folk they tried tae kill was a lassie fancied by ane o' the medical students."

"And they're hangin' 'em tamarra, ye say?"

"Aye. There should be a rare crowd for that, or I miss my guess."

Tam didnae let on that he kent aught aboot it, o' course. He simply lay there on the hearth and kneaded his paws in and oot and purred and thought o' the possibilities a hangin' crowd might present tae an enterprisin' cat about town.

Pardon the heavy dialect please but I've been reading a lot of folk stories from the Scottish Travelling people, who tell stories of the "Burkers," or body snatchers, known by that name because of the most famous, Burke and Hare. Hence the Traveller cat who does not roam the countryside but makes the entire city his territory.

WHAT THE CAT DRAGGED IN

Janet Dawson

THE TIGER-STRIPED cat appeared at the edge of the clearing one afternoon while Hattie Ballew was chopping wood. Hattie's brothers, Ned and Tom, had gone hunting, for the same reason Hattie labored at the wood pile. They needed plenty of fuel and game stored before autumn gave way to winter. Snow had already fallen in the upper elevations of the Sierra Nevada. Days were shorter, and the nights had turned chilly.

Perhaps that was why the cat showed up, seeking more comfortable quarters. To be sure, she looked scrawny, her ribs showing under the brown and black fur. She meowed, beseeching Hattie for something to eat.

The need for a cat came on Hattie, as sharp as the big ax she'd been hefting. It would be nice, she told herself, to have something soft and warm to doze in her lap in the evening.

Hattie set down the ax and went inside the cabin. She scraped the leavings from the pan of stew they'd had at midday into a chipped crockery bowl and carried it back outside. The cat waited at the edge of the clearing. Hattie set the bowl down on the ground, then backed off and watched. The cat didn't hesitate. Hunger propelled her toward the bowl, where she consumed every scrap. Then she sat back, pink tongue darting as she licked the residue from the fur around her mouth. The expectant look in her wide green eyes, followed by another meow, told Hattie the cat was waiting for more.

"Got no more," Hattie told the cat. "Not now, anyhow. But you stick with me, Little Bit. Maybe we'll both strike it rich."

Little Bit wasn't so little anymore. With the onset of winter and regular eating, her coat became thick and full, the sleek brown showing only her black stripes, not her ribs. She slept with Hattie on the crude rawhide bed with its mattress stuffed with straw, both of them curled into tight balls against the winter cold that seeped in through the cabin's log walls. During the days, Hattie and her brothers worked their claim. Ned and Tom used pickax and shovel to loosen the earth along the creek's banks, while Hattie shoveled the dirt and gravel into the rocker and poured water over it, using the apparatus to sift and search for the glittering bits of gold.

While the Ballews worked, Little Bit sunned herself on a flat stone near the rocker. Or she'd go off into the woods to stalk small animals and birds. Sometimes, when she caught something, the cat would haul it back to the cabin to display her trophy.

"Look what the cat dragged in now!" Hattie cried many an evening as she was greeted by a half-eaten jay or the fluffy tail of a squirrel.

Little Bit was certainly one for dragging things all over creation, and more often than not it was out of the cabin as well as in. Once, Hattie saw the cat trotting into the woods carrying an apple core that Ned had tossed away. Another time it was one of Tom's thick woolen socks, which Hattie retrieved before the cat disappeared into the woods. Hattie figured Little Bit had a place out in the woods where she hid the things she had taken.

"If we're not careful, she'll thieve our gold," Hattie told her brothers, so the Ballews took care to hide away their bags of dust and nuggets, lest the cat find one and drag it to Kingdom Come, spilling out the result of all their labors.

They hadn't struck it rich yet, not like some of the others working the Mother Lode. But they weren't busted either. They'd found plenty of color in the stream running through their claim, enough to keep them, and Little Bit, in food, enough to send some home to the folks, enough to keep their hopes alive.

The creek was called Cibola, just like the town that had sprung up on its banks, in a sloping valley between the Mokelumne and Calaveras Rivers. If you could call that rough mining camp a town. It sure didn't look like the towns Hattie was used to back in Missouri. Cibola had been thrown together from tents and lumber in the spring of 1849, when the world, lured by the seductive promise of gold, rushed into California.

Early in 1848, a man named James Marshall found gold at Sutter's Mill on the American River. Gold fever spread up and down California and into Northern Mexico. It wasn't until later that year that the news filtered back east. In August there was a story in a St. Louis newspaper, and that folded piece of newsprint came back to the Ballew farm in the back pocket of Pa's britches.

"Well, I'm going to California," Hattie declared when she'd read the story. "Get me a pile of gold and live like a queen."

"I never heard the like," Ma said with a snort, as she dished up bowls of stew and handed them around the table. "You're not going to California."

"Yes, I am. What do you mean, you never heard the like?" Hattie folded her arms across her chest and squared her jaw. "Why, the Ballews have always been fiddlefooted, and the MacNeills too." She turned to her father. "Wasn't it you who walked all the way from Virginia to Kentucky, through the Cumberland Gap?"

"That's a fact." Pa nodded, sucking on his pipe.

Now Hattie looked at her mother. "And wasn't it your

grandparents who came across the ocean a hundred years ago, without any idea of what might lie ahead?"

"They knew what was in back of them," Ma said. "English soldiers, after anyone who'd fought on the side of the Bonnie Prince." She frowned at Hattie, her eldest. "But that was different. They were families, not unmarried girls, all on their own."

"She won't be all on her own," Ned piped up from the other side of the table. Tom was at his side, mouth full of cornbread, and both boys had eagerness flashing in their eyes. "We aim to go to California too. We can look after Hattie."

"Look after me? I never heard such nonsense." Hattie glared at her younger brothers over the table. "It was me taught the two of you how to shoot. I can look after myself, without the pair of you under my feet."

Pa threw his head back and laughed. "She can, at that. I'd bet on it."

"That's not all you'd bet on." Ma shook her head in exasperation. "Land sakes, the gold fever's got all of them." Ma reached for Hattie's strong brown hands, and cradled them in her smaller, work-roughened fingers. "I'd hoped you might marry Dan Cullen. He's been courting you this summer."

"Oh, Ma," Hattie said. "He's a nice enough feller. But I'm not ready to settle down. I won't be twenty till next spring."

The Ballews argued about it all winter. But come April of 1849, Hattie, Ned and Tom set out for Independence, where they joined a party of goldseekers heading overland to California. It was a hard trip that took them four months, but they made it.

When they found Cibola, there was nothing to the little valley but the creek and two miners digging for gold along its banks. The one who had arrived just a week earlier and staked his claim on the north side was a tall Kentuckian named Jack Murdock. He was a handsome, well-spoken fellow, Hattie thought, with blue eyes and a head of curly black hair, a handlebar mustache and a full beard.

The one whose claim stretched on the creek's south bank had been there longer, a month or so. He, too, was pleasant to look at, dark eyes in a brown face and a wiry muscular figure. "My name is Miguel Santos," he told the Ballews. "I am from Sonora."

"The town farther south?" Hattie asked.

"No, *señorita*." Santos tipped his sombrero and bowed as though she were a great lady instead of a rawboned farm girl from Missouri, with a battered straw hat atop her lank brown hair, riding a horse, astride, and decked out comfortably in Ned's shirt and trousers and a pair of Tom's old boots. "The state of Sonora, in Mexico. There are so many of my countrymen here in California that they named the town for us."

She smiled at Santos, who grinned back, his eyes sparkling up at her as he stood leaning on his shovel. "I like the look of this place," Hattie told her brothers. "Let's scout up that crick, and find us a claim."

The Ballews went farther upstream, a half mile or so, and staked a claim on the south side of the creek. They built a cabin with one big central room and two sleeping rooms on either side, one for Hattie and the other for the boys.

Cibola grew quickly as summer wound into fall, once word got out that there was color in the stream. Gold there was, glittering in the crevices along the twisting creek. The Ballews didn't find lumps as big as their hands, but they did all right. That's what she told her mother and father and the young'uns in the monthly letters she wrote by candlelight, snug that winter. They bought a small cookstove and a rocking chair, and it felt good on a winter's night to sit by the stove with Little Bit in her lap, Hattie's hands stroking the tiger cat's fur, feeling the vibration as the cat purred, listening as Ned played the fiddle and Tom picked his banjo. Sometimes their neighbors

would join in, Miguel Santos with a guitar and, more infre-
quently, Jack Murdock playing the harmonica.

"Why did you name the place Cibola?" she asked Miguel,
one afternoon in the spring of 1850. She'd come to town for
supplies. Now she and Miguel stood in what passed for a store,
a flimsy structure built of planks and canvas. "Been meaning to
ask you that all winter. You could have named the place after
yourself, since you was the first to stake a claim here."

Miguel didn't answer her right away. He frowned as he read
the front page of a copy of the *Alta California*, the newspaper
published in San Francisco.

Hattie glared at the shopkeeper, who was making money
hand over fist by charging miners what the market would bear.
"Land sakes, what they're charging for eggs! You'd think they
was lumps of gold. I've a mind to get me some laying hens."
But she wanted eggs, to make a cake for Ned's birthday, so she
watched the shopkeeper like a hawk as the man weighed out
the necessary gold dust for her purchase.

Miguel set the newspaper on the counter and turned to her.
"My dear Hattie, have you not heard of the Seven Cities of
Gold?"

"Not a word." Hattie wrapped her eggs carefully and put
them in the basket she carried over one arm. "Are they somewhere near here?"

"They do not exist, as far as I know," the Sonoran said as
they left the store. He took her arm and steered her away from
a group of rowdy, rough-clad men who'd spilled out the doors
of a nearby saloon. "If they do exist, I suppose California is as
good a place as any. The Seven Cities of Gold are a legend,
and Cibola is one of them. Coronado searched the Southwest
for them, but didn't find gold." Miguel laughed. "Unlike those
of us who journeyed to California. There is an old Spanish
fable about California. It's supposed to be an island paradise,
full of gold and precious stones, ruled by the Amazon queen
Calafia."

"What nonsense." Hattie shook her head as she surveyed Cibola's only street, rutted and muddy from the tail end of the winter's rain. A man rode by on a mule, its hooves kicking up mud that soiled Hattie's trousers and shirt and splashed on her chin. Hattie scrubbed at the splotches on her bosom, making the mess worse. She gave up and looked at Miguel. "Does this look like an island paradise?"

"Perhaps not." Miguel took out one of the linen handkerchiefs he always carried. He used it to brush away the mud on her chin. Hattie looked at the initials "MS" embroidered on the corner and wondered if they'd been stitched there by Miguel's sweetheart back in Mexico. She'd never asked him. "California is not an island, as the legend promised," he continued. "But the gold is here. We just have to dig for it. And you, Hattie, perhaps you are the Amazon queen Calafia, here to wrest the gold from the earth."

Hattie's face turned red, from her chin to the roots of her drab brown hair. "What nonsense," she said again, her voice roughened to hide her embarrassment. Why, she felt such a fool when he talked like that.

Hattie knew it seemed strange to people that an unmarried woman like her was in these mountains, working a claim. There were other women in the rough mining camps of the Mother Lode, married to miners, some even working the claims with their husbands. Others ran boardinghouses and shops, cooked for the miners or took in washing. There were other kinds of women too, the ones people called soiled doves. But the men by far outnumbered the women. A lot of them wanted to get married, if only to have someone cook and clean for them, Hattie thought. She'd fended off men ever since she'd hit the Overland Trail for California. And more since she'd arrived, much to the amusement of her brothers, who couldn't fathom why anyone would want to hitch up with their sister.

The marriage proposals she dealt with easily enough, with a

shake of the head and a firm "no," or even more words from a tart tongue if that became necessary. That was all it took to discourage Patch Turner, the red-faced Pennsylvanian who'd staked a claim about a mile south of town. He'd made a play for Hattie right after he got to Cibola, but she'd put him in his place smartly enough. As for the other sort of advances, she had a Colt revolver and a shotgun, and she knew how to use both.

Not that Hattie would have minded if Miguel came courting. He was a fine looking man, educated, with good manners, who managed to keep cleaner than most, and he always treated her like she was a lady, even if she hadn't worn a skirt since she left Missouri.

It was Patch Turner who told her the news, hailing her that April afternoon as she walked back up the creek to her cabin. He was at the edge of a knot of miners, wearing the colorful patched vest with brass buttons that gave him his nickname. She saw Jack Murdock, and Shorty LaRue, the Cajun from the Louisiana bayous, and a couple of Iowa farm boys, Johnny and Pete Brubaker.

"Did you hear about the tax?" Patch said as he hailed her.

"What tax?" She kept her distance. She didn't much like Patch, and she didn't want anyone to jostle her market basket and those expensive eggs.

"Why, the territorial legislature's passed a tax," Patch declared, mopping his florid face with a dirty gray handkerchief. "Against the foreigners. About damn time, too. The damn Mexes and Chinee coolies are thick as flies, outnumbering the Americans. Taking gold that rightly belongs to Americans."

"Gold don't belong to nobody till it's found," Hattie said sharply. "And it don't matter to me who finds it."

Patch was talking nonsense. There were all sorts of people here in California and she liked it fine that way. Plenty of people had come from back east, like the Ballews. There were lots of Mexicans, like Miguel, and she'd once met a fellow from a place called Peru, way down in South America. There was an Englishman up in Mokelumne Hill, a bagpipe-playing Scot in San Andreas, and an Australian down in Angel's Camp. She herself had met a Frenchwoman who, with her husband, worked a claim in Fiddletown. And the Chinese in their strange pigtails were a familiar sight in all the rough towns up and down the Mother Lode.

"Some don't agree with you," Murdock told Hattie, his deep voice slow, and carrying the flavor of his Southern roots, as well as evidence of his education. "The legislature's decreed that only native or naturalized citizens of the United States will be permitted to mine in California, without a license, that is. All foreign miners must have a license, which costs twenty dollars a month."

"Twenty dollars!" Hattie's eyes widened with astonishment at the figure. "Why, that's . . . that's . . ."

"A princely sum," Murdock finished. "It will drive a lot of them away."

"Sounds like a damn fool notion to me," Hattie said, regaining her composure. "What if they won't pay it?"

"There'll be trouble," Patch said, with a laugh, almost as though he relished the thought. The Brubakers joined in.

There was already trouble in the Mother Lode. Shootings, stabbings, robberies, and even murders, were common in the mines, as the hordes of goldseekers competed for the glitter that drew them to California. Hattie heard Americans blaming the Mexicans for these crimes, but from what she could see in Cibola and the other towns she visited, troublemakers came in all nationalities.

"Truth be told," she said to Little Bit when she returned to the cabin, "there's too damn many of us, scratching for gold all over these mountains."

Little Bit paid her no mind. The tiger cat was dragging an item of clothing from Hattie's room into the main room of the cabin, heading, no doubt, out the door to her cache. Hattie left her basket on the table and rescued her last clean pair of underdrawers, not so clean now that the cat had been at them. She shook them free of dust and hung them on a peg near her bed, then returned to the main room, removing her precious cargo of eggs from the basket.

She remembered how it was last year when she and her brothers had arrived on the banks of Cibola Creek, just the three of them, Jack Murdock and Miguel Santos. Now there were hundreds crowding the little valley. If she multiplied that by the number of gold camps scattered throughout the Mother Lode. . . . She stopped, shook her head, and spoke again to the cat, who'd jumped up on the table and was eyeing those eggs. "Don't you dare, Little Bit." Hattie moved the eggs out of danger. "Why, there must be thousands more in the diggings than there were last year. When you get that many people crowded together, there's likely to be trouble."

There was.

She heard about it from her brothers, who'd been in Sonora when it happened. The foreign miners, outraged by the tax, refused to pay it. Several thousand of them gathered and paraded through Sonora. In response, several hundred American miners organized an armed force.

There was a murder, Ned told Hattie. Maybe two, Tom chimed in, and a few arrests. After this conflict, an uneasy peace settled over the Mother Lode. In the camps, and on the pages of the newspapers, arguments about the Foreign Miners' Tax continued.

"What do you think of this tax?" Hattie asked Miguel at his claim, a few days after the Sonora incident.

He'd been digging with his pickax and now he stopped, mopping his brow with one of his monogrammed handkerchiefs. "All of California used to belong to Mexico, until the Bear Flaggers took over Sonoma in 1846, and the *Americanos* occupied Monterey. My cousin Juan and his family have a *rancho* near San Luis Obispo. They are old *Californios*, who have been here for more than a hundred years. Why should we be called foreigners? It wasn't so long ago that people from the United States were foreigners."

"I know," Hattie said. "But Sonora ain't the last of it. Some Chinese miners up at Angel's Camp got burned out last night. I heard Patch Turner and those Brubaker boys spouting off about it when I was in town just now. They were sayin' all the foreigners better get out of Mother Lode."

"Especially 'the Mexes and the Chinee coolies.' And if we don't, Patch will do for all of us." Miguel shook his head. "Ah, Hattie, there are too many of us. Those three are blowhards. Get a little whiskey in them and they'll say anything."

She reckoned he was right, as she walked home. But all the time Patch and the others had been laughing about the fire that burned out the Chinese miners, she'd wondered if they'd been responsible for setting the blaze. When she heard the next day that Pete Brubaker took over the claim the Chinese had abandoned, she was convinced that they had.

The following Monday, Hattie rose later than usual. The boys had already made mush for breakfast, leaving cornmeal all over the table. But where was the letter she'd been writing to her mother? She'd left it right here, folded into a neat square and tucked into the addressed envelope. Perhaps Ned or Tom had taken it to town, where miners left letters at the store to be picked up each month by an expressman, who then took it to the post office in Sacramento, the first stop in the mail's long journey to San Francisco, then by steamer to Panama. But the expressman wasn't due in Cibola until tomorrow.

She reached for a rag to wipe the cornmeal off the table, then stopped when she saw the paw prints. "Little Bit. I'll be bound. That cat's dragged off my letter."

Hattie walked upstream to where her brothers were working the claim. "About time you got here, Miss Slug-A-Bed," Ned joshed. "You were sleeping so sound you didn't hear us getting our own breakfast."

"Must have been, since you make considerable noise most of the time." She turned to include Tom in her gaze, "Did you take that letter I was writing to Ma?"

"No," Tom said. "It was there on the table when we left."

"It's gone now. Had to be Little Bit, then." She didn't know whether to laugh or grumble.

Ned grinned. "If you find her, maybe you'll find that tobacco pouch I lost in March."

Hattie crossed to the north bank of the creek and walked downstream to where Jack Murdock was sifting dirt, gravel, and water into a rocker, staring intently at the contents as he looked for gold. "You seen Little Bit?" she asked.

He looked up. "Your cat? No, I haven't."

She'd never known Little Bit to wander as far as Cibola, so she crossed the creek again and headed for Miguel's cabin. Before she reached it she came on Patch Turner, digging a trench, a pickax in his meaty hands.

"What are you doing on Miguel's claim?" she demanded.

"Why, howdy, Miss Hattie," he said cheerfully. He stopped digging and leaned on the shovel, taking a cigar from the pocket of his disreputable patchwork vest. He ought to give the thing a good wash, Hattie thought, wrinkling her nose in disgust. Why, it's greasy and torn. There's a button missing and a corner's been ripped off that patch of red and yellow calico.

"I asked you a question," she said.

"And not very polite at that. This ain't Miguel's claim anymore. It's mine."

She put her hands on her hips and glared at Patch. "What have you done with Miguel?"

"Done nothin' with him. He upped and left last night. The claim's abandoned, so I'm takin' it."

"Abandoned." She shook her head in disbelief. "He wouldn't do that. He was the first one to stake a claim in this valley. Besides, he wouldn't leave without telling me."

"Well, he's gone for sure. Johnny Brubaker saw him riding

out of town, heading south. No doubt he's gone back to Mexico where he belongs."

"I don't believe it," Hattie said. She wouldn't believe either of the Brubakers if those boys swore the sun came up in the east.

"Suit yourself," Patch told her, and went back to digging.

Hattie left off her search for the cat and walked into Cibola. Sure enough, Johnny Brubaker told the tale as Patch Turner had described. He swore he'd seen Miguel Santos pack up all his belongings and ride south.

"It's not like him," Jack Murdock said later, when all three of the Ballews walked down to where he was working, to share the news. "Without a word. I can't believe Miguel would just leave."

"He hasn't left," Hattie said grimly. "Someone's kilt him. I'll be bound if it's not Patch Turner who's kilt Miguel for his claim."

Tom shook his head slowly. "Better watch your tongue, Sister, before you accuse a man of killing someone."

"That's right," Ned agreed. "I didn't hear any shots in the night."

"Even if it is true, how could you prove such a thing?" Murdock sat down on a stump and stretched his long legs in front of him. "Granted, no one's seen Miguel, but it's possible he left. A lot of the foreign miners have been driven away by the tax."

"Or by other miners," Hattie said, thinking of the Chinese who'd been burned out.

"I'll ride south tomorrow," Ned told her. "As far as San Andreas. To see if anyone saw Miguel. I can take Ma's letter into town when I go."

Hattie'd forgotten all about the letter, when she'd heard the news that Miguel was gone. Now she remembered. The fool cat had made off with the letter and she'd gone looking for it, which was why she was out tramping around instead of helping her brothers work the claim. She walked with them back up to the Ballew claim, then set off into the woods to the south, calling and whistling for Little Bit. She found herself circling to the west, coming out behind Miguel's cabin. She didn't see anything that would contradict Patch Turner's claim that Miguel had simply left Cibola.

Hattie turned and headed back toward the Ballew cabin. When she'd walked a few yards, movement caught her eye. A squirrel? No, it was Little Bit, looking smug and satisfied with herself as she trotted into view from behind a clump of boulders. The cat had something white in her mouth.

"My letter," Hattie cried. She grabbed for it, but the cat eluded her, thinking she was playing a game. Little Bit took off, her prize clamped firmly in her jaws, heading uphill through the pines and oak. Hattie ran after her, puffing from the exertion, in time to see the cat disappear into the gnarled tangle of some tree roots.

"Come on, Little Bit," she wheedled. "You know Ma and Pa and the young'uns look forward to those letters." Hattie got down on all fours and crept closer to the trees. As she got closer, she saw the earth had washed out from under the roots, forming a small cave. Here Little Bit had stashed her treasures. Hattie saw Ned's tobacco pouch, just as he'd predicted, as well as a brass button, the bowl of someone's corn cob pipe, assorted bones, and bits of fur. Little Bit dropped the white scrap on top of this mound and settled down, paws tucked under her and her green eyes glittering. She looked pleased with herself.

Hattie reached in, her fingers searching for the letter. Little Bit hissed at her indignantly. Hattie pulled her hand away, but what she held didn't feel like paper.

Hattie stared down in alarm. It was part of a handkerchief, torn raggedly in half, stained with dirt and something brown and stiff. Was it dried blood? The monogram in one corner told her that it belonged to Miguel Santos.

She reached again into Little Bit's cave, ignoring the paw

that swiped at her, and pulled out the brass button. It had a string of white thread clinging to it. Hadn't Patch Turner's vest been missing a button when she saw him earlier today? She tried to recall if the buttons on his vest had been sewed with white thread.

She got to her feet. Jack Murdock and her brothers would say this proved nothing. Miguel Santos was still missing, and Little Bit could have gotten these things anywhere. The cat was notorious for her thieving ways. But where had she found the handkerchief and the button?

Hattie whirled and went back the way she'd come, searching for the boulders where she'd first seen the cat. There they were, some fifty feet from the back of Miguel's cabin. She heard voices coming from inside the cabin as she crept around the big rocks. Sounded like Patch Turner and the Brubaker boys, drinking whiskey early this afternoon.

Behind the rocks Hattie found a gully. It looked as though someone had been dumping dirt and gravel here, the leavings from working a claim. One spot looked as though something had been digging at the pile, probably Little Bit. The cat had followed her back to this spot. With a proprietary meow, Little Bit poked a paw at the place where she'd been digging earlier. Hattie knelt and scrabbled at the dirt with her hands.

When she saw the cold stiff hands, one of them clenched, she recoiled. Then with renewed urgency, she brushed away more dirt until she saw Miguel's dead face and his chest with the blood-caked wound where he'd been stabbed. Hattie gritted her teeth and peered closer, trying to see what was hidden in Miguel's hand.

Quick as a wink, Little Bit's paw reached out. One claw snagged the edge of a piece of cloth and teased it from the dead man's closed fingers. Before the cat could run away, Hattie grabbed her by the scruff and pried the cloth away from her. It was red and yellow calico. Hattie knew where she'd seen the pattern before.

Quickly she covered the body again, then got to her feet, shooing Little Bit ahead of her as she moved quickly through the woods, toward the Ballew cabin. Tom and Ned were there, washing up outside the front door.

"Where have you been?" Ned called. "We found the letter. It was on the floor under our bed. Looks like Little Bit knocked it off the table and played with it. She chewed on it some. You're lucky she didn't drag it into the woods, or you'd never find it."

He and Tom laughed. Then they stopped when they saw the look on their sister's face. Hattie reached into her pocket. She pulled out the button, the calico scrap, and the handkerchief that held Miguel's initials and the stains from his wound.

"Look what the cat dragged in."

Stitches in Time

Debbie De Louise

It was Gina's twelfth birthday, but she wasn't happy. She hated wearing braces. She hated having freckles and red hair. She hated being an only child and the tallest girl in her sixth-grade class. The only things Gina really cared for were her cat Floppy and her favorite subject, history.

She also loved her parents, but no one over ten admits that. Neither her father nor her mother was an abuser, an alcoholic, nor a criminal. Rarer yet, they were still married after 15 years. Her mother, Alice, was a librarian at Chester Public Library located in a suburb of Philadelphia not far from their house on Acre Street. Her father, Luke, was a computer programmer for Datamark, the East Coast branch of a popular educational software company. No wonder their only offspring was regarded as a "nerd" in school. Brightness doesn't score popularity points with preteens.

Thus, Gina spent many lonely after-school hours reading the historical novels her mother brought home for her from the library, with Floppy curled at her feet or playing with the tassel of her bookmark.

This particular afternoon, as Gina was studying for her American History test while waiting for her parents to come home from work to take her out to celebrate her birthday, her cat stood up suddenly with raised ears and let out a low growl. A sure sign someone was approaching the house. Gina's first thought was that her parents were surprising her by coming home early, but when she went to check, she saw a UPS truck driving away. Opening the door, she found a small brown box addressed to "Miss Gina Garrett." She thought it odd that there was no return address, and that the UPS driver had not knocked and asked for a signature as he usually did when delivering packages for her father. Floppy was circling her legs, sniffing at the brown box with legendary cat curiosity.

"It must be a present for my birthday, Flops," she told him, carrying the package to the kitchen table where she used a knife to cut the packing tape. Before she lifted the lid, though, she noticed that the underside was marked "Magnetic Material" which was the term usually stamped on her father's packages. She debated with herself about whether she should reseal it and wait until her parents came home. Floppy's head, however, was already under the packing material, as he played with the end of the loosened tape.

"Good, now I can blame you," Gina said as she moved the cat aside and reached below the shredded newspaper. She felt a square plastic case that she recognized as the type that usually contained a CD-ROM. Extracting it from the box, she saw that it did. The label on the disk read "Virtual Time Travel." Gina laughed. Ever since she'd won first prize in her history class's Back to the Future essay contest, for her story about a software program that could transport its user to any time period in history, her father had been bombarding her with time-travel computer games. She had always preferred her mother's historical novels, which relied solely on the reader's imagination (in her case, a wild one), to the razzmatazz of modern technology with all its bells and whistles. She had never had the heart to tell her father that. He was like a kid in a candy store when it came to software. He expected her to share the same enthusiasm, but her generation was too accustomed to digital hijinks and multimedia magic.

Floppy bounded after her on white boots as she took the CD into her father's office and loaded it onto his Pentium machine. The opening screens showed scenes from historic events—Christopher Columbus sailing to America; the Founding Fathers signing the Declaration of Independence; the bombing of Pear Harbor; headlines from the Vietnam War; the first Moon walk; Bill Gates introducing Microsoft Windows—a chronology of people and places familiar to her from reading and watching television, yet as unreal as characters and settings on a movie screen. She clicked the left mouse button to start the game. Floppy was sitting to the right of the keyboard, his yellow eyes wide, waiting for his chance to "catch" an image on the monitor or issue an undesired command by pressing one of the keys.

The main menu consisted of a listing of dates. Gina chose 1776 because the Colonial period was her favorite. Just as she was about to hit the "enter" key to transport herself to Early America via the Virtual Time Travel CD, Gina heard her parents' car pull up in front of the house. Floppy turned his head at the sound but didn't move. Gina ignored the interruption and pressed "enter."

GINA DIDN'T know where she was. The moment she'd pressed the "enter" key on her father's computer, she'd felt a strong jolt flash through her, from her fingertips to her toes. She thought she'd been electrocuted, but then she realized she was no longer in her father's office. She was in a hot, dark room, almost completely in shadow except for a flickering candle on a long table, at which sat a woman in a long black dress. Lying upon the table in front of the woman were half a dozen wooden spools of thread, of various colors, and a white garment that looked like an old-fashioned man's shirt, with a ruffled collar and high neck buttons, one of which the woman was repairing.

"Oh, there ye be, Ginny," the woman said looking up from her sewing. "When I'm done, can ye bring this down to Dr. Franklin, and let Stitches out on your way there?"

Gina was startled. Could the man this woman was referring to be Benjamin Franklin? If so, could the woman be Betsy Ross? Had the Virtual Time Travel CD actually transported her back in time to 1776?

Gina tried to recollect her history lessons. She realized that if the seamstress was the proposed maker of the first U.S. flag, she was wearing black because she was still in mourning over her husband's recent death in the militia explosion.

A cat cried from the front parlor, and Gina turned to see Floppy enter the room.

"Stitches," the woman exclaimed, "be patient until Ginny lets ye out."

Gina didn't remember reading in any of her history texts that Betsy Ross had ever had a cat, but it was likely. Gina had visited the Betsy Ross house on Arch Street in Philadelphia with her fifth-grade class. She recalled the beautiful fountain in front that featured the names of the thirteen colonies at its base, around which two stone cats played—one from whose mouth water spouted. She had wondered then if the famous seamstress had been a cat lover.

The woman stood, holding up the white garment. "All done! Now, Ginny, please take this to Dr. Franklin. He's already paid me for it, but he might have a shilling or two for you. He's always so kind to young apprentices."

Gina didn't know what to do. She took the shirt the woman handed her and walked into the front parlor.

"Don't forget Stitches," the seamstress called after her, but the cat was already at Gina's heels.

As Gina approached the front door, she noticed another table on which rested a long white cloth that seemed to be in some stage of preparation. Nestled on its center were several blue stars.

"The flag," she thought. "This must be the summer of 1776." A thrill went through her unlike anything she had ever felt. This wasn't a game. It was real. She wasn't reading about the past; she was living it. She wanted to touch the material Betsy Ross was using as the first flag's canvas, but she was afraid the woman would see her.

Gina opened the door and stepped out into eighteenth century Philadelphia, her cat behind her. As she walked down Arch Street carrying Benjamin Franklin's shirt, Gina was like a child again, absorbing all the new sights and sounds of Old Philadelphia. She watched as horses clopped down the narrow street and people in colonial garb stepped out from storefronts to hawk their wares or greet their neighbors. There was the wafting smell of freshly baked bread as she passed the bakeshop; the noisy clang of horseshoe drilling from the blacksmith's.

Gina didn't know where to find Benjamin Franklin. She knew he had a print shop in the area where the presses had once rolled for his *Poor Richard's Almanac*, but she had no idea of its location. As she wandered down the cobblestone block, scanning each doorway, she suddenly stopped when she noticed Floppy, AKA Stitches, had left her path. She didn't want to lose him back in the past before she was able to find her way forward to the present. She looked around for the cat, trying to figure out which name he'd respond to, but before she could call out to him at all, she saw him sitting on a doorstep, gazing at her with the inscrutable, wise regard of cats that inspired Mark Twain to say—later than this time but earlier than her own—"If man was crossed with the cat, it would improve the man, but deteriorate the cat."

Gina was about to pick up Floppy when the door, above which hung a bronze plaque inscribed with Carson's Needlework, opened and a stout, gray-haired woman shouted, "Scat, ye vermin! Go home to your mistress. I won't abide the likes of any Ross by my doorstep."

Gina assumed that the woman was so preoccupied by the cat that she hadn't noticed Gina standing in the shadow of the alleyway that formed a rather uninviting entrance to the needlework shop. Garbage spilled over from sacks that may once have contained potatoes or flour. Some pigeons were picking at some of the debris, and Gina could imagine rats gathering there at night. No wonder Floppy had chosen this place to stop, but he didn't seem interested in the birds. It took two swipes of the old lady's broom to get him to move from the doorstep.

Gina stepped back into the shadows, as Floppy dashed to her side. She didn't want the old woman to see her, but the lady had already turned her back and was speaking to someone behind her in the house.

"Have ye been feeding that cat again, Catherine? How many times have I told you it's as wicked as that Betsy Ross who takes our livelihood away from us with her fancy needlework."

"But mother," a feeble voice replied, so low Gina was surprised she could hear it. "It isn't Betsy's fault she hath such skill."

"She hath no more skill than you. She just advertises better. A widow still in black, and she threads the garments of half the men in Philadelphia. They tip her a pretty pound, too."

"Mother!" The girl's exclamation was louder this time.

"Don't mother me, Catherine Ann Carson," came the woman's bitter voice again. "If you listen to me, we'll both be rich and famous like her and not living in this poor house your father left us in when he went away with another woman of Betsy Ross's kind."

There was a pause. Gina felt her heart thump and heard Floppy meow as he circled her legs. She knew she should go before she was caught, but she wanted to hear more. What was Mrs. Carson planning?

"Don't you want to sew for Dr. Franklin and General Washington?" she continued. "You should've been the one asked to make the flag for the United Colonies. But 'tis not too late. I know Betsy will attend the Patriot's dinner at the State House tonight. If we can get in her house and take the flag, I'm sure you can finish the work and get it to General Washington before she hath the chance to make another."

Gina almost cried aloud, but her exclamation would have been muffled by Catherine Carson.

"Mother, you can't do that! Betsy worked so hard for this honor."

"The only reason she got the job is because her late husband's uncle works with General Washington, and we both know that."

"Mother, that isn't true. Betsy is a wonderful seamstress. She will make a fine flag."

"Believe that, and you'll never get anywhere, Catherine. If we don't get some work soon, we won't be able to live. Making the flag will convince all of Philadelphia to use our services."

"Then what will happen to Betsy?"

"She'll probably marry again and find a rich husband. That will never happen to you." The old woman's voice lowered suddenly and became softer. Gina had to strain to hear her next words.

"We must think of ourselves, Catherine. 'Tis the only way. We are alone in the world except for one another, my dear daughter."

Gina could scream. What a horrid woman to plant a guilt trip on her daughter like that and to even conceive of stealing the first flag of the United States! What if this woman got away with it? How would she and her daughter finish the project? Would the flag still resemble "Old Glory"? Would it even be red, white, and blue? Surely, this couldn't happen. The flag was never stolen by a jealous old woman named Carson. Unless. Gina had a thought that frightened her. What if she and Floppy had actually been here in 1776 as the famous seamstress's apprentice and pet? What if they had been sent back to complete a mission—the saving of the flag?

The door to the Carsons' shop closed, and Floppy scurried away. Gina followed him, clutching Ben Franklin's shirt and trying to keep it from wrinkling in her shaking hands, as she considered what she had to do.

Deep in thought, Gina didn't realize she'd made a turn off Arch Street. Following her cat, as if in a trance, she found herself on Market Street standing in front of a small shop that faced the white steeple of Christ Church. An aged man with ink on his trousers came out of the shop. Gina recognized him immediately from the pictures in her history books. Her heart began beating fast. Talk about meeting VIPs. First, she'd met Betsy Ross; now she was about to meet Benjamin Franklin, one of the most famous men of the eighteenth century.

Floppy ran up to Franklin who reached down to pet him. "Greetings, Stitches!" He looked up and spotted Gina. "Ah, Miss Ginny. 'Tis good to see ye with my shirt. Please come in. I was just printing some flyers for tonight's State House meeting."

Gina could barely speak, but the urgency of her time-travel mission cleared her throat and, as she handed Franklin the shirt with trembling fingers, she stuttered, "Dr. Franklin, I can not stay, but there is some news I must bring you. On my way here, I passed the Carson shop and overheard Catherine's mother making plans to take Mrs. Ross's flag while she is at the State House tonight."

Gina didn't know what reaction to expect from her declaration, but it wasn't amusement. Franklin laughed heartily. "That crazy woman," he said. "She's always starting trouble. Last winter, Mrs. Carson tried to make off with my long johns which Mrs. Ross was stitching. I would have frozen off my britches if Mrs. Ross hadn't caught that jealous old bat."

Gina was shocked. "Dr. Franklin, if Mrs. Carson is a thief, why isn't she in jail?"

Franklin laughed again. "With the War of Independence raging around us, we have more important things to worry about than a bitter old woman. Although, I must admit, Mrs. Carson goes a bit too far when she threatens the American flag. Don't worry, Miss Ginny, I'll warn Mrs. Ross to keep the flag in a safe place tonight, and I'll keep a closer eye on Mrs. Carson. As I always say, 'Tricks and Treachery are the practice of fools, that have not wit enough to be honest.'" Franklin smiled. "Thank you, Miss Ginny and Master Stitches." He bent down and patted Floppy's head again. "You may go home now, and I'll see that the flag is safe."

As Gina turned and started back the way she came, a nagging doubt assuaged her. With so many important things on Franklin's mind, what if he forgot to issue the warning to Betsy? Initially, Franklin had not even seemed to take Mrs. Carson's threat that seriously. Gina realized it was up to her to prevent a crime that would change American history. Then somehow, some way, she and her cat would find their way back to their own time.

Floppy walked ahead sniffing the trail as Gina followed. She hoped they were headed in the right direction. When they turned onto Arch Street and were passing Carson's Needlework Shop, Gina knew Floppy had correctly retraced the scent of their steps. The cat paused on the doorstep of the rundown house. This time, Catherine Carson opened the door and stepped out to greet Floppy. The girl was alone and sounded as if she were crying as she spoke to the cat.

"I don't know what to do, Stitches," Catherine sobbed. "Mother saw Betsy at the milliner's when she went to look at some hats to buy and overheard Betsy say she was on her way to run some errands before her apprentice returned from delivering a shirt to Dr. Franklin. Then mother decided to steal the flag this afternoon while Betsy's house is unoccupied instead of tonight during the State House meeting. I tried to stop her, but I couldn't."

Gina listened in dismay to this turn of events. The seamstress's daughter, unaware that anyone but the cat had heard her, closed her door after giving Floppy a farewell scratch under the chin. The moment the door to the needlework shop closed, Floppy scurried off like a bolt of gray-and-white lightning. Gina had no choice but to run after him.

Floppy's wild dash down the street turned into a flying leap when he encountered a solid object traveling at a similar speed in his direction. The leap allowed him to land with front paws spread on top of the object. Gina was not as lucky. She collided full force with the center of the object causing both she and the object to fall onto what she now realized was the front lawn of Betsy Ross's house.

"Ouch!" said the object, now recognizable as Mrs. Carson. The woman had been on her way down the path from the house, with the stolen flag in her arms. When Floppy had landed on her head at approximately the same time Gina had knocked the wind out of her, the flag had fallen to the ground.

Gina wasn't sure how to handle the situation. An apology to a thief just didn't seem right, but Mrs. Carson was bleeding slightly from a cut caused by Floppy's claws before he'd jumped off her head.

"I'm sorry," Gina said. "Floppy, I mean Stitches, didn't mean to hurt you. He just seems to have a thing against thieves."

Mrs. Carson wiped away the blood from the scratch over her left eye.

"It is I who am sorry, Miss Ginny. I've been an old fool trying to make trouble for Mrs. Ross but only because I've wanted a better life for my daughter."

Gina, startled by the sincerity of the apology, was saved

from a reply by the voice of Betsy Ross, who had returned home to this awkward scene.

"What has happened here, Ginny?" Betsy asked, as she saw her apprentice and a bedraggled Mrs. Carson lying in the grass with the flag and the cat between them.

Gina and Mrs. Carson got up at the same time and both began speaking in unison. Betsy couldn't understand a word being said.

"Stop!" Betsy yelled but not at the two who were talking. She was addressing Floppy, who had settled himself on the flag and was kneading the material beneath his white paws.

Mrs. Carson went over to the cat and gently lifted him off the flag, making sure his claws had not pulled up any threads.

"'Tis all right, Mrs. Ross. No harm be done. I would suggest applique on the stars, though. They will hold better."

Forgetting her question to Gina, Betsy approached Mrs. Carson, who was holding out the flag to her.

"Thank you, Mrs. Carson. I wanted to use applique, but I never seem to make them the same size. This is one of my most important projects, and it must be perfect. I just wish I had more time to devote to the work. Ever since John died I've just had so much to do."

"'Tis a shame. My daughter's specialty is applique, and we have too much time on our hands."

Gina, who had been listening to the exchange, broke in with a suggestion. "Mrs. Ross, is there any way you and the Carsons can work together?"

Betsy smiled. "Of course. What a great idea! If I could send some work out to Catherine and Mrs. Carson, it would be a great help." She turned to the older woman. "Would that be acceptable to you?"

"Very much so. I will go and tell Catherine straight away." She paused, glancing at the flag in her hands. "I must first make a confession, Mrs. Ross."

Before she could continue, Gina cut in again. "What Mrs.

Carson wanted to tell you is that she was planning to surprise you by bringing the flag home so that Catherine could fix the stars. I had told her they were a bit loose, and she asked me to give her the flag while you were away so she could finish the job before you returned. I was doing that when you caught us. Stitches got a bit upset and tried to protect the flag by pouncing on Mrs. Carson. I got in the way and that's how we all ended up on the ground."

"That's an interesting story," said a voice from behind them. The three turned to see Benjamin Franklin crossing the street toward them. Gina's heart was in her throat. What if Franklin divulged the earlier story she had told him? Even though Mrs. Carson was guilty of trying to steal the flag, Gina realized she didn't deserve to be treated as a criminal. Life had been rough for the Carsons. Maybe a partnership with Betsy Ross would benefit all three of the seamstresses. Indeed, if Catherine Carson could fix the stars on what was to become the American flag, then perhaps Gina's mission had actually been to secure this alliance. She couldn't let her warning to Dr. Franklin interfere with what she believed was now best for all. She was about to comment when Franklin continued.

"Yes, quite a story. I shall tell it tonight at the State House when I announce the partnership of the three best seamstresses in all of Philadelphia. I have been hoping for this for a very long time." Franklin looked at Gina with a twinkle in his eye.

It was then that Gina realized Floppy was missing. In all the excitement, she had forgotten about him. As Betsy and Mrs. Carson made their partnership plans with wise counsel from Ben Franklin, Gina slipped away to look for the cat. She spotted him turning the corner of a street off Acre that she hadn't noticed before. When she rounded the corner, she stumbled on a cobblestone. The last thing she felt as she fell forward into darkness was Floppy's tail.

* * *

GINA AWOKE in her bed at home with Floppy beside her. She wasn't in her nightclothes, and it was still light outside.

"Why didn't you come when I called?" her mother was asking her from the doorway. "And you know better than to leave your father's computer on in his office after you leave the room. Besides, that CD you were playing with must have been damaged in shipping. Your father says it doesn't work. He's been in there trying to fix it while I went to find you. Do you know who sent it? We saw the UPS box when we came in, but there was no address." Her mother paused, not noticing Gina's disorientation. "Never mind. Are you ready for dinner?"

Gina nodded, still having a hard time believing she was back in the twentieth century.

"Good, then go get your father. I'll freshen up and meet you both in the car."

Gina stood on wobbly legs and went down the hall to her father's office. Floppy followed her, sniffing the familiar scent of his home.

As Gina went in the office, she saw the computer was still on, with the Time Travel CD displaying a flashing "1776." Her father was nowhere in sight. Floppy jumped up on the leather office chair and raised a hesitant paw to the monitor that sat next to her parents' wedding picture on her father's desk. Glancing at the photo, Gina noticed for the first time how much her father resembled a young George Washington.

The Cat and the Kinetophone

Jon L. Breen

THESE DAYS, YOU hear a lot about Alzheimer's Disease. Years ago, when old folks' mental powers started to slip, they just called it senility. Whatever you call it, it's one of the biggest fears of those who are really old. Now personally, being ninety-seven myself, I don't start getting really old until the century mark at least, but most of you probably peg it at about eighty—I hope none of you in this age of increasing longevity would put it any earlier than that.

Anyway, people like me and my fellow residents of Plantain Point, a truly splendid retirement community, do worry about keeping their memory sharp—and the cliché that older folks can remember vividly what happened to them fifty years ago but not what they had for breakfast has at least a grain of truth in it. To keep vital at an advanced age, you need exercise, both physical and mental. Some of my fellow residents take care of the mental part by doing crossword puzzles or reading old detective stories. As for me, getting online and exploring the information superhighway, safer for a man my age than the real driving I gave up several years ago, helps keep my mental reflexes nimble, as well as helping me keep current in the waning years of my own private century. Some of my friends here, however, people lots younger than I am, go slack-jawed and glassy-eyed at the very idea of using a computer.

Anyway, memory is important to us. If we feel it going, it scares us. If our pride in our memory is challenged, we defend it. That will explain why two friends of mine, both quite mentally alert, got so heated in arguing something that may seem relatively trivial to one who doesn't understand their mindset.

How many people alive now remember silent movies first-hand? Not very many, you may think, but at Plantain Point, a lot of us do. Myself, I *worked* in the industry in the silent days, but that's another story. (Many other stories, if you care to listen some time.) Ricardo Gomez and Jerome Goldberg (Rick and Jerry), old pals of about the same age, early eighties, really got into it one morning out on the sun deck. It started fairly calmly.

"Silents," said Jerry, "really look stupid now. How'd we ever watch that stuff?"

"Some of them were great art," Rick replied mildly.

"But they were so fast and jerky."

"No, no, that's just when they're played at sound speed. Show them at the right speed, the way they were intended, and they're fine. When we used to go see them, they didn't have that phony jerkiness."

"The hell they didn't. I *remember*, Rick."

"Oh, and me, I'm losing my mind, huh? Got old-timer's syndrome, do I? When I used to see silents, the speed was realistic, appropriate to the action, none of that herky-jerky stuff."

"Well, when *I* used to see them, they were exciting to a kid, sure, but they jumped around like Mexican jumping beans."

"Is that by any chance a racial reference, Jerry?"

"Ah, stop acting like a kid, Ricardo."

"A kid?"

"Yeah, a kid. You think you'll never grow old if you never

grow up. Well, it won't work. Silents were herky-jerky fiascoes, stuff you'd be embarrassed to watch today."

"They were great art, and they didn't jump around like rabbis at the Wailing Wall, either."

"What did you say, you lettuce-picking anti-Semite?"

"You heard me."

They were raising their voices, and getting red in the face. Some of the others sitting around on the deck were looking nervous. Fistfights, though rare at Plantain Point, have been known to happen, and they aren't a pretty sight. More likely than fisticuffs, one of them—or one of the onlookers—might keel over from a heart attack. Anyway, I felt like it was time for somebody to jump in, or as near jumping as I can manage at ninety-seven.

"Come on now, guys, we all know you like to needle each other, but some folks look like they're taking this seriously. Let 'em know you're kidding."

The two of them glared at each other.

"Sure, we're kidding all right," Jerry said unconvincingly.

"Yeah, big joke," Rick said. "You know all about this stuff, Seb. Tell this over-the-hill seasoned citizen I'm right."

"In a way, you're both right," I said casually. "'Course, I love hearing folks talk about the old days. Reminds me of when I saw my first talking picture."

"*The Jazz Singer* with Al Jolson," Jerry said, confidently.

"You're wrong again," said Rick. "That was a part-singing picture without much dialogue. First real all-talkie was *The Lights of New York*, 1928."

"Think you know everything, don't you? Jolson talked, and it was '27."

"Now you're both wrong," I said, and the two of them gaped at me. "I saw my first talking picture in 1913!"

YEARS BEFORE the Warner Brothers bet their future on sound in the twenties, there were various experiments with talking pictures. But in 1913, they were another vaudeville act—and not a very good one. An Edison invention called the Kinetophone was introduced in New York, Chicago, and a few other cities on February 17 of that year. The idea was a simple one, really the same one as the Vitaphone process the Warners used: sound on a phonograph record kept in synchronization (sometimes with great difficulty) with a movie on the screen. Sound on film didn't come in until around 1930.

I guess you could say the Kinetophone was just another Edison phonograph, except that it played longer and louder, and had a lever that let the operator speed it up or slow it down. The machine itself was placed next to the screen at the front of the theatre, and the operator controlled it from the rear by means of a fishline. While he was busy doing that, another fellow operated the projector, so it took two to get the job done. Before the Kinetophone vanished from the circuits less than a year later, for very good reasons I'll be telling you about, Mr. Edison's latest wonder made a stop at the vaudeville theatre where I was working that summer.

My town was big enough to get a good standard of vaudeville—not the top acts maybe, but some pretty decent ones. My job there the summer I was thirteen was vaguely defined. I just did whatever I could to make myself useful, and I guess it was enough that they kept me around—come to think of it, I've had a lot of jobs like that in my life. Most of them paid better than this one, though—in fact, I'm not sure the manager of the theatre, Mr. Cranmacker, paid me at all. I was enamored with the show business, and just being around the performers was pay enough for me.

When I wasn't engaged in my various gofer duties, I spent as much time as I could talking to the entertainers who passed through, usually for two- or three-night engagements. Ambitious without being really focused, I always tried to learn the specialty of whatever artiste I'd talked to most recently. Most vaudevillians were friendly and helpful to a novice, but it didn't take me long to learn I was no acrobat and no musician. I couldn't sing or dance worth a damn. I was a little better at doing simple magic tricks, but I didn't think I'd be the next Thurston—don't remember Thurston? He made more money on the circuit than Houdini.

There were always plenty of animal acts in vaudeville, often opening the bill while the customers were still finding their seats. Most were dog acts, as you'd expect, but I can remember sea-lion acts and even a goat act. Unfortunately, the only animal available to test my training ability on was Polonius, the theatre cat—he'd been left behind a couple years before by a Shakespearean company who'd finally decided cats weren't designed for the road. Mr. Cranmacker claimed to hate Polonius, but he couldn't have meant it because the old tabby managed to stick around—and I noticed whenever he was missing for more than an hour of so, it would worry Mr. Cranmacker more than anything except short box-office receipts.

I never succeeded in training Polonius, but I kept trying. Some of the animal people who passed through claimed it was impossible to train a cat to do anything, but others assured me there were at least some successful cat acts in vaudeville. For example, in the last century an act called Cat Piano had a guy who supposedly played music by pulling the tails of a bunch of cats. That one doesn't really count, though. Actually, the cats just sat in their boxes; the tails were phony and the performer, an animal imitator, provided most of the meows and yowls himself. Later I heard about Tetchow's cats, thirty of them, very much pampered, but able to do only one trick each. (The best one must have been pretty spectacular, though—the star cat would run out of the wings, scurry up a rope, jump in a basket that was attached to a parachute, and float down to the stage.) I also heard about an act called Nelson's Cats and Rats, where they actually had the felines and the rodents working together in the common cause of audience amusement, a strange-bedfellow combination that sounds too unlikely to believe.

Anyway, one night that summer in 1913, a touring operator of Edison's Kinetophone, a somewhat taciturn and worried-looking fellow named Forsyth, brought talking movies to our theatre for what was intended to be a full week's stand. But it would be cut short.

The morning after the first performance, in a little storage room where Mr. Cranmacker was letting Forsyth keep his machine, the cleaning lady, Mrs. Ferguson, found an even bigger mess than she was used to. Sometime during the night, somebody had taken a heavy object—a baseball bat maybe—to the Kinetophone and its operator, killing both.

Mrs. Ferguson called Mr. Cranmacker, who in turn called the police. Soon all the artistes currently on the bill had been rousted from their boarding-house beds and told to come to the theatre. They all sat out front, along with us regular employees, to hear local police detective, Cyrus Wallace, pace back and forth in front of the stage doing his best imitation of Sherlock Holmes.

"Did anybody here know this Forsyth before he got here yesterday?" We all shook our heads. "Did anybody talk to him yesterday?"

Mike Fanning, who operated the movie projector, said, "Sure, I talked to him. We had to get our jobs straight."

"How did he strike you?"

"Nervous, worried, like his boss would take it out of his hide if anything went wrong. He was real careful about the machine. At one point when we were setting up, Mr. Cranmacker's cat—"

"Not my cat," Mr. Cranmacker muttered from force of habit.

"—started playing with the fishline that led to Forsyth's machine and I thought he'd strangle the poor little guy." Mike chuckled. "If he could have caught him, that is."

"Anything else he might have been worried about that you know of?"

"We didn't have a personal conversation. It was just business."

"Did you like the guy?"

"I didn't like or dislike him. Having personal feelings about somebody you work with for one night or maybe a week tops wastes too much energy."

"What about the rest of you?" Cyrus said.

I spoke up then. "I tried to ask him about how his machine worked, but he didn't have much to say." I wasn't sure anybody heard me; I was used to being as anonymous as the furniture.

"What about you, Cranmacker?"

The manager shrugged. "I said hello, introduced myself, mentioned a few of the house rules. That was all."

"And what about the rest of you actors?" Cyrus said, turning his attention to the assembled performers. "Any of you crossed paths with this Forsyth in other towns?"

They all shook their heads.

Then Cyrus told us his theory. "This Forsyth apparently didn't know a soul in town, so why would anyone want to kill him? A personal motive? No, I think not. I think it was more of a professional motive."

He paused dramatically and looked over the assembled actors, his knowing gaze moving from face to face. We had a pretty strong bill that week.

There were the Martinelli Brothers, Claude and Billy, a couple of acrobats in their twenties—them I liked. It wasn't their fault they couldn't teach me to do a backflip. Then there were the O'Hoolihan family, a husband and wife and five kids of various ages and temperaments who did songs and scenes from sentimental plays—some of them I liked, especially a girl named Minnie, who was close to my own age. Singer on the bill was Freddy Dobbins, a skinny tenor with a big voice and a fancy way with words. Willie Ford was a Dutch comic—that really means German dialect. I imagine he switched to Yiddish come the First World War. Like a surprising number of comics, he was morose and unfunny when not performing, as if he shed his sense of humor with the comic accent. Mona and Lester Keeler were a dance act—she was beautiful, and he always looked worried; there may have been a connection. Our headliner was Walter Blane, a bald female impersonator who (typical of his kind in those homophobic times) was about as aggressively masculine (now we'd say macho) offstage as you could imagine.

"You actors felt a threat to your livelihood in this invention of Mr. Edison's, didn't you?" Cyrus hammered out in an accusatory tone. "If both images and sound could be recorded, what need would there be for you folks? The top acts would do their turns once for a camera and a recorder in New York and be seen all over the country. The lesser acts wouldn't be able to keep up with the competition. So this invention of Mr. Edison's had to go, didn't it? That's why one of you came in here last night and took a club to the—what's it called?—Kinetophone. Mr. Forsyth unfortunately surprised the culprit in the act and got his own skull crushed for his trouble."

Freddy Dobbins raised a hand. "Ah, tell me, Inspector, did you have the somewhat dubious pleasure of actually witnessing the unfortunate gentleman's act last night?"

"No, couldn't say that I did," Cyrus replied with broad sarcasm. "I'm usually a little too busy keeping law and order to go to the theatre."

"Well, if you had, you'd know that the Kinetophone presents no great threat to the vaudeville actor."

"Freddy's dead right," Walter Blane chimed in. "The novelty wears off after about a minute, slightly longer maybe if the sound goes out of synchronization."

"Like it did last night," Freddy said. "Watching Mike and

Forsyth struggling to catch up with each other was funnier than your whole act, Willie."

The Dutch comic just grunted.

Mike the projectionist smirked. "Forsyth blamed the cat again, but I never saw the little guy after the show started."

Freddy went on, "The poor audience member, who comes here to relax and forget his troubles, doesn't want to have to strain his ears to hear a tinny, mush-mouthed voice almost drowned out by static."

Mike said, "It's not possible to play the recording loud enough in a theatre this size for enjoyable listening. The louder the voices are turned up, the louder the accompanying noise gets."

"I'm honest enough to admit the New Yorker singing 'Danny Boy' at the top of his lungs on that Kinetophone is a better tenor than I'm likely ever to be," Freddy said with rare modesty, "but the audience enjoyed me singing in person much more than they did him on a recording."

Cyrus turned to Mr. Cranmacker. "Is this guy right? Didn't the people like the show?"

"They seemed to. They applauded. I wasn't going to send Mr. Forsyth out of town on the next train, I can tell you that."

"The reception to the presentation was polite," Walter Blane said judiciously, "since this is a well-mannered community, but Freddy's right. No one who saw it could think for a minute that my colleagues and I were threatened with obsolescence by this contrivance."

"And even if we were," Freddy pointed out, "destroying one Kinetophone would hardly do the job. Mr. Edison has others, I believe."

"Then why was Forsyth killed?" Cyrus demanded, as if assuming someone there could tell him.

I ventured to speak again. "Where's Polonius?"

"Behind the arras usually," said Danny O'Hoolihan, a smart

aleck three or four years older than me, "but we're not doing Hamlet this week."

"Or any week," one of his sisters giggled.

"What the hell is an arras?" Cyrus demanded, but no one enlightened him.

"Maybe we should send the kids out," Mr. Cranmacker suggested.

"Kids?" Danny protested. "I've shaved twice already this week, and ask Mona if I'm such a kid." Mrs. Keeler turned red, husband Lester looked at her like a comic cuckold, and Danny added weakly, "You two aren't married, are you?"

Before things could get out of hand, I repeated, "Where's Polonius? The cat. Hasn't anybody seen him?"

"He can take care of himself," Mr. Cranmacker said quickly.

"I saw him," said Mrs. Ferguson. "When I opened the storeroom, before I found . . . what I found. He shot out of there like Lucifer and all the hounds of hell were chasing him."

"So there's a witness to the crime," said Mrs. O'Hoolihan.

"Don't be silly," said Mr. Cranmacker, protesting way too much. "Why, if I never see that cat again, I'll be happy. Now, Cyrus, I don't mean to tell you your business, but shouldn't you be asking us all where we were—?"

Not being paid attention to was sometimes an advantage. While Mr. Cranmacker was posturing, I'd fed a line to Minnie O'Hoolihan, the friendliest of her family—at least to thirteen-year-old boys of all work.

"Oh, it was terrible," Minnie said, with more conviction than she usually brought to her lines in the family dramatic presentations. "The poor, poor kitty."

Mr. Cranmacker didn't react, but Cyrus said, "What do you mean?"

"Poor, poor Polonius. Run over by a milk wagon. I saw it this morning on our way here. It was so sad." Her parents and siblings looked at her quizzically but didn't contradict her.

"That's impossible," said Mr. Cranmacker, looking shaken. "It must have been some other cat. It wasn't Polonius."

"How do you know, Mr. Cranmacker?" I asked mildly.

"He's safe in my room, that's how I know."

"What's he doing in your room, sir?" I asked, as innocently as I could manage. "I thought you hated cats."

"I wanted to put him where he couldn't do any more damage." Listening to himself, my boss must have realized how lame that sounded. "Cyrus, I have a lot to do. I need to wire the Edison company to let them know about this tragedy. Could I be excused? If you need me, you can find me—"

"I need to see this cat," Cyrus said. "He can't testify directly, but he may have other ways of telling us something. Even if the cat did nothing in the nighttime." He had read his Sherlock Holmes. "The rest of you folks make sure Officer Gilfoyle, who's out in the lobby, knows where to find you—and none of you leave town."

"Where's that bat of yours that used to lean against the wall just inside the stage door, Mr. Cranmacker?" I asked.

"What'd you say, kid?"

"The baseball bat. It was always there."

He grinned weakly. "I gave up baseball years ago. You know that, Cyrus. And I wasn't much loss to the team, was I?"

"But I thought you carried it around with you when you checked the theatre after hours," I said. "For protection in case of burglars."

Cyrus looked at him. "What about it? That could have been the murder weapon."

"Why, so it could," Mr. Cranmacker said, like a great light had dawned. "You and Gilfoyle probably should search the theatre for it, shouldn't you, Cyrus? It may have been hidden somewhere. Meanwhile, I'll go over to my room and get the cat, bring him back for you to look at, though I can't imagine what you think he could tell you."

I was thinking fast. Like Cyrus, I had a theory but no evidence. And who'd listen to me anyway? Still, I could see my vision of the truth as plain as day—or maybe I mean as plain as melodrama—and every word out of Cranmacker's mouth convinced me I was right.

What, if Forsyth, who thought Polonius was responsible for ruining his act, found the cat in the storeroom late that night climbing all over his precious Kinetophone? And what if the worried Forsyth snapped and decided to take revenge then and there? And what if Mr. Cranmacker, who loved that cat for all his protestations to the contrary, came along in the course of his nightly security rounds, bat at the ready to protect him against intruders, and discovered Forsyth in the act of trying to throttle Polonius? What if Cranmacker took his own revenge both on Forsyth and on Mr. Edison's invention?

An unlikely scenario, you think? Maybe not. There had been no sign of breaking and entering. Who else but Mr. Cranmacker could have been in the locked-up theatre for a legitimate reason? And what other motive could there have been for the crime?

I think Polonius was scared by the violence and hid somewhere in the storage room where Mr. Cranmacker couldn't coax him out. Then when Mrs. Ferguson made her fearsome discovery, and Polonius came shooting out of the door, Mr. Cranmacker caught the tabby and removed him from the scene, hoping to downplay his possible role in what had happened. Only my concocted milk wagon story, and the fear that some disaster might have befallen his beloved cat, shook Mr. Cranmacker enough to reveal what he had done. It was the kind of dramatic slip that would have hanged him in a play or a story, but maybe not in real life. It was enough for me, but Cyrus, who was every bit smart enough to be the official cop in a bad stage detective story, seemed about to let him go, either to destroy the evidence or escape town altogether. If I was right, the bloody bat would be back in my boss's room, along with Polonius.

I thought about offering to accompany Mr. Cranmacker to his room, help him bring Polonius back to the theatre. But by that time, he must have realized I was suspicious of him. When Cranmacker had gone, I tried to sneak out and follow him, but Officer Gilfoyle spotted me and insisted I stay. I had the feeling Mr. Cranmacker was going to get away with murder, and there was nothing I could do to prevent it.

About an hour later, we all learned what had happened.

Mr. Cranmacker was seen by several witnesses that mid-morning leaving his rooming house. He was heavy laden, a struggling tabby cat under one arm, an unidentified object wrapped in butcher paper under the other. As they came down the steps, the cat got away from Mr. Cranmacker and set off running. Polonius was headed home for the theatre, and he eventually arrived. But Mr. Cranmacker, chasing him into the street, was not so lucky. He was run down and killed, not by my imagined milk wagon but by a farmer's going-to-town Ford traveling at a more than stately pace down the middle of the street.

Poetic justice for Mr. Cranmacker, you might say. But if you think the tabby cat was the cause of everything, there was poetic justice for Polonius, too. Minnie O'Hoolihan had fallen in love—not with me, darn it, but with the cat. Even her no-nonsense father couldn't refuse her anything she really wanted, so the O'Hoolihans adopted Polonius and, for a time at least, he was back on the road. Which I know he hated.

BY THE time I finished my story, Jerry and Rick were listening so intently, they seemed to have forgotten their quarrel. In fact, I caught them turning to each other and sharing a laugh at some points. They'd stay pals, and no senior-citizen blood would be spilt that day at Plantain Point.

However, they weren't ready to let me off the hook.

"Okay, Seb," Rick said, "that was a good story, and you got us calmed down like you wanted. But what do you mean we were both right about silent pictures? I know they weren't speeded up and jerky."

"And I know they were," Jerry said, with interest but no heat.

"You were a city boy, right, Rick?"

"Yeah, okay."

"And, Jerry, you grew up in a small town."

Jerry nodded. "Outside of one actually. We were farmers, but I got to the big city of ten thousand inhabitants almost every weekend, and I sure saw my share of movies."

"In the big cities, at the first run houses, silent pictures were projected at normal speed, the way they were intended. So Rick is right. But when they went to the minor circuits, the second run and small town houses, they'd often be cranked faster so they could squeeze in more showings and sell more tickets, thus the jumps and jerks. So Jerry is right, too."

"My pop always said, that theater manager was a crook!" Jerry, exploded, now mad at somebody deep in the past rather than his best friend. "Seymour Desmond was his name. He always wore plaid vests. His wife's name was Daisy, and she wore the shortest skirts in town." Jerry smiled suddenly. "You know, fellas, I was afraid I was losing my memory!"

TINSELTOWN FOLLIES OF 1948

Bill Crider

ON THE SILVER screen, Amanda Ballew was "America's Hometown Girl!" She looked as if she'd been raised behind a white picket fence in a small town in, say, Kansas, where she'd helped mom in the kitchen, had a pet dog, been a majorette with the high school band, and eaten apple pie every day.

Offscreen, it was a slightly different story, or so the rumors had it. I don't think the one about the USC football team (and all the trainers, not to mention the entire coaching staff) was true, but maybe it was. It wouldn't have been out of keeping with all the other stories I'd heard. According to one of them, she'd slept with the male lead in every picture she'd done, even the ones she'd made when she was underage. And with most of her directors. Some cameramen. A stagehand or two. A couple of gaffers. But not with any of the horses in *Ten Rode South*. That was a gross exaggeration, or so I'd been told by the head of Gober Studios himself.

He put it like this: "Goddamnit, Ferrel, she might be a little oversexed, but she'd never stoop to horses!"

I thought about asking just exactly how he meant the part about the horses, but I decided there wasn't any profit in it for me. After all, he pays me a nice retainer to see that none of his contract players gets into trouble, which is of course an impossible job. What he's really paying me for is to get them out of trouble and to keep the press from finding out about it. The pay's so good that I don't mind it when he calls me "Goddamnit" instead of my real name, which is just plain Bill. Anyway, as it turned out, there was something worse than messing around with horses. Amanda Ballew kept a diary.

"Can you believe it?" Gober asked. He was trying to stay calm, but even at the best of times his voice was so loud that it vibrated the office walls. "A goddamned diary! What kind of a woman keeps a diary?"

I was sitting in Gober's studio office in a chair that was sunk halfway to the arms in the carpet. I think he had to have a guy come in once a week to mow.

"Lots of women keep diaries," I said. "They like to have a little record of their daily lives, and—"

"They don't have daily lives like Amanda's! And they don't work for Gober Studios! And if they did, they'd have sense enough to keep the goddamned diary locked up in a safety deposit box!"

I could see that we were getting to the real problem now.

"Did something happen to the diary?"

"That's what I like about you, Ferrel," Gober said. "You're quick on the uptake. Something happened to the diary, all right. Some son of a bitch stole it."

"Uh-oh," I said.

Gober looked at me coolly. "That's one way of putting it."

"What I meant was, I'd better find out who took it, and quick. Before it gets into print or something."

"Oh, I doubt anyone could print it," Gober said. "We don't have to worry about that. There are laws about pornography, you know."

I could tell sarcasm when I heard it. And I knew as well as Gober that there could be plenty of heavy hinting without actually using any forbidden words.

"I think I'd better find that diary," I said.

"So do I," Gober said. "And soon."

AMANDA BALLEW lived in a pink stucco apartment building designed to look like the set of one of Gober's Casbah
movies. There were palm trees all around, and nothing missing
but the camels. I almost hated to park my '42 Chevy on the
street out front. It spoiled the whole picture.

But I parked and went to apartment two, which had its own
little oasis around the pool in front. Gober had called Miss
Ballew, who opened the door practically as soon as my knuckles connected with it.

If she looked good on the screen, she was a knockout in
person, all that strawberry blonde hair, blue eyes, dimples, and
a smile that would light up the Hollywood Bowl. Not to mention a shape that would make a vicar kick his vows.

"Come in, Mr. Ferrel," she said.

Her voice made icy fingers run up and down my . . . well,
let's say it was my spine. I stepped inside a room that was so
full of cushions and rugs it looked as if it had been designed for
a Rudolph Valentino film. Except for the three cats that made
a beeline for me and started arching their backs and rubbing
themselves against my ankles and calves. She should have had
a few dogs, instead. They might have barked and scared off
whoever took the diary.

"My cats like you," Miss Ballew said. "Isn't that sweet? I'm
sorry they're shedding."

I resisted the urge to sneeze and said, "I don't mind. I love
cats."

I didn't, not exactly, but a little white lie never hurt anyone.
It certainly didn't discourage the cats, who kept right on rubbing and purring.

"Mr. Gober told me you were going to find my diary," Miss
Ballew said.

"I'm going to try."

"That's wonderful. I just know you'll find it. It has some things it in that might be just the teensiest bit embarrassing to me and to . . . some other people if anyone printed it."

"Do you have any idea who might have taken it?"

She took my hand and those icy fingers got to work again. She led me over to a cushion and gave me a little push. I landed softly, and the cats came running, bumping their heads on my legs and rubbing against me.

"I don't know who would do a thing like that," she said.

"Do you know when it disappeared?"

Miss Ballew sat on a cushion near me, crossed her legs gracefully, and said, "I was outside this morning for about an hour, swimming in the pool."

I'd seen her in a bathing suit in *Co-Ed Capers*, and I could only imagine how much better she would look in the flesh. But I forced the image out of my head. I had to concentrate on the diary.

"Did you see anyone enter or leave your apartment?"

"I think maybe I did. My door wasn't locked. I never lock it when I swim. And I think I saw someone coming from the apartment."

"Do you have any idea who it was?"

"I'm not really sure. I was in the pool, remember? I had water in my eyes. But I think it might have been that awful Tommy Reynolds. When I checked around the apartment, my dairy was gone, and that's when I called Mr. Gober."

I didn't blame her for calling Gober. Tommy Reynolds was big trouble. Not because of who he was, but because of who he worked for, *Inside Secrets* magazine, a genuine scandal sheet, the same one that had ruined Heather Young, one of Gober's stars just after the war. That had been right before I'd started working for the studio.

Heather was unwise enough to have too much to drink at a popular night spot, where someone had convinced her that it would be a great idea to strip off and walk home nude. It was bad enough that she'd snarled traffic and caused a couple of wrecks, but what proved even more devastating was that *Inside Secrets* had revealed Heather's most closely guarded secret: she wasn't a natural blonde.

"Did Reynolds know about the diary?" I asked.

"I don't see how. I never told anyone about it, except for my best friends of course."

According to the papers, her best friends were Laura Holmes and Sally Tuggle, both of them Gober starlets, and two of the biggest gossips in town. Telling them was almost as bad as telling Louella Parsons. It wouldn't be much of a shock to discover that they'd said something about the diary to Tommy Reynolds.

"You know how vicious Tommy's magazine can be," Miss Ballew said.

I shifted on my cushion and tried to nudge the cats away discreetly.

"Indeed I do," I said. "*Inside Secrets* would love to shine a little light on your love life."

"Do you think you can stop them?" Miss Ballew asked.

"I'm not sure. First I have to prove that Tommy Reynolds has the diary."

I didn't really have to prove it. I just had to find the diary. I guess maybe I was stalling. Maybe I was hoping she'd say that she'd do anything—anything!—for the man who brought that diary back to her.

But she didn't. She said, "What if he doesn't have it?"

"Then we're in even more trouble than you think," I said.

I LEFT the apartment after Miss Ballew answered a few more questions. The cats, whose names I'd learned were Poppy, Aster, and Rose seemed sorrier to see me go than Miss Ballew.

I drove to the L.A. business district, where the *Inside Secrets* office was located. I figured that if Tommy Reynolds was the one who'd taken the diary, he'd have gone straight to his type-writer.

And there he was, sitting in front of his old Underwood, pecking away with two fingers, a cigarette dangling from his lower lip. The ashtray by the typewriter was full of butts.

There were two more desks in the office, but no one was sitting at them. There was another office, where Reynolds' boss worked, but the door to that one was closed.

"Hey, Tommy," I said. "Turned over any interesting rocks lately?"

He looked up, took the cigarette out of his mouth and crushed it in the ashtray. He was thin as a hoe handle, and he had a nose sharp enough to open letters with. He was wearing a dirty white suit, and there was a white hat sitting on the desk near the ashtray.

"Well, if it isn't old Bill Ferrel," he said. "The poor man's Sam Spade. Or maybe I should say the poor man's Sidney Greenstreet, considering your size."

"Ha ha," I said. Not that I'm sensitive. "I'd like to ask you a few questions."

He leaned back in his chair and put his feet up on his desk. He pulled up on his pants legs to settle them the way he wanted.

"Ask away. I don't have to answer you, though."

I knew that, but I asked anyway.

To my surprise, he answered. "Amanda Ballew's apartment? Me? Let me tell you something, Ferrel, if I ever broke in there, it wouldn't be to steal anything." He leered. "Do you get my drift?"

"I get it," I said, and the worst part was that I believed him. Oh, I didn't believe that he wouldn't steal a diary. He'd do that quicker than a producer would lie. But I did believe that he hadn't broken into Amanda Ballew's place.

I don't know why. Something in his tone, maybe, or something in the assured way he said it. It could have been the look in his eye. But I was sure he was telling the truth. He hadn't been in that apartment.

And of course I was disappointed as hell. I kept on poking and prodding at him, but it didn't do any good. I couldn't budge him, and I hadn't expected to. I finally gave it up, and turned to leave.

"I'll tell you what, Ferrel," he said to my back. "Now that I know there's something missing, I'll do my best to find out what it is. And if it's as good as I'm thinking, you can bet that *Inside Secrets* will have all the details."

The son of a bitch would, too. I could count on it. And I could also count on what Mr. Gober would do. I wondered if anyone in outer Mongolia would be needing a slightly balding private detective.

I turned back, intending to make some crack, but I never got it out because the door of the boss's office opened and a guy came out, wearing a huge grin. He was about Reynolds' size, and he was wearing a suit almost the same color of the one Reynolds wore. There was a paper bag in his right hand.

As I was giving him the once-over, I suddenly realized why I'd believed Reynolds' story, and I made a run at the guy with the bag.

Reynolds saw me coming, and stuck out his leg. I'm pretty agile for a guy who's built a little like Sidney Greenstreet, so instead of stumbling over the leg, I gave Reynolds a little kick that set him to spinning around in his swivel chair. Then I was past him and grabbing the paper bag from the other guy's hand. Then I turned and ran back the other way.

"Hey!" he yelled, which of course didn't slow me down at all.

What slowed me down was that he caught up with me and jumped on my back, putting a choke hold on me. I staggered across the room with the bag clutched to my chest like a football. I felt like Red Grange, headed for the goal line with one tackler hanging on his back, except that the Galloping

Ghost probably wouldn't have had as much trouble breathing as I was.

The guy on my back was skinny, but strong. He kept squeezing on my windpipe, until I began to see little black spots in front of my eyes. But I had enough momentum to run right over Reynolds, who'd gotten out of his chair and taken up a position right in front of me.

He was standing there like a traffic cop, with his hand up and the palm out, as if that would slow me down. I didn't even slacken my pace; I just kept right on going as if he weren't there and flattened him out. I think maybe I stepped on his chest as I went over him. He screamed something at me, but I couldn't tell what it was.

Then I was out the door and on the street. My old Chevy was only a few yards away, but I wasn't sure I was going to make it there. The guy on my back was about to pull his forearm right through my throat. I was gagging, and my head was spinning.

I couldn't think of anything else to do, so I came to a sudden stop, bending over and sort of coming up on my toes at the same time. The guy flew over my head, feet first, nearly taking my ears off as his arm came loose. He flipped over in the air, and his head hit the front fender of the Chevy. The fender rang like a bell, and the guy slid to the curb as if all his bones had dissolved.

I didn't wait to see if he was all right. I opened the door, threw the paper bag on the passenger seat, and jumped in the Chevy. By the time Reynolds got out to the street to help his pal to his feet, I was already half a block away.

I looked over at the paper bag. I was going to be pretty embarrassed if there was a pastrami on rye in there.

"WELL, FERREL, you did it again," Mr. Gober said.

We were in his office, me sitting in the same chair, still sunk in that overly plush carpet of his. Both of us were feeling a lot

better about things this time, however, especially me, since the
bag had held the diary and not someone's deli lunch.

The diary was sitting on Gober's desk right in front of him.
He hadn't opened it. In fact, he hadn't even touched it since
taking it out of the bag and laying it on the desk.

"Are you going to read that thing?" I asked.

He looked down at the diary, then back at me. "Of course
not. That would hardly be gentlemanly."

I couldn't recall that anyone had ever accused him of being
a gentleman, but maybe he had a natural sense of delicacy —
like me. After all, I hadn't even opened the diary myself.

Or maybe it wasn't delicacy, exactly. Maybe neither one of
us really wanted to know what was in there. As long as we
didn't read the words written in Amanda Ballew's own hand-
writing, there was some part of us that could believe she was
still America's Hometown Girl.

"How did you figure out who'd taken it?" he asked.

"Cat hair," I said.

He didn't say anything, just looked at me as if he thought I
might be a little crazy.

"I knew Reynolds hadn't taken it, but I didn't know how I
knew. Then I realized it was cat hair."

He kept on looking at me. He didn't think I was a little
crazy now. He thought I was a *lot* crazy.

"See, Reynolds didn't have any cat hair on his pants," I said.
"When I went in Miss Ballew's apartment, those cats were all
over me, rubbing against my pants legs. They're not shy about
it. Whoever took the diary got the same treatment.

"And the cats are shedding pretty bad. Cat hair sticks to
fabric. Look." I held up a leg. "See? It's all over me."

"And there wasn't any on Reynolds?"

"That's right. But it was sticking to the guy with the bag. I
could see it from across the room."

"Those cats are pretty good watchdogs," Gober said.

I nodded. "A lot better than I thought."

"Very well, then, Ferrel. I'll see that you get a little bonus for this."

I knew that I was being dismissed. I stood up and said, "Want me to take that diary to Miss Ballew? It wouldn't be out of my way."

"I wouldn't want you to go to the trouble," Gober said. "I'll see that she gets it."

I left then, wading through the carpet. As I was closing the door, I thought about turning back to have a look, just to see if Gober was taking a peek inside the covers of the diary.

But I didn't. My natural sense of delicacy was in control. I winked at Gober's secretary and went outside. It was one of those perfect California days, with a sky so blue and clear that it seemed to be a thousand miles high. I brushed some cat hair off my pants and drove back to the office to sit in my chair and dream about America's Hometown Girl.

THE DEATH CAT OF
HESTER STREET

Carol Gorman

"FIFTY TIMES I'M telling you, Herman Epstein can make you happy!" Rose Bochlowitz said. "He's a good man, Lena. He's also a butcher, of course, so every day you'll never go hungry. Did you see the way he looked at you?"

"Oh, Mama," Lena said, pushing away a stray wisp of dark hair that had escaped the knot on her head, "let's not talk about it again. It's too hot."

Lena and Rose Bochlowitz, carrying their sacks sewn from coarse cloth, made their way along crowded Hester Street, weaving around pushcarts and wagons. All around them, a clamor of voices called out in Yiddish, German, English, and Russian as peddlers and buyers haggled over the price of potatoes, pumpernickel and suspenders. The air was still and rank. Above them, residents of the tenement apartments sat on fire escapes, sipping water or cheap beer and waited for a cooling breeze that never came.

"Five cents everyone pays the butcher to cut off the chicken's head, but Herman Epstein won't take it from you!" Rose said, stepping around a pile of horse manure in the street. "He looks at you with such affection, *Lenale*. It's good I happened to meet you there to see such a thing."

Rose and Lena plodded on, their cotton skirts swirling

around their legs. Sweat wetted their underarms and stained their shirtwaists.

Lena blotted her forehead with a handkerchief. She was not only hot, but tired. She had spent ten hours on her feet at Gibson's dress shop with only one twenty-minute break for lunch. As the manager, she watched over the cash girls and sales girls and worked as hard as they did. At least it was the dull season. During the fall and winter, she worked a twelve-hour day before returning after supper to do the bookwork until midnight or later. But then she didn't have to deal with this heat. It was a heat that could suffocate, that could drain a person's energy and strength in less than an hour.

The shadows were lengthening along the street as people headed home to apartments to fix their evening meals.

"One thing more I will say, and then I will say it no more," Rose said. Lena rolled her eyes upward, and Rose waggled her finger at her daughter. "Better you should marry Herman Epstein now and eat, than wait for God knows who and starve."

"Mama, this is America," Lena said. "Women in America marry for love."

Rose ignored her. "Esther Rossman is getting married, and she's twenty-two years old. In one year, maybe she'll have a baby! Twenty-six you are—may you live to be a hundred—and you have no man, no nothing. Maybe you'd like Nathan Samuelson. I saw him and his mother, the fortune lady, this morning on Hester Street. Such a nice young man! I told him about you and how well you're doing at Gibson's—"

"Mama, I'll find my own man. Lots of men come into the shop."

"To buy something for their wives or lady friends," Rose said. "No man walks into a dress shop who isn't taken."

"Well, I won't marry a man I don't love. If I don't find the right man, I won't get married."

Rose looked horrified. "*Bays di tsung!* Of course, you'll get married. God forbid such a thought should enter your head!"

A white cat, its fur darkened and matted with filth, suddenly appeared at their feet, streaked over Lena's shoe, scrambled across the street and disappeared behind an ash can left for the dumping cart.

"*Gottenyu!*" Rose screamed, grabbing Lena's arm protectively. "Turn your face, Lena! Don't look at the cat! Come with me, come, come." She dragged Lena into a shoe-repair shop where she collapsed against the wall, her breath coming in ragged gasps.

"What is it?" Lena asked, her eyes wide in horror. "Mama, you look as if you've seen a ghost. It's just a cat."

"It touched you, Lena? Tell me—"

"It ran over my shoe—"

Rose gasped and clasped her hands together. "The fortune lady, Mrs. Samuelson. We must see her!"

"Whatever are you talking about?"

"A terrible thing, that cat," Rose said. "It's the Death Cat."

Lena frowned. "The Death Cat?"

Rose was still breathing heavily. "It showed up, the cat did, the, the day Mrs. Solomon got the first signs of consumption."

"Oh, Mama, that was just a coincidence."

"A coincidence she tells me!" Rose said, exasperated. "I haven't said everything there is to tell. Now listen. Mr. Levi fell down the stairs and broke his neck. That terrible thing was there, too."

"Mama—"

"And what about poor Mrs. Gitelson? Walking she was, minding her own business, and the Death Cat jumped out, and she fell right down on the street and died! Someone should kill the evil thing and bury its body in a place far away."

"Mama," Lena said, "there's no such thing as a Death Cat. It probably eats its weight in rats every day." She smiled. "We shouldn't kill it; we should invite it into the apartment."

Rose grabbed Lena's arms. "Don't get near the cat again. Promise me, Lena, promise me."

Lena sighed. "I won't go near the cat, Mama."

"Now we talk to the fortune lady," Rose said.

"Why? Mama, I have to go home and pluck this chicken."

"Chickens can wait. The fortune lady will tell us what we need to know."

"Mama, if you're playing matchmaker again—"

"Who said anything about her son Nathan?"

"You did. Not two minutes ago. Besides, we don't have the money to pay for a fortune."

"Five cents. So I won't get the scissors sharpened this week. I can sew shirts with dull scissors. My daughter's life is more important. Come."

The fortune lady lived on the fifth floor of a brick tenement house on Orchard Street. Odors from clogged toilets, left unattended by the landlord, and garbage smells from the air shaft, hung in the still air and mixed with the aromas of dinners cooking.

The women climbed flight after flight of dark, creaky steps. The temperature rose the higher they climbed, and at every landing, Rose stopped to catch her breath.

"Mama, this is crazy," Lena said at the fifth floor. "Just because a cat—"

"A terrible thing, that cat," Rose said again, leaning heavily against the clammy wall.

"Have you asked Mrs. Samuelson for a fortune before this?"

"Once I came with Ruth Frank," Rose said. "She told the truth: that Ruth's daughter would marry in a year, and she did!"

"Oh, Mama."

"Well, so maybe it was two and a half years." Rose shrugged. "But she got married! That's the important thing." She pointed down the hall. "Over there."

A handwritten sign outside the back right apartment said Fortunes Told.

"Here," Rose said and rapped on the door.

After a moment, the door was yanked open. A small, stooped woman stood in the doorway. Her dark hair was threaded with gray, braided and pinned in a circle on her head.

"Mrs. Bochlowitz, twice in one day I see you," she said in Yiddish.

Rose answered her, in Yiddish, "Mrs. Samuelson, a fortune is what we want for my daughter, Lena."

The woman motioned them to come in and led them through her small kitchen and into her parlor. The room was very dark and hot. Lena moved quickly to the window, hoping for a breath of air. She was disappointed. Five stories below was a narrow concrete courtyard, surrounded with tall, brick buildings that blocked the sun and any breeze that might be stirring outside.

Turning from the window, Lena gazed around the dimly lit room for the first time. It was nearly empty; the wooden floor had been swept clean. The walls were bare except for a clock that ticked softly on the far wall. The only furniture was the tiny wooden table and two chairs standing next to her at the window. Two plain pieces of thin cotton, stretching across the window, served as a curtain.

"Come," Mrs. Samuelson said. "Sit."

She took a chair and sat at the table. That left only one remaining chair, and Rose gestured for Lena to take it.

"Mrs. Samuelson," Lena said in Yiddish as she sat, "my mother thinks—"

"Five cents," the woman said in English, tapping the table. Then reverting to Yiddish, "Put it here."

Lena felt resentment toward her mother for insisting on this fortune that they couldn't afford. She frowned at Rose and pulled the nickel out of her knotted handkerchief. She laid it on the table.

"Where's the crystal ball?" Lena murmured in English, and the woman looked up at her sharply.

"I must go into a trance now," she said, and closed her eyes.

"Mrs. Samuelson—" Rose said anxiously.

The woman opened her eyes. "So how can I go into a trance if you talk to me, eh?"

"I have to know," Rose said, drawing closer. "Is my daughter in danger? The Death Cat touched her just now."

"The Death Cat?"

"A terrible thing, that cat," Rose said, worry lines deepening in her forehead. "It appears and people die."

The woman peered closely at Lena. "And you touched this thing, this Death Cat?"

"A white cat ran over my foot," Lena said, waving a hand impatiently. "I don't believe in such things. My mother is a little super—"

"A white cat?" Mrs. Samuelson said. Her voice became soft and she stared out the window. "Like a ghost."

"Mrs. Samuelson, I really don't think—"

"Silence," Mrs. Samuelson said, closing her eyes once more. "I'm going into a trance."

She began to hum in low tones and rock back and forth. Lena glanced at her mother, who bent over the fortune lady, her eyes wide with fear.

Lena sighed heavily. It had been a long day, and she still had to pluck and dress that chicken.

Mrs. Samuelson let out a groan. She stopped rocking and, with her eyes still closed, said, "It is night. A warm night. I see a shop—"

"Yes, yes!" Rose cried. "Gibson's! I told you about it this morning. Lena works there."

"The dress shop—" Mrs. Samuelson said, nodding. "Someone is moving in darkness."

"Outside the shop?" Rose whispered.

"No, I see inside. Someone is—yes, someone has broken in and is robbing—"

A look of horror crossed the woman's face. "No, no! Terrible! I can't watch! It's awful, terrible, terrible."

Her eyes flew open and she leaped to her feet. "Go!" she cried. "Now. Both of you. You must leave my house."

"But what did you see?" Rose cried, her face ashen. "A thing so terrible you can't watch? But my daughter! What will happen to my Lena?"

Lena watched with a mixture of horror and fascination. Whatever it was that Mrs. Samuelson imagined she saw, it was enough to frighten the woman terribly and send a chill up her own back.

The apartment door opened, and a young man walked in.

"Hello," he said and smiled. "Mrs. Bochlowitz, is it?" He looked at Lena then and opened his mouth to speak, but then he saw the horrified look on his mother's face. "What's going on?"

"Go!" Mrs. Samuelson said again to Lena and her mother. "And never come back here!"

"Mother!" the young man said. "What's wrong?"

"It's all right," Lena said, holding up her hand. "We're going, Mrs. Samuelson."

She walked Rose across the parlor floor, out the kitchen door and into the hall.

Lena bustled Rose down the five flights of steps and out into the busy street.

"Lena, I'm so frightened!" Rose cried. "A terrible thing is waiting to happen. You heard Mrs. Samuelson."

"No, Mama," Lena said. "It was just in her imagination."

"But the Death Cat always comes before a terrible thing!" Tears welled in Rose's eyes and she clutched Lena's arms. "*Lenale*, you can't go back to the dress shop! Especially at night."

Lena steered Rose toward their apartment on Broome Street and began walking, her arm around her mother.

"Of course I'm going back. I can only get the bookwork done after the shop has closed. There's no time during the day."

"Some terrible person is going to rob it!"

"Mrs. Samuelson doesn't know anything," Lena said.

"The police," Rose said. "We must tell the police."

"What? I thought you didn't trust the police."

"What's not to trust? My daughter is in trouble."

"I'm not in trouble!" Lena said. "And what are you going to tell them, Mama? That we saw a white cat and a fortune lady went into a trance and saw a burglary? How can I tell them that?"

"You speak," Rose said. "You have a mouth. They'll listen."

"They won't listen," Lena said. "They'd think we're two crazy ladies."

Rose turned abruptly and headed across the street.

"Mama, where are you going?"

"To the police," Rose said, walking straight ahead. "So they think I'm crazy. I'll protect my daughter."

"Not now, please," Lena said wearily, hurrying to catch up. "It's hot and I'm tired, and I have to pluck this chicken."

"Always with the chicken!" Rose said, continuing on her way. "I worry about my daughter's life, and she talks to me about chickens! Come. We'll talk to the police. Later we pluck the chicken."

DETECTIVE GABRIEL Goldman, leaning back in his desk chair, listened to Rose's story. No expression crossed his face. Occasionally, he glanced at Lena, but his face didn't give a clue as to what he was thinking.

He was a handsome man, Lena observed. But he was laughing at them behind that mask of his, she was sure of it. She felt the heat rise in her cheeks.

"So, of course, we came to the police," Rose concluded. "You will make sure Gibson's is not robbed by that horrible man, and my daughter will be safe." She nodded once, sat back in her chair and folded her arms across her lap, a gesture that put a physical "period" at the end of her story.

The room at the police station was crowded with desks and people. For a moment, Goldman said nothing, and Lena was suddenly aware of how noisy the room was.

Goldman stared thoughtfully at Rose. Then he shifted in his chair.

"Uh, Mrs. uh—" he glanced at the paper on his desk, "—Mrs. Bochlowitz, I appreciate your concern for your daughter."

Here it comes, Lena thought. He thinks Mama's crazy.

"But you understand that I can't put officers around a shop simply because of a dream—"

"What dream?" Rose said, "A *trance* it was! Mrs. Samuelson goes into a trance. Don't ask me how she does it, she just does it. And she sees things. She saw something terrible."

"And the Death Cat brought this on."

Lena, her face flaming, rose from her chair. "Come on, Mama, I told you he wouldn't believe you."

Goldman leaned forward in his chair and caught Lena's arm. "Now, I didn't say I didn't believe it."

Lena stopped and stared at him. "You believe Mama?"

"Well—no," he said, "but I didn't say it. Up until now, that is."

Lena shook her arm free. "Come on, Mama." She gently pulled Rose to her feet. "I won't have him laughing at us."

"Miss Bochlowitz," Goldman said seriously, "that's the last thing in the world I would do to you."

Lena glanced at him to see if he were making sport of them, but his face was boyishly earnest.

"Thank you for listening, Mr. Goldman. But I think we've taken up enough of your time."

"Lena, he has to help us," Rose said. "You can't go back to Gibson's. Something terrible will happen!"

"Miss Bochlowitz—"

"Come on, Mama." Lena pulled her mother across the crowded room and outside.

"But what will we do, Lena?" Rose cried. "There's danger at the shop!"

"That's nonsense. I don't believe a word of it."

"You can't go back, Lena."

"I'm sorry, Mama, but I can't quit my job. Positions are too hard to find. It took me eight years to work up from cash girl to manager. Do you have any idea how many girls would give everything they have to get out of the factories or give up their pushcarts? I'm one of the lucky ones, Mama."

"No job is worth the danger that waits for you, Lena. So you don't believe the fortune lady. You must believe the Death Cat!"

The argument continued through the evening as they plucked and dressed the chicken, browned the onions on top of the coal stove for *paprikasch* and during the cleanup after their meal.

"I'm going to go back to the shop now," Lena said, drying her hands on an old, worn towel. "I must catch up on the bookwork, and I don't want to hear a word about it."

"No, Lena!"

"It's too hot in the bedroom," Lena said. "Why don't you sleep on the fire escape tonight? Maybe there will be a breeze. I'll join you after I get home."

"So how can I sleep if my daughter is getting herself killed?"

"I'll be back before you know it."

"It's too dangerous. Please, Lena."

Lena washed her face at the kitchen sink, used the toilet outside the apartment in the hall and returned to the parlor where her mother paced.

"I'll wait until you're settled on the fire escape," Lena said.

"Please don't go, *Lenale*."

"Mama, I have no choice. I've always gone back to do the bookwork at night. I won't stop now because of some silly—"

"Who knows how the fortune lady sees things?"

Lena sighed heavily. She helped her mother into her night

shift. Rose washed up at the kitchen sink, all the while fretting aloud about the Death Cat. Then she left to use the toilet.

After the kitchen door closed behind her mother, Lena moved quickly into the bedroom and dropped to her knees. She reached under the bed, heard a scurrying and snatched her hand back. A rat.

She hurried to the kitchen and lit a candle. Grabbing a broom in the corner, she tiptoed back into the bedroom and shoved the broom under the bed. The broom was the weapon they always used for killing rats in the apartment. Now, though, Lena only wanted the rat out of the way so it wouldn't bite her.

She tipped the candle carefully to see under the bed and grabbed a ball bat that she'd used as a girl to play One O'Cat. The rat scurried to a dark, far corner. "I'll get you later," Lena whispered.

She leaned the bat against the wall next to the doorway leading to the kitchen.

Rose returned, and Lena helped her mother out the parlor window and onto the metal fire escape, still warm from the heat of the day. She handed Rose a blanket and pillow.

"Good-night, Mama," Lena said. "And don't worry."

"Don't worry she says. My daughter is going to be robbed or killed, and I'm supposed to be happy." Her face etched with anxiety, Rose reached out to take Lena's hand. "May God go with you, *Lenale.*"

LENA REACHED into the dark bedroom and grabbed the bat just before leaving the apartment. She descended the two flights of stairs and pushed open the heavy wooden door to the outside. At the corner, she turned south onto Orchard where the peddlers were packing up their wares. Some were already heading down the street toward the pushcart barn, talking and complaining about the heat. Overhead, residents sat or lay on the fire escapes, quietly waiting for sleep to come.

Lena walked a block and turned right onto Grand. The shop fronts were dark, but overhead the new electric streetlights were casting a buttery glow over the neighborhood. Lena tucked the bat under her arm and reached into her purse for the shop key.

She didn't exactly believe the fortune lady's vision. Her mother believed in a lot of superstitions, and Lena usually laughed about them. But once in a while, her mother would predict something, and weirdly enough, it would come true. At least often enough to make her cautious. Lena felt a little silly carrying the bat with her, but it was somehow reassuring to feel the weight and density of the hard wood under her fingers.

Lena unlocked the shop, tiptoed inside and locked the door behind her. She stood in the gloom and waited for her eyes to adjust to the darkness.

Gradually, inky forms took shape, standing like cemetery statues around the room. Mannequins dressed in Gibson's finery posed in shadowy groups of twos and threes. Dresses hung from hangers on wire racks. Tables featuring Lena's artistic displays of scarves and jewelry squatted around the room looking like so many hunched monsters in the darkness.

The quiet was unnerving.

Still, hot air hung heavily around Lena. She wiped sweat from her chin and forehead, then walked quickly over the wooden floor to a small window at the front and lifted it a few inches. A faint breeze wafted inside. Lena squatted next to the window and let a whisper of air cool her face. She took a few deep breaths, then returned to the back of the shop where the cash table stood.

Like most of the shops along Grand, Gibson's was still using gas lanterns inside. Lena rested the bat on the table, picked up the leather-bound book that contained the shop's financial figures, and reached up to turn on the lights. She had put a quarter into the meter on the wall just yesterday, so all she had to do was turn the switch.

The front shop door rattled softly. Lena froze and listened. The sound came again, and she grabbed the bat and crouched behind the cash table. She rose slighty and squinted over the cash register into the darkness. On the other side of the glassed-in shop door, was the figure of a man hunched over in the gloom. A small sound of breaking glass pierced the quiet, and in moments, the door swung open, and the man was inside.

Lena gripped her bat tightly and kept low. Surely the burglar's first stop would be the cash register; he was already heading in her direction.

Lena scrambled quietly to the end of the cash table and rounded the far side just as the intruder reached it.

The register drawer opened with a loud *jang!* that rang through the silent shop. Lena peeked over the cash table and watched as the robber stuffed money from the drawer into a bag. Maybe he would take what he wanted and leave. Maybe if she were very quiet and kept low, he wouldn't see her. After he was gone, she would be safe.

When the register was empty, he slammed the drawer shut and moved to the table where Lena had carefully arranged a display of jewelry and accessories. In a crouch, she moved behind a mannequin, putting a little more distance between herself and the robber.

With one broad stroke of his arm, he swept all of it—the necklaces, bracelets, rings and hair clips—off the table and into his bag.

That's when something changed inside Lena. He was so greedy, so callous about these treasures that customers saved for and bought with their hard-earned pay from the sweatshops or their factory jobs. How dare he steal from Gibson's where she and her girls worked so hard! Would Mr. Gibson fire a few of the girls to make up for the loss? Would the rest of them have to work that much harder to make up for fewer shop girls to wait on the customers?

Rage boiled inside of Lena. She would *not* wait quietly and let this horrible person walk off with Gibson's money and merchandise.

She brought her bat, and she would use it. But she would have to be closer to the robber.

Her heart hammering her ribs, she moved once more, this time around the mannequin, toward the shadowy figure that was now stuffing shirtwaists from a rack into his bag.

Lena gripped her bat and moved closer—and stepped on her skirt. She tripped and fell forward into the mannequin which toppled onto the floor, sending a hat flying and spreading its dress in disarray.

In a moment, the man was on Lena, grabbing her from behind. She was so frightened, she forgot for a moment that she still held the bat at her side. By the time she remembered, it was too late to raise it. "And who is *this?*" he said, yanking her to her feet and spinning her around. The streetlight shone behind him, and his face was in deep shadow. The beer on his breath was nearly overpowering. "Well, well, were you waiting for me, eh? We could have some fun tonight."

And that's when it happened.

A small form scrambled out of the darkness and ran between the robber's legs. The man's toe caught on the creature, and he lost his balance, falling to the side, letting go of Lena.

"Rrreowwwwww!"

Lena had just enough time to raise her bat and bring it down on the back of the intruder's shoulders and head.

The man slumped to the floor and lay there without moving.

Lena stared at him, clutching the bat to her chest.

"Miss Bochlowitz! Are you there?" The voice came from outside the shop. The door burst open, and a man entered. "Miss Bochlowitz, it's Detective Goldman. Are you all right?"

He walked around a display, and saw Lena with her bat and the dark form of the man stretched out on the floor. He scratched his head. "I'd say you're doing all right for yourself, Miss Bochlowitz. I thought I'd walk past the shop on my way home, and I saw the broken glass—"

Goldman turned the man over. Lena leaned down and peered into his face. She gasped. "It's the fortune lady's son!"

"BUT TO bring that terrible thing *home*, Lena!" Rose said. She stood over the kitchen counter where she was chopping onions for chicken soup.

The white cat crouched over a dish on the floor and greedily ate the chicken livers Lena had given it.

"Mama, the cat saved my life, climbing through the window that way! That's a big accomplishment for such a small creature."

"I don't like it, this cat being here. It's a feeling in my stomach. And my stomach never lies."

"I think she'll bring us *good* luck, Mama," Lena said. "She's already killed a rat."

Rose's eyes opened wide. "This mangy Death Cat is a *she?*"

"I think I'll call her Miss Pluck. She certainly has a lot of it."

"And dirt. This cat has a lot of dirt."

A rap sounded at the door. Lena crossed the tiny kitchen in three steps and opened the door.

"Mrs. Samuelson!" Lena stepped back. "Please come in," she said in Yiddish.

"Mrs. Samuelson?" Rose wiped her hands on a rag.

The fortune lady took a couple of timid steps into the kitchen.

"I'm sorry to disturb you," the woman said. She looked at the floor. "My son—I'm sorry."

"It wasn't your fault," Lena said. "There's no need for you to apologize."

"Yes, I must." The woman began to tremble, and Lena

pulled out a chair for her. She sat. "You see, in my trance I saw the robber."

"Yes, you saw him in the shop."

"But I saw his face. My son's face. It was terrible. I saw blood dripping from his ears. I saw him, and I knew he would rob the shop." A long moment passed. "I was frightened for him, and I told you nothing."

"You were protecting your son," Lena said.

"A hundred times that night I told him not to go out."

"Children never do what you tell them," Rose said. Lena looked up at her, and she shrugged. "So all right, *some* children never do what you tell them."

Lena put a hand on Mrs. Samuelson's shoulder. "It turned out fine, Mrs. Samuelson. How is your son?"

"He'll be all right," the woman said. "He must go to jail first." She stood. "I'm going to visit him now." She looked down at the floor and gasped. "The ghost cat—"

"The Death Cat," Rose corrected her. "My daughter has invited it to stay with us."

The woman's eyes widened.

"It's a good cat," Lena said. "Thank you for stopping to see us, Mrs. Samuelson."

The fortune lady said good-bye and disappeared out the kitchen door.

"She saw her son's face," Rose said. "You see, the fortune lady knows these things!"

"Yes, Mama."

Rose looked down at the cat who was sauntering into the parlor. "The cat is full of dirt, Lena. My clean house—"

"Mr. Goldman is going to help me give it a bath tonight."

Rose gasped. "The policeman? He's coming here?"

Lena's cheeks reddened. "Yes. He says he wants to see me again. We'll bathe the kitty and then go for a walk."

"This is a romantic evening, washing a flea-bitten cat?"

Lena beamed. "It's a start."

Rose sighed. "What's with young women in America, eh? They marry for love; they clobber robbers over the head; they wash filthy cats for a little romance." She glanced up at Lena. "They aren't interested in butchers."

"You're right, Mama," Lena said, smiling.

Rose shrugged. "So my daughter loves a policeman—"

"I don't love him, Mama! We just met!"

"So my daughter just met a policeman. If that's what she wants—"

"Mama," Lena said, covering her mother's hand with her own. "Maybe I'll fall in love; maybe I won't. But I'm happy."

"So my daughter's happy. The policeman can't support her as the butcher can, so maybe they'll starve. We have a Death Cat living with us, eating chickens at sixteen cents a pound. So, maybe we save money, eh? Instead of paying the butcher five cents to cut off a chicken's head, we can bring home the live chicken and let the Death Cat kill it. As long as my daughter is happy."

"Oh, Mama!" Lena laughed.

Rose shrugged and smiled. "As long as my daughter is happy."

ST. MARGARET'S KITTEN

Doug Allyn

I WAS DYING but I wasn't sure why. I'd chosen a busy corner in the market square of the Scottish border village and
chatted up passersby as I uncased and tuned my lute. With five
kings contending in Scotland and the Lionheart abroad, traveling minstrels are a rare sight in the outlands north of the
Tweed nowadays and I soon drew a small but friendly crowd
'round me.

I opened with "The Song of Roland." It's a ballad from the
time of Charlemagne, a tale of a hero who throws his life away
for honor. I sing it well and the village folk responded with
hearty applause and a few shouts of encouragement.

They offered no money, of course. Pennies are in short supply in the borderlands, hard enough to acquire at sword's
point, to say nothing of a song.

No matter. In the wandering trade I follow, a good meal is
as welcome as a few coppers. With luck, I'd earn an invitation
to sup with a village family and perhaps gain an introduction
to the steward of the local stronghold.

It was a fair day for late October, brassy and bright as a
Saracen gong. I followed Roland's song with a gentle love
ballad popular among the gentry of London and York. Some of

the women in the crowd went dewy-eyed as the song wound
on, and I knew I was reaching them.

Moments like these, singing in a new town for an attentive
audience, are the true wages of a troubadour, fair payment for
the chancy life of the road and the loneliness. I was enjoying
myself mightily, happy as a bear at a honeybee's bridal feast.

Then suddenly my day began coming undone. I chose a
ballad I'd written myself, "The Battle of Aln Ford." It's a bold
tale of a desperate battle of Englishmen against a wolf pack of
Norse raiders. The fight had occurred not many leagues northeast within recent memory, so I thought the story might be
familiar to some of the locals. But instead of winning me the
smiles and nods of recognition I expected, my song had the
opposite effect.

A dozen verses into the ballad I sensed restlessness in the
crowd. I glanced around for the cause, approaching soldiers or
perhaps a quarrelsome lout, but the trouble seemed to be with
the song itself. The more I sang, the more uneasy glances were
exchanged and folks began to move off. One moment I was
enjoying a golden afternoon's performance, the next I was dying, living a performer's nightmare as my audience melted
away from me like beeves from a barn fire.

The cold sweat of disaster beaded my brow. I tried to
shorten the song, eliminating the penultimate arc of the saga
altogether. Too late. By the time I rang the final verse to a
close, I was almost alone in the square. I couldn't have frightened them off more effectively if my lute had been a leper's
bell.

Only two remained, a wee girl who'd been hovering near my
knee since I began and a stripling youth who'd been watching
me from the shadow of the village well.

The child stared at me with brimming eyes and quivering
lip. She was barefoot and dressed in coarse linen but her face
was clean and she looked well fed. Not a serf's whelp then, a
local craftsman's daughter, perhaps. A miller or a smith. She

was holding a small sack. Food? My mouth watered. I'd not eaten in two days.

"Why do you cry, child?" I said, kneeling to face her. "Did hearing of the battle frighten you?"

"No, sir," she said, swallowing. "It were the song before, the one about the dying princess. It was very sad."

"Even so, it was only a song. Cheer up, it's too fine a day for frowning. What, um, what do you have in your bag?"

"My kitten, see?" She opened the mouth of her sack and hauled out a tiny, snow-white kitten by the scruff of its neck. It looked about a month old, weaned, but not much beyond that. The kit hissed and clawed at her. "I named her Maggie, for the saint," she said, offering it to me. "She liked your singing ever so much. I could tell. You may hold her."

"Thank you," I said, taking the kitten, which immediately sunk its needle talons into my tunic. "She looks to be a fine . . ." But the girl had turned and scampered off. "Wait little miss, your kitten—"

"You may keep her," she called over her shoulder. "My ma told me to drown her." She held up the empty sack as proof, then broke into a run and vanished between two huts.

"Be grateful for the free kit," the youth said, stepping from the shadow of the well. "If one of Milord's guardsmen had heard that last song you might have earned a thrashing instead."

"A thrashing? Surely I didn't sing all that badly?" I sized him up. Sixteen or so, freckle-faced with a mop of unruly chestnut hair, he was clad in a short green tunic trimmed with squirrel fur, belted at the waist. A noble? No, he hadn't the look and wore no dagger.

"It wasn't your voice that was amiss, minstrel, only your lyrics. The Fight At the Ford is well known in the area. Sir Denis de Picard, the hero of Aln Ford is master here at Wansfeth. That's his stronghold at the river bend."

I followed his eyes. The local castle stood on a mound of

raised earth at the east end of the town. A stout stone fortress fifty feet high with the river on three sides, it was built in the early Norman style with corner towers for bowmen and surrounded by a crude wall of earth, stone, and upright logs. To the south, in England, it would have been unimpressive, but here in the hinterlands it seemed formidable.

"What did you say the lord's name was?"

"Sir Denis de Picard. It was his song you sang, and quite well I might add, though you had the story wrong. It was Sir Denis who led the charge that broke the Vikings at the ford, not his cousin Ranaulf."

He sang a verse of the ballad for me, quite different from the one I'd written years ago. His voice was clear and strong, and his intonation was true. A promising talent, if a bit raw.

"I've not heard that particular version before," I said carefully, "but sometimes songs change over time and distance. You have a fine voice, sir. Are you a minstrel?"

"I hope to be one day. I sing reasonably well, but I'm only a novice on the lute. My fingers are like sausages. May I examine your instrument? I've never seen one with so rounded a body shape."

"It's called a turtle-back," I said, passing it to him. "It's derived from the Italian style." He cradled it, as reverently as a sliver of the True Cross, and for a moment I recalled another singer handing me a similar instrument in York many years ago. Was I ever so young?

"It's beautifully crafted," he said wistfully. "Did you carve it yourself?"

"Nay, I traded a hard-used sword and buckler for it. I was a soldier in the years before I took to the road as a singer. Some say I've injured more folk with my voice than I ever did with a blade. My name is Tallifer, of Shrewsbury and York."

"Elwood Chisolm of Wansfeth," he said, accepting my handclasp. "I'm a ward of Milord de Picard's. My parents died when I was a tad, not much bigger than your kitten. With no heir of age, our land rightfully reverted to Sir Denis but he took me along with it and made me welcome in his household."

"He always had a weakness for strays—dogs, cats or children."

"You know him?"

"I did once, many years ago, if it's the same man. Picard's not an uncommon name on either side of the border. But if he was at the ford and he's truly Ranaulf de Picard's cousin, then yes, I knew him. Whether that's still true is another matter. Men can be as changeable as songs."

"Not Milord," the youth said positively. "He's as constant as yonder hills. Come, I'll take you to him. He's always happy to welcome visitors from the south."

Carrying Maggie the kitten ensconced comfortably inside my tunic where she could peer out, I followed Elwood through the village toward the castle.

Wansfeth Town seemed prosperous enough for a border backwater. It had its own mill, a smithy, and a chapel crafted of carved stone. The huts were mostly of wattle and daub, but seemed stoutly built and well-tended.

The castle was another matter. It was large, but had a rude, unfinished look, as though the Norman craftsmen who'd raised it a century before had only finished their work a few weeks earlier.

There was no moat but the long stairway to the main gate was guarded by two men-at-arms with pikes and chain-mail tunics. Elwood waved at the sentries and they passed us through without a challenge.

The inner courtyard was abustle with visitors. A dozen horses, still dusty from the road, were tethered to a rail outside the stable, which was nearly filled. Grooms and servants were brushing down the mounts and unpacking their loads.

"What is all this?" I asked. "Christmas is more than a month away."

"A festival," Elwood said. "The feast of Saint Margaret."

"Margaret? The child said her kitten was named Maggie after St. Margaret, but I know of no such saint."

"St. Margaret Canmore of Dunfermline, the widow of old King Malcolm," he explained. "She's not been properly canonized by Mother Church as yet but folk hereabout consider her a saint and pray to her. She died a decade ago in November. With the harvest laid by and winter not far behind, it's a good season for a feast. Come this way."

Elwood led me into the great hall used for feasts and formalities, courts and councils of war. At the moment it was a madhouse. A number of newly arrived guests were being fed at the low tables. Seated at high table on the raised dais, the lord was complaining to his pantler about provisions.

Sir Denis de Picard? Definitely. His blond beard was shot with gray now and he'd gone a bit paunchy at the waist but otherwise he was much the same, a rangy sort with a coltish look about him. His tunic was of dyed wool but his cloak was silken and blue as an angel's eyes.

He nodded curtly as we approached, then hesitated. Frowning, he eyed me more critically.

The minstrelsy is not bound by custom to a particular code of dress but most of us affect multihued garments that set us apart from the common. My clothing marked me as a musician and perhaps that's what confused him. But not for long.

"I know you, don't I?" he said, rising and waving his servant away. "Tallifer? Is it you?"

"Milord," I said, bending the knee to prevent any confusion of protocol. "When last we met we were both soldiers."

"My God, you old dog, I thought you'd be dead in a ditch by now, brained in some nameless campaign or gutted by a jealous husband." Grinning, he raised me by the shoulders, reading my face. "How long? Fifteen years?"

"And a few more. It appears you've made your fortune since last we met."

"Hardly. I'm lord of a fleabitten outland that Prince John expects me to hold with little more than my charm. As my father's fourth son, I used to pray for land of my own. Beware of prayers. Sometimes God hears and answers. And then laughs."

"Even so, there were times in the old days when a prayer was all we had," I said.

"Aye, there were," he said, stepping back, a trace of wariness in his eyes. "What brings you to these parts now? Do you seek a place as a man-at-arms?"

"No, the road is my home now, milord. I gave up soldiering not long after our last campaign together against the Vikings. I'm a wandering troubadour these days."

"And a good one," Elwood put in. "I heard him sing in the village."

"Bah, you'll find scant profit caroling for these northern clods," Denis grumbled. "They wouldn't part with a penny to ransom Christ from the cross. I can offer you employment, though. I've guests to entertain and perhaps later we could talk about old times. It's hard to carry on a civil discourse with the gentry hereabout. All these Scots care about are breeding sheep, bairns and blood feuds. I swear some days I wish I was landless again and back in London."

"But never back at the Aln, I imagine. With the Vikings howling for our blood across the river?"

"No, never there." He measured me a moment with his eyes. "My life here may be a curse but I needn't scratch my ear every few moments to be sure my head's still attached. Do you remember those days fondly, Tallifer?" The question seemed innocuous, yet there was an edge to it, and I sensed a hint of danger.

"I remember them as little as possible," I said warily, "and none too clearly, milord. It was long ago and I've found that over time my memory of old times tends to be . . . uncertain."

"Well said," he nodded, satisfied. "You still retain your wits, I see. Good. I have need of a clever man. Elwood, take the minstrel's pack. He can board with you in the barracks room. Walk with me, Tallifer."

His tone brooked no argument and he was lord here. I tossed my paltry shoulder bag to Elwood who bowed and trotted off.

With a hand on my shoulder Denis led me out of the room to the corridor. "Perhaps it's an omen that you've come, Tallifer. I find myself in a . . . difficult situation."

"In what way?"

"My wife died three years ago—"

"I'm sorry."

"Don't be. I'm not. She was older than I by a decade and horsefaced to boot. I married her to gain this fief and I earned every damned acre of it. I only regret that she died barren. Left me without an heir or the memory of a single night's pleasure."

"Perhaps you could marry again, milord. You had a way with women as I recall. Is courting such a cross to bear?"

"Courting?" he snorted. "Along the border, mates are chosen like breeding stock. Still, when in Rome . . ." He smiled without humor, a nervous habit I remembered well from the old days.

"After considering the local prospects, I've decided the logical choice is Muriel, the daughter of Eoin of Mangerton. She's plain as a brain pudding, but sturdy enough to bear stout sons and she brings a substantial dowry."

"Then your problem is resolved?"

"Hardly. Nothing in this godforsaken border country is ever simple, Tallifer. My northern neighbor, Tormod the Mackinnon has a younger sister, Fiona. She's quite a stunning creature actually, though a bit headstrong. Unfortunately, the lass also fancies a match with me."

"A woman in hand and a beauty in pursuit? Some men would be on their knees giving thanks for problems like yours."

"It's no laughing matter, minstrel. These Scots will slaughter one another for generations over a strayed pig, to say nothing of an offended lady. I tell you it's a damned tricky situation. This Fiona already has a serious suitor, a young hotspur from the Bewcastle Wastes named Lindsay."

"Then I don't see the problem. If you're not interested in the girl . . ."

"It isn't that I don't find her attractive. She's fair as a May morning and clever as a fox. When we first met I admit I was as smitten with her as any young idiot. But I'm neither young nor an idiot, I hope. Fiona's lovely, true, but she's not worth a damned border war."

"I don't understand. A war with whom?"

"Her suitor, Lindsay, is totally enthralled by the girl and ready to fight for her. The Mackinnon would like nothing better than for me to slaughter the lad in a duel. He'd snatch up Lindsay's land and perhaps nibble up some of mine while I'm busy battling Lindsay's kinsmen."

"Still, if the girl's as lovely as you say . . ."

"I'm not fool enough to be drawn into a fight over a pretty face! I didn't endure the mockery of my first marriage to throw away all I've gained over a slip of a girl, however fair."

"I see," I said slowly, and I was beginning to. It had been fifteen years and more since the fight at the ford, but Denis hadn't changed much. He was still a bit . . . overcautious, to put it kindly. "What would you have me do?"

"Distract the lass. Sing her ballads about the joys of young love. Make her see that Lindsay's the better choice for her no matter what promises she thinks I made earlier. What man hasn't said things in the heat of passion that he can scarce recall later, if you take my meaning."

"But if the girl's attracted to you, milord, aren't you in a better position to straighten the matter out?"

"Nay. If I should misspeak and offend the lass I could wind up fighting her brother and Lindsay both. You always had a clever tongue, Tallifer. You were a poet, for god's sake. Do me this service. For the olden days. You'll not find me ungrateful."

"As you wish, milord," I said, smothering a groan. As a rule, I dislike entertaining private audiences. Give me the open air and a noisy crowd, preferably drunken. Still, I'll admit I was curious. A woman whose charms could trigger a duel or even a border war? There have been a thousand songs written about such beauties from the *Iliad* to our own time; I've sung quite a few of them myself. On the other hand, I knew at least a dozen ballads about unicorns too, yet I'd never met one.

Until that day. When Denis ushered me into the airy chamber occupied by a young lady and her maidservant, I was struck immediately by the girl's loveliness. Her eyes glittered sapphire bright and her smile could melt a snowdrift in the dark of February. Her woolen gown was dyed a brilliant green that set off her eyes and the fire of her auburn hair.

Denis introduced me and lauded my skills at some length. I doubt I could have managed more than a babble in those first moments. But after he made his excuses and left us, the girl's smile faded as though a cloud had passed over the sun.

"Are you come from the south, from England, minstrel?" she asked, not bothering to conceal her annoyance.

"Yes, lady, I'm originally from Shrewsbury and York." I uncased my lute and began tuning it hastily.

"Milord said you've lived in London as well?"

"Aye, I've spent time there. Perhaps you'd care to hear a ballad—"

"Spare me your singing, minstrel. In truth, I've no ear for music. I couldn't tell your voice from the mewling of that kitten I see peering out of your jacket. Let me see her."

I hesitated.

"Are you deaf? I said give her to me."

"It's just that she's not properly tamed, lady. She may scratch."

"Not more than once," she said, taking Maggie from my

arms. The kitten snuggled to her breast without a by-your-leave. I envied her. "You see? Cats and I understand each other. Which is more than I can say for your lord. He said he's known you long years. Was he always so . . . inconstant?"

"I'm not sure I understand," I said carefully.

"I think you do. A month ago at my brother's stronghold, Lord Denis all but begged me to be his bride. Now, under his own roof, he pretends that I somehow misunderstood him."

"Perhaps that's so. You are very young, milady. And not very experienced in the ways of men, I would think."

She stared at me as though I were an insect she'd found in her pudding. "Do you take me for a muddlehead, minstrel? Because I'm a woman? And young?"

"No, lady," I said, swallowing, my mouth suddenly dry. Lovely or not, this girl was no child. She was sister to a border lord and for a moment his steel flashed in her eyes.

"Look at this room," she said, indicating the tapestry and intricately carved wardrobe. "Milord de Picard apologized for it. He said his uncle had rooms far finer in their estate outside London. Is that true?"

"I . . . have never seen his uncle's holdings there, but his family is wealthy and many homes of the gentry are as fine as this or moreso."

"I thought as much. My family is not poor and our blood is as blue as any, but compared to this, my brother's house is a pigsty." She broke off at a minor commotion in the hall. At her nod, the servant girl hastened to the door and peered out.

"It's Neil Lindsay, milady," she said. "He asks if he may visit you."

Fiona considered a moment, then nodded, with a vixen's smile. "Show him in. What a pity he's not interrupting anything improper. Play something romantic, minstrel. It might lighten my guest's mood."

She took a seat near the narrow window, and in the golden pool of its light with the kitten in her arms, she was a vision out of paradise, glowing like an angel. I stood by the fireplace, strummed my lute gently to check its tune, then began to play a brooding Celtic melody I'd learned years before in Strath-clyde.

Fiona's maid ushered in a young man who was probably only a year or two older than Elwood, but a man grown nonetheless. Broad-shouldered and beetle browed with a square, strongly handsome face, he bore a savage scar along his jaw and an-other across the back of his left wrist. Sword gashes, by the look of them.

I doubt he was a day past eighteen, but boyhood ends early in the borderlands. This lad was already battle hardened, I knew the look well. He was prosperously dressed in soft doe-skin breeches and a doublet with a fine fox collar. Chain mail would have suited him better. He was a border wolf in a gen-tleman's clothing.

"Neil," Fiona said sweetly, "how good to see you. You've arrived at a perfect time. My maid and I were just listening to some music. This is Tallifer of York, a musician Milord Denis brought all the way from London to amuse me. He's performed for all the finest families of England."

"I've no taste for any music but the pipes," Lindsay growled, giving me a dark look. "Still, if you fancy his songs, let him play on. Enjoy it while you can."

"What do you mean?"

"I've heard a wondrous rumor, milady. It's said our host will announce his engagement tomorrow. To Muriel, the daughter of Eoin MacDonald of Mangerton."

"That's a damnable lie!" she said, flushing. "He could never choose to wed that—cow!"

"Possibly not," Neil nodded. "Rumors aren't always true. But this one may well be. I've put it about that I'd challenge him if he asked for your hand, and unless I'm greatly mistaken, Milord de Picard has seemed less . . . devoted to you than before."

"He's not afraid of you, Neil, nor any other man. Only a fool would imply it. He's a great warrior. They even sing songs about him. Do they sing any about you?"

"Not yet," he admitted, "nor would I call any man coward without just cause. Still, that battle the minstrels sing of was so long ago you were scarce born when it happened. And any man who would give you up rather than fight for you, well. We've a name for a man like that along the borders. And it's not milord. Hear me out, Fiona. I know you're much taken with all these trappings, tapestries, and singers and such, and I know my own holdings are not so large as this—"

"As this?" Fiona interrupted, annoyed. "Neil, your fief is half the size of my brother's and *our* lands are half the size of Milord de Picard's."

"Even so," Lindsay pressed on stubbornly, "there are other things than wealth. What of love, Fiona? Milord de Picard is an old man. He can never care for you as I do, nor can he warm your bed with fire that I feel for you."

"Men," Fiona said, shaking her head ruefully. "Always so concerned about how warmly we ladies sleep. If my bed feels chilly, Neil, I don't need a man to warm it. A kitten will serve every bit as well. And you see?"—she held up Maggie, who hissed at Lindsay—"I already have a warm bedpartner."

"You may need that kit, lady," Lindsay said grimly. "I swear on my family that I'll send de Picard to the great sleep before he ever lies with you. On the other hand, if he passes you over, maybe I shall do so as well. I don't like settling for another man's castoff. I have my pride, after all."

"Then let your pride warm your bed on a long winter's night. If it doesn't, maybe you'll recall how spitefully you've spoken to me today. But you needn't lose sleep over it. I'm not one to hold grudges. Anytime you need your blankets warmed or want someone to hold in the night, come to me, Neil. And I'll gladly . . . lend you my kitten."

She warmed the room with the same demure smile she'd

offered earlier to myself and Milord de Picard, and Lindsay was as helpless against it as we had been.

"You are the most troublesome woman I've ever known, lady," he said, shaking his head slowly. "But in truth, you're the only one who's worth killing for. Or dying for."

"Killing and dying, indeed. You've such a romantic way with words, Neil. No offense intended, sir, but I think I'd prefer to hear the songs of this minstrel now. And since you've no ear for any music but the pipes, you may leave us. Perhaps we'll see you this evening at supper."

"That you shall, lady. Do you know any laments, minstrel?" he asked.

"One or two."

"Good. You may need them before this week is out." He wheeled and stalked out. Fiona's smile vanished with him and she turned on me.

"The vile lie Lindsay mentioned, of de Picard marrying Muriel, the Mangerton cow; have you heard aught of it, minstrel?"

"I'm—afraid I only arrived here a few hours ago, milady."

She eyed me thoughtfully, stroking Maggie's tiny head. It was a strangely unnerving experience. Fiona was a lovely girl and Maggie was but a kitten, yet their stares seemed uncannily similar, frank curiosity without pity or humanity. They weren't mistress and pet. They were sisters.

"Odd," she said at last, "I would have thought a storyteller would make a better liar, sir. You didn't answer my question. Or perhaps you did? Enough. Take your wretched animal and go. I've had a tiring day."

"As you wish, milady," I said, taking the kitten from her. I offered my best bow as I exited, though I doubt she noticed.

In the hall, I asked directions from a servant and found my way to the barracks room; a spartan stone chamber with rushes on the floor and nearly two dozen cots crammed into it. Elwood was sitting on one, lost in thought. He glanced up as I entered.

"Ah, you're back, Tallifer. Here, I've saved you a bed and brought you food and a cup of wine."

He tossed me a trencher, a slab of hard oaten bread flavored with beef drippings, and I fell on it like a wolf.

"No need to thank me," he said dryly, "you're milord's guest, after all. But I wonder if I might ask a favor of you?"

"What favor?" I mumbled around a mouthful.

"A simple question. I've been thinking on that ballad you sang in the village earlier today, about the Battle of Aln Ford?"

"What of it?"

"There's a verse near the end that goes 'This song was writ by one who counted friends among the dead, his arm near severed.' That man was you, wasn't it? Milord said he hadn't seen you since that campaign and you have a scarred forearm."

"Many folk have scars. It's a dangerous world." I swallowed the last of the bread and washed it down with the cup of wine Elwood handed me.

"Please don't treat me like a child, Tallifer, I haven't been one for some time. Are you the man who wrote it or not?"

I nodded, too tired to lie.

"Then I have a second question. Why is the version you wrote so different from the song Milord de Picard taught to me?"

"It was a long time ago and battles are chaos. Men's memories of events often differ, and tend to vary even more over the years. Tales, told and retold, sometimes change."

"I understand how some details might fade but not the central facts of what happened. So I ask you, which version is the right one? Did Milord lead the charge against the Vikings? Or was it his cousin Ranaulf?"

"You task me unfairly, boy. How old are you?"

"Sixteen," he admitted. "Why do you ask?"

"Then you're old enough to understand the rudeness of asking improper questions. Which version is true? The truth is,

Ranaulf died of his wounds long years ago and I'm a guest in
Lord de Picard's home."

"That's no answer."

"It's all the answer you get, my lad, and a damnsight more
than you're entitled to. Now, if you don't mind, get your young
carcass off my cot so I can rest awhile. I have to sing for my
supper tonight and I'm expecting stormy weather."

I never spoke truer words.

THE GREAT hall was nearly filled, mostly with the kinsmen
of Milord de Picard's two noble guests, the Mackinnon and the
family of Eoin of Mangerton. De Picard had spared no ex-
pense. All six trestle tables were muslin-covered and the high
table was draped with linen embroidered with Sir Denis's coat
of arms. The feast was equally rich, hare and venison served on
trenchers, pastries filled with raisins or marzipan, and mead
and wine aplenty.

Ordinarily, Scots at a feast are a pleasure to entertain, as
long as you don't have to compete with the main course.
Though they pay scant attention while feeding, later, with full
bellies and fuller cups, they're a cheerfully boisterous lot, bait-
ing one another with no offense intended or taken. But that
night the air in the hall felt more like the eve before a battle,
fairly crackling with tension.

Milord Denis had wisely separated the Mackinnon and
Mangerton clans at the opposite ends of the high table with
himself between them as a buffer. He needn't have bothered.
His two ladies-a-waiting ignored each other completely. If
there was any competition between Fiona and Muriel for de
Picard's attention, you couldn't tell from their behavior.

Muriel of Mangerton seemed a pleasant, bovine creature,
dressed, or perhaps overdressed, in a rich azure gown of raw silk
trimmed with lace which accented her plumpish figure.

In contrast, Fiona Mackinnon's simple muslin gown
wouldn't have been inappropriate in church. Her only adorn-

ment was a sapphire comb in her fiery hair. Yet she drew the eyes of the menfolk like a lodestone.

Her brother, Tormod, was seated with Neil Lindsay beside him. The Mackinnon was a wild-haired Scot with eyes as black as flints and a mood to match. He and Neil had little to say to each other, but both were clearly on edge. As a rule, guests don't wear weapons at a meal, but I noted that the Mackinnon's clan dirk was nearly the size of an old Roman *gladius*. If de Picard chose this evening to announce his engagement to Mangerton's daughter, I expected the room to erupt in open warfare before he'd finished speaking.

But while Milord Denis may not have been the boldest soldier I ever knew, he was no fool. He acted the perfect host, dividing his attention among his guests equally and taking care to avoid giving any offense.

When it came my time to play, I made my way to the center of the hall feeling like a forest deer trapped on a moor between the hounds and the deep blue sea. Though two previous performers had been courteously received, the audience was growing restless.

It was nearly a disaster. As I struck a ringing chord on my lute to announce myself, Fiona Mackinnon rose and called out for the "Ballad of Aln Ford." I affected not to have heard, and sang the "Cattle Raid At Cooley," an Irish ballad of thievery and battle.

The song seemed to please the crowd but, even as I sang, I was desperately seeking a way out of my predicament. Intent on stirring trouble, Fiona was certain to call for the Aln Ford song again. Unfortunately, I knew only the original version which rightly lauds Ranaulf and scarce mentions Denis de Picard, yet if I sang it, especially on this night, I'd likely earn a thrashing for my troubles. Assuming I wasn't slaughtered outright.

Then, just as I was finishing my song, Maggie the kitten saved my life. Afraid she'd wander off from the barracks room,

I'd left her in the corridor wrapped in my lute's sheepskin case. But apparently she took the job of being a minstrel's cat seriously.

Midway through my song, she marched unsteadily into the hall, looking about with wide-eyed curiosity. An uneasy murmur rose among the guests, for a number of de Picard's hunting hounds were wandering loose through the room, seeking scraps.

I'd no choice. With a silent curse I scooped up Maggie and thrust her inside my doublet. A ripple of laughter echoed around the room as she hissed angrily at me and clawed at my face.

It was the first light moment of the evening and I seized it. Taking Maggie out of my coat, I held her aloft and scolded her like a child, then I cuddled her to my cheek and sang her a lullaby followed by a love ballad. There was a noticeable easing of tension in the room as the songs progressed. Milord's guests began to look more to their cups and ignore their weapons, thanks be to God. Or St. Margaret.

I closed my set with a sprightly tune about a magical kingdom where all is harmony and light. Not to be ignored, Maggie joined in on the last chorus, yowling impatiently to be put down.

I exited to hearty laughter and applause. Glowing at the crowd's response and damned grateful to be alive, I made my way back to the barracks room, promising to make an offering to the new Scottish saint at my first opportunity.

The feast must have ended soon after I finished, for some of the guests began drifting into the barracks before I'd fallen asleep. Neil Lindsay was among them. After tossing his doublet on his cot, he spotted me and threaded his way through the clutter of temporary beds to mine.

"You sang well tonight, minstrel," he said agreeably. "Very amusing, especially the business with the kitten. I prefer the pipes myself, but the folk seemed to like your voice well enough. Perhaps you'll visit my freehold at Bewcastle some-time. It's not as grand as all this, but the land is green and the folk are friendly. You'll be welcome."

"I'll remind you of your offer if the wind ever carries me in that direction, sir."

"That's your life then? Wandering with the wind?"

"I've done other things at other times. Wind-drifting suits me for now."

"But have you no home? No family?"

"I had both when last I saw them. But I'm a sixth son, and my father's holdings are not large. It's better for all that I make my own way in the world."

He nodded absently. I sensed he wanted to ask me some-thing, perhaps what Fiona might have said of him after he left, but if so he thought better of it. He bid me a pleasant good night and made his way back to his own cot near the door.

I lay there awhile, staring up at the rough-hewn ceiling beams, considering the events of the day. Maggie clambered up from the foot of my cot, nestled in the hollow of my throat and instantly fell asleep. And in two beats of her little heart, I followed her to the land of kitten dreams.

Sometime in the night I felt Maggie stir and tense. I opened my eyes warily. In the dim light of the lone oil lamp, I saw Neil Lindsay up and stretching. Too much wine, perhaps. He pulled on his doublet and wandered out to find the lavatory. Otherwise the night passed peacefully.

It was the last peace I would know in this place.

Seduced by the luxury of a soft bed and a cuddly—if not romantic—companion, I'd intended to linger beneath my blankets in the morning. No such luck. At first light I heard an unnatural stirring in the castle, footsteps pounding down corri-dors, distant voices shouting alarms. Something was amiss.

I roused myself, slipped into my leggings and boots just as Elwood burst into the room. He pushed his way through the other cots to mine, his eyes alight with excitement.

"What's happened?"

"A duel! A fight to the death. Neil Lindsay's been killed outside Fiona Mackinnon's chamber. He was trying to break in, to carry her away with him. Milord Denis heard the uproar, confronted him and ordered him off. When Lindsay refused to give way they fought, but it was over in a heartbeat. Lindsay was no match for Sir Denis."

"Really?" I said doubtfully, remembering Lindsay's stout, scarred wrist. And the invitation he'd offered me when last I saw him. No. That wasn't the last time. Thanks to Maggie's restlessness, I'd seen Lindsay leave the barracks room in the night . . . to find the lavatory. Or so I'd thought. "Where is he now?"

"Sir Denis is in the great hall with his guests—"

"No, I meant Lindsay. Where have they taken his body?"

"I'm not sure. I suppose they carried him to the chapel. Why?"

"Just curious. You're fairly jumping out of your skin with excitement, boy. Go back to the great hall. Sir Denis may need you. Thank you for bringing me the news."

"You're welcome." He wheeled and trotted off, but at the doorway he turned back a moment. "Tallifer? Do you think we could write a ballad about this? Together, I mean. It would make a grand gift for Milord Denis."

"Perhaps," I said. "We'll talk about it later. Get you gone."

Elwood hurried off, leaving me alone with my kitten and my thoughts. But even the ingenuous charm of St. Maggie couldn't distract me from a shadowy image in my memory. I dressed myself and wandered out, hoping to smother the uneasy questions that were troubling me.

The chapel was not large. Reserved for the use of the lord and his family, it was well-appointed, with richly embroidered tapestries, carved pews and even a cross of gold. A larger, less ornate parish church in the village served the common folk.

The silent room was deserted, save for a lone mourner pray-

ing in the shadows of the nave. I wasn't surprised. A man slain
during an attempted abduction would have few friends remaining. Especially in the stronghold of the lord who killed him.

Neil Lindsay's corpse lay at the foot of the altar on the stone
floor, wrapped in a winding sheet. I blessed myself and genu-
flected, then made my way slowly to the body and knelt beside
it.

Lindsay's face was uncovered. It looked oddly peaceful and
much younger than in life. The sheet was stained red over his
heart, nowhere else. A clean kill. A single thrust, the mark of
a master swordsman. Like the hero of Aln Ford.

Curious now, I tugged the sheet open a bit. His hands were
folded on his chest but the only marks on them were old scars.
The death wound was narrow, barely more than slit—

"What are you doing? Have you no respect?" The voice
from the shadows was a low growl, startling me. Its owner
stepped into the ring of light offered by the altar candles.
Tormod, the Mackinnon. His eyes were as wild as his mane of
dark hair and he was armed with both sword and dagger.
Though they were still sheathed, I've seldom been closer to
death than at that moment. He was in a killing fury, with the
fire of combat barely contained.

"I'm sorry," I said, rising. "The sheet was disarranged."

"No it wasn't. I know you, you sang at supper last night. To
the wee kitten. What were you looking for just now?"

"As I said, the sheet—"

"Don't bandy words with me, minstrel, that's my friend lying there. The road to hell is lonely. Perhaps Neil would like a
companion to sing his way down."

"I swear I meant no offense. Lindsay and I spoke last evening—"

"What about?"

"He invited me to visit his freehold in Bewcastle. He said he
cared only for the sound of the pipes himself, but that his
family might like my singing."

"And that's all he said? Nothing else? Nothing about my sister or . . . anything at all?"

"Nothing else, truly. We only spoke a moment. He seemed in good spirits and he was civil to me. I liked him. I'm saddened by his death."

"Are you? I should think there might be profit in it for you, minstrel. Doubtless Sir Denis will pay handsomely for a new ballad about this great victory."

"Perhaps, but not to me. I see nothing to sing of here, unless perhaps a lament. Shall I sing one?"

"Nay, not for Neil. As you said, he only cared for the song of the pipes. Go now. Leave us in peace."

"As you wish." I backed away from him warily, but I needn't have feared. When I made my last genuflection he was in the shadows again, kneeling, praying for the soul of his friend.

Elwood was waiting for me in the corridor outside. "Milord de Picard sent me to find you. He wants to see you right away."

We found Sir Denis in the great hall amid even greater chaos than before. Servants were fairly flying about, men-at-arms were on the run, something was obviously afoot. Lord Denis himself was fairly glowing, smug as a goose the day after Christmas. He was wearing a shirt of finely crafted chain mail beneath a surcoat which bore his coat of arms. Dressed for battle, or more likely, a celebration. A conquering hero. Once again.

"Ah, Tallifer, old friend," he said, seizing my forearm before I could bend the knee. "Walk with me. I must talk with you a moment." He led me to a corner of the room away from the others. "You've heard what happened?"

"Everyone's heard, milord."

"But what have they heard? What are they saying?"

"That there was a fight. And that young Lindsay was no match for you."

"Yes, yes, that's exactly how it was. I was totally in the right, yet you know how these damned border Scots are. Lindsay's kinsmen may seek revenge. I don't fear them, of course, but my lady is in terror for me."

"Your lady?"

"The lady Fiona Mackinnon. We're to be married. In London during the Christmas holidays. We're leaving straightaway for the south and England. I want you to come with us."

"Me, milord?"

"That's right. As a member of my household. Damn it, Tallifer, I need someone near me I can trust. You'll receive an ample stipend and your board, of course. What do you say?"

"I . . . you're most generous, milord. But why me? You already have a fine singer in your service."

"You mean Elwood? He's just a boy. We share a history, you and I. The old days."

"Those days seem very long ago to me, milord. Too long, perhaps. I'm sorry, but I'm afraid I can't accompany you. I've given my promise to be elsewhere."

He eyed me a moment, then shrugged. "In that case, go and be damned. And the sooner the better."

"As you wish, milord. But before I go, let me congratulate you on your . . . victory, and on your engagement as well. May you and your lady have all of the happiness you both deserve."

His face darkened and, for a moment, I thought I'd gone too far. He started to speak, then thought better of it and stalked off.

I made my way out of the great hall, stopping for a last look from the doorway. Sir Denis had returned to the hasty preparations for his journey. He was a wealthy, powerful man, surrounded by vassals, and would soon wed the most desirable woman I'd ever seen. Yet I did not envy him. Not even a little.

Elwood found me in the barracks room, folding my few belongings into my pack.

"Milord bade me give you this," he said, tossing a small purse to me. "For your performance at the banquet last night."

"Thank him for me. He always had a generous heart. I'd like to ask a favor of you, Elwood. I fear Maggie the kitten's too small to survive a life on the road. May I leave her in your care?"

"Of course, but could I ask a favor in return? I know Milord offered you a place. Why aren't you coming with us?"

I fitted my lute carefully in its sheepskin sheath, considering how much to tell him. Truth is a valuable commodity, because it is so rare in this life. Still, he'd befriended me, and would care for Maggie well . . .

"Fair enough," I said, turning to face him. "A favor for a favor, the truth is that it's the kitten's fault."

"The kitten?"

"She wakened in the night and I saw Neil Lindsay go out in search of a lavatory."

"Or so you thought. Actually, he must have been going to see the lady—"

"You're not listening," I said, cutting him off. "I assumed he was going out to relieve himself because he put on his doublet against the chill, but nothing more. He didn't arm himself, Elwood. I'm an old soldier. Believe me, if he'd strapped on a blade or even his dagger, I would have noticed."

"What are you saying? That Milord Denis killed an unarmed man?"

"No. That was my first thought, so I went to view the body. Lindsay died of a single thrust through the heart. He was a seasoned fighter yet there were no other wounds, no cuts on his hands or arms as there might have been if he'd tried to defend himself. He was struck cleanly. Tell me Elwood, if an enemy caught you unarmed, would you offer your breast to his blade? Never. You'd run for your life or fight for it just as Lindsay would have. But if he'd done so, he wouldn't have died unmarked."

"I don't understand. You claim Lindsay was unarmed, yet he didn't run? Or fight?"

"There was no fight. Because there was no abduction. I believe Lindsay went to Lady Fiona's chamber at her invitation. And he died there. Love is blind they say. For Lindsay, it was fatally so."

"You mean Fiona . . ."

"Was in a desperate situation. She's a woman of great beauty and even greater pride. Milord de Picard was obviously smitten with her, yet he was about to pass her over for fear of young Lindsay. Instead of snaring a noble husband, she would return with none, and her pride could not bear that. And so she invited Lindsay to her room . . ."

"And struck him down? That slip of a girl?"

"The fatal wound was narrow, the kind a lady's dagger would make. And to whom else would Lindsay offer his heart? Don't be deceived by her manner. She's the sister of a border lord and a she-wolf is as fierce as any male. When it was done, she doubtless sent her maid to fetch Sir Denis and made him an irresistible offer: herself as his beautiful young wife, and a chance to play the hero once again."

"A false hero, you mean," he said bitterly. "As he was at the Aln Ford."

I hesitated, surprised.

"Come now, if he'd been the hero that day, you simply would have said so when I asked instead of babbling on about battles being chaos and men's memories fading. Milord wasn't the hero of the ford, was he?"

"No," I conceded. "His cousin Ranaulf left him with the rear guard because he feared for him. Milord Denis was never much of a swordsman."

"And he's lied about it since," Elwood mused. "I should have known. I've never seen Milord Denis wield a blade for anything more desperate than carving a bird on the Feast of Stephen. He's a fraud, isn't he? And always has been. Sweet Jesus." He shook his head sadly.

"Why not come with me, Elwood?" I said abruptly. "The

wandering life might suit you. You have a fine voice already and I can teach you the lute. There's much to see in the world, much to learn."

"I'm sure there is," he said with a wan smile. "But no, I can't go with you, Tallifer. Fraud or no, Milord Denis is still the man who treated me like kin when he owed me nothing. I cannot leave him now. He thinks he's won the day, but I fear that after he marries his border lady his troubles will multiply like rats in a pantry. Besides, if I go with you, who will be left to care for St. Margaret's kitten?"

I eyed him a moment, then nodded slowly. "Odd. When we first met I mistook you for a youth. I see now I was mistaken. Take care of yourself, young sir. And my kitten too."

"I will. But Tallifer, how can I face him now? How can I sing songs that praise him, knowing the truth of what he is?"

"What truth? The truth is, songs are never about men as they are, only as they were once, sometimes only for a moment. Everything in this life changes. Heroes fail and cowards find courage. That lovely kitten you hold will grow fangs and become a mighty killer of mice and, in time, grow old. But if you would sing Maggie's song, wouldn't you sing of her as she is now, at this moment, beautiful and virginal and pure?"

He nodded without speaking.

"Well, then, when you were a boy, Sir Denis treated you kindly. So when you sing his songs, don't sing for the man you see now. Sing them for the man you remember."

He walked me through the village gate and down the road a ways. We parted on a hill. I headed northeast, into the Wastes toward Bewcastle. When I looked back I could see him standing there with Maggie the kitten nestled in his arms and the long afternoon shadows of Wansfeth Castle stretching out to him as the sun lowered behind its towers. As I see them still.

I pushed on into the dusk. The leaves of the forest were turning, amber and russet and gold, and they seemed to light my path with the glow of their dying. Just before dark, I came on a copse of cedar and made a bed of boughs beneath it, sheltered from the wind.

But sleep would not come. Perhaps I'd been enclosed within stone walls for too long. No matter. Warm in my cloak, with the air scented by the fragrance of cedar and the nightwind whispering through the limbs above me, I mulled over the events of the past days as their images flickered in the pool of my memory.

Elwood telling me my ballad was amiss. Lord Denis, haggard and fearful in the heart of his own stronghold. Young Neil Lindsay, battle-hardened at eighteen, confident in his own strength and skills, yet so unwise in the ways of the world. Undone by love.

And later, Tormod praying in the chapel for the soul of his fallen friend. And for his sister as well, for I'm sure he'd surmised the truth, as I had.

And last of all, the lady herself. Fiona. Her image was branded in my mind; haloed in the golden light of her chamber window with St. Margaret's kitten cradled at her breast. I've sung a thousand ballads of beauties worth dying for, but I'd never met one until that day. A girl with the exquisite comeliness of a kitten, yet with no more humanity than a marble Venus. In her own way, she was perfect, and worthy of a melody of her own.

I sat up most of the night with my lute, snug against the cedar bole, half dreaming, composing her song. Visions came to me out of the dark, of ghostly figures dead long before Lindsay, of fools who'd killed and died for love, of pale kings and princes . . . .

English seemed too harsh a tongue for the song of such a merciless beauty, but in French, the lyrics flowed like a caress.

"La belle dame sans merci . . ."

SLIGHTLY GUILTY

Morris Hershman

CARL WEST HATED getting into this cheap all-wool suit with that tight vest and two-button jacket that never fit right because the padded shoulders dragged down to his arms. It made him feel like he was still working for some two-bit twerp instead of being his own boss.

Bunny, watching him, smiled impishly. "I won't go out with you later tonight if you put on cheap clothes like that."

Carl didn't have to tell her that he was only doing it because he never wanted the boys to think he was high-hatting them by going to the distillery when he was dressed like a million.

Instead he buttoned his fly disdainfully and told her what she needed to know. "You ain't going with me later on."

Bunny's face didn't exactly crumple, but her cherry-red lipstick seemed to shiver a little. "I thought we'd both get dressed for that ritzy place you want to go to."

"I'm going out now on business and then I'll come back and go out alone to the Yard Boys Dinner." The Yard Boys was an organization of New York City hot-shots who raised money to sponsor cultural events in the city "for a happier 1926," as somebody always said at a speech, naming the current year.

Carl got a kick out of pledging ten thousand to help pay for a performing visit by the Russian ballet, for instance.

Bunny said softly, "Gee, just think how great we'd look, with me in my French crepe and—"

"You gotta work," he said briskly. "Remember?"

"Mr. Grady said I can take a couple of nights off if I want." Bunny was a dancer at Revels on the Roof, popping out of a giant cardboard cake while people swilled illegal liquor in the town's best known speakeasy. Sometimes, though, she felt as if this was the night for her to be discovered as an artiste, another Marilyn Miller or Ann Pennington.

"Don't bother taking time off," Carl snapped.

"You mean you really don't want me at that big dinner?"

"Now you got it." A high-pitched meow near his feet was enough to annoy him, like it always did. "And I wish to hell you'd get rid of that cat before I do."

He had told her a few times that he'd needed to sleep close to a lot of goddam cats in his days of being flat broke, and he hated seeing even one cat in this high-class Fifth Avenue apartment.

"I'll keep Ziggy out of your way," she promised for the hundredth time and believed it. The red tabby had been named for Mr. Florenz Ziegfeld, who produced the stylish yearly editions of the Follies. Bunny had never been near the great man, but she liked calling the cat by Ziegfeld's nickname. It made her feel like a show business insider.

She was snuffling as she picked up the growling red cat and moved slowly into the hall and then to her own room. Ziggy padded back just as Carl was irritably climbing into a cheap black cowhide jacket. He aimed a kick at the beast and missed by a mile.

HE LIKED his city car pretty well, a Rollin two-seater that could get thirty miles to the gallon on a good day. He kept a Pierce Arrow Runabout at his other home in Saratoga Springs where he lived in racing season. A different girl decorated that place, a girl demure and stylish, a girl who talked good English, the right sort of a girl for a guy who was nearly rich.

He drove out to Castle Hill Road in the Bronx. Eventually he pulled up at a garage he knew was as cold as an icebox on the inside. He paid a dime to have a boy drive it in. A three-block walk brought him to a two-story gray brick building where workers had made his current easy living possible. It was a distillery licensed to produce medicinal whiskey only. A mint of money had bought the place and fetched the needed permits to produce and sell the stuff—not for medicinal purposes, really. Profits came in so soon that he'd been happily repaying loans in no time.

"Maybe trouble will come tonight," the assistant told Carl solemnly in stiff book-learned English a few minutes after he walked in. The assistant, Sergei Ivanovich, claimed he had been a Grand Duke in Russia before the Communist revolution. His bony face reminded Carl of the President of the United States, Silent Calvin Coolidge himself. "There is talk of a jacking very soon."

"So Ned Reese thinks he'll hijack even a drop of my booze! Well, put two boys on the truck to ride shotgun with tonight's shipment along with the usual four. We'll fix Reese."

"Where will I get two men?"

"Take one rifle yourself and offer fifty bucks for—" he looked around at the shabbily dressed workers busily packing whiskey bottles in large cartons "—the closest one."

That worker turned slowly. He was thin, and only the frames of his glasses were thick. Carl knew him.

"You're Four Eyes Fred Fitch! I'm pretty sure my girl friend introduced you to me a while ago."

"Bunny Hatton, yes. She said you'd be an important guy, but I thought she was dreaming again like she usually does."

"That time she wasn't dreaming. Stick around and you'll

have more money than you'd expect. Fifty bucks extra goes to you for tonight's ride."

"If you remember me at all, you know I don't carry nothing heavy and I don't hurt nobody."

"You better carry a rifle and ride tonight if you want to be here tomorrow—got that?"

Four Eyes was quiet.

Carl was already putting on the cheap wool cap he wore for these visits in winter. Gesturing Sergei Ivanovich to follow, he strode to the door and turned to talk quietly.

"That Four Eyes will never put an eight-ball in the side pocket. He's a flopperoo, a guy who'll be broke forever." Carl didn't add that he wanted nobody working for him who had known him even casually during hard times. "After he does the extra job tonight, fire him."

HE TOOK off that cheap cap and jacket at the first traffic stop and put on his plaid lined coat. His mind was roaming, which happened to be unusual for him. It was hard to keep wondering, for instance, how soon the state government would get done building that bridge from Fort Lee in Jersey over to Fort Washington in uptown Manhattan, a sure time-saver for everybody when it got done. Now that he thought about motion, he made a mental note to put down a bet on Bubbling Over for the Kentucky Derby when the time came.

He was humming *I found a million dollar baby in a something-or-other*, not remembering the words five-and-ten cent store, when he reached Fifth Avenue again. In front of the garage he used, he called for an attendant to park his car. In respect for the young man's snappy uniform, Carl paid out a quarter this time.

Before going upstairs to his apartment he tore up the crossword puzzle magazine that Bunny had left in the car. Bunny enjoyed that new fad because she was sure it improved her vocabulary. Leave it to Bunny to waste her time and think she was improving herself.

He had taken off the cheap clothes and jammed them into his hall closet only a few minutes after he got back to his apartment. Deciding that his skin was rough, he spent a few minutes with his fancy new vibro-shave electric razor, keeping one foot on the new saddle-seat toilet top all the time. He had put on a stiff white shirt and bow tie with his knife-crease tuxedo pants and was trying to decide which blackskin shoes to wear for the charity dinner tonight when he heard the front door.

Ready to bawl out Bunny for coming home early as if she could change his mind about not taking her to the dinner, Carl charged into the hall. There must have been steam coming out of his ears.

The door had opened on—he didn't believe it!—Four Eyes Fred Fitch. Four Eyes was walking in slowly, practically tiptoeing as he closed the door behind him and turned.

He was facing Carl West.

Carl knew from experience just how to deal with people who didn't have as much money as he did: surprise them. Smile when they expected scowls, for instance, or use the fists before they could guess what they had done wrong. The trick was to keep poor simps off-balance.

"Come in here," he said roughly, knowing that Four Eyes was expecting to be pitched out.

Carl gestured the intruder into his living room and walked in behind him. Four Eyes gaped at the mirrored walls that reflected both of them along with the hard angular furniture. In particular Four Eyes stared at the loudspeaker radio console, showing admiration for the item rather than for the man whose shrewdness made it possible to own such a treasure.

"Give me the key," Carl said, trying not to show he was annoyed by the misplaced awe as well as by the intrusion. "You got in with it, and I want it. Then I'll have all the locks changed."

The key was handed over, a warm metallic chunk without lettering on the stubby part. Carl made sure that the metal would let somebody into his apartment.

"Where'd you get it?" he snapped, striding back to his living room.

"Made it," Four Eyes said with furtive pride. Even the reflected light in his thick glasses glowed with his pride. "I can put a blank into any door and punch out the pattern without ever leaving the outside hall."

"I don't believe it."

Four Eyes took out a cloth handkerchief from a coat pocket. Half a dozen small instruments gleamed when it was opened. Carl had never seen the likes of them. If he'd had those pieces and ·had known that trick only a few years ago, he wouldn't have needed to sell logs that had been washed ashore from the Hudson River as firewood. On the other hand, Four Eyes had probably known the key trick for years, but was now shaking in his shoes at being alone in Carl's presence. While Four Eyes was running to get out of the road, in other words, Carl was riding over him.

"I suppose you figured to sneak in if I wasn't home and to take some of my stuff," Carl said with lofty understanding. "You must have been so set up at using those tools that you convinced yourself I wouldn't be here and I guess you were sure you could lie your way out of trouble if you got caught. Okay, go ahead and lie. Let me hear how an idiot punk does it."

"I guess I wasn't thinking clear." Four Eyes swallowed. "I knew I wouldn't be working for you after I told that Russian guy I won't carry a rifle to get a shipment of booze where you want it to go. Before I left town to get away from your boys, I figured I might as well—you know."

"Uh-huh. Steal, you mean—hey, what the hell—"

Carl had been in complete control up to that point, showing his classiness, proving how much smarter he was, as well as being better off. No human being could have made him lose control, and no human did. It was a cat which made the difference.

ZIGGY, THE red tabby who caused Bunny to giggle occasionally and say she belonged to him, had originally jumped to the base of the window from here. On this, a favorite perch, he would usually gaze out at the blurry sky and the tall buildings. Every so often, usually in spring or summer, he had a chance to scare off a pigeon who paused on the outer ledge. He would make some clicking noise which the bird certainly couldn't hear, but it was enough to send the youngest of birds back into the air. Bunny, giggling again, would say, as if she believed it, that darling Ziggy gave those little birds their flying lessons.

As soon as he sensed the rising tenseness in the room, Ziggy did what every cat is programmed to do in the case of quarrels among humans: he ran for the exit. He didn't stop, even though his person's person was standing close to the door. Ziggy put on as much speed as Bubbling Over would hopefully put on in the Derby, getting away from that nasty human.

Carl turned the air purple with profanity. To have seen some animal whose species reminded him so much of his own hard times in the past was bad enough. For that beast to have nearly defiled his soup-and-fish—Ziggy had come as close as a whisker—was nothing less than the outside of enough.

Carl was instantly proved wrong in his assumption that nothing could be worse. When a red rim of anger cleared from in front of his eyes and he focused on Four Eyes again, he saw a glint of amusement behind the man's thick glasses. Four Eyes was clearly amused by Carl's discomfort and anger. Disgusted, Carl made up his mind to be sure that any sign of pleasure was wiped off the features of this bozo who did donkey work, wiped off forever.

He kept his voice calm. "Four Eyes, I guess you want me to forget what happened here and even forget that you refused to do your whole job for me, maybe even give you another chance to work for me and I'll swear you never again get asked to ride shotgun with booze or anything else. Isn't that what you want?"

Four Eyes turned serious again. "What would you expect from me in exchange?"

"Catch that cat," Carl said, smiling more widely, "and kill it."

Four Eyes put up a hand in front of his face. "I wouldn't use violence against any creature, and that means I wouldn't wring a cat's neck."

"Who said anything about wringing the damn animal's neck?" Carl was good at making believe he was being perfectly reasonable. "What you do after you catch him is you take him into Bunny's room—there—open the window and throw him out."

"I couldn't do anything like that, either."

Carl swiftly reached back of the standing azure pillow of the nearest soft chair and brought out a gleaming Colt. He pointed it toward the ceiling, but made sure that chandelier lights reflected from its oily surface. Four Eyes couldn't miss the sight.

"Turn down that simple request, Four Eyes, and I might soon be telling my friends the cops that I shot a burglar with a police record. I'd be awfully sorry if I killed him."

"You'd do all that over a cat?"

It wasn't a cat for its own sake, but Carl wouldn't justify himself. He simply glowered.

Four Eyes nodded unwillingly and started down the hallway after that red tabby. When he walked back into Carl's view, the cat was complaining loudly in Four Eyes' clumsy grip.

He said doggedly, "I don't want nobody seeing this," and closed the door of Bunny's room behind himself. The window was opened. The feline squeals came to a stop suddenly. The window was shut.

Slowly the door opened a little way. Four Eyes had to squeeze himself out of there.

"Open it all the way and don't never let me see you again."

Even as Four Eyes hurried to the outside door, in response to Carl's crude gesture, he murmured, "I knew you'd double-cross me."

A draft of wind from the opening hall door opened the door to Bunny's room. Carl, glancing inside, saw the damned cat eating hurriedly from its dish. No doubt it had quieted down when Four Eyes put him there; Carl had originally insisted that the animal's food dish be kept in Bunny's room, and the pan in her bathroom.

The next seconds were a nightmare for cat and man. Ziggy sped away from tension, taking the only possible space to freedom by scooting out between Carl's legs. Carl, seeing his tuxedo actually desecrated with cat hair, making his hand shake in fury, fired down at the cat with what had to be less than perfect aim. . . .

Bunny hurried into the apartment by the back way, the front key having got jumbled up in her ring. Maybe she was too excited to pick it out. There was a good reason for that. After her night's work in the chorus at Revels on the Roof, a British producer had asked if she'd like to work for him. He must be an important producer, about that much she felt sure.

Thank heavens that Carl had insisted she go to work instead of being taken to some society dinner. He'd sacrificed himself for her career. She should think of that as one favor he had done for her. He wasn't always easy to live with. Now that she could help herself in her career, she realized he was sometimes rough on her, very rough on her.

Another girl, a girl who wasn't so forgiving, might've been glad to get out of this arrangement, to be the one who broke it off. Another girl would almost be looking forward to saying those necessary goodbyes.

She stopped to coo at Ziggy on the kitchen windowsill, looking a little—she thought—guilty for some reason. Making her face serious as was fitting for this occasion, Bunny walked to the front of the apartment.

She didn't scream at what she saw there.

OF PERSEPHONE, POE,
AND THE WHISPERER

Tom Piccirilli

IN SUCH A sweet-scented autumn, with the distant cries of
ravens declaring a grievous winter on the front, October of
1817 saw the arrival of two new students to the mist-veiled
village of Stoke Newington. Their approach up the long gravel
path, past the leaning gate of jagged iron spikes, seemed
equally morose as the sullen church bell striking noon the
instant they appeared on the step of Manor House.

Complete strangers as they reached the front door, and despite three years difference in their ages, the boys could well
have passed themselves off for twins. Indeed, at first I had
difficulty in differentiating them adequately, and became so
distracted by their mirrored countenances that I often lost my
train of thought. They each maintained a mop of curly black
hair, worn in a manner accepted in the ungrateful Americas
but not in our small suburb of London, and I immediately
ordered them shorn. Both were of an extreme pallor, with skin
of a near-translucent quality, more like the film on the surface
of a pond than a healthy child's pigment. Worst were their
deep, unsettling, dark eyes, as though they'd witnessed an
equivalent portion of dismay and sorrow in their young lives.
Each possessed a slightly troubled, melancholy demeanor, perhaps best explained by their respective plights as orphans at an

early age. They both had found themselves the beneficiaries of quasi-adoptions by well-to-do families, households who refused to pursue full legalities to make the boys their heirs, yet who provided for the children, and provided quite commendably.

Though both youths proved to be bright, witty, and amicable, each exhibited traits to forgo full acceptance by their classmates. William Wilson, due to either a condition of throat or merely persona, spoke only in a dull susurration and soon became known as "Wilson the Whisperer." Edgar Poe, one of the most naturally discerning and earnest students to attend Manor House in my nine years as principal, experienced bouts of disquietude and apparent grave depression, which often offset the others' attempts to welcome him into either sport or game. He did not seem to mind at all, preferring to spend his free time reading the classics in Latin or Greek, and writing at length in his many notebooks.

Another distinction to separate the boys from their classmates, and thus prove an even greater binding force between them, soon became apparent in the svelte and lissome form of my late sister's beloved cat, Persephone.

A remarkably large British Blue, sagacious to the extreme, and entirely black except for a white splotch covering her chest, she always remained nearby my person, perpetually on hand and under foot, a mysterious and eternal remembrance of my sister, Lenore. Though most animal gazes appear scintillating, luminous, and even fiery, Persephone's eyes blazed hotter than expected, the left eye only slightly brighter than the right, a trait unnoticeable to anyone not seeking such an aberration.

At the end of their first week in attendance, after second Mass, I called William and Edgar into my office in an effort to belay any fears or apprehension on their part. Though Wilson had already entered the realm of his teen years, and thus should have desired a certain common deference from the underclassmen, it was he who remained several steps behind the younger Poe, like a shadow falling from his heels. Though I addressed them impartially and made futile attempts at conversing evenly, I soon found myself speaking only to Edgar. With Wilson so similar in feature and attitude, observing interestedly but not partaking in the discourse—not even with his unnerving whispers—it seemed more efficient to address the flesh and not the shade.

As I'd noticed in the past several days, Poe said very little of a personal nature. Still, he showed a warm empathetic temperament and seemed to wish to broach the subject of my sister's recent death. He regarded the many glass baubles and trinkets on my shelves and desk—the chess pieces, figurines, candle holders, and paperweights, as well as the various plaques, medals, and degrees that also decorated my small office. Poe appeared to instinctually understand that Persephone had belonged to my lost sister, Lenore, and so he watched the roaming black cat keenly, even as Wilson did, awaiting the proper moment to speak.

"Well," I said. "I'm certainly glad to hear that you've had no real difficulties with your transition to Manor House, Edgar. Some American children find British decorum a bit too fastidious for their tastes, but you've proven yourself an admirable resident. Please feel inclined to call upon me for any reason, if the need should ever arise."

"Thank you, Reverend Bransby," said Edgar. Unlike his counterpart, Poe's pre-pubescent voice was notably rich and resonant, which stood to reason since his mother had been an actress—as had been his maternal grandparents—though none very accomplished.

"Of course, of course." I had to force myself to confront Wilson, who stood in the background and merely stared, most often at Persephone, his face composed of unreadable expression. "And you as well, William. No need for an appointment, my door is always open." He whispered what I assumed to be his assent.

"Fine, fine then. Will there be anything else, gentlemen?"

Poe considered each word carefully, weighing it upon the next and the prior. I'd never seen a boy so in love with words. His lips set in a bloodless line, those brooding eyes not only haunted but in some bizarre fashion managing to haunt as well, he leaned forward as if to speak confidentially, and said, "I admire your glassworks."

"You are most kind to say so, Edgar, for I made them myself. I apprenticed with a glassblower many years ago before my call to the Church, and on occasion still pursue the art, though I freely admit I am not as skilled as I once believed in my arrogant youth."

Edgar nodded, and finally found it within himself to mention the recent misfortune that had befallen Manor House. "I'm sorry for your loss, sir."

"I truly appreciate your condolences, Edgar."

"My father followed the entire dreadful story in the daily papers quite closely, even in Richmond, and while traveling through Ayrshire."

Though I'd never discussed any element of the circumstances with the students, I became oddly and unduly forthright with young Poe—and thus with his silent duplicate, as well. "Yes, and with understandable reason. No father would wish his son to attend a school where a murderer might lurk. However, the whole ugly matter has been put to an end."

"Yes, sir."

The boy sparked a certain paternal inclination on my part, sentiment perhaps, or concern. For whatever reason, I reached over and pressed my hand to the soft fold between his shoulder and neck, an exceptionally rare, affectionate gesture on my part, having been raised by such stoic and impassive parents. "Thank you."

He raised his chin and looked at me then, sagely and squarely, turning that black, burning gaze on me with a knowing depth that perhaps only one as disassociated as he could possess. It shook me, and I drew my trembling fingers away as if seared. "What are you staring at?"

"Nothing, sir."

"Are you sure everything is all right?"

"Of course."

I'd heard tales of John Allan, the Scotch merchant who had taken in the infant Edgar due to his wife's beseeching and through no empathetic nature on his part. In my few scant meetings with the man I'd found him aggressive but fair, brusque, yet with a leaning toward virtuosity if not blatant kindness.

But the way Poe froze beneath my touch, as if a shard of ice or the very hand of death had been set upon his warm neck, and his turning those flaming eyes upon me, I wondered what kind of a homelife he might have endured to cause him to cast such a fervent gaze.

"You'll have a fine future here at Manor House, Edgar. And you too, Wilson. I look forward to our time together."

And though the Whisperer's thin mouth curled into a shrewd smile, and his lips parted as if to speak, only Poe gave voice. "As do I, Reverend Bransby."

That look—as if peering into the very marrow of my soul.

SOME DAYS later I realized that Persephone had begun spending less and less time looming in close proximity; no longer did she sleep stretched out before my office door, curled over my desk, or lying sluggishly on my bed. Though perplexed and distracted by Poe's odd glare, I'd noticed that the black cat had taken an especially enthusiastic liking to William Wilson. When I went in search of Persephone I found her seated at the boy's side, paws crossed about his ankle as though clenching a lover, gazing up most solemnly at him, and each of them on occasion tilting their heads as if to gain better perspective of the other.

"You've made a new friend, William," I said. "She is an

adorable creature, and one with a most discerning and critical disposition, though I see she's clearly taken you to heart."

He agreed that such was the case.

Too easily could one falsely believe that William Wilson "muttered" or "mumbled" or "murmured," or spoke thusly out of a lack of intellect. No, he most unquestionably *whispered*, and though I could usually make out his words, it often took a great effort of engrossment and focus, a keener diligence than I possessed. Poe, though, seemed to maintain a nearly supernatural concentration, and would often answer Wilson from across the room when even the student nearest the Whisperer was forced to lean in to ask him to repeat himself.

"I didn't realize just how attached I'd grown to her in these last several weeks after the loss of my sister," I said. "She reminds me greatly of Lenore, that is to say I am constantly reminiscing, recollecting happier times, for my sister cherished the animal above anything in the world."

He agreed that she was a prize to cherish.

"Ah . . . yes, yes." I bent to retrieve the black cat, gesturing her to me excitedly. I recognized how comical I must have appeared in my glossy school robes and powdered wig, acting so resolute in chasing a silly cat, the way Lenore had so often done. "Come, come here, my girl, come here now." Persephone ignored my clawing hands, and remained steadfastly affixed to Wilson's ankle. "Ah well, if she diverts you from your work, simply let me know. We can't have your grades slipping due to my over-affectionate pet."

He agreed that he would.

But Persephone didn't return.

Not that night, nor the next, nor the next.

By day she spent the hours woven about Wilson's feet, as he attended his classes, at meals, while studying, and during prayer. Even when walking the irregular and extensive grounds, the black cat adhered to him like mist clinging to the weeds. I asked him time and again to return Persephone to my care, and time and again he reminded me that he did nothing to provoke or illicit such endearment from lost Lenore's pet.

Despite his claims and protests, I grew more and more agitated with this increasingly confounding turn of events, and felt certain that the Whisperer or Poe must have some hand in Persephone's complete and total abandonment of me.

EDUARDO, OUR former handyman, gardener, and groundskeeper, had been imprisoned for the crime of murdering my sister with his bare, hairy hands. Her white and lifeless body had been discovered in a field not far from the shack where he spent most of his leisure time, sharpening his tools and practicing his minimal writing skills. Lenore had provided unparalleled aid to him in teaching the fundamentals of literacy and English propriety.

A soft, bluish hue tinted her strangled alabaster face.

Though Eduardo professed his innocence in broken English, with numerous Portuguese pleas, entreaties, and epithets cast among his cries, several pieces of my sister's unique and precious jewelry were found in his quarters. All that she wore on the day she breathed her last had been recovered from beneath his bed, save one relatively minor treasure—a small diamond earring half the size of a pinkie nail, one of a set bestowed upon her by our mother, and worth more to her than all the relics and remnants within the walls of Manor House. Even so, it proved to be the least costly of the stolen items, and the Prefect of Police suspected that Eduardo had in all probability given the earring to some harlot in London he fancied, in an effort to win her wares.

Having devoted my life to the Christian faith, I did my best not to believe in capital offense, and so sought reprieve for Eduardo. Denied that by reason of what the court called "justice by divine sanction," I appealed to his jailers and asked to be at hand in case he might wish to unburden himself of any of his trespasses. Reluctantly, they allowed me this course of action. His three guards, with only the merest attempt at concealed meaning—and yet revealing in no uncertain terms—promised they would kill Eduardo without hardly any provocation on his part, if such was my desire.

In prison, wearing yards of chains, with his hairy back arched beneath the streaming light from his small cell window, hands raised as if he wanted to choke the life from me, Eduardo suddenly fell to his knees and wept. His massive, muscular arms rippled beneath the weight of his shackles. With my hand upon his shoulder, praying aloud for his soul, he implored me and spoke in that same halting English, "Was not me! No, no, Reverend, I'm a good man!"

"Everything will be all right, Eduardo."

"It is the truth!"

"Repent and all our trespasses are forgiven in the eyes of the Lord."

"Not me, not me! Jesu Christo! It is the truth, Reverend!"

I left him there sobbing in the dust, unable to think of anything except my sister's blue lips.

Eduardo's replacement, Charles Franklin of Russell Square, proved to be his complete physical opposite: small—in fact, one might even say petite—with tiny fingers like a china doll's. A man of dubious character, though, with an inclination toward partaking of the grape in the early hours directly following supper, but who also had a tendency to tire easily and bemoan his state as solitary hired hand.

At Edgar's own urging, I allowed the boy to work side by side with Franklin, gardening and fixing the many minor but ceaseless problems arising about Manor House; Poe established himself to be quite adept at woodwork, and appeared tireless in replastering weakening walls, doing mortar reconstruction, and restoring the ancient stone fence surrounding the grounds. The number of creaking floorboards, rotted rafters, wind-ruined shingles, and broken bricks lessened considerably. In no time at all he became proficient as a jack-of-all-trades repair-man.

Manor House—my father's house, the home I spent my boy-hood in—had been bequeathed to my sister upon the death of our parents some ten years ago. At my constant urging, and after a good deal of bickering, she eventually converted the Elizabethan mansion into a school, and under my direction it had risen to great prominence in only a handful of years.

I knew from experience that the cat enjoyed the house too much to ever leave its confines for even a full night—its high, receding oak ceilings, incomprehensible subdivisions, innu-merable nooks and crannies all proved to be a domain in which Persephone regaled. I was exceedingly familiar with all its dark recesses, and sought through them hunting for her at the oddest hours. I'd sit watching both boys sleeping, some-times until nearly dawn, tracking through the rooms and dor-mitories of Manor House, and yet never did I find her. More and more extreme grew my urgent sense of disavowal and re-nunciation.

The Whisperer told me he had made every effort to disasso-ciate himself from the black cat, but that Persephone proved to be of a singular and independent mind.

Much like my sister.

And yet, in the morning—each and every morning, perhaps only minutes after I gave up my fruitless exploration and pur-suit—there sat Persephone, once again lying in the open for all to witness, huddled near Wilson, and both of them observing me with abject dissatisfaction. As I stalked off, the veins throbbing at my temples and writhing like venom-stuffed asps in my neck, so fell the shadow of Edgar Poe, stepping out from some unseen doorway to pass directly in front of my path.

THE FOLLOWING Sunday, after first Mass, I wandered about the graveyard and entered Lenore's tomb. Memories of my sister, our childhood, our parents, and images of all the weekend carriage rides, picnics, and beachcombing at the seashore came pounding against me like the roiling surf. My thoughts dipped and bobbed: I fell into reflecting on how life changes most drastically from our early years, and tragedy seems to follow tragedy, like insects coming to feed—of my parents' deaths, of their bitter bequests, and Lenore herself dying in the sweaty grip of rage.

I dropped against her crypt heaving, my face pressed to the cold stone, tears squirting from my eyes, alone in the shadows with my mediations. Turning at last from her tomb to find my students playing beyond the churchyard in a rush of garrulous wrestling and sparring.

All save for two, who stood by patiently watching—staring, forever staring as only gargoyles should—Poe and his whispering double . . . and between them, comfortably crouched and yet also glaring at me, the black cat.

Wilson hissed and Poe responded . . . another hiss and again Poe's grunt of a reply, too low to be discernible. And once again the sudden anger pervaded me like a sword fills its sheath. I shoved toward the exit to escape the dismal confines of the crypt and came within earshot.

Poe, without emotion, stated succinctly, in agreement with the Whisperer. "Yes, William, what you say is true. How like laughter a man's wracked sobs can sound."

THEY HAD changed, those boys—perhaps the black cat had brought about such a transformation in them, the vile creature. How they went from dire but witty children to cruel bastions of misery.

I managed to return to Manor House unnoticed and spent an hour probing the nook where Edgar resided.

One notebook, set aside as if for his most deeply private thoughts, contained only a single page of tight and perfect print: *We undo our selves. We are the villains. The enemy resides within. Our mementos verify our flawed natures.*

Perhaps not his personal journal after all.

No, no, perhaps a message.

I had earned that cat in ways that most men would never dare to even dream. I would never release her or allow someone else to ridicule my efforts, taunting me with their pitiless scorn beneath my very nose, after all I had endured. Though there were times long past when I'd weakened to a most dire condition—my parents had witnessed such sporadic moments—never had I been laid low.

I had suffered from a thousand unseen wounds, from barbs, indignities, and outrage that would have broken lesser men and driven them mad. I refused to be mocked with such impunity.

And it fell upon me that if I could not take the cat back under the Whisperer's ever-watchful scrutiny, then I would be forced to murder the boy.

At the very least, I was assured that he would die quietly.

IMPOSSIBLE—SHE couldn't hide from me in our own home, despite its inconceivable branches and abundant apartments and chambers. I stared down at Wilson and came within a hair's breadth of sealing someone else's fate with my own fists. Poe knows—by God in heaven, to look into that boy's face— he knows! Demonic children, where is she? At times, perhaps only in the dreams of my feverish brain, I can swear I hear those purring sighs, and her cautious, supple uncurling movements somewhere just beyond my reach.

AND TOO, that Sunday, I heard Lenore breathing in her crypt—my sister's gasps and slow movements, as if turning and stretching like her own pet, attempting to rise from beneath the stone shield covering her—my pounding heart sounded not like a heart at all, but the tolling of the church bell, a death-knell meant for me on this occasion. And still I perceived the dire breathing as I backed away slowly for the doorway, shuddering so badly until I was unable to move any more, not even when my back brushed the cold, damp wall and I began the slow slide to the floor. The sounds of my sister's moaning prevailed now in the darkness, as well as that of the stone lid moving, as if gripped by excessively weak, tiny hands. Unable to contain myself any longer I cried, "Lenore, Lenore! Forgive me! I couldn't control myself! Forgive me, forgive your brother! Forgive me, God!"

Amidst the abrupt noises of much puffing and gurgling could be heard a sudden shattering of glass, and then, lapping from around the crypt, spread a widening pool of crimson.

"Lenore, you brought the end upon yourself! If only you ever showed mercy upon me! But no, but no! Oh God!"

Franklin stumbled forth from the gloom, rubbing the back of his hand across his wet mouth, and said, "Edgar? Is that you? You promised me more wine. Why have you brought me to this cold place? Who's there? Let a poor hardworking man sleep! Wine should be warm! Edgar! What's this of murder?"

Wheeling, I watched as the courtyard before the church filled with the citizens of Stoke Newington, staring at my sweaty, tear-streaked face, for my cries had been carried on the wind. They pointed and peered, women wrapping themselves more tightly in their shawls, and soon the Prefect of Police emerged, listening intently at what the others had to tell him.

I ran back to Manor House, past all the boys who simply gawked, as if they had played no part in this strangely affecting game . . . no, more like a ritual, an unmasking at the end of the masque—pretending that they had not sensed the ever-tightening threads of maleficia spun by Edgar Poe. Rushing into the foyer I heard Persephone, finally, yes, yes, leading me to the Whisperer's wall, where at last I could reach in and find the false barrier put up by Poe in the dead of night, painted and refined to perfection because he knew—so, this was her lair!—he knew from the moment I touched him on the neck that I was a murderer, he knew from the instant he laid his own fiery gaze upon that of the one-eyed Persephone, for he recognized immediately—the clever, gifted boy!—that one of her luminous eyes was indeed made of glass . . . made by me! . . . to house the shining bauble of my sister's diamond earring, which I'd plucked from her even before she'd breathed her last beneath my tightening fists.

The house filled with the oglers and those who slumped with their mouths agape, and the police pushed through with their enraged faces—more at the thought of now having to apologize to the innocent Eduardo than at having been deceived—and all the many white-faced ladies fought to gain entrance into my home but then fluttered feebly in the arms of their husbands.

And behind them all, as if only a mere spectator of these grotesque events, stood Edgar Allan Poe. In those eerie, ochre eyes, he spoke a clear and pealing question, and asked without asking, *Why?*

How to explain the thousand injuries I had borne as best I could?

"For the love of God!" I said as the Prefect of Police fought his way forward through the crowd, handcuffs open and waiting like steel jaws ready to snap, for it was my only suitable response. "You think this is the fall of Manor House? We shall meet again! Wilson, where are you, boy? I shall have my Persephone someday! Do you think she will love me again?"

Edgar turned away, washing his hands of the entire matter as only a boy destined for fortuitous ends, unlimited success, and boundless happiness could, for he would never know the depths and horrors of degradation and shame that a man like myself had suffered beneath the wrath of the world.

And in a loud and profoundly deep voice, so similar to Poe's, with Persephone twining about his feet the way she'd done with the lost Lenore, the Whisperer whispered no longer, and uttered one word like the booming cry of Heaven itself.

"Nevermore."

A WARM NEST

Shirley Kennett

FRANK JOHNSON RODE his bike along the road to the Hillsburg Munitions Plant, which everybody in town called simply the Plant. He had taken the back road, the one the trucks used. Chunks of gravel flew up behind his wheels as he struggled to stay upright. He was riding the crown between the two deep ruts. A slide to one side or the other would put him ankle deep in dirty water edged with ice. The moon was full and straight ahead of him, tugging him onward and making his mission seem even more urgent. When he came to the fence, he pulled his bike off the road and hid it among the dense undergrowth of the woods that surrounded the Plant.

He made his way along the fence to the point where he knew the wire was loose. He crawled through the opening, catching his knapsack on the wire and twisting to free it. A window rattled in its frame and yielded to pressure on the lower left corner. He reached in and turned the bolt on the door next to the window.

Wind whistled angrily until he shut the window. It was warm inside the converted tin-can factory. The building had once been at the core of the small southern Missouri town of Hillsburg where Frank had spent all of his fourteen years. It had sat idle for years, until lucrative ammunitions contracts had brought it to life, so that money flowed into the pockets of Hillsburg residents again. Only this time, it was women and old men who made up the work force. The town's young men were overseas, some in Europe, some in Africa, some in the Philippines. Frank's dad, George Johnson, the mayor's son and by all accounts one of the shining lights of Hillsburg, was on some God-forsaken island fighting the Japanese.

Frank's mother Margaret worked at the Plant. So did the mothers of all of Frank's friends. Next year, if the war lasted that long, Frank would be old enough to take a few shifts a week himself.

He hadn't sneaked out after his bedtime just for a midnight ride on his bike, although he did that from time to time too. Tonight he had a mission.

He made his way down the corridors between machinery, finding his way unerringly by the light of the moon that filtered through the dirty windows. He knew that at this time of night the watchman would be taking the first of two naps. Old Mr. Winchell, who was also the town barber, had already made his rounds and wouldn't be walking the place again until near dawn. Frank came to a spot in the large, lightly used room where office supplies were kept. He pulled aside some boards and boxes that concealed a hiding place under the stairs.

Inside the cozy place were a mother cat and her three kittens. Mama Cat, who was barely beyond the kitten stage herself, was curled protectively around her litter. Recognizing Frank, she greeted him with a soft rumble that aroused her kittens from sleep and sent them nuzzling into her fur.

"Hello, Mama Cat," Frank said warmly. "I've got something good for you." He rummaged in his knapsack and came out with a dish that he had wrapped securely in a towel. When he put it down, Mama Cat was up in a flash, her face buried in the scraps of fried chicken he had saved from dinner. When she was finished, and rubbing against his legs, he unwrapped the second package from his bag. It was a small bottle of milk, which he poured into the dish. The milk had gotten such a shaking on the bike ride that the cream had mixed back into it. Glistening dots of milk fat swam in the white puddle in the dish. Mama Cat stopped rubbing and began lapping.

As she gave the dish her attention, Frank stroked the kittens. They were three weeks old now, fat and fuzzy, eyes deep blue, tiny claws as sharp as Mr. Winchell's razor. Mama Cat was black with white paws, sleek on the sides, pendulous underneath, and always damp from her kittens' seeking mouths. One of the kittens was all black, one black with a white belly, and the third, Frank's favorite, a wild orange-black-and-white calico. He lifted each one, petted it, and returned it to the blanket he had brought to make a warm nest.

Three weeks ago Frank's mother had come home and told him over dinner that someone had found a dead newborn kitten at the factory. *What a shame,* she had said. *The mama put her dead one out of the nest, the way cats do. There are probably more, but no one knows where they are.* Had he imagined that note of challenge in her voice? She hadn't really come out and said it, but he knew what she meant. Frank's father loved cats, and he would have found a way to help. Now it was up to Frank.

He made his way into the Plant that very night, and searched for a couple of hours before he saw it, that movement at the corner of his eyes, a black streak, a shadow among shadows. It took two more hours to locate her nest under the stairs. She was raggedy and distrustful, and slashed at him with her claws. Her remaining kittens were barely moving, their mouths open, mewing silently. She wouldn't accept his gift of meat until he moved far away into the darkness. Then hunger drove her to the dish.

He had come every night since then, his mother turning a blind eye as he pocketed food or set aside milk.

Frank put out a second serving of chicken for Mama Cat to eat later on. He gathered his things and replaced the boards and boxes. As he made his way back to the rear door, he heard something. A shuffling noise.

Someone was in the building with him.

Assuming it was Mr. Winchell, he hid behind a tool counter. When a couple of minutes passed with no more noise, he rose up high enough to peek over the counter.

A woman was near the door. He could see her silhouette against the window, the light of the full moon falling on her brightly enough to leave a shadow on the floor. Her back was to him. She was wearing a full-length coat, and as he watched, she put a scarf on her head, knotting it beneath her chin. Then she turned the bolt, opened the door, and stepped out into the night. Cold air swept toward Frank, raising swirls of dust on the floor. He held his breath, gooseflesh rising on his arms and back, and listened as a key was inserted, locking the bolt from the outside.

When he rode home that night, he put his foot down into the icy water in the ruts twice, and got home with his shoes squeaking from the damp.

THEY ARRIVED one by one at Margaret Johnson's house, the workers from the Plant, the sensible ones she felt could be trusted with what she had to say tonight.

Her feet ached as they always did after a day of standing on the concrete floor. She was a Quality Checker, one of several responsible for making sure that the ammunition that left the Plant didn't let the soldiers down when their lives were on the line. In spite of her fatigue, she had pushed aside furniture to make space in her small living room, and gathered chairs from all parts of the house. She had made sure Frank had plenty of work to do upstairs, supplementing the teacher's assignments with a few of her own.

She was expecting a dozen people, and they all showed up. Some brought hot dishes, which Margaret accepted with the

easy grace of a transplanted farm wife, brought to town of
necessity while her man was gone.

When her living room was full to overflowing, Margaret
served herb tea, her own blend she grew and dried, the
bunches hanging from nails pounded in over the kitchen windows. Imported tea was hard to come by, coffee even more so,
and the group appreciated a hot drink on a chilly November
night. Margaret was nervous talking in front of more than one
person at a time, but she launched right in.

"I've asked you all here tonight because of something I've
noticed at the Plant," she said. "Something that affects all of
us." There were nods around the room, and all eyes were focused on her. "I think someone's deliberately trying to put the
Plant out of business. One of the people who works there is a
traitor."

There were sharp inhalations of breath, and eyes grew large
and round. Then everyone started talking at once.

"Wait, wait, let me finish. You all know I'm a Quality
Checker, just like you, Bernice," she said, nodding at a slight
woman in the corner. "Over the past few weeks, I've noticed a
pattern. Too many rejections. And you know I only check a
percentage of the rounds. That means more duds are getting
through."

One of the women spoke up. "What are you doing about it?
Have you told anyone?"

"I haven't gotten to that yet. I don't know what to do. First,
I want to ask Bernice if she's noticed the same thing."

Heads swiveled. Bernice started to shake her head, then
sighed. "Yes, I have. I didn't want to say anything about it."

"I'm sure you all see the problem," Margaret said. "If we
speak up and tell Mr. Aster, there's no telling what will happen. The Plant would probably close, temporarily or permanently. We all need the money. What would we do without
our jobs? So we keep quiet." Margaret nibbled her lip, her
anguish leaking out in the flash of her eyes and the twining of

her hands. "We keep quiet, and bad ammunition goes out. I've been having nightmares about George not being able to fire his gun. About being responsible for him . . . dying. Or some other husband or son."

Mr. Aster, the plant manager, was a volatile man who used his authority and power like a whip. He knew he held the livelihood of his workers in the palm of his hand, and he wasn't above crushing his hand into a fist. If he found out that there was tampering going on, the least that would happen would be a purge of the current employees. There were plenty of people in the county who would drive to Hillsburg for a weekly paycheck.

"Why do you think it's deliberate, Marge?" said Arlene Letters. "Couldn't it just be a batch of defective powder or something like that? Aren't you getting a little hysterical?"

Margaret regretted inviting Arlene. The woman had a knack for putting her in a bad light. Besides, there were rumors about Arlene, that she was sleeping with another man while her Arnie was in the trenches in Europe.

A thought ran through her head that perhaps Bernice, the other woman in the room besides herself who knew the truth, had a reason for not wanting to say anything about it.

Margaret dropped her second bombshell. "I've seen evidence of tampering," she said. The room was as quiet as a church after the wedding's over. "Boxes opened and resealed. Scratch marks on the casings. And I think I know who's doing it."

The room erupted in a babble of voices, indignant, frightened, worried. All of them wanted to know whom it was Margaret suspected.

"I'm not sure I should say yet, since I don't have absolute proof."

"You can't do this," Arlene said angrily. "You can't bring us all here and tell us we're going to lose our jobs, and then not tell us who's responsible!"

"Yeah," chimed in JoAnne Evers, her voice dangerous. Margaret knew she was the most impetuous of the group. "Tell us who the traitor is. We'll show her a thing or two!"

There was a chorus of agreement. "I brought you here to decide what type of rational action we can take," Margaret said. She feared that the group she had brought together harbored a depth of feeling that she couldn't channel. The meeting seemed to have a momentum of its own now. "Not to be a lynch mob. Calm down, everybody."

"Tell us!"

"Who is it? We'll fix 'em!"

Margaret put her hands over her ears. All the pressure she'd been feeling for the past weeks bubbled up, her mouth opened, and she spat out a name.

"Lillian Hogan. It's Lillian Hogan!"

Her hand flew to her mouth. The room got quiet as the name was absorbed. Judged. Condemned. Margaret raised her eyes to the ceiling, as if she could summon her words back from the air. Her eyes met and locked with Frank's. Her son was watching, and listening, from the landing of the stairs.

Margaret was doubly ashamed now that she knew her son had witnessed her indiscretion. She hadn't intended to blurt out the name. Had she? There was a murmur in the room now, and she heard out the word "traitor."

"I said I didn't have absolute proof."

"Well, what do you know?" It was Arlene again. If anyone was going to pin Margaret to the wall, it would be Arlene.

"First of all, the tampering started just about the time Lillian moved to town. She said she was a widow from Tennessee, but none of us really knows her or any of her kin."

"That's true," said Bernice. "But none of you knew me, either, when I moved here two years ago. Just because she's new in town doesn't make her guilty."

"That's not all," Margaret said. Her voice was raspy and low. Accusatory, in spite of her mixed feelings. "I was working late last week, you know, with the rush order? I had to go to the bathroom, and from my station, that's a long walk over to the east side. On the way, I saw Lillian. She was taping up boxes that were on the belt. The boxes were going to be packed the next morning in the shipping crates. That's not proof, because I didn't catch her with the boxes open. But it's the next best thing."

"Did you say anything to her?" JoAnne asked.

"Of course not. I was too shocked. She didn't see me. Anyway, she had a knife which she must have been using to slit the boxes."

"Are you saying she would have used the knife on you?" JoAnne said.

"Oh, God. It's her. I just knew it." Bernice's voice wafted from the corner of the room.

Arlene rounded on her. "Just what do you know about this, Bernice? And why haven't you come forward with it?"

"Nothing. I . . . I didn't really see anything." Bernice shrank under Arlene's full-bore glare, and it was obvious that she was holding something back.

"We're agreed, then. The Hogan woman's a traitor. She's cutting our throats, and getting our men shot, too," JoAnne said.

"If it's true," Margaret said, "and I still say if, what are we going to do about it? If we go to Mr. Aster, he'll have to report it. There will be inspectors swarming all over the place and the Plant will be shut down until they get to the bottom of it. And they may decide not to reopen it. I've heard those rumors about relocating to Carlisle."

"We could confront her," JoAnne said. "Tell her we know what's going on and she'd better quit. Or else."

"Or else what?" Margaret said, aware of her son's eyes watching her expression and her words crossing the distance between them.

"Or else something bad will happen to her," JoAnne said.

"What, like getting tarred and feathered and run out of town?" Arlene said derisively.

"No. Like getting killed."

The words bounced off the walls and came to rest in the center of the group. There was a long silence.

"Of course you didn't mean that," Margaret said. Things were way out of her control now. Even worse, she wasn't quite as shocked as she would have been just an hour ago.

"Maybe I did," JoAnne retorted.

"I think we should all sleep on it," Margaret said. "We're not going to come up with any useful suggestions tonight. Let's get together again on Friday, and maybe we can discuss things more calmly."

Not everyone agreed, but Margaret prevailed. When the living room was empty, she turned to talk to her son. Frank was gone from the stairs.

THE NEXT night Frank was anxious as he stroked the kittens. He was abrupt with Mama Cat, once stepping on her tail accidentally. She picked up on his distracted mood and soon returned to nursing her babies. When he tried get in a farewell pat as she lay curled around them, she whacked his hand away, leaving bloody marks of her ill temper. It was time to go, and take his troubles with him.

As he cautiously returned to the rear door, stopping farther away than he had the night before, he again spotted a female form ahead of him. From what he had overheard the night before, he guessed that it was Lillian Hogan, and that she was up to no good. She certainly wasn't feeding homeless cats. The woman tied her scarf and then opened the door. As she went outside, another figure stepped from the shadows. The light of the moon fell on her profile, and Frank was shocked to recognize his mother.

The two women spoke in low tones. The woman he thought was Lillian Hogan began to gesture angrily, and Frank's mother responded by raising her voice. Frank caught "traitor" and "Kill you", and those were words he didn't like to hear coming from his mother's mouth. Suddenly the woman shoved his mother hard, sending her sprawling backwards. While his mother was on the ground, the woman strode off toward the interior of the Plant. She passed within a few yards of Frank, as he held his breath and noticed that one of his shoes was immersed in a pool of moonlight. She should have seen him, but she didn't.

It was Lillian Hogan, he was sure of that.

His mother got to her feet slowly and left. Frank wondered if she had come to warn the woman, or if there was more to it than that. He wondered how soundly Mr. Winchell slept. Perhaps the old man knew about Frank's nightly visits but saw no harm in them. Did he also know about Lillian's? Had he overheard Margaret Johnson threatening to kill the woman, as Frank had?

It would be good if that woman was out of the way. Frank didn't want his mother to lose her job, and he certainly didn't want his dad, or any other soldiers, to die because of Lillian Hogan. He hesitated in the gloom of the factory floor. He knew his way around very well, and he was a big, strong boy, almost as tall as his dad.

The Plant could be a dangerous place at night. Lillian Hogan could have an accident.

AT SIX A.M. the next morning, as Margaret was sliding a pan of biscuits into the oven for breakfast, there was a knock on the door. Wiping her hands on a towel, she went to answer it, but Frank beat her to it.

It was Ansel Waterman, Hillsburg's police chief and only member of its law enforcement department for the past four decades. Frank opened the door wide, and Ansel swept in, bringing the cold, bleak morning in with him.

"Good morning, ma'am, Frank. Could I have a word with you both?"

Margaret nervously led him to the kitchen, where she could keep an eye on the biscuits.

Hat in hand, Ansel sat at her table and delivered his news in his blunt way.

"A woman was found murdered last night at the Plant. I believe you know her, Margaret. Her name was Lillian Hogan."

"Oh, my," Margaret said. Fear rooted her to the spot. In her home last night, death had been discussed, and now it had happened. She looked at Frank, and what she saw in his face troubled her greatly.

He wasn't surprised.

She wasn't sure if Ansel saw it or not, but a mother's eyes couldn't possibly miss it.

She told Ansel everything about the meeting in her home, told him anything she thought would draw attention from Frank. She didn't mention going to the Plant the night before, seeing Lillian, and getting pushed to the ground. Throughout, her son was silent.

The facts were that Lillian's body had been found by the watchman, Mr. Winchell, on his dawn rounds of the Plant. She had been hit with a blunt instrument, probably one of the hammers that were always lying around to use when sealing crates. There had been a struggle. There was blood under her nails.

Margaret closed her eyes. It seemed too intimate, what Ansel was telling them. She didn't want to think about Lillian's last moments, or who had shared them with her. When she opened her eyes, she caught sight of the scratches on Frank's hand, and inhaled sharply. She tore her eyes away so that Ansel wouldn't follow her gaze. She had lost a minute of the conversation. He was talking to Frank now, focused on him.

Abruptly she realized that Ansel had come to talk to Frank, not to her. Her heart froze.

". . . long have you been going to the Plant at night, son? Mr. Winchell knows all about it, so don't bother to deny it."

"About three weeks, sir."

"And what do you do when you're there?"

"I feed the cats. There's a cat and her kittens living under the stairs in the supply room."

"Feed the cats, eh? Gone soft like your old man, I guess. I'm going to have to ask you to show me those cats, just so I know you're not making this up."

"Yes, sir. I'll be happy to. But please don't do anything to them."

Margaret watched, unable to say anything, to think of anything, as her son walked out with the police chief.

FRANK LED Ansel Waterman through the Plant and pulled the boxes and boards aside. He stepped away and let the man look. From his side view, he could see that Mama Cat was arched and hissing, standing over her kittens and prepared to lay down her life. It tugged at his heart. He would try to make it up to her later.

"What's that colored thing in there, that thing with the fringes?" Ansel asked, peering into the nest. He moved away and let Frank get a good look.

Frank shook his head, puzzled. "I don't know. It wasn't there last night when I fed her." He knelt and reached toward the thing, which was tucked into the blanket he had brought on the first night. Mama Cat objected, and he snatched his hand away quickly.

"Looks like she's scratched you before," said Ansel.

"Yes, sir. I stepped on her tail last night, and she didn't much like it."

"Cute kittens. Here, let me try."

Frank turned and looked at the man. His face had softened

and his eyes gleamed with memories of a special cat purring under his rough hands. Ansel knelt and spoke quietly to the cat. In a few minutes, he was able to draw the item from the blanket with a minimum of hissing.

It was a woman's scarf, rudely stained with blood.

"Something the cat dragged in," Ansel said.

"It wasn't here when I . . ."

"I believe you, son. Don't worry." He rose to his feet heavily. "I may just have to sign your cat on as deputy. It looks like she's collected a crucial piece of evidence."

Frank wanted to snatch the bloodied scarf from the man's hands and get rid of it. Burn it. Tie it in a sack and throw it in the river. He couldn't take his eyes off it, and he could hear its mute accusations.

THE NEXT few days were torture. Frank couldn't concentrate on his schoolwork, although he kept up pretenses. His mother did too, bustling around with her dust rag and mop, and going off to work. He kept waiting to hear bad news, waiting for the police chief to descend on his house. When the knock finally did come, it was almost a relief.

Ansel was at the kitchen table again. "A cup of that tea you make sure would go down well now," he said, rubbing his hands. A cold front had moved in, and last night there had been an ice storm. Frank had walked to the Plant, slipping and sliding, to find the kittens rolling and biting each other while Mama Cat looked on and occasionally pinned one down for a good washing.

"Are you sure everything in there's legal?" Ansel asked as Frank's mother brewed the tea. He sipped appreciatively. Frank impulsively reached across the table and grasped his mother's hand. She returned the squeeze, letting him know they were in it—whatever it was—together.

"Lillian Hogan was murdered because she was a traitor to this country," Ansel said. "Not that the killer should get away with it. There are laws for that sort of thing, and she should have been brought to trial."

Frank's mother cleared her throat. "Do you know who did it?"

"I do, thanks to the scarf Frank's cat found. It was Mr. Aster."

Frank looked at his mother. There were bright tears in the corners of her eyes.

"I know what you two thought," Ansel said. "And you couldn't be further from the truth."

Frank was speechless. He just nodded, overwhelmed that his fears were unfounded.

"It all started at the meeting at your house, Margaret. Arlene Letters was there, and she was convinced that Lillian was guilty. She wanted to do something about it, so she went straight to her . . ." Ansel glanced at Frank, uncertain, then apparently made up his mind to continue. "She went straight to her lover, Cornelius Aster. Arlene wanted him to fire her and make her move away. I interviewed everyone at the meeting, and Arlene just came right out and told me about it. I think she was a little bit proud."

"I never should have had that meeting."

"I'll agree with you there. You should have come to me instead. Aster followed Lillian Hogan to the Plant last Tuesday night. He heard your argument with her, Margaret. That's another thing you should have come to me about."

Frank's mother lowered her eyes to the table, but she couldn't stop herself from smiling with relief.

"When you and Frank were both gone, he went after Lillian. He had sharp words with her, and she told him he didn't have any proof. He shoved her, and she scratched his face. He picked up a hammer and hit her. He didn't go there with the intention of killing her, but that's the way things turned out."

"What about the scarf?" Frank said.

"He wiped the blood off his face with it and tucked it in his pocket. He took the hammer, too. Somewhere on his way out of the Plant the scarf fell out. He went back for it, but couldn't find it. We know why." Ansel stopped long enough to finish his tea. "I sent that scarf to the police laboratory in Jefferson City. You up on your science, son? There were two blood types found on that scarf. The first belonged to the victim, who was Type A. The second was Type B. Couldn't have come from the same person.

"I knew it wasn't Arlene. Oh, she talks big, but she couldn't do a thing like that. Cornelius Aster, though—that man has a temper, we all know it. When his doctor confirmed that his blood was Type B, I went and had a talk with him. His conscience must have been screaming in his ear, because I wasn't in the house five minutes before he showed me the hammer."

At the door, Ansel turned to Frank. "If you haven't got homes for those kittens yet, I'd like to put in a claim for one. Maybe two would be better, so they'd keep each other company."

"Yes, sir! I had in mind," Frank said, glancing sideways at his mother, "that I might keep Mama Cat and her little calico."

"I think that's the least we can do for that cat," his mother said. "We owe her a debt, and besides, I think your dad might like a couple of cats around the house when he gets home."

FUR BEARING

Brett Hudgins

THERE WAS A poem called *The Rime of the Ancient Mariner* which Gilles Demers knew he would probably never read. He had neither the patience nor the bilingual literacy. However, in the eight years since its publication in 1798, Coleridge's verse composition had achieved such fame that Gilles frequently heard it discussed by travellers.

The chilling example of the Mariner and the albatross had convinced Gilles that he too lived under a curse, though his was bovine rather than avian in nature.

He was six feet tall, muscular—ruggedly handsome, even, if the admiring Métis women could be believed. In short, he was miserable, for there was nothing Gilles wanted more than to be a *voyageur*. Braving the wilderness of his Canadian homeland, shooting frothing white rapids in a *canot du nord* loaded with beaver pelts, singing songs, smoking pipes, passing the days with good friends and hard work.

Except he was too big for the boat.

The ideal *voyageur* was short, thick-set, and possessed of limitless energy. His arms and shoulders were developed out of proportion to the rest of his body. His wide, cheerful face bore testament to brawls and animal maulings.

The last thing he ever did was compromise the efficiency of

his canoe with a pressing need for leg-room—the way Gilles would have.

Hence Gilles's curse.

He was stuck living a sort of half-life at Fort William, formerly Fort Kaministiquia, on the northwest shore of Lake Superior. The fort was the western headquarters of the North West Company, a coalition formed in 1783 by independent traders to compete against the huge Hudson's Bay Company. Each summer all furs obtained from natives and collected at outlying posts were brought to Fort William by *voyageurs* in their North canoes. At the same time brigades of *canots de maître* arrived from Montreal laden with essential supplies and trade goods. The necessary exchanges were made.

Gilles was scorned ceaselessly by his boisterous heroes for the ungainly size of his body, and his dreams.

Yet the devastating truth was that a man could not escape his own body. The one time he'd tried, a blazing summer afternoon, he'd gotten so involved in racing his shadow that he'd hurtled into the wall of the counting-house. Explaining that he thought the building could use a window hadn't saved him from his nickname, his albatross. *Le Taureau*. The Bull.

Gilles had a single refuge against the contempt of his idols. His only solace came from a most unlikely friend, an animal he would ordinarily have ignored: the fort's communal cat. Gilles had named his confidant *Chat du Nord*. North, for short.

Snow-white, sleek and swift as *La Vieille*, the wind that ruled the waters, North displayed an unswerving willingness to spend time with Gilles and listen to his fantasies, as long as the human reciprocated with quality pampering of the sort he had previously reserved for his most prized possession: his paddle. A *voyageur's* paddle, individually decorated to its owner's tastes, was his most distinctive badge of office. Gilles had made one for himself in a burst of wishful thinking and occasionally toted it around when he needed to feel valued.

To his surprised delight, he received the same affirmation of his worth—as well as a great deal of fur on his pants—by petting his cat.

As if sensing his thoughts, North twined around his booted ankles, purring. Thoughts of poems and curses fled before real-life spectacle. Together, man and cat watched a North canoe approach from the mouth of Kaministiquia River. As usual, the *voyageurs* were paddling hard, maintaining their daily average of forty strokes a minute from dawn till dusk. A typical North canoe was eight meters long and over one meter wide. This particular vessel carried a crew of seven men and just over a ton of bundled furs.

Singing raucously, attracting many of the fort's inhabitants to vantage points on the long lakefront wharf, the *voyageurs* put on a burst of speed, paddles striking the water like broad, painted lightning bolts.

The spectators tossed an ebullient chorus of cheers, praise, and questions at the returning travellers, along with more practical anchor lines, as the canoe glided to a halt.

Four Métis women, taken as wives by four of the men the previous summer, rushed to embrace their husbands. Three presented young children to proud fathers for the first time.

Gilles struggled to avoid being trampled by the overly festive crowd and moved to help unload the canoe. The crew's *bourgeois*, a partner in the North West Company and the designated law and order during the rough expedition, tossed Gilles a tumpline and imperiously directed him to get to work.

"I missed you too, Etienne," Gilles muttered, fitting around his forehead the harness which helped him hoist and balance a heavy fur bundle.

"At least the Bull has a strong back, no?" laughed one of the *voyageurs*.

Five red woolen *tuques* bobbed with laughter as paddles slapped the water in appreciation of the jibe.

Still hoping for elusive acceptance, Gilles could not help

but answer pleasantly. One caught more flies with honey than with vinegar. "I see you fellows had a good trip."

"Thanks to me!" one man boasted. Even though he was a near duplicate of his comrades in his deer skin leggings, moccasins, and blue capote, Pierre Dumond never failed to distinguish himself with his abrasive, self-important manner. Gilles would never forget this braggart who had given him his nickname. Massive ego aside, however, Pierre was a hell of a trader.

"The richest fur trade I have ever made and we almost missed it. How do you suppose that happened, *bourgeois?*"

Etienne Gauthier shot the *voyageur* a look that invited him to work now, talk later. To the amusement of his partners, Pierre managed to do both, firing back a stream of colorful profanities while affixing his tumpline.

Gilles sighed wistfully at witnessing another special moment in which he could never share. "I wish I could have been there," he said softly to North, who merely lashed his eloquent tail back and forth.

Pierre appeared before him, looking up solemnly. "I, too, wish you were of smaller stature, my friend."

"Really?" Gilles gasped.

"*Oui.* Then I would not have to reach so high to do *this!*" He gave Gilles an open-hand smack to the head and the dock exploded in laughter.

"The Bull must have dull horns for you to abuse his head so, Pierre!"

Almost choking on the sudden lump in his throat, Gilles let his tumpline slip to the dock, picked up North roughly, and lumbered blindly away.

For perhaps the first time, *Le Taureau* genuinely saw red.

GILLES AWOKE with a strip of sun across his eyes and North happily kneading his stomach with needle claws.

Of the two, the light hurt more, as if his contracting pupils controlled an inversely proportionate pressure within his hungover head.

He sat up slowly, swaying with the throbbing in his skull. Reaching out to pet his cat, he missed on the first two tries, then rubbed the wrong way and got his hand bitten. This good-natured feline violence helped him pry his eyes open wide enough to recognize, not his lodging-house room, but a stone cell with a single barred window.

Bars. Strip of sun. In his melancholy rage he'd apparently drunk enough to end up in Fort William's jail, known among the *voyageurs* as the *pot au beurre*, the butter tub. As his reputation around the fort was already well-colored by his hero-worship, Gilles supposed it wouldn't be the end of the world if he were accused of emulating one more facet of *voyageur* behavior: sleeping off a drunken revel.

Having abandoned Gilles's stomach when he sat up, North had just finished working his lap to the proper consistency when Gilles upset the whole process by lurching to his feet, dislodging the cat entirely.

Gilles smiled at his hissing friend. "Don't worry, I'm thinking of you. Keeper!" he called. "I think I've got my head together, such as it is. Can I get out of here and feed my cat?"

He blinked in surprise when Fort William's magistrate, Samuel Desjardins, appeared before the cell, accompanied by the *bourgeois* Etienne Gauthier. Where was the ordinary keeper?

"Finally awake, eh Bull?"

"I guess I got a little carried away yesterday," Gilles said sheepishly, *having* to guess because he certainly couldn't remember. "All right if I rejoin the world?" Puzzled by the two men's stern-faced scrutiny, Gilles added, "It won't happen again. I don't even know what I was drinking."

"A *little* carried away . . ." Samuel echoed faintly.

Etienne was much more vocal. "He goes too far, claiming not to remember!"

"Remember what?"

Etienne stepped so close the bars framed his nose. "Do not act the innocent. You bludgeoned Pierre Dumond to death!"

Gilles sat down hard, not noticing what was beneath him. Fortunately, nothing meowed or fought back. "Pierre?"

Etienne threw up his hands and let Samuel step forward. "Last night," he began somberly, "well after midnight, as the revels died down, one of the clerks who had been up cataloging the new pelts was returning to his quarters when he stumbled over the body."

"He looked as if a tree fell on him!" Etienne spat each word like a bullet of outrage. "Several times!"

"We found your paddle, splintered and bloody, where you dropped it a few feet away. You yourself managed to stagger only a few extra meters. We found you slumped against the powder magazine."

"The stone walls were rough and cold," Gilles muttered, vaguely remembering his collapse, though nothing more. He looked up. "My paddle?"

Samuel pointed to a table behind him on which rested the murder instrument.

At the sight of his most prized possession, Gilles could only shake his head in silent denial. But in this matter, silence wasn't, could not be, sufficient. "I would never use my paddle to commit such brutality."

"No?" said Etienne. "Your laughable pretensions are a crime against all *voyageurs*!"

"That's enough, Etienne," Samuel cautioned.

"He murdered one of my men."

A hundred protests clogged Gilles's throat like a logjam. He might have squeaked.

Samuel resumed. "Gilles. Everyone saw Pierre taunting you. Maybe he brought this on himself, but the fact is that even your temper must have a limit. Your jealousy of *voyageurs* is well-known."

"Envy, not jealousy. I. Am. Not. Bitter."

"Regardless. You have the only motive. I'm sorry, but you're in a great deal of trouble." He shook his head sadly. "You may not have lived your dream but you had a good life here, Gilles. You shouldn't have thrown it away." With that pronouncement, it seemed he could no longer look Gilles in the eye. "I'll go see if I can find you something to eat."

"For North. I have no appetite."

Etienne followed the magistrate, casting smugly venomous looks at the prisoner on his way out.

Gilles found he didn't even have the energy to get off the floor. Furthermore, it seemed fitting that all his doubt and worry would settle with him, allowing him to sift through it at his muddled leisure. He was deathly afraid that he might unearth the one crumbly clod of guilt which would confirm that he had indeed murdered Pierre Dumond.

WHEN SAMUEL and Etienne finally returned, the sunlight had traversed half the floor. The most depressing difference between the light and himself, Gilles reflected, was that the light stood a much better chance of leaving the cell by nightfall.

It had also usurped his position as North's companion. The cat would settle in the beam and bask, wake up in shadow, reposition himself, and repeat the cycle. Gilles wished he were a cat.

"Etienne wants to prosecute you according to trail rules," Samuel said with no preamble. "Where he's the boss. Because Pierre was under his supervision, and because the evidence against you is so positively crushing, fogged memory or not, I've agreed."

"You *will* regret succumbing to the heat of the moment," Etienne promised. He waved his arms theatrically. "Dozens of punishments suggest themselves to me."

Untempered by mercy or understanding, Gilles supposed

bitterly. Then again, who was to say he did not deserve such treatment?

"How did you let everything get out of hand, Gilles?" Samuel had regained his sincerity and willingness to make eye contact. He exhibited an almost paternal manner.

"I swear I don't remember. I know that doesn't speak highly of me, but I don't think I've ever been blind, dead drunk before; how could I anticipate murderous tendencies or a mental blackout? I just wanted to deaden my emotional pain, not eradicate its source."

"And your paddle?"

Gilles glanced at the table. "What about it?"

"Should I not aid in the questioning?" Etienne interrupted coolly. "It is my responsibility, and I am less interested in the murder weapon than I am in determining the Bull's fate."

"If the paddle was so important to you, Gilles," said Samuel, "why did you put those scratches in it? They predate the bludgeoning."

"Scratches?"

North meowed loudly, responding to the word, and stalked from his sunbeam to the bars, slipping through lithely. He launched himself easily to the tabletop, positioned himself on the paddle, and began scratching vigorously. Sinewy forelegs dragged razor claws through tough wood, leaving more furrows of the sort Samuel had questioned.

"Oh," said the magistrate.

Gilles laughed, and felt his mood lighten a fraction. "Yes. Some time ago North settled on my paddle as the perfect tool on which to sharpen his claws. I indulged him. Now, when I take it out, I make sure I display the undamaged face." He blinked. "That is, when I used to take it out . . ."

Samuel sighed. "I suppose it isn't doing any good on that table, nor can you use it from your cell. Etienne, would you get Gilles his paddle?"

"I will not coddle a murderer."

"Then do it as a favor to me."

"I must object—"

"I insist."

"Very well," Etienne mumbled. He walked to the table, his steps almost mincing, and reached for the paddle. As soon as his fingers touched the handle, North exploded into a white blur of fur and claw.

Etienne shrieked and jumped back, cradling bloody hands.

"I should have mentioned," said Gilles innocently, "that North doesn't like to have his scratching interrupted."

"May you find *merde* in your moccasins," Etienne snarled, if not at Gilles, then at the world.

"I apologize, Etienne," said Samuel contritely. "Here, let me have a look."

"I am fine."

"Etienne . . ." Samuel grabbed his hands for a closer examination. "This is odd. In addition to all the fresh scratches, there are a number that are just beginning to scab over."

"I . . ."

"As if you've tried before to wrest this paddle from this cat," shouted Gilles in a rush of understanding. "Perhaps last night in my quarters, before framing me for murder!"

"Nonsense. I got these picking berries."

"You've been hostile to me from the beginning."

"Because you murdered Pierre."

"No, because *you* did!"

"Gentlemen," Samuel interjected.

"I remember when Pierre was bragging on the dock, you gave him a dirty look. What did you resent him for?"

"Nothing! He was part of my crew."

"Etienne . . ."

"Come now, Samuel. You cannot take *Le Taureau* seriously."

"I take a murder seriously." He swept his penetrating gaze over both men, settling on Etienne. "You may be a big man out in the wilderness with only your crew, but I'm the law in this fort, and I want answers. Neither of you will leave this jail until we clear up this matter."

Gilles regarded the fidgety Etienne serenely and said, "Perfectly acceptable."

"I have done nothing wrong," Etienne said petulantly.

Gilles thought hard about the previous afternoon, willing to relive a painful past for the sake of his future. "Samuel, besides humiliating me, Pierre was bragging about an extremely lucrative fur deal. Maybe Etienne is upset a mere *voyageur* was taking credit for this."

North meowed and hopped from his scratching paddle to rejoin Gilles.

Etienne looked as if he wanted to kick the cat. "He had no business making that deal," he said between gritted teeth.

"Why?" asked Samuel.

"Because I was saving those furs."

"For what purpose?" Samuel bore in relentlessly.

"So I could pass the information on to the Hudson's Bay Company and one of their legitimate agents could return and close the deal. Are you satisfied?" Etienne kicked disconsolately at the floor planks, seeming more ashamed by his confession than by what it revealed.

"You work for the competition?"

Defiantly: "With exceptional skill. You Nor'Westers probably do the same thing among Bay men."

"Maybe," Samuel conceded. "But I doubt we make ourselves conspicuous by committing murder."

"That arrogant Pierre—I was seething! I had to do *something*. The Bull, his paddle, his reputation in general, provided the perfect cover for my revenge."

"Poor Etienne. You should have paid more attention when you were stealing my paddle." Gilles affectionately bumped foreheads with North. "One look at my sad little bed would have shown you how much cats like destroying covers."

A ROMAN OF NO IMPORTANCE

Elizabeth Foxwell

*I have invented an invaluable permanent invalid called Bunbury in order
that I may be able to go down into the country whenever I choose.*
—Algernon Moncrieff, *The Importance of Being Earnest*

I, THE VERY real Bunbury, was contemplating the use of
thumbscrews on my own personal millstone, Algernon Moncrieff, when the letter arrived. My invaluable man, Slade,
brought it to me in the conservatory as I fumed in my Bath
chair. I ripped open the envelope. Slade's eyebrow lifted, and
he tucked the silver salver under his arm with disapproval at
such excess. But instantly my mood changed.

10 March 1893

Dear Mr. Bunbury,

You may recall the occasion when you brought the murderer of
my father to justice. Because of your encouragement, my first
play, "The Passion of Cleopatra," will open at the Royal Adelphi
in a fortnight. Could you come to see me? I should be grateful for
your presence.

Yours sincerely,
Maud Greystone

Oh, I remembered the Hon. Maud Greystone. She would be difficult to forget. In the Greystone morning room, she and I had . . . The faint scent of roses wafted, and I held the envelope to my nose. Unforgettable. Miss Maud's gratitude was something to cherish, if somewhat . . . bruising.

"Are we off, sir?"

I performed a quick self-inventory. Patterned silk waistcoat and trousers of a darker gray—good. One must always make a dignified impression upon the fair sex. I stripped off my dressing gown and tossed it at Slade, and he exchanged it for my frock coat. "Yes, Slade. London. The theatre. Would you fetch my topcoat, please."

"Yes, sir. I shall pack our false mustaches, sir." He bowed and stalked out. The theatrical profession offended Slade's considerable dignity. Slade believed the lower orders should set a good example for the unregenerate gentry.

But he packed our bags with his usual swift efficiency, including the invaluable portmanteau he tucked away behind my chair, and wheeled me out to the carriage. We do not as a rule refer to the affliction which confines me to a Bath chair; it would be bad form.

A few hours later, we alighted at the Adelphi. I straightened my tie hastily as Slade wheeled me into the passage to the stalls. A rehearsal was in progress, with a collection of actors declaiming in a fantastic combination of bedsheets and breastplates across a landscape of fake rock, scattered sand, and the occasional pyramid. Yet my attention was drawn to a slender, dark-haired girl in a graceful brocade skirt and lace-trimmed shirtwaist, twisting the cameo brooch at her throat. She saw us, and heedless of her beautiful clothes, leaped into the orchestra pit and flung her arms about me. Slade cleared his throat, but I was too—occupied—to regard it. Miss Maud made very—er, free—with her hands. When she finally rose, I was surprised to see that they trembled—she of the perfect composure.

"Dear Mr. Bunbury, how good of you to come," she said, smoothing her bodice.

"Your servant, Miss Maud." I answered correctly, although my arms felt empty without her.

Her eyes shifted behind me, and craned upwards. My valet is of considerable height. "It's nice to see you again, Slade."

Slade unbent under her easy recollection of his name. "Good afternoon, Miss Greystone."

"Come and meet the cast."

"I don't wish to disturb your rehearsal—" She grimaced, and I lowered my voice. "Is there something amiss?"

Her hand pressed my shoulder. "If I could speak to you, later—"

"Since Miss Greystone the Artiste has already interrupted our work—" declared a small figure wearing a breastplate and beret.

("The actor-manager," Maud explained, rolling her eyes. "Playing Caesar, appropriately.")

"—I suppose we must break for tea."

She curtsied in mock obedience and I smiled. Despite her agitation, the forthright Maud had not changed one whit. Caesar snorted, tossing the tail of the sheet over his shoulder.

Tea arrived and was laid out in the orchestra. Slade busied himself with distributing cups and cakes to the actors who drifted over to the edge of the stage. Maud conveyed me to a seated centurion, who was unbuckling his breastplate and mopping his beefy face with a handkerchief.

"Signor Angelo, this is my good friend Mr. Bunbury."

"Signor Bunbury." He doffed his helmet without unsettling the incongruous yellow cat reposing on his shoulder. The creature and I regarded each other coolly. She turned her back on me and butted her head against Slade in the most disgusting fashion.

"Roma likes you, signor," pronounced Signor Angelo with a

fine grasp of the obvious. "She is most particular with her affections."

Slade looked pained. Already a clump of fur had appeared on his immaculate black sleeve.

"Angelo plays Marc Antony's lieutenant-general," Maud explained. "And very good he is too."

"I was actor in my home country," he informed me. "From great family. I play La Scala. But I come to England to find my young sister, and work for great Tree."

There was no vegetation on stage. My brow creased.

"Beerbohm Tree," supplied Maud. Herbert Beerbohm Tree, the distinguished actor-manager; that made more sense. But I did not see how a lowly spear carrier would have the means to leave Italy and work for The Great Tree or lowlier Branches.

"And your sister?" I said aloud. The jovial features lengthened.

"I do not know. She came here with our aunt when our mother died. *Pauvra bambina.*"

I drew out my cigarette case and offered it first to Maud, then to Angelo. Maud accepted, her eyes flashing appreciation; I had recalled her fondness for smoking. Angelo refused. The cat did not approve, apparently.

An older woman in diaphanous costume, her eyes heavily outlined with kohl, oozed over, seeking a free cigarette. I held out the open case to her.

"Too kind," she gushed. As I lit her cigarette, her hand brushed against mine, rings flashing in the light. Maud's face tightened.

"Our Cleopatra," she said coolly. "Mrs. Helena de Winton. Mr. Bunbury."

"How do you do. Such a distinguished-looking man, Maud," she added to her playwright. "I can see why you've concealed him." She slinked away to Caesar, leaning heavily and co-quettishly on his arm. The costume billowed distractingly.

"She wants to be in his Hamlet," Maud said, exhaling irritated smoke. "Panting to play Gertrude, and other things. A most excellent actress, on—and off—stage."

"Maud, *bella*," chuckled Angelo, patting the cat, which sunk its claws appreciatively into his shoulder. "Signora de Winton is just—as you say—high-spirited. All great actresses are so."

She flushed. A sweet-faced blonde drifted over, wound in a sheet tied Grecian-style around her slim waist. Two young men were hard on her heels. Maud smiled and patted her hand.

"Marc Antony's wife Octavia, Miss Lucia Granville; Marc Antony, Mr. Mortimer Deane; and Caesar's General Taurus, Mr. Simon Harbury."

I bowed, and Octavia blushed. The young men inclined their heads coldly.

"Is there an asp?" I inquired, eyeing a basket on stage with some trepidation.

"There's half a dozen I could name," interposed a light drawl. I looked over my shoulder and beheld a large figure approaching in a long, fur-collared overcoat, with hair that was a little longer than was fashionable.

"This is the playwright who has taken such a kind interest in the production, Mr. Bunbury," said Maud. "Mr. Oscar Wilde."

"It's terribly convenient to my new rooms at the Savoy, and the divine Maud has adopted the Grecian style of dress for the cast, which I cannot but approve. Mr. Bunbury." He bowed. "Bunbury. Seems familiar . . ."

I shuddered; Algernon had much to answer for. "I know you, sir."

"Few do not, sir."

I repressed a sharp reply. Mr. Wilde had achieved his fame by flamboyance, including the recent publication of a scandalous play called *Salome*, not for any noble achievement. "I believe we have a young friend in common. Mr. Moncrieff."

"Such a dear boy, Algy. So amusing. Lovely tenor."

"And easily led."

The languid eyes held mine, and I had the jolting impression of a tiger of an intellect beneath the surface. It was unsettling. "It is much more pleasant to be led than to lead, Mr. Bunbury. A rosier, and far more inhabited, path." He raised his voice. "My dear Caesar, I must speak to you about your untidy performance in the second act." Coat fluttering, he put a massive arm around the actor-manager, dwarfing him, then kissed the hand of the simpering Cleopatra.

"Somewhat excessive, isn't he?" said Maud, and drew my chair away, a little apart from the others. I seized the moment's respite.

"You were nervous when I arrived," I observed. "What is it, Maud?"

She bit her lip. "No doubt you will think me very foolish. I have a dreadful premonition of doom, Mr. Bunbury."

I jerked my head at Slade. He nodded and headed for the backstage area. He would ascertain if anything irregular did exist behind the scenes.

Signor Angelo's massive head nodded. He appeared to be napping. The cat leapt from his shoulder and sauntered to Cleopatra, nudging her leg imperiously. She pushed it off with an oath, still hanging on Caesar's every nugget of divine and short-tempered wisdom. It did not go unnoticed by Maud.

"Earlier she was feeding herring to Roma," she observed. "Every inch the Gracious Queen—especially when an opportunity presents itself."

"Such as Mr. de Winton?"

"Never made his acquaintance. Perhaps he did the wise thing and fled the country." Her hands twisted. "Oh, I do hope it will go well."

The men were still hovering around the demure Octavia. Angelo sagged.

"I shouldn't worry, my dear," I said aloud. "It's probably just an onslaught of opening-night nerves."

My diagnosis was overly optimistic. Octavia screamed, and swooned into Antony's ready arms. Cleopatra and Caesar gaped. I shot forward, sweeping Maud behind me.

The centurion's head lolled, and his large frame slid fully to the floor. I glimpsed the protruding tongue, the glazed eyes. Signor Angelo would not work for The Great Tree again, but instead would be planted under one.

"How unique," commented Wilde, bending from his thick waist toward Angelo like an inquisitive ostrich. "A corpse in the cast."

I gripped Maud's wrist. "Go fetch Slade. Quickly, dear." The blessed girl did not faint or scream, only nodded once, very pale, and raced backstage. I examined the body as the actors crowded round.

"This is a disaster," Caesar declared.

"Undoubtedly," I muttered.

"Who can I engage to play a general at this late date?" His beady eyes fastened abruptly on me, and I jumped. "You. You're perfect." He pushed the helmet on my head and the wooden sword into my hand. I glared from around a leather earflap.

"You're mad."

"Gifted," Caesar corrected, sizing me up. "Costume should fit."

I was considerably slimmer than Angelo, but that was not the point. "I'm in a Bath chair!"

"So we slap a bush in front of you."

"I sincerely doubt bushes existed in ancient Egypt."

Maud reappeared with my valet, and Slade slid adroitly through the little knot of actors. He knelt by the body, and glanced up at me in his usual unruffled fashion. "Poison, sir."

"As I suspected."

Slade wrinkled his nose. He knew I had suspected no such thing, but a confident countenance inspires the innocent and confounds the guilty. "Shall I fetch the police, sir?" he inquired.

"Police!" chorused the cast.

"Failure of the heart," decreed Caesar. "Or suicide."

"Rubbish," Maud retorted.

"So—one less extra. And a foreign one at that."

Maud hissed like Cleopatra's asp, and I touched her wrist in warning. As much as I sympathized with her, I did not wish her to jeopardize the production of her first play nor become a likely suspect.

"Indeed," drawled Wilde. "One cannot be too certain what the odd foreigner will do. Most of them are perfect geniuses."

Then I remembered—he was Irish.

Caesar remembered, too; he reddened at his insult of such a prominent gadfly. One negative word from Wilde in the right ear and Caesar would be playing the hurdy-gurdy in his next engagement at the Empire. The idea had its appeal and placed Mr. Wilde in a more flattering light.

"I'll fetch them, Bunbury," he volunteered. I looked at Slade and was reassured by a minute shake of his head. Wilde—at least here—was innocent.

"Thank you, Mr. Wilde."

He headed for the back of the house and the office.

"Well, hail and farewell," remarked Cleo. "May I have another cigarette, Mr. Bunbury?"

I obliged, and asked, "You did not like Signor Angelo?"

"A dead bore." She inhaled smoke with a flourish.

I addressed Antony and Taurus. "Did you share the same opinion?"

Antony shrugged. "Decent enough, if somewhat flashy and garrulous. Not uncommon in the theater."

"Always buying rounds for us," added Taurus. "Meals as well. Generous fellow."

More than a simple centurion. The plot thickened. I beckoned to Slade and whispered in his ear, "How was the poison introduced? The tea?"

"I don't believe so, sir. A real puzzle. I distributed the tea, as you recall, and saw no one slip anything into Mr. Angelo's cup. And it could not have been in the pot itself, as we would all now be in some considerable distress."

"Indeed. Nor do I carry poison about my person."

"I was not including you among the suspects, sir."

"Generous of you, Slade. Let us have another look at the body."

He wheeled me closer to the unfortunate man, and I studied him with pursed lips. "Would you pull his sleeve up? But have a care."

From the invaluable portmanteau Slade removed a pair of white gloves, slipped them on, and applied himself gingerly to the sleeve. The skin below Angelo's right shoulder was inflamed, and my eyes met Slade's.

"Is there a snake in the basket, Slade?"

"Not in the real one, sir. Stuffed." He picked up something caught in the cloth and held it up to the light. "But there seems to be a literal one."

"What are you doing?" boomed an official voice, striding down the aisle with a constable and Wilde in his wake. The Law had arrived.

"Ah, Inspector," I said calmly. "Good. Name's Bunbury. I think I can clear this little matter up for you."

The cast froze, like a tableau—*The Fateful Announcement*.

"Oh, bravo, Bunbury," said Wilde, clapping. "Do Reveal All. I will take notes."

I ignored him, and the inspector folded his arms. "Well, I like a good play. Proceed, Mr. Bunbury."

"Thank you." I turned my chair, and steepled my fingers, in approved Sherlock Holmes fashion. "The Hon. Miss Greystone felt that there was something wrong here, and she was correct. A poison of a spiritual, and physical, nature. Signor Angelo undoubtedly died by a lethal agent—the most lethal."

"Such as?" inquired the inspector.

"*Cherchez la femme*, Inspector," I said. "Or whatever it is in Italian."

"*Cercaré le femmina*," supplied the informative Slade. I glanced at him.

"Er—yes. My man and I concluded that it could not be the tea, for we all drank that, with no ill effect. The cyanide capsule was introduced through the skin, opened by the claws of a feline." I turned to Miss Granville. "Your first name is Lucia—clearly Italian."

Marc Antony's fists clenched. "Look here—what are you insinuating, Bunbury?"

"It's my grandmother's name," she whispered, eyes wide.

"—who died in Italy," I finished in triumph.

"—who appears three nights a week at the Tivoli," she amended.

Wilde had a faraway look in his eyes. "Ah, Lucia Beale," he murmured. "Not the Jersey Lily, of course, but a charming songbird."

High praise from the Aesthete, and distressingly conclusive. I quickly changed tack and addressed Cleo.

"It's obvious," I said. "You are the sister of Signor Angelo."

Cleo laughed. "Do you actually think before you speak?"

Maud shook her dark head. "Sorry, that can't be right. His sister was his junior."

"So much for The Great Detective," Cleo snorted.

Slade coughed. He is not fond of those who question my abilities. I made a mental note to supply Slade with another rise in salary.

The cat rubbed against Cleo's leg, and Slade's faith was not misplaced. "No, I don't suppose you are the sister," I said, and leaned back in my chair for effect. "That was just . . . my ploy to trick you. Yes indeed. You're the aunt, of course."

She sucked in her breath, and the cast members stared at her, appalled.

"You must have changed your appearance somewhat to deceive Signor Angelo—dyed the hair and so forth. You are an excellent actress, after all. But the cat obviously knows the aunt who visited Italy years ago, despite your cigarette habit, which it normally takes great pains to avoid. Was the herring an early reward for work well done?

"How does a spear carrier obtain a passage to England and secure work with the Great Tree? Regularly treat his fellow actors to drinks and dinner? There must have been a legacy." My voice dropped. "Where is the girl?"

She sprang for my throat, surprisingly agile in her clinging garments. For one fearful moment, I thought I should be throttled in my own chair. But I had discounted the contents of the invaluable portmanteau, and my valet's lightning reflexes.

"Step back, ma'am," said Slade, a sturdy revolver clapped to Cleopatra's temple. "And do please keep your hands in plain sight. I've an unreliable hand with firearms." He gazed down at me. "Are you all right, sir?"

I wheezed an affirmative from a prone position. The blasted apparatus seemed to have stuck. Maud restored the chair back and I thanked her, rearranging my abused necktie. The other cast members and the police applauded and I waved a feeble and modest hand.

Slade sniffed. "I saw a newspaper in Mrs. de Winton's dressing room," he said pointedly. "The young Italian lady met with an unfortunate accident. A remarkable coincidence."

"An excellent performance," concluded the inspector. "Thank you, Mr. Bunbury. I think Mrs. de Winton should come with us and assist with our inquiries." He grasped her arm, and motioned to the constables, who attended to and carried out the unfortunate Angelo.

"Meddler," she hissed at me. "I needed that money. I am an

actress and my public expects me to maintain a certain life-style."

"I doubt your public expects you to clutter the landscape with bodies," I answered coolly. "Inspector, I should look into the mysterious disappearance of Mr. de Winton. It might prove—instructive."

Cleo swept her sheet around her and was conducted firmly out. Octavia slipped her little hands around my arm. "How clever of you, Mr. Bunbury," she breathed. Such a perceptive child.

Maud tapped her foot but Antony anticipated her, pulling the actress away. "It's all over, my dear."

"Poppycock," snorted Caesar. "We have much work to do, since Miss Granville is our new Cleopatra."

Her eyes grew round. "ME?!"

Caesar took firm possession of her arm. "Miss Greystone!" He swept off with Antony and Taurus hovering at their heels. Maud cast her eyes heavenward as if appealing for succor, murmured a promise to return forthwith, and dashed off in their wake. Slade and I were alone, and I massaged my stiff limbs.

"Are you all right, sir?"

"Stop mothering me, Slade," I answered with irritation, and suddenly thrust upright, standing on my two legs without so much as a waver. "Damn, that chair can be cramping."

Suddenly there was the sound of two hands, applauding. Wilde moved from the shadows of the wings as I stood frozen in place. "Oh, well done, Mr. Bunbury," he purred. "This surprising third act is a trifle overdone but pure genius. You present me with an intriguing—scenario. Most intriguing, sir. Oh, don't concern yourself. I shall dress it up sufficiently so you may rail in public at the vagaries of the playwright and do—or not do—as you please." Winking, he disappeared in a swirl of his coat, and I collapsed into the chair—no dissemblance on this occasion.

"Sir?" Slade fanned me with his handkerchief as if I were a swooning matron. "Shall I fetch the smelling salts, sir?"

"Sarcasm does not become you, Slade."

"No, sir. Do you think he will keep his word, sir?"

"I don't know," I said, grabbing his handkerchief and mopping my perspiring forehead. "Providence is a feckless creature."

Maud finally reappeared and I moved my feet hurriedly back onto the footplate. "Well, I've rendered unto Caesar what is his—for the moment."

I glanced around the set. " 'All the world's a stage, and all the men and women merely players.' "

Maud placed her hand gently in mine. " 'They have their exits and their entrances; And one man in his time plays many parts.' Does that mean it is your time to play the general?"

"If it means honoring Angelo's memory, and preserving your play . . . yes. Although I am not certain just how Caesar will conceal the chair."

"Don't underestimate the Imperial will or its devotion to the box office."

My eyes moved to Slade, who was edging away from the affectionate cat twining around his ankles. "Slade, do attend to that animal."

His face froze. "Sir?"

"Well, Roma did oblige us with the final clue. Bathe her claws—well—and feed her, or play with her, or do whatever it is that cats require."

He gave me a look which promised retribution on a future occasion, but lifted the cat and held her at arm's length, her tail swishing. "Very good, sir." He stalked out, accompanied by the creature's plaintive cries, and Maud and I were finally alone.

Her fingers tightened on mine. "The show will go on, and once again, I am indebted to you."

"Always at your service." I patted her fingers. I had much

experience as the kindly uncle. "Will you dine with me? Cafe Royal?"

"How kind." Eyes sparkling like champagne, she bent and laid soft fingertips against the back of my neck. Sometimes the uncle routine wore thin. *Very* thin. "But wouldn't you rather dine in this evening?"

I was—persuaded.

CONNIE

Bentley Little

NOW SHE WANTED to be a hippie.

It was too much. Al had put up with her previous whims and caprices, her brief foray into the fashion world, her flirtation with the mod life of the jet set. But he wasn't about to allow those dirty, smelly, bearded, long-haired, tire-tread sandalled freaks to overrun the house merely because Connie now wanted to align herself with the dregs of humanity who, for some ungodly reason, seemed to be the nation's current cultural bellweather.

"The people." That was her phrase of the moment. She wanted to be one with the people, help bring power to the people, to stop the war that was being foisted upon the people. The people, the people, the people . . . No matter that she was a rich bitch living in her momma's mansion who hadn't done an honest day's work in her life and wouldn't know a real person if he came up and bit her on the ass. Once again, she had seen the light, and she was going to make herself over in this new image as a champion of the common man, a revolutionary for her time, supplying financial backing to groups and organizations that were too forward-thinking and progressive for mainstream America to recognize.

She would probably be over it in six months, on to something else, the next trend, but while she was a hippie she would be committed. She was nothing if not dedicated. She immersed herself fully in her newfound interests, no matter how transitory the infatuations turned out to be, and this would prove no different.

Only he wasn't going to go along with it this time.

It wasn't just that he found flower children aesthetically repellant (though he did), it was their value system he objected to, their rejection of everything he held dear. And he didn't approve of all their anti-war activities, their . . . agitating. His own son Jimmy was over there in Vietnam, and he was proud of the boy. But lately, he'd been made to feel embarrassed for his beliefs, for morally supporting his own child—and he didn't like that one bit. Just yesterday, a girlish boy wearing raggedy dungarees and what looked like a cutoff section of his mother's muu-muu had started a shouting match with him, eventually getting Al to admit that he didn't know why American troops were continually being sent over to Vietnam. It didn't matter, he tried to tell the kid. When your country asked you to do something, you did it. That's what it meant to be an American. But a small secret part of him felt discomfited that something—anything—the kid said had made sense—and that the boy had actually been able to wring an admission of that from him.

He felt disloyal to his son. As strong as he knew himself to be, even *he* was being corrupted by the radicalism sweeping the country.

Which was why Connie's sudden embrace of this lifestyle stuck so much in his craw. Connie was weak, drawn like a pin to the magnet of any fad that came along. Only this flower-power fad was much more dangerous than the ones that had come before. It was not merely cosmetic, a matter of appearances. It involved modes of behavior, ways of thinking.

There was a note from Connie on the kitchen counter, and Al picked it up without looking, shoved it in his coat pocket.

He walked out to the foyer to pick up today's mail. He glanced at the family portraits on the curved wall as he passed by.

Her mother had been a star. As had her aunt. But Connie was famous merely for being famous, and she enjoyed all of the perks while possessing none of the talent. She'd half-heartedly gone to a few auditions—for Blofeld's confidant last year in *You Only Live Twice*, for bit parts in *Duffy* and *Sebastian* earlier this year—but she hadn't gotten the roles and she hadn't really wanted to. She didn't know *what* she wanted to do, and that was the problem.

It was also part of her charm.

And Connie could be charming.

It was why he'd stayed around as long as he had, why he had endured the frustrating years of aimless adolescent indulgence, the endless avoidance of adult responsibility. Connie, when she wanted, was fun to be around, and most of the time, he genuinely liked working for her.

The basket beneath the mail slot was empty. Mavis or Kate had obviously picked up the mail, and he found a pile of envelopes stacked on the small table beneath Connie's portrait.

He grabbed the letters and bills and invitations, started sorting through them—

—and the doorbell chimed.

Al stiffened. He looked up at the door but something had come over him, and he stood there dumbly, mail in hand, unmoving, making no effort to answer the door until the bell chimed again.

He walked slowly forward. He did not know why he thought this was bad news, but he did. It could be Velma. Or Hank. Or Robbie, Audrey or Cheryl. It could be a group of those filthy hippies come to mooch some food. But something told him that it was none of those, and he opened the door to find a man holding forth a Western Union telegram.

"Al Johnson?"

His heart sank in his chest.

No, he thought. Don't let it be.

He took the telegram, closed the door on the man, ripped opened the envelope, and read the message, not knowing what to think, not feeling anything, stunned but somehow not surprised.

Jimmy had been killed outside of Da Nang.

His body would be flown home Friday.

He felt empty inside, hollow, as though every bit of living tissue within him had been scooped out. The only thing that told him he was alive was the fluttering of the telegram in his shaking hand.

He reread the message. It was simple, to the point, and gave no details, but his mind was already filling in the gaps. He imagined his son's last thoughts, imagined what part of his body was hit and how intense the pain was.

He forced himself to derail this train of thought before it went too far. Breathing deeply, he folded the telegram and slipped it into his coat pocket. His fingers touched the thinner, flimsier paper of Connie's note, and he brought it out, reading it for the first time, trying to distract himself with the mundane minutiae of everyday work.

He looked over the list of Connie's specific and typically detailed instructions: buy three ounces of patchouli oil, a dozen sticks of sandalwood incense, two sand candles, enough plastic beads to replace the mansion's interior doors, a bean bag chair and three sitting pillows, a strobe light, a black light, and four posters—fluorescent Adam and Eve on a mountaintop, any Peter Max, Bogie from *Casablanca*, and W.C. Fields from *My Little Chickadee*. Shop for groceries, but only buy organic foods and don't buy them from Thriftimart, it's owned by a right-wing war-supporter—

Al crumpled the instructions, throwing the wadded ball of paper on the floor, the emptiness inside him replaced by anger. Rather than distract him, his work—catering to Connie's every frivolous whim—brought home to him how much he had

truly lost, made him realize what his inability to properly pri-
oritize his life had cost him. He thought of Connie, and he
imagined her lying langorously on her bed, staring out at the
bay or half-watching some pathetic soap opera. He was filled
with tremendous rage, a blistering red hot anger unlike anything else he had ever experienced. He glanced up at Connie's
portrait, and he realized how much he hated her face. Her
face? He hated everything about her, and, his own face still
flushed with fury, he took the winding staircase two steps at a
time, striding purposefully down the long hallway at the top to
her room.

The door was open, and Connie was lounging on the bed,
casually washing her tail. She smiled up at him when he entered, but said nothing, and her thoughtless, dismissive attitude enraged him even further.

He walked directly over to her bed, picked her up, smiled
tightly. "Nice kitty," he said. "Nice kitty."

And then he wrung her neck.

HER MOTHER HAD PLAYED PYEWACKET IN *Bell,
Book and Candle,* her aunt had had the title role in Disney's
That Darn Cat, and both of them had been gracious, kind, and
generous. But Connie had been spoiled, a brat from the beginning. Interesting, yes. Fun, yes. But basically a selfish, self-
absorbed, overgrown baby, and even after the heat of the moment, after the anger had worn off, he did not really feel guilty
for doing what he had done.

She had deserved it.

He should have done it long ago.

He buried her body on the grounds, in the far corner of the
rose garden, where no one but the gardener ever went. He
waited until nearly midnight, long after the day help was gone,
when the rest of the live-in staff was asleep. There'd been a
frantic search for Connie around dinnertime—that cat never
missed supper—but Al told Mavis that she was out in the

Haight with her new friends, and no one questioned it. Plates were cleaned, food was sealed in Tupperware and refrigerated, and Al retired to his room where Connie's stiffening form lay in a box in his closet.

There was no problem getting the body out of the house, no false scares or close calls, and he walked directly to the rose garden where earlier in the evening he'd left a shovel. The burial itself went just as smoothly. He dug the hole, dumped Connie's body, folded the box and put it over her, and filled in the hole.

Walking back to the tool shed afterward, to return the shovel, he was acutely conscious of every nightsound, every hint of movement in the dark. He'd prepared an alibi in case someone spotted him, but it was not particularly believable, and he wasn't sure how well he'd be able to deliver it. Fortunately, it looked like he wasn't going to have to use it. All of the lights in the house were off: there were no cars out on the street, and even if there had been, the grounds were gated and not visible from the outside. He was alone out here—

There was a rustle of leaves from off to the left.

He stopped in his tracks, holding his breath. Were those glittering eyes he saw under the bushes, watching him? He didn't want to think so, but he turned around, saw that there was a perfect view from here of the spot where he'd buried Connie's dead body.

He rushed the bushes, swinging the shovel before him, making much more noise than he should, but willing to take a chance on waking someone in the house if it would flush out whoever was under there. He stopped, waited, listened.

Nothing.

He crouched down, checking again, just to make sure, but if he thought he'd seen something the first time he must have imagined it because there was nothing beneath the leaves except shadow.

He hurried back to the shed, returned to the house.

Once inside, he carefully closed and locked the door, then started down the side hall toward the closest bathroom in order to wash up. The chandeliers were turned off and there was only one table lamp on, shining a faint dim yellow that illuminated nothing clearly but provided enough light to manuever by. He crept quietly down the carpeted corridor, past the closed morning room, past the linen closet. His eyes on the darkened rectangle of the open bathroom doorway ahead, he passed the lamp on its table and an adjacent chair.

In the silence of the sleeping house, he heard a low catwhisper: "Murderer."

He stopped, turned, looked around. Glittering eyes looked up at him from the cushioned chair. It was Leon, the Persian Connie had been seeing, the pinko pussycat who'd led her into this whole hippie thing.

Al's heart was pounding in his chest. What was Leon doing here? And at this time of night? Sure, the Persian sometimes came to see Connie, sometimes spent the night, but he hadn't been at the house since Tuesday. Why was he here now?

Leon knew.

Murderer.

Al took a deep breath, tried not to panic. The two of them stared at each other in silence. Cat faces were so hard to read. It was impossible to tell whether or not the expression on Leon's face was one of accusation. Especially in this light.

He'd just imagined it. He hadn't heard what he thought he'd heard. He was feeling guilty and nervous and—

"Murderer."

He hadn't imagined that one, and Al immediately lunged at the animal, moving quickly, but Leon sprang nimbly off the chair, adjusting his trajectory with a touch of backfeet to armrest, and was off, down the hall, toward the foyer and the cat entrance.

Al ran as fast as he could, his heavy feet thudding on the carpet, not caring how much noise he made. He reached the foyer just in time to see a tail disappear through the small swinging cat door. He unlocked and threw open the human door, ran down the walkway, through the gates and out to the sidewalk, but he knew even before he was halfway there that it was no use.

Leon was gone.

THERE WERE no cats allowed at Jimmy's burial service.

A WEEK passed.

A month.

It was still with him, the killing, but its memory faded a little with each day. Connie was young, had had no will, and while the lawyers sorted through the business of her disappearance, he and the other full-time staff remained in the house, on the payroll and working.

Surprisingly, amazingly, Connie's body had not yet been discovered. He'd assumed the gardener would find it after a few days, but roses were trimmed, pruned, watered, fed, the surrounding dirt raked. And that was it. There was no reason to dig up the dirt. If he was lucky, Connie might never be found.

And Leon had disappeared, afraid, hopefully, that Al would come after him.

Things were shaping up.

He finished unloading groceries, then settled down to read the newspaper as he waited in the kitchen for Mavis. Ronald Reagan had sent National Guard troops to quell an anti-war riot at San Francisco State, and Al silently applauded the governor's move. He read the lead paragraphs of the article, then glanced over at the accompanying side-by-side photos. On the left was Governor Reagan at his desk, looking stern and unyielding. On the right, holding picket signs and placards, were the leaders of the demonstration.

And Leon.

Al's breath caught in his throat. He held the newspaper

closer to his face, though it did not allow him to see the scene more clearly, only fragmented the image into pixeled inkblots. It was Leon. Of that he was sure. The cat was in the arms of a buxom hippie girl, staring straight at the camera.

And he looked angry.

Al put down the paper, feeling cold.

Why hadn't he gotten a job working for a *person*? Or even a dog. Lassie, maybe. Rin Tin Tin. Dogs were such stupid creatures. They could be trained, but a man *owned* a dog, was a dog's *master*. It wasn't that way with cats. In the human/feline relationship, cats were the ones calling the shots. They were the masters and it was their human caretakers who were required to toe the line. People on the outside thought that a pet was a pet. Hell, he'd thought that himself at first.

But it wasn't that way.

He'd learned that from Connie's mother.

Mavis walked into the kitchen, and he quickly folded the paper, covering the photo, pushing it away from him on the table. The cook frowned at him. "You all right, Al?"

"Fine." He forced himself to smile. "I'm fine."

LEON KNEW.

He should just let it be, but he could not. The more he thought about it, the more he was convinced that Leon had seen something. Not the killing itself, but the coverup, the burial, the disposal of Connie's body. He recalled those glittering eyes seen beneath the leaves of the bushes, the cat waiting for him in the hallway, on the chair.

Murderer.

The only question was: why hadn't Leon done something about it? Why hadn't he gone to the police—or gotten his caretaker to go to the police?

Al didn't know. And it bothered him. So he spent his free days, his time off, roaming the Haight-Ashbury district, walking around, keeping his eyes open.

Looking for Leon.

There was revolution in the air, Connie had told him the day she'd died, and he'd put it down then to hippie propaganda, but he thought now that she might have been right. There was something different in the feel of the city. He sensed it. An unpleasantness. An anger. A rage. The possibility and potential for violence.

He was on an unfamiliar block of an unfamiliar street. The whole damn place was a slum, but this area seemed particularly menacing to him. He thought briefly about heading home, but his need to find Leon outweighed his reservations about this section of the city.

What would he do if he found Leon?

Kill the cat. There was no doubt in his mind about what he needed to do, although it occurred to him that if he was caught the police would consider him some sort of sickie, while the government considered Jimmy a hero for the fact that he'd killed dozens of human beings.

He pushed that thought out of his mind. It was the argument that the girlish kid had used on him, and he felt disloyal to his son's memory for even entertaining such logic.

He passed a dilapidated Victorian rooming house. A Siamese in the lap of a scruffy student sitting on the front steps glared at him as he passed by, and it was hard not to think that the cat knew who he was, knew what he'd done and was . . . *watching* him.

He turned after he'd passed, and saw the animal still looking.

Across the street, two other cats had stopped rooting through an overturned garbage can to stare at him.

He was just being paranoid. He'd been reading a lot of Poe lately, and all that guilt and those cats and those premature burials had obviously been swirling around in his subconscious and mixing with the reality of his own situation and Connie's death.

He reached the corner, turned right. Behind him, he heard a loud high-pitched meow, a cry that was taken up by felines on both sides of the street.

Al quickened his pace. He didn't want to admit it, but he was getting a little nervous. They were meowing because they wanted to communicate among themselves, without humans understanding. And the relay nature of the repeated sounds indicated that a message was being passed from one animal to another.

He saw movement out of the corner of his eye and looked left. There was a bearded hippie crossing the street, a heavily tanned barefoot guy smoking a pipe.

And carrying a cat.

To his right, on the stoop of a flophouse, a stringy haired girl was bent down, listening to an orange Persian, looking at him from an angle and scowling.

Al walked faster. They were emerging now from side yards and porches, from within garages and permanently parked vans. Cats and their people. He broke into a jog. He tried not to show the fear he felt, but it was becoming increasingly diffi-cult not to acknowledge that something strange was going on here. This was not imagination, not paranoia. This was a legit-imately strange occurrence that was rapidly escalating into a direct threat.

The humans were running after him now, the cats leaping out of cradling arms and sprinting toward him in their quick animal way. He was being chased through the Haight, but no one seemed to notice, no one seemed to care. He prayed for a cop cruiser to drive by, legitimate help that he could flag down, but the street was empty save for occasional passing cars.

He turned right into an alley and realized almost instantly that that was a mistake. Momentum had already propelled him one house in and by the time he saw the people and cats at the opposite end of the alley and turned around, the way he had come was blocked.

There was an open gate to his left that led into a small backyard overgrown with weeds. He dashed through the narrow opening and looked quickly around. There was no way around the house. The backyard's high fence connected directly to the side walls of the home, blocking off access to the front, and he was too out of breath to climb or jump it now. But the rear door was open, only a rusty screen keeping him out, and he took the porch steps two at a time, yanked open the screen door, and dashed inside.

He had time to notice cat dishes on the floor of the kitchen next to the refrigerator, then he was in the living room, heading for the front door.

A huge Hell's Angel opened the door, walked inside. He slammed the door shut behind him and stood there, arms crossed, glaring at Al.

There was a calico perched on his shoulder.

"It's him," the cat said in a clear high voice.

A chill sped down Al's spine, spreading outward through his bones. He looked around. Marijuana plants grew in the pots on the windowsill next to bushy bunches of catnip. The filthy room smelled of rotted food and uncleaned litterboxes. From somewhere in a back room came the sound of kittens laughing.

This, he realized, was exactly where they'd wanted him to go.

His eyes were still darting quickly about, searching for an escape route, but he knew already that it was no use, and in the kitchen he heard the screen door open and close. There was the sound of movement in the hallway to his right, footsteps on the stairs leading up to the second story.

He said nothing, did not try to get away. They surrounded him, the cats and their people, and soon he was in the center of a circle in the middle of the room. There was a parting in the ranks, and a Persian stepped into the breach.

Leon.

The cat walked up to him, stood before him. Al was tempted to kick the animal and send him flying across the room, but he had the feeling that the only way he was going to get out of this situation alive was if he played it cool.

"So is this why we're here?" someone said. A girl. "This guy?"

"He murdered Connie," Leon said coldly. "And he tried to murder me." The cat looked around at the assembled faces. "And he supports the war."

That turned the tide. They were all looking at him now in the same way that Leon was looking at him, with anger, with hatred, and it occurred to him that he might not get out of this at all.

He glared at Leon, trying to intimidate the cat into turning away, but Leon met his gaze and held it.

"Cats only," Leon said.

Abruptly, the people left, the hippies turning and walking out the doors through which they'd come until there was only himself and about thirty cats left in the room. The cats moved around, changing locations, arranging themselves in even rows behind Leon.

There was something formal and ritualistic about the repositioning of the cats, and Al suddenly knew what they planned to do. Before him was a tribunal of Connie's peers. Connie had told him the week before she'd died—

before he killed her

—that she and her freaky newfound friends had participated in just such a tribunal where they had tried Lyndon Johnson and Robert McNamara, in absentia, for war crimes and crimes against the American people. Of course, they had both been found guilty, and Connie had been ecstatic over the outcome of the farcical proceedings.

He did not intend to subject himself to any such nonsense,

and before Leon could even mention the charges against him, Al said, "I strangled Connie and I'm glad I did."

"I have not even stated why we are here," Leon admonished him.

"I know why we're here. Because I killed Connie and you saw me bury her body and you want me punished for it." He smiled cruelly. "But no one cares. She was a spoiled rich brat, and your hippie friends have probably already forgotten she ever existed. Besides—" he paused "—she was just a cat."

"I loved her!" Leon shouted.

Al's smile broadened.

Leon made an effort to control himself, then looked back at the other cats, meowing once. He turned back around, took a deep breath. "Al Johnson, we hereby sentence you to death for Connie's murder."

"Surprise, surprise."

"We will not kill you but will allow you to sacrifice yourself in order to atone for what you have done. Your death will further the cause of peace and aid the anti-war movement you so virulently oppose so that at least some good can come from your miserable murdering life."

"Poetic justice, huh?"

"If you like."

"I thought you peaceniks didn't believe in violence."

Leon smiled, motioned toward the doors through which the hippies had left. "They don't." His smile grew wider, exposing fangs. "We do."

Leon nodded.

And then the cats were upon him.

Al screamed as frenzied felines leapt onto his body, sharp claws rending flesh, tiny teeth biting skin. It had not hit home that this was really happening until the pain hit. He'd been panicked while being chased, but once caught, once in the house, there'd seemed something . . . silly about it all. Something comical. He hadn't had any concrete plan, any ideas for escape, but he realized that, somewhere in the back of his mind, he'd intended to fight his way to the front door and run out, kick his way through the animals and take off. But the cats were stronger than he'd expected. And there were a lot of them. Leon remained on the floor in front of him, staring, smiling, but the others attacked him from all sides, jumping onto his back, attaching themselves to his arms, crawling up his legs, climbing onto his head and digging razorclaws into his scalp.

The pain was unbearable, and he tried to fight back, tried to swat the animals away, but he lost his balance and toppled backward, hitting his head hard against something immoveable and irregularly shaped.

And then he was out.

HE AWOKE several times, feeling pain in his head, in his limbs, in his abdomen, in his back, feeling metal beneath his body. He didn't know where he was or what was happening, but there was the sense of being jostled about, and he thought he was probably in the back of a travelling van.

WHEN AL finally regained full consciousness, he was tied up and on the ground, surrounded by a crowd of moving, shifting, marching bodies. He was outside and it was night, but there were lights from somewhere and quite a few of the people around him were carrying torches. Everyone seemed to be chanting in unison, and though he could not make out the words, he knew that he was in the middle of some type of rally or demonstration.

Had he just been dumped here? Was it over? He struggled, trying to sit up, and then he heard Leon's voice next to his ear. "Awake, huh?"

Al turned his head, saw the cat leap nimbly onto a wooden platform, then jump smoothly onto the shoulders of a long-haired young man. Leon whispered something into the young man's ear, and then both of them hurried over to where Al was still struggling on the ground.

"Let me up!" he demanded. It hurt his scratched face to form the words.

Leon snickered.

"Help!" Al screamed at the top of his lungs. "Help!"

But his voice could not be heard above the chanting of the crowd, and the long-haired guy pulled a bandanna from his pocket and used it to gag Al's mouth.

"Let's do it," Leon said.

Leon's person reached out behind him and someone handed him a mask. A Ronald Reagan mask.

Al was lifted and held suspended in the air. For a few brief seconds, he could see everything. They were at Golden Gate Park, on some type of stage. Before them were thousands of people, many of them holding signs and placards denouncing the war. He was shocked to see that the demonstrators were not all hippies. He saw some middle-aged adults, some old couples, some men who looked like himself.

Then the mask was pulled over his head and the only thing he could see was the limited view from the small eye-holes. He was turned, carried, and brought over to the wooden platform Leon had jumped upon.

It was a gallows.

Out of the corner of his eye, he saw the torches, and he suddenly understood what was happening.

Governor Reagan was being burned in effigy.

And he was the effigy.

The rope was attached to the ropes across his midsection, and he was hoisted high. Before him, on the shoulders of the others on the stage, he saw cats, dozens of them, eyes glittering.

The bonfire below him was set.

Ironic, Al thought as the blaze grew around him, as his pants caught fire and the flames moved up his body. Connie's

great-grandmother had had a brief walk-on in the old Ronald
Reagan film *Hellcats of the Navy.*

Hellcats.

If he hadn't been gagged, if he hadn't been in so much pain,
he might have laughed.

LIVING THE LIE

Marc Bilgrey

"WILL YOU MISS me, Dave?" said Sally, as she looked out the passenger side window of the light blue Packard.

Dave held the steering wheel tightly and kept his eyes on the road. For a minute he forgot his name. Since he'd only had it for six months, it was an easy mistake to make. He kept telling himself it was Dave, like *Davy Crockett*, the hottest program on television.

"Sure I'll miss you," said Dave, staring at a police car in the rearview mirror. His heart began beating faster. He watched the patrol car drive up behind him, then silently turn onto a side street and disappear. Dave let out a deep breath, glanced at Sally sitting next to him, then at a passing sign that read Train Station, 1/4 Mile.

"It'll be the first time we've been separated," she said.

"Oh, come on, it'll only be for a week. You make it sound like you're going on a trip around the world."

"That's what going back home feels like to me. And now with Mom being sick . . ." her voice trailed off.

"She'll probably outlive us all." The train station came into view. Dave glanced at the imposing, dirty, stone building, then slowed the car down as he navigated between taxis.

"You won't forget to feed Scooter, will you?"

"How many times do we have to go over this? I'll stop by your place every night and feed the cat, don't worry."

"Okay," said Sally, as they pulled up in front of a cab which was dislodging a group of tourists.

Dave got out, opened the trunk, pulled out Sally's suitcase and placed it on the sidewalk. Sally put her arms around Dave and kissed him.

"I'm gonna miss you so much," she said.

Dave looked into her sparkling green eyes and said, "Just don't be talking to any of those Midwest guys."

"Oh," she said, playfully slapping him on the arm, "you're impossible."

Dave kissed her cheek and said, "Me and Scooter'll be counting the days."

She smiled, picked up her suitcase, turned around and walked into the station.

ON THE drive back, Dave turned on the radio. The Platters sang, *You've Got That Magic Touch*. Dave thought about Sally. It occurred to him that he really would miss her. He was already starting to feel lonely. The feeling surprised him. He'd vowed to himself when they'd met that he wouldn't get too involved. She was there to pass the time with, to have some fun with, interchangeable with a hundred other women. Though he had tried to maintain his emotional distance, he had realized early on that it was a losing battle.

A police car with flashing lights appeared behind him. Dave felt his throat go dry as he gripped the steering wheel so hard his knuckles turned white. The police car passed him and then zoomed down the highway. Dave swallowed and relaxed his hold on the wheel.

If it hadn't been for Sally, he'd probably have left a month or two earlier. He knew he was pressing his luck. They hadn't called him Doc for no reason. He'd been the brains, the logical one who thought things out. There was no place for emotion, he'd told them. And yet, here he was, ignoring his own advice.

Dave slowed the car down as he passed a movie theater. There was a new Bob Hope picture playing. It looked good, but, he decided, he just wasn't in the mood. He considered going back to his apartment. What was the point of that? Just to sit and stare at the four walls or watch his new television set? Besides, at this hour, all that was on was *Howdy Doody* or *The Lone Ranger*. He pulled up to a bar and found a parking space.

INSIDE THE bar it was dark and reeked of stale cigarette smoke. He found an empty stool and sat down. An old man at the far end of the bar nursed a drink. The bartender asked Dave what he wanted. He ordered a beer and then chewed on a couple of pretzels from a bowl next to him. The jukebox was playing Doris Day singing *"Que Sera Sera."*

The bartender brought his drink, collected on it and then went to the other side of the counter. Dave took a sip of beer and looked at his reflection in the mirror behind the bar. He had dark circles under his eyes. And no matter how many times he saw his mustache and beard he couldn't get used to them. He'd stopped shaving the day after he'd begun his new life. And even so, there'd been a few close calls.

In Boston, a year earlier, a man in a hotel lobby had called him by his old name. They'd gone to high school together. "You must be mistaking me for someone else," said Dave. He left Boston that night. It was probably just an innocent, accidental meeting, but why take chances?

One time, when he was living in Chicago, a newspaper ran an article on the case and printed his picture. He was out of town before the afternoon edition. That's why it was so odd to stay where he was. He'd taken to moving even when there were no incidents. He took another sip of his drink and watched the bartender ring up a sale on the cash register. His thoughts drifted back to *that* day a year and a half earlier. The armored car, the bundles of neatly wrapped new hundred dollar bills. "See you guys back at the warehouse," he'd said. Then he'd gotten into his car and driven away. He wondered how long it had taken them to realize that he wasn't coming back. A day? A week?

"This seat taken?" said a voice.

Dave snapped out of his daze and looked to his left as a burly man in a rumpled suit and tie sat down next to him. Dave shrugged.

"Bartender," said the man, "I'll have a glass of your best whiskey." Then the man turned to Dave and said, "When I say life insurance, what comes into your mind?"

Dave got up, placed a quarter on the bar and headed toward the door.

"Hey," said the man, "you don't have to be downright rude."

Dave walked out of the bar and back to his car. A minute later he was driving through the streets. He stopped at a red light and forgot where he was. He was used to it. After awhile, everyplace started looking the same. The greasy spoons, the gas stations, the drive-ins.

He hadn't realized that it would be like this. When he'd taken the money he'd thought that he'd be able to retire and just lie by a pool somewhere, surrounded by palm trees and nubile young women in bathing suits, but it hadn't worked out that way. A few days after he'd left, he'd gone to Florida, rented a house, bought a sports car, a boat, new clothes. A couple of weeks later, he noticed that one of the local cops seemed to always be driving around his house. That was when he realized that he'd never be able to sit in a chaise lounge with a cold drink in his hand and watch the world go by. Oh, the money was safe. He'd buried it in a secret place, that wasn't a problem, not for Doc. Nor was coming up with fake I.D. and a new life history. That wasn't a problem, either.

What *was* a problem was always having to look over his shoulder.

Even Sally had noticed it. He'd told her that he was neurotic. Phobic was more like it. A fear of cops or feds, or anybody in a uniform, or in a suit and tie, that looked a little too serious.

But what he was really worried about was the old gang. After what he'd done, he knew they'd never stop looking for him. When he hadn't returned to the warehouse that night, it was no longer about just the money. He'd even thought about giving the money back, but he knew it wouldn't solve anything. They'd still hunt him down. At least with it, he had a fighting chance.

Dave stopped the car in front of a boarded up nightclub and walked across the street to a small park. He sat down on a bench under a shady tree. A couple of teenagers in leather jackets went by. A woman wheeling a baby carriage strolled past, followed by a young couple holding hands.

Dave thought about Sally again. He'd met her six months earlier at the diner where she worked. He thought she looked beautiful in her white waitress uniform. He started going back to the restaurant just to see her. Eventually he asked her out. She'd believed his story about being a financial consultant. At first Dave thought it was just a fling, a casual liaison in a strange town. Then, as the months went by, he actually wondered if he should tell her the truth. Finally, he decided that the best thing for both of them was to live the lie.

But he couldn't deny he had feelings for her that went beyond the physical. "Doc don't feel, he just thinks," was what one of the guys used to say. And for the most part it was true.

"Bang bang!" yelled a child.

Dave turned and saw two little boys wearing coonskin caps, and pointing toy muskets at each other. He got up and walked back to the car.

A few minutes later, he pulled into the parking lot of a

supermarket and got out. Now what the hell was it that Scooter eats? he thought, as he walked into the store.

He found the cat food section and stared at the different brands. They all had colorful labels and cute names. Then he remembered that Sally had mentioned that she had stocked up on cat food before she'd left. What was he doing here? He shrugged. Maybe Scooter would want some kind of special treat. If Sally were Scooter's mother, then he was an uncle, and wasn't that what uncles were for, to spoil kids?

Scooter was a shaded golden Persian that Sally had gotten as a kitten seven years earlier. She'd seen an ad in the newspaper about him. Scooter was the runt of a litter of purebred show cats. Scooter had been real sick and there was some question about whether or not he'd live. Sally had taken him in and nursed him back to health.

Dave would often watch the cat and study his behavior. Dave noticed a lot of things about Scooter. Like how right before it rained, Scooter would start jumping around and scratch the walls and stand up on his hind legs. Then, as soon as it did rain, he'd calm right down. Sometimes Dave would watch how Scooter would sneak up on a spider and then pounce on it and hold the insect under his paw.

And Scooter was always happy to see him. Whenever he'd visit, Scooter would run over and rub up against his leg. Until he'd met Scooter, he hadn't really liked cats, but Scooter was different. Scooter was a real friend. And he wasn't that way with everyone. If Sally had someone over to fix the sink or a squeaky door, Scooter would run and hide.

Dave picked up a few cans, went up to the cash register and paid for them. Then he got back into his car and drove out of the parking lot.

On the way to Sally's house, he stopped the car by the bay, got out and watched the sailboats go by. He wondered if the people on them were happy. He took off his jacket and glanced at the sun. Even though it was going down, it was still as warm as it had been earlier in the day. Dave adjusted the gun in the small of his back. On hot days it felt heavier than usual. He looked at the water in the bay and thought about tossing the weapon into it. It was something that had occurred to him many times before. He gave up the idea as he saw a police launch cruise past him. Then he turned around and got back into his car.

A few minutes later, he pulled up to Sally's house. She lived in a residential neighborhood on a quiet, tree-lined street. Dave walked up the path to the house, put the key into the lock, and opened the door.

"Hey, Scooter, Dave's here!" he said, stepping inside and closing the door. No response. "I've got treats for you," he said, shaking the bag of groceries. Still nothing. Dave looked around the living room and saw Scooter under one of the chairs. Scooter tensed up. Dave stood silently. He listened, but didn't hear anything. Then he placed the bag on the floor and pulled out his gun.

As soon as he did he heard a floorboard creak in another room. His heart began pounding. He turned and noticed that one of the windows was open. He took a breath, then tiptoed to the sofa and crouched behind it. He said in a loud voice, "So, how you been Scooter? Good kitty, I've got some food for you."

Just then, a shadow appeared on the wall. It came from the direction of the bedroom. Dave kept talking. "Good boy. I know you like tuna."

A man wearing a dark coat and hat and holding a gun peered out from behind a wall. Then he stepped into the living room. Dave squeezed the trigger of his gun. There was a flash of light and a loud cracking sound as the man moaned, grabbed his stomach and fell to the floor.

Immediately another man with a gun appeared. Dave shot him twice in the chest. He dropped to the carpet and stopped moving. Seconds went by. No one else walked out. Dave looked in the bedroom and then the kitchen, but they were empty. He went back into the living room and stared at the two men. One he recognized. He was the cousin of one of the guys in the gang.

Scooter came over and rubbed up against Dave's leg. Dave let out a breath and said, "You saved my life, boy, you know that?"

Scooter mewed.

"C'mon, Scooter, we have to get out of here."

He grabbed Scooter, got Sally's cat carrier out of the closet and put Scooter inside. Holding the carrier, Dave cautiously walked outside and back to his car. He stuck Scooter's carrier on the seat next to him and turned on the car's ignition.

Five minutes later, Dave was on the highway heading north. How had they found him? he wondered. He must have done something careless. He'd stayed too long in one place, he'd been spotted by someone, he'd—Sally. Sally. She had just co-incidentally gone to visit her poor sick mother in Cleveland. Sally. He'd trusted her. Somehow they'd found him and had bought Sally off, or scared her, and she'd cooperated. Could she have known about what they'd intended to do? Maybe they'd told her that they were federal agents, something like that. Anyway, she'd gone along and . . . Dave noticed Scooter looking out of the window of the cat carrier.

Scooter's eyes were big, like he was scared, but he wasn't mewing. Dave glanced back at the road, then at Scooter again as he saw him pushing his paws through the slats in the carrier. It was as if Scooter was in his own little prison, thought Dave, a travelling prison. Dave pressed down on the gas pedal. He wondered where the road would take him and what the next town would be like. Then he realized that it didn't matter. Even though it all seemed like wide open country, everywhere he looked there were locks and guards and iron bars.

MAIL-ORDER ANNIE

Gary A. Braunbeck

HE WAS BEING followed.

John Nitzinger wasn't sure by whom—or possibly *what* (his aunt had often written to him before her illness with stories about the wildcats that came down out of the mountains when winter began)—but for the last hour his horse had been skittish as hell and the hairs on the back of his own neck had been standing on end from something more than the freezing night wind and swirling clouds of snow.

And so John Nitzinger, age thirty-seven, a man who'd been alone on the plains for most of his life, riding fences for a succession of ranchers, a man now with no one to call family, who felt the chill of the winter slowly making itself a part of his soul, rode on with weary deliberation through the December night in the year 1888, his eyes looking from one side of the darkness to the other, while his right hand rested on the stock of his Spencer rifle.

It was so cold that his breath turned to iron in his throat, the hairs in his nostrils webbed into instant ice, and his eyes watered and stung. In the faint starlight and bluish luminescence of the snow everything beyond a few yards of his gaze swam deceptive and without depth, glimmering with things half seen or imagined. He listened beneath the low, mournful call of the wind and there could detect no sounds save for those made by himself or his horse. Everything else in the world might have died out there in the cold.

"Sometimes you are one damned cheerful fellow," he muttered to himself.

His horse chuffed its agreement, its metal shoes making lonely sounds as they struck against the cold-hardened ground and occasionally smashed through patches of silver ice. Even in this Godforsaken temperature the horse stank of frozen sweat and manure. Nitzinger figured that after these last three days of riding he probably didn't smell much better.

He was going to be right pleased to see the lights of Cedar Hill in a few hours, even if it was just another town full of strangers.

I will warn you, Johnny, his aunt had written in her last letter, *that you might assume this town to be just another shabby little place where miners and outriders lay down their burdens for a few days before venturing back out to their labors, leaving the wives and children to fend as best they can on what meager earnings the men bring back with them, but this is not a sad place at all. You will find the people are quite friendly after they get used to you, and in many ways become outright protective of you once they realize you are here to stay. I hope you will stay on here, Johnny. Your mama would have wanted for you to have a home. I know that I do.*

His reverie was broken at the same instant as the chill night silence.

Something in the frozen landscape nearby released a long, loud, unearthly yowl that rose above Nitzinger's head and spooked his horse.

He tried to pull the Spencer from its case but had it only halfway out before his horse reared back, cried out, and threw him from the saddle. He landed with an unflattering thud on a sizeable snowdrift and felt the wind ripped from his lungs.

Whatever had made the sound made it again and started out of the shadows for him.

Nitzinger scrambled to his feet, slipped on a patch of ice, and fell face-first into the snow.

The unearthly yowling was closer now, and Nitzinger silently cursed his foolhardiness at deciding to travel on during this night, for now he was about to perish—none too neatly, he imagined—at the claws and teeth of a cougar before he could get to Cedar Hill and claim the generous inheritance his late aunt had bequeathed him.

Not with my face in the snow, he decided.

If he was going to die, he'd do so facing his enemy.

Nitzinger took a deep breath and pushed himself up onto his knees, ready to die like a man.

Five feet away from him, sitting on its backside as if watching a mouse struggle in a trap, a dirty-gold tomcat no bigger than a man's forearm stared at Nitzinger's actions, then slowly, with what looked to be great pity, shook its head, rose, and sauntered away.

A boisterous laugh exploded from Nitzinger's chest with such force it knocked him back down into the snow.

A stray cat.

Good thing he hadn't muttered a prayer for his immortal soul before throwing himself into battle; the Good Lord probably wouldn't take too kindly to a man who was feared of a pet. No room for them nervous types in Heaven.

He laughed again at the thought of the cat's reaction (and at the odd notion that something about it seemed familiar to him), shaking his own head. His horse stood a few yards away, staring at him and leaning forward.

"Like to thank you for your bravery," Nitzinger said through his laughter.

"Hello?" came the echo of a female voice. "Hello? Is anyone there?"

Nitzinger got to his feet and mounted his horse, making sure the Spencer was secure, and rode to the top of the rise.

She stood at the edge of the passenger platform above the

train tracks. A single lantern hung over a bench behind her, giving off very little light. She was small, thin, and looked to Nitzinger from this distance to be a bit blanched. Her coat wasn't near heavy enough to keep a body warm on a night like this, and as he started down the rise toward her, Nitzinger hoped that she hadn't been waiting out here too long.

She leaned forward, peering into the darkness, then stepped back quickly when she finally caught sight of him.

"I know I must be a frightful sight, miss, but I ain't gonna bother you or nothin' like that."

"Are you all right, sir?" she asked. "I heard the most terrible ruckus a few moments ago."

"That'd been me engaging in a life-or-death struggle with a tomcat."

"*Oh*," said the young woman, trying to suppress her grin. "I wondered why the poor thing seemed so rattled."

Nitzinger looked behind the young woman and saw the dirty-gold cat perched comfortably on an old sea-trunk.

"That yours? The cat, I mean?"

"No sir. I saw it for the first time just a few moments ago. After your . . . encounter with it."

"*Encounter*," said Nitzinger, dismounting his horse and tying its reins to the station's post. "Mighty nice way to put it."

"To have put it any other way would risk insulting your pride, sir, and I gather that's been wounded enough for to-night."

Smiling to himself at her unusual directness, Nitzinger brushed the snow from his person as best he could and started up the steps. Mounted on the wall at the top was a badly tarnished brass plaque declaring that this station had been one of the monitor stops for the great Tom Thumb race in 1829 on the Baltimore and Ohio.

And though this place can't lay claim to much history, his aunt had written, *it is selfishly proud of what history it can call its own.*

Nitzinger silently wondered why, if they were proud of their history, the plaque was so badly in need of polishing.

He nodded a greeting to the cat, then removed his hat, pulled back the scarf he'd been using to cover his ears, and extended a gloved hand. "John Nitzinger, miss."

"Amanda Jakes," she replied, shaking his hand.

Even through his heavy woolen gloves, Nitzinger felt how cold her own gloved hands were. He blinked to clear his eyes, and saw then that her face wasn't blanched at all, as he'd mistakenly thought, but flushed from the cold. Her ears looked ready to fall right off from freezing and she was having a time of it keeping her nose from running all over her lip and chin.

"You mind, miss, if I ask exactly how long it is you've been waiting here?"

"Do you have the time?"

Nitzinger dug into one of the pockets of his duster and fished out the silver turnip watch his aunt had given him for his thirty-fifth birthday. Popping the cover, he turned into the dim lantern light and said, "Looks to be about 5:40."

"Then I have been here six hours."

"*Six hours!*" He snapped closed the watch and immediately removed his scarf. "Hell's bells, miss—pardon my language—but it's a wonder you ain't froze to death. Here, you take this and wrap it around your neck and ears—"

"—there's no need for you to—"

"—not in a state of mind for arguin' with anyone, miss. Can't believe the stationmaster'd go off and leave a body out here in this weather."

"There was no stationmaster on duty when the train arrived. There weren't even any porters. I was the only passenger who disembarked at the stop."

"Still," Nitzinger mumbled as he tried the station's sole door. "They ought to have left the waiting room open if they knew a train was comin'."

The door was locked.

He brushed a circle of snow and ice from one of the glass panes and looked inside. A padded bench, a potbellied iron stove, and three dark lanterns.

He bent his arm at the elbow and smashed in one of the panes, then snaked his hand through the opening and fumbled around until he found the latch and unlocked the door.

"Let's get you inside, out of this wind."

Amanda Jakes—appearing not in the least offended by his actions—nodded her thanks, picked up a small carpetbag and cardboard box, then went inside.

The dirty-gold cat followed, immediately curling up next to the iron stove, then yowling its displeasure at finding no heat waiting there.

"Sit yourself down right over there," said Nitzinger, striking a match taken from his pocket and setting flame to a lantern wick. "I gotta get some stuff from my horse, then I'll be right back."

He took from his horse his own bedroll and well-used pillow (hand-sewn, another gift from his aunt), a rusty coffee pot and sack of coffee beans, a dented cup and plate, a small satchel containing dried beef, a small slab of bacon, his last two eggs, a griddle, and, as an afterthought, his spare Navy Colt pistol. He thought about taking her something to read, but all he had were a couple of old and well-thumbed copies of *New York Detective Monthly* and didn't think a lady would find that proper material.

He made sure to cover his horse with its blanket. "Rest up for a bit, then we'll be on our way."

Back inside, he emptied the small satchel and used it to cover the spot where he'd smashed in the glass pane, then found the station's water closet (which to his surprise had a working gravity toilet) and cleaned himself, then started a fire in the stove with some of the coal from a bucket near the ticket-counter door (that made the cat very content), and set about making Amanda comfortable while he fixed her up something hot.

While he tried his best to make the food look halfway edible, she began humming a soft tune to herself.

"Pretty song," he said over his shoulder. "What's it called?"

" 'Waltzing With You.' I'm afraid I don't know the words. To be honest, John, I'm not even sure where I heard it. It just suddenly popped into my head."

"That's all right. Some things is pretty enough they don't need words." He checked the pot on the stove. "Afraid my coffee ain't as tasty as the restaurant-bought kind, but it's hot."

"Then it will be some of the best I've ever had," she replied.

Realizing he'd forgotten to bring in a fork and knife, Nitzinger was getting ready to go back out to his horse when Amanda removed the lid from her cardboard box and produced the items.

"I didn't have enough money to afford but one meal aboard the train," she explained. "So I packed myself enough makings for two additional meals, thinking, naturally, that three meals would be all I'd need."

Nitzinger piled the eggs and bacon onto the plate, poured the steaming coffee into the cup, and set everything on the bench next to Amanda.

"Looks delicious," she said, then took a sip of the coffee, made a nasty choking sound, and started coughing.

Nitzinger ran a hand through his hair, embarrassed. "Guess it's a bit strong."

"It's . . . it's fine, really," Amanda croaked, her eyes tearing.

The eggs and bacon went over much more successfully.

As she was finishing the last of her meal, Nitzinger cleared his throat and said, "Not that it's any of my business, miss—"

"Call me Amanda," she said. "Any man who cooks for me has my permission to be on a first-name basis."

He smiled at her and she smiled in return and for a minute

they just sat like that smiling at each other and making Nitzinger feel like a love-struck schoolboy.

Finally he said, "I was just wondering who it was that was supposed to meet you."

"The man I'm to wed."

He tried to tell himself that the pit that opened in his chest at that moment was just his being tired and nothing more. "Oh. He got a name?"

"Yes, it's . . . uh, well . . ." She shrugged, then reached into her carpetbag and removed a bundle of papers. "I'm not a stupid woman, John—may I call you John?—it's just that I'm exhausted from the trip and the weather and that my marriage is, well . . . an arranged one."

Nitzinger shrugged. "Arranged?"

Amanda found the paper she'd been looking for. "Yes. For the sum of five hundred dollars and the deed to some land in Oklahoma, Mr. Cletus Walters of Cedar Hill has bought himself the right to my hand."

Nitzinger looked at the cat; he could have sworn the thing hissed at the mention of Walters' name.

Amanda offered the paper to him. "When I turned twenty-seven it finally occurred to my father that he was going to have a spinster on his hands if he didn't do something about it."

Nitzinger looked over the paper, reading slowly, and without being aware of it muttered, "A Mail-Order Annie."

"I beg your pardon?"

"I'm sorry, miss—uh, Amanda. I said 'Mail-Order Annie.' That's what my aunt always called ladies in your position."

She cautiously sipped more of his coffee and said, "I don't know whether to be offended by that or not."

Panicked, Nitzinger spoke rapidly. "I meant no offense, really, it's just what my aunt always called mail-order brides on account of, well, my mother was one herself and her name was Annabelle. She was one of the women who sailed on *The Angelique* to California with Eliza Farnham in 1849. She married my father there. He was a miner. Mama always used to complain in her letters to her sister that the life of a mining-camp wife was lonely in the extreme and my aunt, she used to write back that that's what my mother deserved for becoming a 'Mail-Order Annie.' There weren't no harshness in the words, understand; my aunt, she had herself a pretty sharp sense of humor. She raised me after my mother died. Summer of '57, a cholera epidemic took out half the mining camp where we was living. Mama, she sent me here to Ohio right when the first case was reported. Said she didn't want to take no chances with her boy. I was only six then, and I didn't know it was gonna be the last time I saw her or my daddy. Anyway, my folks, they both died that summer and my aunt kept me on. Whenever she used to talk about my mother, she always called her 'Mail-Order Annie,' and I guess that just sort of stuck in my mind. I really didn't mean for you to think I was lookin' down my nose at you or anything."

"Do you remember her, your mother?"

"Some. I remember her laugh and how dark her hair was." He looked down at his hands. "Years go by, though, I keep less and less of her in my memory. Not from lack of trying, you understand?"

"I do," said Amanda, petting the dirty-gold cat that had crawled up into her lap. "And I take no offense, Mr. John Nitzinger. I don't think it's in you to purposefully offend a lady."

"Thank you."

She smiled at him again. "You're most welcome. So—are you here to visit your aunt?"

"In a way. She owns a boarding house and restaurant in Cedar Hill. I ain't seen her in, I'll bet, ten years."

"You must be very excited."

"She died a couple weeks ago. I got a . . . a letter from her lawyer tellin' me that I was her sole beneficiary and she'd left the place to me."

Amanda took in a sharp breath, placed a hand over her mouth, then reached out with the same hand and took hold of Nitzinger's. He could still feel the warm traces of her breath on her skin.

"I am *so* very sorry, John."

He nodded his head. "She was one great lady. I miss her already." He looked into Amanda's soft gray eyes. "But don't you . . . don't you fret none about that. We stayed real close, wrote to each other all the time, so I got no hard regrets about things. Besides, we got to figure out what we're gonna do about your situation and that rude Cletus Walters."

"Now that I'm warm and fed," Amanda whispered, not removing her hand from his, "I think I can survive until morning in here. My guess is that the road from town must be fairly high with snow. A man couldn't very well get a wagon through on a night like this."

"It wasn't night when you got here, and a man who's takin' on a new wife ought to have enough damned sense to bring a shovel along in his wagon during winter. You ask me, this Mr. Walters had better have himself one powerful excuse for treating you this way."

There was something more in her smile and her eyes than there had been before as she said, "I suppose it's not the most promising start to a marriage, is it? But you know what they say. 'A spinster can't complain.' "

"Don't you be saying that, Amanda—hell, if you was coming here for me I'd swim across a damn river to make sure I was waiting to greet you when you stepped off that train."

"Thank you."

"No need to thank me," he said, rising and gathering up his coat, hat, and gloves. "I'll ride on into Cedar Hill and find your Mr. Walters. Now, there's still some bacon left in the bag, and some dried beef, and my awful coffee. You're welcome to use my pillow and bedroll if you can stand the smell. There's plenty of matches and coal for the stove, so you won't freeze.

Lock the door behind me and—oh, yeah, almost forgot." He handed her his spare Navy Colt. "You know how to use a gun, Amanda?"

"I do. My father taught me how to shoot all manner of firearms."

"This is just in case any animals come wandering down from the mountains."

She gestured over her shoulder. "Like our bloodthirsty friend here?"

Nitzinger grinned and blushed, looking down at his feet. "Don't remind me."

Just then, another loud yowl echoed in from the coldness, and the dirty-gold cat jumped off the bench and clawed at the station door until Nitzinger let it out.

It bounded off the platform and across the snow to where another cat, this one much darker, sat waiting. Instead of circling one another like most cats did, each animal regarded the other as if it were a long-lost friend, someone they'd known all their lives. They stared at one another for a moment, then set off, side by side, in the direction of town.

With a greatness of purpose Nitzinger didn't usually associate with such creatures.

"My father was a road engineer," said Amanda beside him. "After my mother passed on and my three younger sisters all married, I traveled with him to many exotic countries. That autumn when the British were in Egypt, when President Arthur was raising dust about the tariffs, Father was advising the British on some construction. A woman who did the cooking told me a story about cats, that many people regarded them with great awe and respect because they were the form our loved ones who'd passed over took when they returned to this life to watch over and protect us. I always used to think that there were certain cats that just automatically took to you for no good reason—like that cat did to me."

Nitzinger stared after the cats. "I swear to you that thing's been following me for the last few hours."

"Maybe it has. They are very mysterious animals." She poked his arm and Nitzinger turned to look at her. "Maybe that cat was your aunt, come back to make sure you found your way safely."

"A night like this," he replied, "I wouldn't dismiss anything." He finished readying himself for the ride into town—a good hour and a quarter, at least—and was starting out the door when Amanda removed his hat from his head and wound the scarf he'd given to her around his head to cover his ears.

"I'll hear no arguments from you, John. It's cold out there." She put his hat back on his head, thanked him again for all his kindnesses, then gave him a quick, warm, polite kiss on the cheek.

When she pulled away, though, she didn't let go of his hands—nor did he wish for her to do so.

John Nitzinger figured he'd probably relive this evening over and over in his mind for the rest of his days, and would find it as wondrous then as he did right now.

"A man would be right proud to have a woman like you for his wife."

"A woman would be a fool to think she could do better than you, John."

They regarded each other tenderly in the warm silence of the station, their eyes betraying all that words would have only diminished.

Then Nitzinger went outside, mounted his horse, and began his journey toward Cedar Hill.

"John!" Amanda called from the doorway.

He turned back and waved.

"Remind me sometime," she called to him, "and I'll tell you the story of my life!" Then she laughed. It was music in his ears.

"If I can't find your Mr. Walters, I'll rent a wagon from the livery and come back here to get you."

And, with great purpose, he snapped the reins and his horse broke into a trot.

COVERED CANDLES gave Cedar Hill's main street a soft glow. The little church at the end of the street was aglow with yellow light and the sound of a choir rehearsing Christmas carols. The people who walked past on the boarded sidewalk between the one- and two-story frame false-fronts seemed pleasant enough; several of them even offered a small wave or a tip of their hat to the stranger who was riding into town.

Nitzinger figured that maybe the Christmas season softened their suspicion of strangers a bit. It was easy to see why his aunt had liked living here so much.

His flattering first impression of the town was dampened considerably by the reception he got from the livery manager, a cantankerous old man who made no attempt to hide his displeasure at having his dinner interrupted in order to take in Nitzinger's horse; his manner became downright cool when Nitzinger made an inquiry about Cletus Walters' whereabouts.

After that, what he found waiting for him at his aunt's establishment was a blessed relief.

The first thing that hit him when he came through the door was the smell of the food from the kitchen; roasted chicken and buttery potatoes and fresh peach pie. His mouth watered at once.

He approached the lobby desk slowly, wanting to take in the sights: the ribbons and green pine garlands that decorated the stairway; the cluster of mistletoe that hung over the entrance to the dining room; the splendid way the restaurant patrons were dressed—the men in three-piece suits, the women in dresses of silk and organdy. Low-hung Rochester lamps cast a homey glow down onto the tables while a tall, gallant-looking Negro man in pressed-whites glided from table to table with a frosty pitcher of ice water to refill patrons' glasses. At the far end of the dining room another Negro man sat at a piano—a baby grand, not an upright—while his graceful hands played sweet Christmas music.

Nitzinger had always imagined the place would be like this, but had never dared hope.

Most times, riding the fences, you found that dreaming about things made it all that much easier to be disappointed by their reality.

He turned away from the dining room and approached the short, stoutly attractive woman who was checking a ledger behind the desk. He removed his hat and stood there for a moment, not wanting to interrupt her.

After a moment she sniffed at the air, made a face, then looked up. "Something I can help you with, mister?"

"I hope so. My name's John Nitzinger, I'm—"

"Ethel's boy!" the woman cried out, then slammed shut her ledger and came gliding around to the front of the desk. Before Nitzinger knew what hit him, she had him in a hug that would have made a bear cry out for mercy or death.

"We was all wondering when you were gonna get here," said the woman, releasing him and stepping back to get a good look.

Nitzinger pulled air into his lungs and felt to make sure she hadn't broken any ribs.

Little lady's stronger than she looks, he thought. *Hell, she's stronger than I look.*

"Ma'am?" he said to her.

"Oh, no. You'll not be 'ma'am'-ing me. I'm Sarah Cobb. I manage this establishment for your aunt." She took hold of Nitzinger's hand and squeezed it.

He wasn't surprised that her grip hurt.

"Ethel spoke of you all the time," said Sarah. "She used to read your letters to me—Lordy, was she *happy* whenever something from you came in the post!" Then the woman's eyes filled with tears. "Ain't no one sorrier than me that she passed—except maybe for you."

Nitzinger could feel the eyes of the restaurant patrons on his back. "Um, I'm sorry to be coming in during dinner like this."

Sarah playfully smacked his forearm. "Don't you be apologizing, Johnny. This place is *yours* now. You can come and go as you please."

"Uh, about that . . ." He dug around in his saddlebag and produced the envelope he needed. "I'm supposed to meet with a Mr. Daniel St. James?"

"Danny's out of town, up in New York on some business or other. We expect him back at the end of the week. You *are* planning on staying here, ain't you?"

"For a little while."

Sarah's face wrinkled with concern at his words, but she brushed it away with a wave of her hand. "Well, come on, let's you and me go back into the office and have ourselves a talk."

Before Nitzinger could say anything, she had him by the arm and was pulling him behind the desk and through the doorway just beyond. She then put him in a terribly comfortable padded leather chair and thrust a cup of hot cocoa into his hand.

"I want you to know right now, Johnny, that your aunt was a fine, fine woman—a *splendid* woman. Everybody here in Cedar Hill just thought the world of her."

"She always said real nice things about this place and the folks here."

Sarah smiled at him. "I also want to put your mind to rest on another matter right now: I was with Ethel when she passed, and a more peaceful leaving you couldn't have asked for. Benjamin was down here on the piano, playing her favorite song so's she could hum along, and it was a pleasant night with stars out in abundance, and her room was warm, and Reverend Maddingly was present with his Bible, and all manner of friends stopped in to say their good-byes. She had your last letter in her hand and a picture of you and her sister on her bedside table. Her heart problems had been troubling her something fierce the last few years. The doctor said that most of the muscles surrounding it were shot. And with her coming down with pneumonia on top of that . . . well, it was for the best. But she died as happy as a person can, on that you have my word."

John was surprised to find tears in his own eyes. "That's good to know, Sarah. I don't mind telling you, on the ride here I often wondered about how . . . well, you know, if she had any regrets."

Sarah started crying. "No regrets, Johnny. None at all."

"Well, now . . . ain't that just fine?"

This time, Nitzinger was ready for Sarah's rib-cracking embrace.

And didn't mind it in the least.

Dear Johnny,

If you are reading this then you made it here all right and for that I am most grateful to our Good Lord.

I imagine that Sarah has made herself known to you by now. Don't mind her going on about things like she does, it is just her way. Believe me when I tell you that you will not find a more dependable or loyal friend than she. I have made some last-minute arrangements with Mr. St. James to bequeath Sarah either a small sum of money or a share of the business. The choice will be yours. Please keep her, Johnny. She knows more about running this place than I ever did.

In the small box accompanying this letter you will find what few worldly possessions I truly treasured, a photograph of your mama and you as a child among them. The silver frame was made from materials your daddy mined with his own hands. I'm sorry I don't have a picture of your daddy for you. He wasn't much to look at, truth be told, except when he smiled. Then a more handsome man didn't walk the earth. Until you, that is.

I would strongly advise you to make yourself known to folks around here before they decide to make themselves known to you. I'm afraid you have inherited more than a business establishment, Johnny. You have inherited a town filled with friends who have heard countless stories about you as a boy and a man. I apologize if I told them of anything that you might find embarrassing. I have always thought of you as my boy, and will not be held accountable for boasting of a child as a mother should.

This is your home now, if you want it. I sincerely hope you will. You have been alone for far too long, and in the end a life lived in loneliness is no life at all.

I will stop with my lecturing now. Always remember me fondly. I have loved you as my own and am certain to continue doing so once I am by our Lord's side. You never forgot to write to me and I treasured your letters. Don't go getting all disagreeable with yourself about not being here when I left. You have always been a part of me and so were here with me at the time.

I should mention that you will find all the books in order. That is Sarah's doing. There are no outstanding debts for you to worry about and a goodly sum of money in the bank.

I have had as fine a life as a woman who never married can expect. Finer, in some ways.

Bless you, my boy.
With Love,

Ethel

Damn if this wasn't the second time in as many hours that Nitzinger felt tears in his eyes.

He looked down at the sparse contents of the box which had contained the letter. There was the photograph of himself and his mother in its silver frame, several ribbon-bound bundles of the letters he'd written to his aunt over the years, a few pieces of jewelry (he thought Sarah might fancy a particular brooch), a piece of old rolled-up sheet music, and a wedding ring.

His mother's wedding ring, sent to his aunt a few weeks after his parents had died, only an hour apart.

He held it up to the light and reveled in its simplicity: A single stone set into a gold circle.

"Ah, well—*shit*," he whispered, letting go of the tears at last.

A life lived in loneliness is no life at all.

And so, for the first time in his life, John Nitzinger admitted to himself that he was lonely, and had been for a goodly while. His aunt had left behind a legacy that would survive through generations of Cedar Hill children—stories about her and her kindness, the way she could host a ladies' tea in the afternoon and drink any man in town under the table at night, and still retain the respect of both groups; countless other tales and memories people would keep alive—and what would he leave behind? Miles and miles of repaired fences that would surely crumble to dust and be forgotten long before he himself was dead, and once he was gone who would remember him or what he did? Was there ever a man he worked alongside of who could recall his face, the sound of his voice, or any conversation they'd had?

This place was his home, if he wanted one.

A life lived in loneliness is no life at all.

And he wanted it. He wanted nothing more than to live out the rest of his days in a place where neighbors greeted you by name each day and inquired after your health if they didn't see you out and about. He wanted to marry himself a fine woman and raise a family while there was still time to do so.

Amanda Jakes' smile blossomed in his memory, and he felt that pit in his chest open again. He was going to find Mr. Cletus Walters and punch the man right square in the mouth if he didn't have himself a good excuse for abandoning that fine lady out there in the cold.

Without realizing he'd done it, Nitzinger had unrolled the

sheet music and suddenly found himself looking at the title of the song.

"Waltzing With You."

Before the chill snaked down his back, he remembered what Sarah had said: *Benjamin was down here on the piano, playing her favorite song so's she could hum along.*

What brought the chill to him were Amanda's words: *I'm afraid I don't know the words. To be honest, John, I'm not even sure where I heard it. It just suddenly popped into my head . . .*

A movement to his left caught his eye and he turned toward the window of his aunt's bedroom.

On the outside sill he saw the dirty-gold cat sitting, its black-and-white friend at its side, and a couple of other, smaller cats.

Watching him.

He knew then, somehow, that he'd been right: The dirty-gold cat had been following him. But why? Cats weren't supposed to behave like that, were they? Sure, maybe they were good trackers, had inherited that from their ancestors, but weren't they supposed to track by smell? This thing had to have been tracking him by sight.

It didn't make sense.

"John Nitzinger?" came a gravelly voice from the doorway.

He turned, quickly wiping his eyes. "Yes?"

A short, stocky man with reddish-gray hair stepped into the room, removing his hat. "My name's Jack Baines. I'm the sheriff here."

Nitzinger rose and shook Baines' hand. "Can I help you with something, Sheriff? I hope I ain't done nothing wrong, broken a town ordinance or something like that with my horse or—"

"No. Hell no," said Baines, waving his hand. "Nothing like that. I wanted to introduce myself and welcome you. Your aunt, she was a good friend of me and my family. My wife, well, she's been feeling right poorly ever since Ethel left us.

You see, every year about this time, her and your aunt, they'd start in with baking the Christmas goodies, cookies and candies and such. Me and the kids, we couldn't get within five feet of the kitchen until after New Year's. The two of them practically set up armed guards to keep us out of the way." He ran a hand through his hair. "Yessir, the two of them was a holy terror this time of year." He shrugged. "My wife, she ain't so much as whipped up a batch of cakes in two weeks."

"I'm sorry to hear that."

Baines nodded his head. "Yeah, well, I reckon that once she gets wind that Ethel's boy has come to town, she'll perk right up. Probably lay down the kitchen law again and insist you come over for dinner every other night. Needless to say, you'll be having Christmas dinner with us. I'm just warning you ahead of time, you understand?"

"I stand warned."

"Okay, then. What I come here about was—" Baines' words died in his throat when he caught sight of the cats outside the window. "Christ on the cross," he whispered. Then, to Nitzinger: "How long them things been out there?"

"A while, I guess. That dirty-gold one there in the middle, I think it followed me from at least the train station."

Baines said nothing, only stared at the cats.

Something in the sheriff's manner betrayed his anxiety; the man seemed downright *spooked* by the cats.

Composing himself, Baines turned back to Nitzinger and said, "Reason I come is that Raymond from over at the livery came to see me a while ago. Told me about this here fellah that was askin' about the likes of Cletus Walters."

"That was me. At the train I met—"

"Did you know Cletus Walters?"

"Uh, no. Like I was sayin', out at the train station there's— wait a minute. How come you said it like that? *Did* I know Cletus Walters?"

"On account of the son of a bitch is dead."

Nitzinger felt a sudden rush of deep sympathy for Amanda Jakes. "Oh, Lord. Are you certain that he's—?"

"I killed him myself not ten days ago out at his cabin. Two barrels right in his chest and he still kept coming at me." He saw the way Nitzinger blanched, glanced nervously at the cats outside, and said in a low tone, "I think you and I need to go over to my office and have ourselves a chat."

THE FIRST thing Nitzinger noticed in the sheriff's office was the hand-carved chess set, evidently abandoned in mid-game.

"You play any?" said Baines, nodding toward the board.

"Whenever I can."

"You and me'll have to have ourselves a game sometime. You gotta be more of a player than my deputy. Man keeps using checkers strategy even though I keep trying to explain they're two different games. Them pieces're in the same positions they was in a week ago when the idiot came down with a case of the gout. I keep telling the man that if his diet didn't consist solely of bacon, beer, and tobacco, his body might not up and attack him so much, but there's just some people you can't pound any sense into."

Baines poured them both some fresh coffee that was far and away superior to the sludge Nitzinger had damn near killed Amanda Jakes with, and the two men sat across from each other over the chessboard.

"What happened with Cletus Walters?" asked Nitzinger.

Baines leaned over, examining the chessboard. "First thing, Mr. Nitz—ah, hell, can I call you John? I heard so much about you from your aunt I feel like I know you."

"John's fine."

"Your aunt—now *there* was a chess player. Woman beat the pants off me more times than I care to admit."

"I'm finding out all sorts of things about her. I hope she knew how many friends she had."

"She did, indeed." Baines began to move his knight to

Queen's-Pawn 7, thought better of it, and continued to stare at the board. "First thing you need to know, John, is that there's only a handful of folks around here who know the whole story about Walters—Raymond at the livery is one of 'em, and only because I needed extra horses and a wagon after it was over . . . anyway, only a few know about what happened, and I'd like to keep it that way, so what is said here in this room tonight stays here in this room, understand?"

"Understood."

Baines rubbed his eyes, took another sip of his coffee, then pulled a store-bought cheroot from his pocket. "You mind?"

"Got an extra one?" asked Nitzinger.

Baines did, and the two men lit up.

"It started with the cats," said Baines. "Two of them—that dark one, and a smaller reddish-brown one. That dirty-gold cat's a new one. Anyway, when Walters moved here from Oregon a couple years ago, him and his wife bought the old Myers place outside of town and started up their farming. Nice enough folks, but they didn't much socialize with the rest of us. His wife in particular seemed standoffish, but it weren't like she was stuck-up or nothing; she struck me as one of them terribly shy types.

"People who'd go out by their place on the road to Granville always commented on the amount of cats they saw hanging around the property. At first it was just them two cats I mentioned, but as time went on other cats started showing up. Last count, they had something like eight of them. Now, what always struck folks about the cats was the way they behaved. Weren't catlike at all, you ask me. They went everywhere together, real orderly. And whenever they'd stop to sit or sleep for a spell, they always did it together, real close in a circle, like they was resting in some kind of protection formation.

"Okay, so the Walters had a thing for cats. Fine by me. The animals was clean enough, never got into any of the chickens or such on other farms. Long as a pet ain't any problem, I don't bother with it.

"Long about eight, nine months ago, Walters comes into town and hires himself a little Hopewell Indian gal to come out and care for his wife who took sick. Didn't seem odd to anybody around here. Them Hopewells, they got a way with sick folk. So off they go back to the farm, and that's the last anybody hears for a few weeks.

"Hopewell gal came into town all by herself one day to pick up some supplies for Walters, only instead of going into the general store she heads over to your aunt's place, all nervous and scared-acting. Come to find out later that she told your aunt this wild story about how the cats was talking to her and Mrs. Walters. I don't mean opening their mouths and talking like you and I are doing, but inside their heads, right? Told your aunt that the reason Mrs. Walters got all sick was because the cats was warning her to get out before it was too late. So this Hopewell gal, she goes into a dream-trance or some-such nonsense and she asks the cats how come Mrs. Walters has to get out. And you know what she told your aunt them cats said to her? Said they told her that they was the spirits of 'his victims' and was trying to save Mrs. Walters.

"So your aunt, she tells me all this after the Hopewell gal goes back to the Walters' place. Me, I laugh it off, but Ethel, she don't think it's so funny. 'Don't you be making light of others' ways just because they're so different from yours,' she snapped at me. 'Now maybe that Hopewell gal has a few boards missing from her upper floor, but she didn't get any ideas in her head that Mrs. Walters didn't put there in the first place.'

"I decide that maybe old Cletus isn't treating his wife like a God-fearing Christian man ought, so I decide to go pay a visit just to see how things are. I get out to his place and there're all them cats, lined up straight as you please on the hitching post outside Mrs. Walters' bedroom window. I go to the front and raise my hand to knock on the door, and Cletus, he's got it open before my knuckle touches wood.

"Man looked like he'd seen a ghost. He was all shaky and pale and wild-eyed, telling me that I'd best be on my way and mind my own business, they're all down with a fever and best be left alone. If it hadn't been for something I caught out of the corner of my eye, I probably would have believed him. But over in the corner I see this little Hopewell gal, right, sitting there with one of Mrs. Walters' fancier dresses in her lap, mending it. And there's dried blood on the dress. Now, you tell me—why in hell would someone bother mending a dress that's got a set bloodstain on it? Wouldn't you try to get the stain out first, *then* mend the thing?

"I ain't a suspicious man by nature, but something about all this gets me thinking. This is a nice, boring little town, and we like it like that. I don't tell anyone about this except for Ethel, and she says to me, 'Didn't he say he moved here from Eugene?' 'Yeah,' I says. 'Then why don't you send a wire down to see if the sheriff there has anything you might need to know?'

"That's exactly what I did. Six days later I get woke up at three in the morning by a couple of Pinkerton boys who look ready to spit nails and eat the hammer. They tell me to get dressed and come with them out to the Walters' place. Along the way, they fill me in on a couple of things that about turned my blood to ice.

" 'Cletus Walters' wasn't his real name. The Pinkertons had no idea what his real name was, but they had a nice little list of names they thought he'd been using. When he'd been in Eugene, he took advantage of the Land Act—you know, that a married man was entitled to twice the acreage of a single fellah. Him and his wife, they farmed that land for about a year or so, then he just up and sold it for a nice profit and moved on without telling anyone where he was going. The folks who bought the place from him started complaining after a couple of weeks about two things. Guess what one of them was?"

"Cats?" said Nitzinger.

"You got that right. Cats . . . and the smell. So this fellah who bought the place, he eventually runs the cats off and starts digging around the property to find the smell. Well, he found it, all right. Walters had murdered his wife and buried her in her wedding dress under the water closet. When they was finally able to track down the paperwork on her, they found out that she married Walters—he used the name 'Simpkins' then—because of an arrangement he made with her father."

"She was a mail-order wife?"

"Yessir, that she was. According to the work the Pinkertons had been doing, their best guess was that Walters had done this at least three times before, maybe as many as seven or eight. He'd marry himself a mail-order bride on account of there wouldn't be no family of hers nearby, he'd use his marital status to snag himself twice the property he was entitled to then, after him and his wife got the place into shape, he'd sell off the property at a decent profit, murder and bury his wife— he always buried them in their wedding dresses—then change his name and move to another county or state and do it all over again. The man was either damned stupid or damned arrogant. To this day I can't figure if he wanted to get caught or thought that the men on his trail weren't smart enough *to* catch him.

"It was while the Pinkertons was telling me about this that I realized the Hopewell gal had been mending what could very well have been a wedding dress, and I tell 'em this, and they slapped leather to the horses to get to the farm double-quick.

"You never heard such noise as what greeted us that night. There must have been a good half dozen or more cats all around the outside of the cabin, howling up a storm. I could see a light was on inside the house and heard what sounded like a woman screaming. So we jump out of the wagon, the Pinkertons splitting up on either side of the house and leaving me in front with my old double-barrel. I go up near the porch and call for Cletus and all the cats just went quiet—" he snapped his fingers "—like that. Scared me right down to the ground. I call Cletus's name again and the door flies open and this little Hopewell gal comes running out, all beat-up and bleeding and screaming something in Indian at me that I don't understand, and next thing I know here comes Cletus looking like the Devil his own self, and he's yelling something at the cats about how they should just go back to their graves and leave him alone, then he opens fire on me with a set of pistols he's got and hits that poor little Hopewell gal right smack in the back of the head with one of the shots, and she goes down at my feet and I empty both barrels into his chest and he still kept coming. The Pinkertons finished him off, and both of them had to empty six shots each to bring him down.

"He was in the process of burying his wife when we got there. She'd been dead a couple of days at least . . . it was fairly grim. The Pinkertons tore the place up, and they found plenty. Crazy bastard'd kept every marriage certificate. Eight of them. He even kept wedding photographs of himself with each of his brides. And the money. They found something like sixty thousand dollars he'd stashed away from selling off all that land. I did some checking after it was all over, and found out that Walters had been making some inquiries over in Delaware County about land over there for himself and his 'new wife.' "

Nitzinger's blood turned to ice in his veins at the thought of what might have happened to Amanda at the hands of a demon like Walters.

"Sheriff, I don't mean to seem rude, but there's something I gotta take care of as soon as possible."

"Anything I can help with?"

Nitzinger told Baines about Amanda Jakes.

"Christ on the cross," whispered the sheriff. "I wonder if that gal will ever know how lucky she is."

"You think Raymond would give me too much trouble about renting a wagon and couple of fresh horses?"

"Not if I'm with you, he won't."

Nitzinger rose. "I need to get a few things from over at my aunt's place."

"*Your* place now," said Baines. "That is, if you plan on staying put for a while."

"I do," replied Nitzinger. "This is my home. Now."

HE BROUGHT a shovel, and cleared the snowdrifts from the road so that the wagon would have easy passage. As he rode along he sang softly to himself "Waltzing With You." Words and all.

She was asleep when he got there, and so for a few moments, after quietly letting himself into the station, he stood there staring at her soft sleeping face and hoping she'd smile at him when she finally awoke.

She at last wakened when the dirty-gold cat and the rest of its friends began yowling outside; only this time there was nothing mournful or eerie in the sound. To Nitzinger's ears, it almost sounded like they were singing.

It then occurred to him why the dirty-gold cat had seemed familiar to him.

Its fur was the same color as his aunt's hair.

Rubbing the sleep from her eyes, Amanda sat up, saw Nitzinger, and smiled at him with a sleep-blushed face that was, for him, the most beautiful thing he'd ever seen.

"*John* . . . hello."

"Hello, Amanda."

"What time is it?"

"Almost midnight. I would have been here sooner but I—"

"Oh, stop apologizing," she said. "If you apologize to me one more time about anything tonight, I'm going to charge you five dollars each time you say 'I'm sorry.' "

"I got a wagon out front. Road into town's cleared."

"Wonderful. Except that I seem to have been left standing at the altar in a way." She looked him straight in the eyes. "I *have* been left, haven't I?" There was a quiet kind of desperate sadness under her words.

"Yes, you have."

And that was all he ever intended to tell her about it.

"Would you really have married him? A man you never met and didn't know?"

She nodded her head. "Look at the likes of me, John. I'm not as pretty as most men would like, and I am spinster-age. Besides, my father would be very angry if I backed out on a business deal he made."

"I think you're very pretty," said Nitzinger. "I just wish I was more of a Fancy-Dan."

"John," she said softly. "I think you're just fine as you are."

"Good. That'll make this a lot easier."

"Make what easier?"

Nitzinger didn't say anything. He looked out at the cats and gave them a wink, then took off his hat, removed his mother's wedding ring from his pocket, and slowly, with great dignity and purpose, took her left hand in his and got down on one knee.

CARRY'S CAT

Barbara Collins

THE ANNEX IN Wichita, Kansas, was considered one of the finest saloons in the whole country, second only to the Alcazar in Peoria, Illinois. But most people felt the Annex was more elegant, with its marble floor and black onyx railing and cut-glass decanters filled with various liquors that lined a long beveled Victorian mirror behind the bar. Even the walls were unique, the gray stucco blocks imported from the buildings of the 1893 Chicago World's Fair.

It was on one of those walls that hung the focal point of the Annex: a life-size painting of a nude Cleopatra taking a bath, surrounded by seminude Greek and Roman maidens. The picture, in an enormous gilded frame, cost a small fortune, and men came from near and far to ponder its artistic significance.

But none of the opulent (or decadent, according to some citizens of Wichita) decor of the Annex had any effect on Dr. Henry Carlson, who stood at the highly polished cherrywood bar and slammed back a shot of whiskey. He was only interested in the effects of the drink, because after twelve hours of attending Mrs. William Moore, he'd delivered a still-born baby.

Dr. Carlson sighed as the alcohol burned his throat and relaxed his tight neck muscles and began to dull his brain.

225

Then he set the shot glass down and motioned for the bartender, Edward Parker, to pour him another. Parker, a wiry man with a handlebar mustache and slick black hair parted in the middle, filled the glass again with the mind-numbing liquid, picked up the money left on the counter, and moved away from the doctor, down the fifty-foot curved bar, to tend to another customer.

Carlson stared at himself in the mirror. Underneath the black Stetson bowler, his brown hair was graying prematurely, and deep lines were beginning to erode a handsome, if boyish, face. The dark twill serge suit and white linen shirt he had on were rumpled and sweat-stained. He looked like an old man, not the young one he was.

Carlson turned away from the bar and, taking his drink with him, sat at one of the small, round cherrywood tables in the main seating area, where here and there, next to the tables, waist-high brass spittoons also sat, like squat, openmouthed patrons.

There were a few other customers enjoying a drink in the middle of a cold January afternoon. Down at the end of the bar three beefy stockyard workers were having beers, clouding the reality of their lives, liquoring up just enough so they wouldn't go home and beat their wives and children. And at another table two businessmen lingered, left over from a Mystic Order of Brotherhood meeting, deep in whispered conversation. Although alcohol was illegal in Kansas, having been banned from the state in 1880, some twenty years ago, no one paid any attention to the law, from the saloonists to the public to the lawmakers themselves.

An altercation at the bar distracted the doctor from his present languor. An unshaven, shabbily dressed man was trying to order a drink from the bartender. Carlson recognized him as George Johnston, a once wealthy and prominent lawyer in Wichita, before the man became an alcoholic.

"Go on, get out of here," Parker was saying disgustedly to the man. "And don't come back . . . you disgrace my place."

The drunk weaved a little as he stood at the bar, then raised a bony fist and shook it at Parker. "Five years ago, I came in here a healthy young man. You have made me what you see now. So give that drink to me and finish your work!"

Parker scowled and reached under the bar and brought out a Colt .38 which he laid with a clunk on the counter. "Leave, you rummy," the bartender ordered Johnston, "or I'll drain the liquor outa ye!"

Johnston sneered in Parker's face. "You don't frighten me," he slurred. "I'm going. But I'll be back."

From his table, Carlson watched uncomfortably as the drunken man stumbled to the front door and out into the wintry afternoon. He felt a twinge of guilt for succumbing to the whiskey himself; a doctor shouldn't be drinking in the middle of the day. And certainly if his wife, Sarah, found out, she'd have his hide; she was vehemently opposed to liquor.

He stood, buttoning his suitcoat, when the figure of a woman appeared in the doorway. She was unusually tall—at least six feet—wearing a shiny black alpaca dress that most women only put on for mourning. Her head was large, white hair peeking out from under an old-fashioned black poke bonnet with its black satin ribbons tied under her chin. While it was apparent her age fell between fifty and sixty, her face, with its tiny close-set eyes, small bulbous nose, and unpainted full lips, looked like those of a baby's.

Inside Henry's head, a distant bell was ringing; he thought he knew who she was. But because of the mind-numbing whiskey, the bell that was ringing was without a clapper.

A large black cat crawled out from underneath the woman's full, floor-length skirt. The animal positioned itself next to her, by the front door, where it sat as if waiting, eyes hooded.

"Men," she said loudly, addressing the customers, "I have come to save you from a drunkard's fate." Then she turned to the bartender, nodding her head. "How do you do, maker of rummies and widows!"

And before anyone could say, or do, anything, the woman's right hand came from behind her back, holding a hatchet, and she ran to the bar and brought that hatchet down, cracking the beautiful cherrywood counter, while with her other hand she threw a rock at the Victorian beveled mirror shattering it completely. Large shards of glass rained down onto the lovely cut-glass canisters, which in turn broke into thousands of pieces, spilling their contents onto the bartender, who ducked, covering his head with his hands, trying unsuccessfully to avoid the shower of glass and liquor.

The three burly stockyard workers, shouting "Tarnation!" and "Let's vamoose!" tripped over each other as they scrambled to make an escape out the back door, while the two businessmen from the Mystic Lodge took refuge behind the far end of the bar.

Henry stood frozen where he was, at last recalling the woman's name: Carry Nation. He'd read about her in the Wichita *Journal*, how she'd smashed Dobson's saloon in Medicine Lodge last month and put the owner out of business, then did the same to every other joint in that town. She vowed she wouldn't stop until all of Kansas was really and truly dry.

As Carry continued to run up and down the bar, wreaking havoc on the counter with her hatchet, in through the front door came two more women dressed in black. They were younger than Carry (and much more attractive); one had dark hair and the other was blond, both wielding hatchets.

Henry dove behind the bar and hid with the other men— not because he was scared, but because the pretty blond woman was his wife, Sarah.

"Peace on earth! Goodwill toward men!" the two women shouted in honor of the new year, joining their leader in the fracas, smashing everything in their path.

Parker popped up from behind the bar and hollered for the

women to stop, then ducked back down as a whiskey bottle whizzed past his head and smashed into the wall, spraying him with more glass and liquor.

Then the dark-haired woman named Margaret—who happened to be the mayor's wife—jumped up on a chair and punched a hole in the top of the oil painting with her hatchet, and slid the blade down, cutting poor Cleopatra in half.

All through the ruckus, the big black cat had remained motionless by the front door—except for its yellow eyes which seemed to grow large with delight. It now ran toward the bar and jumped up on the hacked-up counter, and stood rigidly next to the bar taps, hissing.

Carry took the animal's cue, and with her hatchet, cut one of the rubber tubes that carried the beer from the kegs on the floor up to the faucets, and grabbing the severed tube, began spraying it like a water hose, all over the walls and the floor, and the cowering men, and even her two cohorts, who were busy digging out the bungs from the beer kegs, flooding the floor even more.

Meanwhile, the cat, its black fur matted with beer, began greedily lapping up the puddles on the counter.

Parker had had enough. He stood and shook his Colt .38 at Carry. "Stop this destruction or I'll shoot!" he told her angrily.

Carry turned the hose on him.

Parker fired the pistol, but missed Carry and hit the cat which was next to her on the counter; it fell over on its side in the beer.

Carry shrieked with rage and ran toward Parker, hatchet raised. He dropped the gun in fear, then turned and tried to flee. But the other men were huddled in the way, and Carry leapt on the bartender's back, as if he were a pony, and the two tumbled onto the rest, Carry somersaulting forward over the heap where she landed on the floor, sitting in a sea of beer, black dress up over white bloomers, black poke hat askew on her head.

Another shot rang out. A Wichita police officer, a big bull-dog of a man in a navy wool overcoat, stood in the doorway of the saloon, his weapon pointed at the ceiling.

"What's going on here?" he demanded as he moved toward the group, sloshing through the beer on the floor.

"Officer," Parker said, his voice shaking with emotion, almost near tears, "these woman have completely destroyed my place! Arrest them!"

Carry picked herself up off the floor, smoothed out her dress, straightened her bonnet. "Officer," she said, and pointed a finger at Parker, "this man is running an illegal hellhole. He's a maker of drunkards and widows. And he killed my cat! Arrest *him!*"

Dr. Carlson, who remained crouched behind the counter, took advantage of the diversion to crawl on his hands and knees in the muck toward the back door and freedom from discovery.

"Hey, you!" the policeman called out. "Where do you think you're going?"

Carlson froze. Then he stood up slowly and turned around. "Uh . . . nowhere."

His wife gasped. "Henry! What are you doing here?"

Henry, like most men caught in a transgression by a spouse, took the defensive. "What are *you* doing here?" he demanded. It was lame, he knew.

"Henry Carlson," Sarah snapped, hands on her shapely hips, "you know how I feel about liquor. Just wait until we get home."

"You're not going home, madam," the officer informed her. "You're coming with me, along with your other two friends." He looked at Carry and Margaret.

"On what charge?" Carry asked defiantly.

"Malicious destruction of private property," he snarled.

"You mean 'destruction of malicious property,' don't you?" Carry responded sweetly.

"That's for the judge to decide," the officer growled. And he herded the three beer-soaked women out—Carry looking back forlornly at her dead cat—leaving the men behind, in what was once the finest saloon in the country.

IN AN upstairs bedroom of his Victorian home on South Main Street, Dr. Henry Carlson got out of his filthy, soggy, beer-stained suit. Then, at a nearby washstand, he poured water from a floral pitcher into a basin and soaped his face and hands and ran a wet cloth through his hair. After putting on a clean white shirt and pair of wool trousers, he went over to a rosewood dresser and withdrew some extra cash from the top drawer, so he could bail Sarah out of the county jail.

He couldn't believe she was mixed up with the likes of that crazy Carry Nation! Although, he thought, that did explain Sarah's strange behavior lately . . .

Six months ago his wife joined an organization called the Women's Christian Temperance Union, or W.C.T.U, as Sarah always referred to it. He thought it was a Bible study group, with nothing more subversive going on than reading modern poetry, or discussing world events. Now it appeared these women got together weekly to discuss a whole lot more. Like wanting to shut down all the saloons in town.

A horrifying thought entered his mind. What if next they wanted the right to vote? Or, heaven forbid, to become doctors themselves? He shuddered and shook his head. With the coming of the new millennium, was the whole world going mad?

It seemed as though Sarah had. Recently, his sweet, docile wife had become very opinionated and bossy. And her dress had become almost immodest—copying the look of those Gibson girls featured in recent *Life* magazines: tight skirts underneath which (ye-gad) her lacy bloomers showed, and form-fitting blouses leaving nothing to the imagination, her long blond hair pulled loosely on top of her head, as if she'd just tumbled out of bed. Furthermore, he caught her several times dancing the hootchy-kootchy when she thought he wasn't around.

If she wasn't so wonderful in their four-poster bed, life could be very difficult, indeed. But she seemed to sense when his blood was about to boil over, and so she would stand, in those fancy Paris undergarments, beckoning him with a finger, untying the satin ribbons.

Damn her! She knew the effect that had on him. And there was nothing he could do—or even wanted to do—about it. How could she be such a wanton in private, and such a prude in public?

Henry sat on the edge of the four-poster bed. Maybe he should take his time in getting down to the jail. Maybe staying in a cell for a bit would take the spirit out of her and give him the upper hand for a while. He gazed at the feather pillows and sighed. Or at least until she beckoned him with a finger, and untied the satin ribbons . . .

Below, a door slammed, startling him. He wondered who it could be. Then he heard Sarah call his name. He ran into the hall and down the banistered staircase.

She was in the parlor, on the brocade sofa, looking sad and weary. But even her torn black dress, beer-matted blond hair, and dirt-smudged face could not diminish her beauty. He sat next to her, and the pungent smell of an array of liquor was enough to make him give up drinking for good.

"The judge let me and Margaret go," she said, looking down at hands folded primly in her lap. "But Mrs. Nation will have to stand trial next week." Then she added, "The W.C.T.U. posted her bail so she wouldn't have to stay in jail."

Henry sighed. "Sarah, I don't understand how you could get involved with that woman."

She looked at her husband. "I guess I can't believe it myself," she said. "But Mrs. Nation came to our meeting this afternoon and gave such a rousing speech about the evils of liquor . . . Then poor Mrs. McCabe stood up and said her husband went on a toot last week and spent all his pay—and her with four little children to feed—and then Mrs. Johnston said she had to throw her husband out of the house because his drinking made him so violent . . ." She stopped to catch her breath, and added emphatically, "If men aren't going to obey the antiliquor law, then women will have to do something about it!"

Henry looked into his wife's tear-filled eyes. "Sarah, you can't fix a law by breaking another. You could have been hurt, or worse."

They fell silent for a moment. Then his wife said softly, "I know why you were there. I heard about the baby. Henry, next time, why don't you turn to me, instead of liquor?"

He smiled just a little. "Don't worry. I saw the way you handled that hatchet."

An urgent pounding at the front door put an end to their conversation. Sarah gestured to her disheveled appearance and jumped up from the sofa and hurried toward the stairs, as Henry headed for the entryway to answer the insistent knocking. But before he could get there, the door opened, and Margaret ran in. She had changed from her black dress into a long green velvet one, her dark hair pulled neatly back into a bun, but her expression was just as wild as when Henry saw her bashing the saloon.

"Something terrible has happened," she wailed, rushing past Henry to the foot of the stairs where she looked up at Sarah, who had stopped, halfway up.

Sarah turned and came down to her friend. "What is it?"

"Someone found that bar owner, Edward Parker, in the Annex saloon hacked to death with a hatchet," she said. "And they've arrested Carry for it!"

IT WASN'T the first time Carry Nation had been in jail. Back in Medicine Lodge, she spent two weeks in a cell for destroying Dobson's saloon, not having the money herself for bail. But at the trial, the judge ("Your Dishonor," she snidely called him) let her go for insufficient evidence, even though half the town had witnessed her "hatchetation." Then the sheriff gave her money and a railway ticket to get out of town, which she did, but she used the money to buy more hatchets and came back and smashed another saloon, and another, until they were all closed down.

But this time was different. She'd never been jailed for murder. With the saloon-smashing, no one dared to prosecute her. How could they? They would have to admit that *they* were the ones breaking the law by allowing saloons to flourish. She was only correcting the situation, acting as an enforcer because they would not. But now, with the bartender killed with one of her hatchets, things didn't look so good.

After the nice women from the local Temperance Union paid her bail money for "disturbing the peace," Carry had gone back to her hotel to freshen up and put on a clean black dress before heading over to the ruins of the Annex Saloon to retrieve her dead cat. She and the animal had been through many a saloon-smashing together and she felt he deserved a proper burial, not to be thrown out with the rubble.

When she got there, the cat was still lying on the counter in a pool of beer and blood, one of her hatchets next to it. She picked up the hatchet so she wouldn't have to buy another, then went around the counter to find a carton or box to put the cat in, and discovered the chopped-up Parker. Then she rushed out to the street, hatchet still in hand, and ran into the two businessmen who had been drinking in the saloon earlier. They were the ones who told the police she had done the deed.

No, this time the situation did not look any so good.

In the cold, gray cell, Carry dropped down off the cot where she'd been sitting and onto her knees. "Oh, Lord," she prayed.

"You told me to call on you in my day of trouble. Well, Sir, this is my day of trouble!"

Then, head bowed, she advanced on her knees around the small cell, a curious practice taught to her as a small child by the God-fearing slaves on her father's cotton plantation.

With her praying done, she returned to sit on the cot. Her thoughts turned back to the cat.

The animal had been such a comfort to her this past year on her crusade. It was after her second saloon-smashing in Medicine Lodge that she noticed the mangy black cat began to appear, watching, waiting, knowing that where Carry went liquor would surely flow.

Some might wonder why a woman opposed to alcohol would keep an alcoholic cat around, but Carry saw the animal as a reminder that creatures both great and small could be affected by the evils of drink.

And the cat was really quite loving (when sober), snuggling up with her in various hotel rooms, keeping loneliness at bay. Carry, after all, had very little family life. Her ex-husband, Charles, had concealed his drinking during their courtship, then, after their marriage, came home night after night drunker than a skunk, eventually ruining his medical practice and their personal finances and finally the marriage itself. Their daughter, Charlien, born retarded, also grew up to become an alcoholic and had to be institutionalized because of her excessive drinking. Often Carry wondered if Charles's addiction had somehow contributed to her bearing a dim-witted child; she remembered the Bible's warning against pregnancy and alcohol.

Softly, Carry began to sing "Am I a Soldier of the Cross?", and after the first verse, a male voice from another cell joined in, and then another, and another, as the sky outside the little cell windows darkened and night moved in.

* * *

IT WAS nearly midnight when Henry Carlson entered the back door of the county morgue, which was in the basement of a clapboard building next to the police station.

He was not the doctor acting as coroner, but knew the man well, and had arranged earlier a chance to see the body of bartender Edward Parker.

The coroner, a small, plump man with a balding head and thick-lensed glasses, opened the door to the back and let him in out of the cold.

A gas lamp on the wall cast long dark shadows, making the room seem creepy even to Henry who was used to such things.

"Don't let the chief know about this," the coroner whispered.

"Don't worry," Henry answered.

"He's over here," the coroner said, pointing to the wooden coffin. "You'll want to hold your nose."

Henry had several reasons for wanting a look at Parker's remains. One was when he'd heard the two men from the Mystic Order of Brotherhood had pointed an accusing finger at Mrs. Nation, he became suspicious of their motives. He knew that the Brotherhood—apparently, like the women's Temperance Union—was not a benign organization. In fact, the Mystic Order of Brotherhood was really a front for the continuing efforts of the liquor industry. But not everyone knew that.

The second reason he was standing in the morgue in the middle of the night, poking at dismembered body parts, was his wife, Sarah, who was completely inconsolable since Mrs. Nation was arrested. She was convinced that Mrs. Nation could not have done such an awful thing, even though the old woman could wield a hatchet with the savagery of an Apache. But if it was one thing Henry couldn't stand, it was his beautiful wife in tears.

"Look there," Henry said to the coroner.

"Where?"

"There."

"I don't see what you mean."

Henry poked some more at the torso. "Where the hatchet went into his heart. Do you see it now?"

The coroner drew in a sharp breath. "My God. Is that . . . a bullet wound?" He looked at Henry. "I'd say this changes everything."

Henry nodded. "I think you'll find that bullet was what killed Parker, and the hacking was done to cover it up and place the blame on Carry Nation."

The coroner's eyes grew larger behind his thick glasses. "You don't think those two men—the witnesses—did this, to frame Mrs. Nation?"

Henry thought for a moment. "I just can't see either of them killing Parker," he said, "but I can see them taking advantage of an already bad situation, if you know what I mean." Then he added, "However, Mrs. Nation certainly has the liquor industry riled, and these are crazy times."

They were moving toward the back door, the coroner turning out the gas light. "Well, if they didn't do it, who besides Carry Nation would want to kill Edward Parker?"

Henry shrugged, then straightened up, half smiled. "I can think of one."

MCNAB'S LIVERY was just a short walk from the county morgue, and Henry hoofed it over there, holding the collar of his wool coat up around his face against the bitter winter night wind, the full moon above watching like a popped-out eye.

John McNab was a patient of his, and he remembered the stable owner once mentioned he let some of the drunks sleep there when it got so cold.

The barn door creaked as Henry opened it, startling a couple of palominos, who snorted and eyed him wildly, until he shushed them quietly and moved slowly by.

He found George Johnston asleep in the last stall, buried beneath some straw. He knelt next to the man, who smelled

almost as bad as the remains of Edward Parker, the combination of liquor and inhumanity almost unbearable.

Henry gently shook the man, whose eyes opened, frightened
as the horses'.

"It's Doc Carlson," Henry said softly. "No need to be
afraid."

Johnston sat up, straw falling away from his frayed coat.
"Doc," the man said, tongue lolling around in a dry mouth,
"have you got any money for a drink?" He held out a dirty
hand.

"Sure, George," Henry replied, and dug into his waistcoat
pocket, then put a coin into the man's palm. "You go and see
Edward Parker tomorrow and he'll give you a drink."

Johnston dropped the coin, like it was a hot coal, and it
disappeared into the straw. His eyes looked frightened.

"I think he treated you badly today," Henry said. "When all
you wanted was a drink."

Johnston's already rheumy eyes took on a wetter look, his
lower lip trembling. "I warned him I'd be back," he said.

"You knew the gun was under the counter and shot him,
didn't you, George?" Henry asked softly.

Johnston nodded and lowered his head. "In the heart . . .
because he had none."

Henry looked at the once wealthy and prominent lawyer.
"You go back to sleep now, George," he told the man, and
patted his shoulder. The police could pick him up in the
morning.

Henry covered up the already slumbering Johnston with
straw, before slipping quietly out.

IN THE parlor of Henry's victorian home, Carry Nation,
wearing her trademark black alpaca dress and black poke bonnet, looking regal as a queen as she sat in a high-backed rosewood chair, sipped the tea Sarah had just served. Henry and

Sarah were across from her, on the brocade sofa. Flames danced in the fireplace.

"I can't thank you both enough for clearing my good name," Mrs. Nation said.

"It was all Henry's doing," Sarah said, looking gratefully at her husband.

Henry smiled, enjoying the moment of adulation in his wife's blue eyes.

"What do you suppose will happen to the two men who tried to put the blame on Carry?" Sarah asked her husband.

Henry shrugged. "That will be up to the judge to decide. But they did admit to seeing Johnston shoot Parker and flee, and decided to use the hatchet on the poor man to make it seem like Mrs. Nation did the awful deed."

The trio was silent for a moment, then Henry asked Carry, "What are your plans now?"

Carry set her cup and saucer on a small pedestal next to her chair. "I'm off to the Senate in Topeka," she announced.

"Oh," Sarah said brightly, "you're finally going to speak to the legislature."

Mrs. Nation frowned. "No, my dear," she replied, "The Senate *Bar*. It's across from the legislature, and all those Republican rummies hang out there . . . So I'm sure they'll get my message."

She reached inside her black cloth purse on her lap. "I'm financing the trip with these," she told them, pulling out a handful of miniature peweter hatchets. "A company in Rhode Island is making them for me. I'll sell them for ten cents apiece—or twenty-five, if I think I can get it."

Henry and Sarah laughed.

Then Carry stood up. "I must be going. My train leaves shortly. Thank you again for all you have done."

"Will you wait just a moment?" Sarah said to Carry. "We have something for you." And Sarah nodded at Henry who left the room.

Soon Henry came back carrying a small black kitten. And when Carry saw the animal her face burst into a smile of joy, and she rushed to it, plucking it out of Henry's hands, and held the furry thing against her face.

"It's not partial to liquor of any kind," Henry told her.

"And I'll see that it never is!" Carry said with tears in her eyes.

After Mrs. Nation left, Henry gathered up the tea cups and carried them into the kitchen. When he returned, Sarah had left the room; he could hear her upstairs moving around in the bedroom.

He climbed the staircase smiling to himself; his heroics should garner a lot of favors with his wife. Like staying out all night, playing poker with the boys, or buying that new contraption Henry Ford had just invented. Yes, for a while, he was going to have the upper hand . . .

He halted in the doorway to the bedroom, where Sarah now stood next to the four-poster bed, in her fancy Paris undergarments, a seductive smile on her face.

. . . or anyway, until his wife beckoned to him with her finger, and untied the satin ribbons.

BYRON

Jack Albert

LYNN CHOSE THE long way, crossing over to the other side
of Beirut with her friend, Byron the cat. They left the Christian side and went by taxi to Damascus, some ninety kilome-
ters away. There, she found another cab with an Armenian
driver who was returning to the Moslem side. Armenians were
considered neutral in the conflict, and allowed to operate in
both zones. She gave him no hint that she understood Arabic.

Her orders were simple. The Commander had given her the
key to an apartment and an address. The information came
from Mossad's resident in Ras-Beirut, who was recently transferred. He owed the Commander a favor. The rest was up to
her.

She looked at herself in her hand mirror. Her hair was
combed and rolled up in a bun. The gray had appeared soon
after she'd stopped using the dye. There were also wrinkles
around her eyes. She wondered whether Boulos would still find
her attractive. She had taken the assignment in order to find
him. Yet, she had no idea where to look for him or whether he
was still alive.

At seven in the morning, the taxi reached Ras-Beirut, and
stopped in front of a two-story building with arcades and col-

umns, and a roof covered with red bricks. Each floor had a balcony looking out on the street.

She stepped out of the Mercedes, her left arm wrapped around Byron, waiting for the driver to unload her two suitcases from the trunk. A man with a white armband came running out of the building, revolver in hand. In broken Arabic, the cabby explained that he had driven the English lady all the way from Damascus.

"I am Aziz, of Security," the man in the white armband said. "Open the luggage."

In the soft nylon suitcase there were dresses and toiletries. The other suitcase had a hard shell and contained shoes and undergarments. Aziz felt with his hand around the bottom of the first suitcase and nodded his head. He examined the bottom of the second suitcase and raised his eyebrows. He pulled a switchblade from his breast pocket when a jeep approached at high speed, tooting its horn. The teenage driver kept looking in the rearview mirror. In the back, a man toyed with an ack-ack gun, aiming it all around, probably trying to impress the local females.

Aziz cursed, and disappeared around the corner. A little later, he came back at the wheel of a noisy half-track, and went chasing the jeep.

The cabby moved the two pieces of luggage inside the apartment. He wrote something on a piece of paper.

"If you need a taxi again, here is my telephone number. My name is Vartkes."

She put on the teapot to boil and stepped out on the balcony. A young woman came down the outside stairs, leading a boy by the hand. The boy carried a tin box. A car stopped in front of the building. A uniformed man jumped out and saluted the woman. She and the boy disappeared down the street.

Suddenly, Lynn heard two bangs coming from the back of the apartment. Seconds later, there was another bang. The apartment consisted of a large living room, a den, a kitchen and a bedroom in the rear. She placed her ear against the back wall of the bedroom and listened. There were no more bangs.

She locked the apartment door, leaving Byron to keep an eye on things. Along the street, the walls were covered with proclamations and hand-painted portraits of Nasser. Four blocks away, she found a cinder-block structure with a sign that read: "Andeel's Supermarket." A young man in an Orioles cap stood at the door, inviting people in.

The store was filled with noisy locals, nervously shopping by candlelight. She was told that the generator was out of gasoline. The smell of rotting fish turned her stomach. She purchased a bottle of Evian water, a few cans of tuna for herself and Byron, and a copy of *The Daily Star*.

"Excuse me, madam," someone said in decent English. "Can I help carry the groceries?"

It was the young man in the Orioles cap.

She smiled and told him she could manage by herself, but he insisted. He said that his name was Usamah, and that he was a freshman at the American University. Since the university was temporarily closed, he was working at Andeel's. On the way, he asked why she was in Beirut. She told him that she was covering the war for the *The London Times*.

When they reached the apartment, she tipped him with a Lebanese five-pound note. He thanked her and told her he could be reached at the store, "should you need anything."

Byron waited at the door, mewing for food. After devouring a can of tuna, he went to sleep on the balcony.

She joined him outside to read the paper. She gazed at the headline: "Presidential Palace Attacked. President Chamoun Safe." She thought about her mission, which was to kill Rustom, the head of a Moslem militia group. She wondered about the mysterious noises she'd heard.

"Come, Byron," she said. "We're going for a little walk."

In order to reach the back of the building, she had to cross a natural barrier of overgrown grasses threaded with morning glory that surrounded a clearing. There was one big wall, and a low window, closed off with cement. There was also a rusty door guarded by a youth in blue jeans. He sat on a chair, snoring, his face hidden under a newspaper. The butt of a pistol stuck out of his back pocket. Her heart sounded in her ears.

Perhaps Boulos was behind that door. She could shout his name, but didn't because of the guard. She went back to her apartment and once more listened at the back wall. There were no noises.

THAT NIGHT, the sound of artillery woke her. The shelling seemed to be coming from the Christian side. It was answered with a barrage of rockets. This sound she'd heard before.

After the next salvo, the building lost its electric power. She heard steps outside her door, one discreet tap, then another. Carefully, she opened it. The beam of her flashlight caught the distorted features of Usamah, the young man from the store. He whispered that he had information that could make both of them a lot of money. He knew where a kidnapped man was being held and was prepared to show her.

Something did not sound right. She told him that she needed time to contact the home office.

"You must come right now," he said. "This prisoner is constantly being moved."

She told him she was going to call her boss, and began to close the door. Usamah shoved his foot in the way, pulled out a gun and placed it against her temple.

"Come with me. Quickly."

A cold sweat trickled down her spine as she thought of her husband, Boulos. Six months before, while on a night mission with eight of his men, he had been ambushed. The next day, they'd found eight mutilated bodies, but no trace of Boulos. Later, there had been rumors that he was held hostage. She started to shiver. Horrible scenes she had read about came back to her, but this time, it was her own dead body she saw dumped with tens of others on the banks of Nahr Ibrahim.

Usamah made her walk three short blocks to an apartment building. The entrance was narrow. He released his grip and pushed her in. She heard the sound of a rat scurrying past, followed by a familiar meow. Usamah followed her in.

From above, Byron suddenly landed on Usamah's head, puffing and clawing. The man tried to fight, but the cat snarled and refused to let go. She kicked Usamah in the groin, and the gun fell on the floor. She picked it up and pointed it at him.

She tied his shirt around his mouth and took him to the rear of the apartment building. She opened a door, walked down a few steps and reached the bottom of the elevator shaft. Using his belt, she fastened his hands to a metal pipe. It would be a while before anyone found him.

As she got near her apartment, she slowed her pace. Byron, who had been following her, slowed down.

"Thanks," she said to the cat.

THE NEXT morning, she woke up at seven. Somewhere, a loudspeaker was broadcasting taped chants of the Moslem morning prayer. The woman from upstairs came with her son.

"I am Madame Rustom and this is my son Antar," she said proudly.

"What a darling boy," Lynn said, playing with his shiny black hair.

The boy opened the tin box and offered her an expended machine gun shell.

"Thank you," Lynn said.

Inside the box were four more spent bullets and two large artillery shell fragments.

"He collects them," Madame said, "and exchanges them with his friends. Antar, stop bothering the lady and leave us alone for a few minutes."

Rustom was here, Lynn thought, the man the Commander wanted dead. Should she complete her mission or disobey the Commander's orders and keep looking for her husband?

Meanwhile, Madame noticed a brass amulet on the wall. It was in the shape of a cat's eye.

"What a nice souvenir."

"It's from Damascus," Lynn said, back in the conversation.

"Do you know the origin of this kind of amulet?"

"No."

"In ancient times, Arab warriors used to wear them into battle, believing they provided protection from harm."

Lynn smiled.

Madame expressed her admiration for the style of Lynn's clothes. She tried to find out which part of England she was from, if it rained there, and why she had come to Lebanon. Lynn told her she was a reporter.

"Very important work," Madame said, showing a beautiful set of teeth. "Come, Antar. We must go."

The boy closed the tin box, in spite of Byron's curiosity about its contents.

Madame shook Lynn's hand, and wished her a pleasant stay.

Lynn waited for them to depart, and made a telephone call to Vartkes.

Next, she had a cup of tea outside. A man in his mid-thirties stood on the upstairs balcony, and waved in the direction of Madame and her son.

Lynn recalled the information of the Mossad agent. Boulos and his men had been ambushed by Rustom. That man probably still held her husband.

Madame and her son disappeared around the corner. Byron became agitated, and went looking for the tin box.

"Come back, Byron," Lynn said. "Back here, Byron."

Interested, Rustom craned his neck over the ledge.

"Miss," he said, "why do you bother with this useless cat?

Many of us are so poor we can't feed our children, while you foreigners have money to throw away on pets."

He pulled out a machine gun and sprayed a hail of bullets in the direction where Byron had disappeared.

"You bloody bastard," she said, her hands on her ears.

"Anyone who starves our people will be treated this way," he said, putting a new clip in his weapon.

She uselessly looked for something to throw.

He laughed and went back into his apartment.

She returned to the rear of the building, and hid in the grass. The youth in jeans was taking a stroll. She threw a pebble a small distance away. The young man pulled out his gun and came to investigate. As he passed in front of her, she stuck out her foot and tripped him. He hit the ground head first, losing the gun. He lay there, moaning softly. She knocked him unconscious with the gun, and used his handkerchief to tie his hands behind his back.

In his pocket she found a key. It opened the rusty door. The only furniture inside the filthy room was a bare metal bed. The smell of urine assaulted her. After she got used to the dark, she saw a thin man lying on the bed. He had a long black beard.

"Boulos?" she said.

There was no answer.

"I am Lynn, your wife."

She came closer and touched his face. She felt his warm tears on her fingers. Slowly, she took him into her arms and helped him stand up. He took a couple of slow steps toward the door. She ordered the whimpering youth to come in, tied him to a post, and filled his mouth with a piece of towel.

"We'll stop here for a moment," she said, opening her apartment door. "To see if Byron is back."

Aziz yanked her gun away, and pulled her inside.

"We were sitting here, waiting for you," Rustom said.

He pointed to Boulos.

"You know him?"

Slowly, she pushed Boulos near where Rustom was standing. She was only a few feet from Aziz.

Rustom asked Aziz for her gun, and pointed to something on the balcony.

"I don't like cats," he said. "Didn't I tell you to get rid of it?" Byron stood immobile on the ledge. Rustom fired at him. Apparently hit, the cat opened his mouth, flailed the air with his paws and fell on his back.

Boulos's face regained some color, his eyes started to blink. He looked around, finally fixing his gaze on Rustom.

Once more, Rustom aimed the weapon at Byron. Boulos jumped from behind, grabbed Rustom's throat and dragged him to the floor. In spite of violent efforts to free himself, Rustom's face was starting to turn violet. His gun went off.

Blood covered Aziz's face and he slowly went down. Lynn took his gun.

Again, Rustom's hand went up in the air, his finger on the trigger. He would fire in her direction, but she calmly shot him in the chest.

HOLDING BOULOS, she slowly reached the street.

"Poor Byron," she said, crying.

Vartkes was waiting for them in his cab. The Mercedes started to shake and bounce over the torn pavement. Suddenly, Vartkes stopped the taxi and stepped out to open the door. Like a small furry ghost covered with blood and dust, Byron limped in and took his place on the back seat.

CLOUD STALKING MICE

Bruce Holland Rogers

Rev. John J. Tiller
Baker City, Oregon
Eighth of September 1899

Rev. W. C. Harris
Oregon City, Oregon

MY DEAR BROTHER in Christ,

You have inquired about my health, and I confess that I am not well. Mary will scarcely let me out of the house except to conduct services. Walking exhausts me, and she says that my face goes purple when I have done no more than cross the room to poke the fire. Long gone are the days when I could count the miles of wilderness walked as well as the scores of souls saved. There are not many miles left in these legs. Even my days as pastor of this church cannot number very greatly.

Bishop Golden was present in Baker City for the Sabbath just past, and he told my congregation that they were fortunate to walk alongside me as I took my last steps toward Home. "There are no heroes like the heroes of the cross," he said, "and no pioneers like the pioneers who brought salvation into the wilderness."

I hope that my flock took comfort in those words. As for me, I find myself without the sure consolation I once had. I do have a cat. He sits upon my lap as I pen these words, and his purring comforts me more than anything the bishop might say. But he is an earthly comfort, and therefore wanting.

I am in despair, William, for the sake of justice.

There are two puzzles that I recently sought to solve. In the first instance, I revealed a murderer. In the second instance, I wrestled with a celestial mystery, one that I had rather left unexamined. Its unwinding has been like the unraveling of a garment that once warmed me.

Were you here, I know that you would demand to know the particulars of my desolation. Then you would endeavor to apply chapter and verse to the wound, and by the Word, heal me. But William, it is by the Word that I am wounded. Raised up, yes, saved from the eternal grave, yes, but wounded also.

This despair of mine has come in stages. In stages, then, will I relate it.

I

You know that I held camp meetings at the Klamath Indian Mission some years ago, but I do not think I ever spoke to you of the experience. From a rude pulpit erected under the pine trees, I held services for some eight hundred red men and women. A Christian Indian was my interpreter. I took as my text the Decalogue, laying God's law before them. I emphasized the "Six days shalt thou labor," for Indian men are especially prone to idleness. I told them also that many white people were not Christians because they themselves were too lazy. I then commenced to unfold for them the Day of Judgment, to describe its terrors. All of this was conveyed with great effectiveness by my interpreter.

In any camp meeting, I have always felt an exultation when, calling all who desired to become Christians to come forward, I should find large numbers prostrate before me and crying for God's mercy. Yet how much more it meant to me when the

Indians' petitions to our Father were answered by their conversions. How they rejoiced, these simple children of nature!
Over one hundred were baptized on that first occasion.

I was never seized with the conviction that I ought to go as
a missionary to Africa, but my experience with the Indians did
produce a similar conviction that I must strive to Christianize
the colored races whenever I encountered them in Oregon.

Thus it should not surprise you to learn that when the last
Conference appointed me pastor to this Baker City church, I
proceeded to study the Chinese residents of the town. There
had once been a great many of them here to build the railroad,
and no small number remained as prospectors or laborers. Now
there were more white settlers here than previously, and the
Chinese were not so much needed for their labor. Such is no
doubt the case in all of Oregon, and in the whole of the country, since the law will not permit more of them to enter. By the
time I had come to Baker City, many had already returned to
China. The rest were expected to return before too long. If I
could effect conversions among them, this might effectively be
my missionary work to China, for they would take the Gospel
with them on their journey home.

But the obstacles to their conversion were considerable. I
spoke not a word of Chinese, and most of them spoke English
but poorly. Also, my experience among the Klamath had
taught me how necessary is the lever of a first conversion. My
interpreter did more than reshape my words to the Indian
tongue. He demonstrated by the example of himself that an
Indian could live by God's laws and know salvation.

For the object of my ministrations I chose a Chinaman
called Kong-Cheong. He suited my purposes well on both
counts. First, he had learned to read, write, and speak clear
English. Second, he was a doctor to the Chinese, well-
respected among them. If I could bring him to Christ, I was
assured that many other Chinese would follow.

I first went out to his cabin to engage him in conversation

and ascertain what he knew of scripture. It was the springtime, and Baker City's streets were thawing to mud. The slope I must climb outside the town was much the same. My boots were heavy with muck and pine needles by the time I reached the stand of trees where the Chinaman's cabin stood. Though I had come slowly, the effort had exhausted me. I labored like a bellows to get enough air.

There was yet a chill to the days, so I was surprised to find the cabin door standing open. No sooner did I arrive at the doorway than Kong appeared in his quilted jacket. Before I had caught my breath to make my introduction, he took me by the elbow and peered up into my face. After a solemn moment, he said, "Too much heat. Your heart, I think it is." Then he leaned forward, as if to listen to my wheezing or smell my breath. Taking my wrist, he felt my pulse for some moments. "Yes," he concluded, "it is certainly your heart."

This made a curious greeting and introduction. All the more surprising, his diagnosis agreed with that of my own white doctor.

"For this," the Chinaman continued, "you must encourage the kidneys. Kidneys rule the heart, and water cools the fire. Come in. Come in." He led me to a rough bench where he bade me sit down. Bending over a table at the back of his cabin, he asked me questions. How often did I pass water? Did I often eat salty foods? Bitter? Pungent?

He began to advise me as to changes in my diet while he assembled dried plants from which I was to brew an infusion. Only when he went to write in his ledger did he ask my name. Without any conscious decision to do so, I had become one of Kong-Cheong's patients.

"I am of meager means," I told him, "and barely able to afford the physician I already have."

"Do not worry for that," he said. "Pay when you can."

I remembered my purpose enough to ask him what he knew of God and holy scripture. He gave me a curious answer. "Look there," he said, pointing to a corner where a white cat lay napping. The animal was tethered by a length of string to a table leg, as was the custom among the Chinese. "There is all the book a wise man needs."

"The cat?"

"Or as easy a bird could be the book. Or a stone."

I thought perhaps some misunderstanding of speech would explain his remarks. "I am speaking of a special book," I said. "I mean the Bible, God's word."

"Words are written in all things," he answered. He brought out a stool and sat before me. "How can one separate a maker from what is made? How would you know your God if you do not look all around?"

"By His word, the Holy Bible," I said, "which is His revelation."

"Perhaps it is," Mr. Kong said. "So is my cat a revelation."

I detected no impiety in his manner and perceived that we had entered into a debate. I decided that we had made a promising start, and I launched from that beginning to an explanation of sin and redemption. I told him of the terrors of judgment and of the personal salvation he could enjoy in Christ. He listened. I could not have misread the interest written upon his face. But at the end he said, "Good and bad are like this: No man is all saved or all damned. Everyone is some of each. How can you separate the sun side of a mountain from the shadow side?"

Pleased to think of so apt an answer and feeling the influence of the Holy Spirit in my words, I said, "The light of Christ shines on both sides of your mountain. By Him is the shade made glorious light."

"Then the shadows are beneath," Kong said, shaking his head. "All aspects are two." In that same moment, I found that Kong's cat was staring at me. The fixity of the animal's green gaze unnerved me.

I looked away from the animal. As I thought of what answer

to give Kong-Cheong, he said, "Forgive me, Mr. Reverend
Tiller. I must go today to see the son of Mr. Halbower, and
then I have appointments in Sumpter. Come tomorrow, if you
wish. Early. Do not neglect to take tea, three times. Drink
water. We must give your kidneys strength to cool the heart."
Then he ushered me to the door.

II

Although I have been blessed with good results in leading
camp revivals, I confess that such revivals were not my favorite
means for winning souls. I am sorry to see the Conference
lately preferring the public shout of revivals to the close
whisper of class-meetings. That many are saved at a camp
meeting I know very well, but of those many converts, how
many will be lost again at the first shadow of doubt? In class-
meetings with a few wayward souls, the preacher is better able
to show the road and the converts are better able to keep it.
One whose step falters will more readily find a Christian hand
to steady him in the class-meeting.

More than that. I miss the class-meeting for the nearness of
the sinners I would save. Class-meetings were conversations.
Revivals are exhortation only. In short, I miss knowing so well
the souls I endeavored to bring to God.

I tell you this to explain why I found myself going almost
every day to the Chinaman's little cabin. Our conversations
recalled the satisfactions of my early ministry, at least in form.
In substance, I was much more successful even in my earliest,
most awkward attempts to preach the gospel than I was in my
efforts to convert Kong-Cheong.

Chief among his beliefs was the dual nature of things. Light
he twinned with darkness, damp with dry, hot with cold, and if
I am not mistaken, good with wickedness. In this last matter,
he was not inclined to give direct answers to my inquiries. "A
man should serve as it is his place to serve," he might say, or

"Rain is good for the earth, but the fire does not love it." His medical opinions ran to the same dualities: too much damp injured the spleen, too much dryness injured the kidneys. When I turned our conversations to the Deity, Kong would sometimes suck on his little pipe and say only, "That is all," by which he meant I know not what. My efforts to draw him out on the matter produced strange questions. Why was it necessary for God to precede creation? Weren't they the same thing?

Most assuredly they were not! I gave him Genesis, but this moved him not at all. He seemed little moved by any words of scripture, or by any proof I gave him that the Bible was God's true word and covenant.

At another time in my life, I might have given up and taken the seed of my evangelism to more fertile ground. Now, however, I made myself fast to Kong's cause. I reminded myself that making a Christian of this man could be a first step in the salvation of countless Chinese souls. And as I have said, I enjoyed our conversations as if they were class-meetings. Besides, I was supernumerary in my service to the Baker City church. My duties were light and left me time to pursue Kong's salvation without fear that my attentions were needed somewhere else.

Kong's medical attentions coincided with God's mercy, and I began to recover my health. I drank the teas he prescribed for me and did certain exercises he taught: swinging my arms a certain way, rubbing my kidneys, describing circles with my hands and suchlike. I did them indoors. Kong said I must have fresh air as I practiced his "chee gong," but Mary overruled, declaring such an out-of-doors display unseemly. Though my physician in Baker City doubted the efficacy of the Chinaman's medicines, he did pronounce me much improved.

Kong and I traded other talk. He extracted from me tales of my life as an Idaho miner and the story of that Cayuse Indian who saved me in a snowstorm. From him I had stories of his family and the famines in China. He told me, too, of his various patients, Chinese and white, and the puzzles their ailments provided. For poisoned blood, ranchers and miners were more apt to call on Kong than on the white doctors in Sumpter or Baker City. Kong often cured it, and he never amputated. Furthermore, he practiced by mail when he could not travel to his patients and they were too ill to come to him. They would describe their symptoms in a letter, and he would send medicine by return post. "That is not best," he told me of prescribing without an examination, "but sometimes it is necessary."

I learned, too, that the name of his white cat was Cloud Stalking Mice. "He moves like this," Kong said, moving his own shoulders in slow circles, stopping, moving again. "He teaches me a new chee gong, I think."

With the arrival of summer, Kong and I moved our discussions outside, sitting in the shade of pine trees. The Chinaman sometimes tied a weight around his cat's neck and brought him out with us, trusting the encumbrance to keep Cloud from roaming far. In China, he explained, not even the male cats strayed from home. They were too useful to lose. He was surprised that cats were not similarly treasured here.

Kong's conversion still did not progress. I had much hope for him, as he was a deliberate and thoughtful man. But that frustrated hope produced in me a state of growing agitation and despair. How often have we seen it that some sinner hesitates in the question of faith, then of a sudden dies before he is enlisted with Christ? My passion to save Kong grew stronger. More than Christian duty moved me. I began to fear for him as I would for a friend.

III

One day as Kong and I sat talking beneath the pines, three black-tailed does made their way from the brush into the clear. We paused in our conversation to watch them as they browsed.

They took no particular notice of us nor of the white cat resting at Kong's feet. At first.

Then Cloud roused himself, stretched from tongue to tail, and walked lazily toward the cabin, which brought him, as if by coincidence, nearer to the deer. The does raised their heads to watch him, them recommenced their browsing. The cat seemed not at all interested in them, and they were not interested in the cat.

But as he neared the cabin and had the cover of some brush between him and the deer, a change came over Cloud Stalking Mice. He lowered his body so close to the ground that the weight tied to his neck dragged across the fallen pine needles. With his gaze fixed on the does, he crept slowly toward them. Little vibrations shook his body and were exaggerated in his tail.

This change in the cat did not go unnoticed by the deer. All three raised their heads. Their noses twitched, and the legs of all three began ever so slightly to tremble. They knew they were being stalked. The creature that had seemed unimportant to them a moment ago was now terrible to them.

Cloud Stalking Deer crept forward just an inch more, and the does bolted. I laughed and admitted my surprise that the deer would perceive Kong's little mouser a threat to them.

Kong did not laugh. He sucked on his pipe, then said, "There is a lesson in the affairs of men," he said, "and perhaps in the ways of heaven as well."

I asked what he could mean by this, and he answered that he did not know, that he would have to ponder the matter.

IV

One of Kong's neighbors was a man known by the name of J. T. Smith, or Old Smith. I had never seen the fellow, though I knew of him from the speculative talk in town. He was very jealous of trespassers and was liable to meet them with rifle in hand, eager to educate them upon the matter of his property rights.

Smith's notion of those rights did not correspond with any recorded deed. Nor had he registered a mining claim, though some of the speculation about him conjectured a small deposit of gold on "his" property since he occasionally bought supplies with the yellow dust. Such a mine was unlikely. There was no stream through Smith's territory, nor any water except what could be drawn from a well, and a man cannot work a deposit without plentiful water.

It was supposed by some that Smith earned his gold from miners at Sumpter. They came to Baker City sometimes for supplies, owing to the high prices in Sumpter. But if Old Smith rendered them some service, none of them ever spoke to reveal its nature.

I chanced to be present when Smith presented himself and his rifle at the doorway of Kong's cabin. At first, I did not know who he was, this big white-bearded man who had stumbled in upon us, gray locks matted against his sweaty forehead. His face was bright red. I perceived a pistol worn on his hip. But then I guessed his identity.

Smith seemed hardly to notice I was there. He pointed his rifle at Kong and said, "I need doctoring."

Kong regarded the gun with calm. "Better you don't shoot me if you need a doctor," he said.

"Just you get me some medicine," Smith said. "I got the bad chills." His hands trembled. "Understand? You give me medicine plenty hurry. You plenty hurry, Chinaman. You plenty hurry or you plenty sorry."

At this point I interjected my opinion that Mr. Smith should sit down and submit himself to Kong's examination. Smith swung the gun in my direction and said, "What I got is the *chills*. I know better than him what I got!" But at last he did sit down and permit Kong to take his pulses and give him a tea to drink.

In the end, Kong and I both helped Smith back to his cabin where he became delirious with his fever, alternately thanking and berating Kong and sometimes seeming to speak to persons not actually present. The cabin was an arsenal, containing an additional rifle, a shotgun, and, upon Smith's rough night table, a derringer. Skins and feathers testified to Smith's success as a hunter, and I wondered if he might not simply earn his mysterious gold by this means.

As night approached, Kong stayed to attend to Smith while I returned to Baker City. Smith apparently recovered his health, for in the following weeks, Kong said nothing about him.

V

My acquaintance with Kong-Cheong might have long continued, even unto his eventual conversion, save for the intervention of just such unhappy circumstance as I might have feared. By which I mean to say that he was murdered.

I learned of his death from the Chinaman who brought me Kong's cat. In sentences of one or two words, he conveyed to me the news of Kong's killing and made me understand that Kong had desired me to have Cloud. I do not know when or how Kong had communicated this wish. Perhaps the Chinese who saw to his affairs had found none among their number who would take the cat. At any rate, Kong's killing made Cloud Stalking Mice my inheritance and remembrance.

The murder of Chinamen is not common here, but it happens more frequently than the assassination of white men. The Chinese of Baker City know that to be found on the streets after dark is to invite the sport of cowboys and other rough fellows. And there have been a few massacres which you may recall. Some years ago, seven men killed a score of Chinese miners on the Snake River and took their gold.

Watching the cat, who returned my gaze with his own

strange stare, I reflected on my failings. Kong-Cheong had died unredeemed when I might perhaps have been less conversational and more exhortative in my efforts for him. I pondered also the wickedness of my fellow men, that we should shoot dead one of our yellow brethren who was a gentle healer, and just when he was first becoming acquainted with the gospel! The injustice of it gnawed at my brain. I could not cease from brooding upon the matter. I even made inquiries of the sheriff, who could tell me only that Kong had been shot twice in the back of the head outside of his own cabin and that the identity of his killer was unknown. He expressed the opinion that the Chinese often settled their differences among themselves and that the killer might never be known.

Again I remind you, William, as I wish I had reminded myself, that earthly judgment is not properly our task. Yet I thought I must do something for Kong. I must make some gesture in his memory. I determined, after my interview with the sheriff, that I would myself find the killer out.

VI

I conceived a theory regarding the murder. I knew that Kong carried some of his patients on credit, for he had done so with me. Thus, a patient owing a substantial sum might have a motive for erasing his debt. From the Chinaman who had brought me Kong's cat, I secured an accounting from Kong's ledger, showing what debts were owed, and by whom.

Interviewing former patients, both Chinese and white, was the work of some days. Kong's practice, and the debts owed to him, were widespread. But the miles I must walk seemed to strengthen, rather than exhaust me.

I continued to take the tea which Kong had prescribed for me, and I began to practice my "chee gong" exercises just as he'd told me to, out of doors, in fresh air. Mary protested daily that the neighbors must think me very queer. But I persisted.

In the course of my investigation, I met a Belgian miner called Heuse who had suffered pleurisy, a rancher called Halbower whose son had suffered a wasting fever, and an Irishman named McBride who credited Kong with saving his arm from the surgeon's saw. And others, among them assorted Chinese. They were nearly unanimous in their esteem for the departed Dr. Kong. The two exceptions, Mr. Kenyon and Mr. Sweet, felt Kong's cures to be ineffective, but they had neither incurred debts nor suffered debilitations sufficient, in my opinion, to engender murderous passions.

For all my efforts, I did not uncover even one definite suspect. At last I made a foray into the camp of Mr. J. T. Smith, but the whole of my interview consisted of my greeting him at the door of his cabin and receiving, at gunpoint, his invitation to "Clear out."

It was at this juncture that the Chinaman who had brought the cat came to me again with a small bundle of papers. These had been found among Kong's possessions, and since I had taken an interest in Dr. Kong's affairs, perhaps I would know what to do about these.

The papers were promissory notes and demand drafts against accounts in the Baker City Bank. Some were years old. I thought at first that Kong may not have understood how to present the drafts at the bank, but, no, the bank employees knew him. They affirmed that they had settled paper demands on his behalf.

William, I pursued my investigation along this new line and found no suspects, but proof instead of something else. Who had written these demands that were never presented? Mrs. Wilbur, who was widowed. Mr. Addams, whose only daughter had the polio. Others, whose travails I knew from my pastoral work. Their accounts in Kong's ledger showed them owing him nothing. He'd kept the demands and notes, but I do not think he ever meant to collect them. I advised burning them.

I knew Kong better than ever, but I did not know his killer.

In memory, I revisited some of the pleasant hours I had
spent with Kong. With Cloud Stalking Mice watching me
from his place near the stove, I thought of how the cat had
seemed a very mountain lion to those three deer. That is when
I conceived a motive for the murder.

VII

I laid my reasoning before the sheriff, but he gave it a skepti-
cal audience. "Well then," I said, "what if we were to test the
matter and see whether or not there is some truth to my sup-
posings?" He replied that he should like to know what test I
proposed.

So it was that I found myself again approaching the cabin of
the well-armed Mr. Smith. I wheezed a grateful prayer as I
spied him at his wood pile, ax in hand and no guns in sight.
Providence might not after all require that I be shot in order to
prove my conjecture, though the ax gave me a moment of
disquiet. He swung it with considerable vigor for a man his
age.

"Brother Smith," I hailed him when I caught my breath, "I
must have a word with you."

He looked up from his labors, startled by my voice. Then he
squinted. "I got nothing to say to nobody," he said. "You clear
out of here."

I approached, but not too close. "You must hear me," I said.
"I am worried for your sake."

"You're what?" He leaned on his ax handle to consider me.

"The man who killed that Chinaman, Kong, is in mortal
danger," I said. "Justice is at hand. I fear for that man. I pray
that he will make his peace with God and ask forgiveness, lest
he meet his maker unrepentant."

"What's that got to do with me?" Smith asked, but I did not
give any plain answer. Instead I kept at my appeal for his
salvation and asked if he would not clear his soul. Was there

anything he wanted to tell me by way of confession? Would he prepare his soul for judgment?

"Just what are you going on about?" Smith said.

I said, "Certain facts, once discovered, must in time be laid before the sheriff."

"What facts?" He stood straight now and hefted the ax.

Of course I did not know. I had not myself discovered whatever it was that Kong had found out, either by hearing Smith's ravings when he was delirious with fever, or perhaps by finding some clue within Smith's cabin.

"Does it matter what facts condemn a man?" I said. "I would have you know the fact by which your soul may be saved! I would have you enlist yourself with Christ before it is too late!"

Smith's face had reddened. "Damn you, what facts? What have you told the sheriff?"

"I've given him no proof of anything," I answered honestly, "for a man's soul is my first concern."

"So you think you know something what will hang me?"

"I know you must ask God for mercy."

"But you ain't told. You ain't told nobody."

"Will you accept your Redeemer? Will you get down on your knees with me to pray?"

"You're a damn fool," Smith said. He advanced with his ax and made ready to swing at my head.

A gunshot rang out. Smith stopped short of my assassination and looked to where the sheriff had emerged from his cover.

What evidence had we of Smith's culpability in the Chinaman's death? None. The sheriff had not heard all of the words that passed between me and Smith. All he had seen was the murderous rage that I had predicted, and that was enough to convince him that Smith's possessions should be searched, as I had urged.

What is it but consciousness of his own sin that possesses a criminal to save a record of his misdeeds, even when that record has nearly trapped him before? Such a man is ripe for conversion, whether he knows it or not.

Among Smith's possessions were papers related to the discharge from the Union Army of one J. T. Canfield. So was his real name discovered. Along with these papers was a clipping from the Walla Walla *Statesman* which detailed the deathbed statement of Robert McMillan. He had been one of the gunmen in the Snake River massacre of twenty-one Chinese miners, and he named his companions in the crime. These were Bruce Evans, Mat LaRue, Frank Vaughn, Hiram Maynard, Carl Hughes, and J. T. Canfield. Also among Canfield's belongings was an ivory knife that was obviously of oriental manufacture. Likewise an enameled mirror.

Now you will perhaps think that I had found Canfield out by an unlikely entrapment, and you would be right except for one thing: I was but inviting him to repent himself.

The deer had known Kong's cat to be harmless until at some moment they sensed a change in him. By his alteration, by his attempt to conceal his interest in the deer, he had instead excited their anxiety.

While treating Canfield, Kong must have made some discovery that made him suspicious. And Canfield, sensing a change, began to fear Kong. And killed him. As he would have killed me.

VIII

I made pastoral visits to Mr. Canfield in the Baker City jail. I urged him to confess and repent. He said to me, "You know what happened up in Enterprise, preacher? They caught three of the men that was supposedly with me on the Snake River. They stood them up on trial. And the jury acquitted every last one."

Then he said, "If I kilt anyone, and I ain't saying I did, the ones kilt was Chinamen."

I feared it might be true that no jury would convict a white man. I feared also that Canfield would not repent his sins and accept heaven's embrace.

IX

I have told you, William, that I have of late been in dark despair. But it is not for the lack of earthly justice. James Thomas Canfield was found guilty of the murder of Kong-Cheong and was sentenced soon after to hang. Canfield might have been right that a white jury would not convict a white man for the death of Chinese miners. But a jury of white patients, or the kin of patients, might convict a white man for the death of their Chinese doctor, even on the weight of circumstantial evidence.

You will think, then, that my despair may come for the loss of Canfield's soul. But Canfield was not lost. After his conviction, I continued to visit him in his cell. I urged him, as his fatal appointment neared, to be conscious of the hand that God reached down to him. I preached the terrors of judgment to him as I had never preached them before. Bit by bit, he achieved his Justification, grew aware of his sinful nature, and was touched by the merciful forgiveness of our Lord. He was lifted up by operation of the Holy Spirit! I knew with certainty that he knew the joys of regeneration, for his face was bathed in the light of glory, and he himself declared how the light had broken into his soul. We sang hymns together.

For him everything was changed. Everything, except that he must still meet his appointment with the noose.

In Canfield's company, I felt the force of his conversion, but away from him, I wrestled with a mystery. Why should Kong-Cheong, who had never wronged any man I heard of, suffer judgment and torment for his sins while Canfield, who was a murderer many times over, was redeemed?

I have never believed, as you have, that God might save

some by their good works. Who has said His mercy is infinite has not read scripture. Matthew 18:3. Luke 13:3. *Except* ye be converted. *Except* ye repent.

Briefly, I conjectured to doubt the Holy Bible. What if God might show mercies not therein described? But if the Bible is not the fullness of revelation, what seals the Covenant?

Nothing can. Without the certainty that scripture is complete and true, there can be no ground for faith to stand upon.

The Bible cannot contain God full and entire, but it contains His word. We have our contract with Him. By that can we know him. What then, must I conclude from what my heart told me, that it was not justice if Canfield and Kong could not *both* be saved?

X

At Canfield's request, I stood with him on the gallows. The executioner had covered Canfield's head, so that we spoke our partings through the black cloth. I soothed him with prayer and with scripture, though all the while my heart tripped and stammered. I was out of breath from mounting the scaffold steps, and no doubt my heart pounded for the fatality of the event. Also, I was thinking troubled thoughts. All mortal men had offended God, and none was deserving of salvation. Only by mercy were a few redeemed, not by justice. But who was God that He should count so little the ministrations of men to one another, and so greatly their acknowledgment of Him?

Canfield, though his face was shrouded in black cloth, radiated the light of his redemption. "I go to Him now! Praise God! Praise Jesus!" He trembled. I do think he trembled with joy.

XI

I have taught Cloud Stalking Mice to sit upon my lap. His purr soothes me even as his strange gaze continues to agitate my soul. In these, my last days, he gives me some earthly consolation. Yet he troubles me, too. I watch him mousing. Some prey he tortures, then dispatches. Others, he lets go. But he knows nothing of them. They are just mice.

I have long since exhausted my supply of medicinal herbs. In Kong's absence there is no one who knows how to resupply me. I have even abandoned the "chee gong" exercises.

William, I have taken a backward step from the ladder of Sanctification you and I first mounted together in younger days. I do not think to be perfected in love. To the ledger of my sins we may add my thoughts of late, but even those will be washed away in forgiveness. I do not despair of my salvation, but of what salvation must be.

By many names is He known. One might be Cloud Stalking Men. I may look upon Him and know ere you read this.

I wish I could rejoice in that.

In His Name,

John J. Tiller

Cat O'Nine Lives

Jan Grape

BULLDOG PORTER, ONE of the finest defense attorneys in the state of Texas, had sent enough business to G & G Investigations to save our bacon more than once. Actually, the first case he sent saved us because the ensuing publicity made our telephones jingle. It seemed only fitting that my partner, C.J. Gunn, and I give Bulldog a party to celebrate his eightieth birthday.

Bulldog's birthday is on All Hallow's Eve and we held an open house in our office in the LaGrange Building in Austin that afternoon. The party turned into a huge success, but finally only our "family circle" remained, enjoying one last cup of coffee and rehashing the fun we'd had. The "family circle" consisted of C.J., Larry Hays, Bulldog and his secretary, Maudie Mae, and myself.

Me? I'm Jenny Gordon, a Private Investigator. Yes and no. Yes, like Magnum, P.I., and no, I usually don't solve cases with my fists, or in an hour's time either.

Larry is currently a lieutenant in the Austin Police Department's homicide unit. He and my late husband, Tommy Gordon, were police cadets together, and partners and best friends. Now he's my closest male friend and likes to be thought of as my big brother. He stands six four and his sandy blond hair and hazel eyes do little to identify his Swedish heritage. His blockhead stubbornness takes care of that.

Maudie is a lovely lady in her late sixties with silver hair and big brown eyes behind her bifocals. She has been Bulldog's secretary almost from the beginning of his practice, and I know for a fact that she's been in love with him for years. Bulldog never acknowledges her affection, or else has chosen to ignore it. Or at least that is my impression.

"Jenny, are you going to ask him?" C.J. wanted to know. My partner's first name is Cinnamon but she prefers to be called C.J. If it were left up to me I'd call her Nefertiti because when she gets that haughty look on her cola-nut face she looks exactly like the Egyptian queen. At six feet tall in her stocking feet, she is statuesque and moves with a panther's grace. A Rice University graduate, she's been a high-fashion model and a policewoman before moving back to Texas and going into business with me.

"Ask me what?" Bulldog looked tired but happy. A spry man for his age and a little shorter than my five feet ten, he has twinkling blue eyes. His salt-and-pepper hair is only gradually turning silver, and it's still dark across his forehead where his widow's peak is most prominent.

"How you got the nickname of Bulldog?" I said.

"Well, that's a complicated story," he said.

"I would not expect anything else," said Larry. He'd been involved in cases we handled for Porter also.

"We all have time, don't we gang?" I looked at Larry, Maudie and C.J., who nodded vigorously. "Our dinner reservation isn't until eight. It's not quite six yet. Why don't you tell us."

Bulldog looked at each of our eager faces and sighed. "Oh, hell, guess it wouldn't hurt. It was during one of my first cases." He looked at Maudie. "Do you remember my cousin?"

"Liddy Mae? Of course. Nice lady. You had a big crush on her didn't you?" Maudie said.

Larry snorted and C.J. said, "King Porter in love, I don't believe it."

"Only when I was a youngster. But she *was* a special person and . . . but wait, let me start in the beginning. In 1936 a man was gunned down on one of Galveston's main streets. Everyone sure thought it was a mob hit but it wasn't really all that complicated. . . .

1936: LEVI Clardy walked out of Mr. Angelo's barbershop at twilight. He whistled a new tune that had recently caught his fancy, called "Music Goes 'Round and Around." The song, a simple novelty tune done by a couple of amiable Fifty-Second Street musicians, had scored an instant hit with the public. The song's pitch worked just right for a toneless hummer or whistler, and suited Clardy to a tee.

Clardy rounded the corner, twirling his index finger and executing a jaunty dance step as he whistled, "the music goes 'round and 'round and it comes out here." Clardy came face to face with a young girl, her red curls the same color as the brick wall. She politely moved to one side and placed her back against the barbershop wall in order for Clardy to pass.

Neither of them noticed the midnight blue Pierce-Arrow sedan coming slowly down the street. Even when the car slowed more and angled over in his direction, Clardy still didn't notice. He kept on whistling, walking past and a few steps beyond the girl. Two small "phfitt" sounds could barely be heard above the man's tune.

Levi Clardy fell. His eyes rolled back into his head and he didn't move as the big car rolled away, fast—burning rubber. The young girl screamed.

She kept screaming until Mr. Angelo, the barber, came running out to see what had caused the racket. As he came around the corner of the building, the girl looked at him wide-eyed, then turned and ran in the opposite direction. Her red curls were the last thing he saw heading around the corner.

"I don't know who she was officer," said Mr. Angelo.
"Never saw her before and probably wouldn't know her even if
I saw her again." His only memory was a skinny little girl with
red hair. Gangland hit, he thought. The less said about it the
better, he thought.

"It was too dark to see good, officer. And I don't know any
kids around here. They never come this way . . . well, maybe
some of the boys do on their way to the pier to fish or something. But I doubt she realized what happened. She thought
he's some old drunk falling in a stupor, you can bet on that."

Mr. Angelo looked across the street. "Other folks walking
over there. Maybe you should talk to them."

The policeman said Mr. Angelo needed to go to the station
house first thing in the morning and give his statement. "But
you can't leave now 'til the dicks get here and talk to you."

The homicide detectives arrived, questioned people who
had been out on the street, but no one noticed anything except that big fancy car. With no one cooperating, the police
put them all in the paddy wagon and took them downtown for
more questions.

Someone finally gave up the sedan's license number and
from that it took only a small leap to discover the car's owner
as one Seaborn Barnito, owner of the Pink Flamingo dinner
club and speakeasy.

Months later, the little girl's identity became known, but by
then everyone knew she'd been too traumatized to speak. Mattie Gillingwater had been struck mute.

1939: "YOU may quote me or quote any intelligent person
you know," King Porter said. "It's a known fact that the Maceo
brothers did not start the rackets, gentlemen. You name the
vice: gambling, the numbers, prostitution, smuggling, bootleg-
ging, rumrunning and loansharking—all of it—has always
flourished in Galveston." The young man paced back and
forth in front of his audience. His white shirt, open at the

neck, revealed a few strands of curly chest hair. Dark hair on his head formed a widow's peak at the center of his broad forehead.

Actually his total audience consisted of one large black tomcat known as Beau. The cat sat regally on a tree stump. Beau also played the part of judge, jury, and prosecuting attorney as well as the audience. The cat took his role most seriously as he yawned and blinked his eyes. He wet a paw and washed above his ear expertly then curled up for a nap.

No one questioned King's remarks and the opposing attorney voiced no objection.

After King had looked into the eyes of several imaginary jurors, he continued. "Before Texas ever became a state, gamblers poured onto Galveston Island from cities such as New Orleans, Houston, San Francisco and points both east and west. They set up tents and gambling paraphernalia on vacant lots and corners of main roads. The city Fathers drew up restrictive ordinances to suppress the games of chance but they learned quickly that restrictions of vices only makes them prosper—at least for some folks. And where is the harm? If you don't want to partake you don't have to. No one holds a gun to your head."

The young man believed so strongly in his scene that he saw all the players in his fantasy courtroom. He walked back to the apple crate masquerading as his defense table, placing himself directly behind his client. "People are going to gamble and you might as well tax it. How do you think our fair city has enough money to pay for paved streets and our excellent police and fire protection? Where does the money come from which maintains our seawall—that protects us from floods and hurricanes?"

King leaned toward his imaginary client, placing a hand upon his shoulder. "It's true that Mr. Maceo has games of chance in his nightclubs. But these are private clubs, patronized mostly by out-of-towners. He never encourages our local population to come in and lose their hard-earned money. His clubs exist purely for entertainment. He brings in the biggest and best singers and comedians in Hollywood today." He looked at each imaginary juror once again.

These men of his jury took their responsibility seriously and he intended to hold them to their oath. His client would be found innocent if a reasonable doubt existed.

He didn't call their names aloud but he knew they often took their wives to see Frank Sinatra and Bob Hope. The men met his look but kept their faces composed. He knew they understood what he meant.

"Mr. Maceo's chefs serve the finest foods and wines," he continued. "If some out-of-towner has a notion to squander a little of his vacation money on a slot machine or at a poker table, we're more than happy to let him leave it in our fair city. This is known as free enterprise, gentlemen, and it keeps our taxes lower. It may be a sin to gamble in your eyes but it's not against the law in our city."

He walked toward the imaginary jury box once again. "Gentlemen, I beg you to find my client not guilty." He turned, walked over to the defense table and sat down on his log.

There was a moment of silence before the courtroom broke out in thunderous applause. "Not guilty," the foreman of the jury shouted, and pandemonium broke out as the news reporters rushed to call in their stories.

He could visualize the morning headlines running across the top of every newspaper around the whole country. Huge black letters: JURY ACQUITS MACEO—DEFENSE ATTORNEY PORTER WINS AGAIN!

"See," King told the cat. "I told you my client would go free." Beau opened an amber eye but otherwise ignored the comment.

The sudden noise of a breaking branch startled the young man and brought Beau to his feet, alert, ears back. King jumped up, nearly falling from his log seat. When he turned, a gawky young girl, looking no more than ten or twelve, stepped out from behind a huge water-oak tree. Thick strands of Spanish moss hung down, hiding the girl somewhat in the shadows.

"You spying on me?"

She shook her head.

"What're you doing then?" he asked in a harsh tone.

She had moved a couple of steps closer to him but paused then like a fawn caught in a car's headlights. Huge tears suddenly welled up in her eyes.

At that moment he thought he recognized her as Mattie Gillingwater, the little girl who had witnessed a man being gunned down in the street when she was only ten years old. He also remembered hearing she had not spoken a word since.

Mattie's fiery red hair fell in ringlets around her lovely face and her eyes sparkled bluer than the Gulf water. A gangly thirteen year old now, he thought. All sharp angles and buck teeth, but he nevertheless recognized the girl had the makings of a real beauty. He smiled again.

"I'm sorry," he said. "I didn't mean to sound so rough. You sorta startled me."

The girl glided over to Beau and the cat jumped into her arms. King couldn't be sure, but thought her eyes reflected pleasure.

The cat's action surprised King. Beau did not suffer strangers gladly.

"That's Beau," he said. "Do you know him? He prowls around nearly every night." If the girl knew the cat it would explain why he'd went to her so readily. "He's a Halloween cat, you know. Because he was born on Halloween night."

Mattie still looked as if she thought he might be a Martian, then nodded solemnly.

"I'm not going to hurt you," he said, wanting to reassure her. "I promise, I'm not."

She snuggled her face into the cat's fur and smiled when

Beau began to purr. Her look indicated she might possibly believe him now. But only to a point.

Reluctant to say any more for fear it might jinx the mood, King didn't want to explain what he'd been doing but Mattie kept looking at him, her bright eyes unwavering until he couldn't resist their stare. "Guess you think I'm sort of weird, talking to myself and all. I'm practicing a summation to a jury. This scene is acting out a real court case."

King continued. "I have my first law exam tomorrow. It will be both a written and oral one. I'm taking law at the University of Texas over at Austin. Practicing keeps me from being so nervous."

She shrugged and gave him a tiny twitch of her lips that may have been a smile.

Just as King began to think she might accept his explanation, she placed Beau back on his tree stump, turned quickly and walked back into and through the moss.

"Mattie. Wait."

But she was gone.

KING HAD opened a minuscule office in the new Santa Fe Railroad Building on Twenty-Fifth at the Strand. The appearance of prosperity helped reassure potential clients. In reality, King's small office barely held a desk, a file cabinet and a bookcase. It did offer a view of Galveston Bay from his window, although ships unloading and loading at the docks were a far cry from sandy beaches and whispering palms. King never cared much for the water and, like many born-on-the-islanders, stayed as far away as possible. The beaches and piers, whether for amusement or fishing, were only there to attract tourists as far as he was concerned.

He stayed busy, mainly with cases relating to the "vices" and an occasional bar-fight killing, but it was enough to pay the rent. As a shrewd and intelligent attorney, King managed to win acquittals for most of his clients and earned himself a reputation in only a few months. He liked to fight for the underdog but it did help when the underdog had resources and could pay the fee. And pay they did, sooner or later, even if it took weeks, because they knew King gave his all to a case and his client knew he had the expertise of an up-and-coming young attorney.

King couldn't conceal his surprise the morning his cousin, Liddy Mae, walked in, dressed to the nines in a dark-green silk dress. A black hat with a green peacock feather on it perched on her golden blonde hair. Her purse and high-heel ankle-strapped shoes were black patent leather. She removed black silk gloves before taking his hand, then placed her cheek near his face for a kiss.

King obliged and breathed in her faint gardenia fragrance. He had forgotten how lovely she was and how he'd always had a big crush on her. Not an unusual state for a young boy with a beautiful older girl cousin.

John Henry Porter, King's father, had two sisters. The younger sister, Ida Lou, had one daughter ten years older than King. The daughter, named Liddy Mae, had married Seaborn Barnito. The family disowned her afterwards because Barnito was of Italian heritage. Porter had never understood such prejudices himself.

When Seaborn had been arrested, Liddy Mae knew her family would do everything to lure her away from him. She knew her father's influence was such that she might be sent far, far away in the hope she'd forget the mistake she'd made. She knew asking him for help would attract attention to her and eventually bring his anger.

Convinced of Seaborn's innocence, she worked and saved extra money for three years just to hire a defense attorney. One day her mother, whom she'd been secretly seeing against her father's wishes, casually mentioned King. "My nephew recently read for the bar of the State of Texas and hung out his shingle." Liddy Mae had almost forgotten she had a male cousin in law school.

"Liddy Mae," he said as they sat, he behind his desk and she across from him. "It's good to see you. Are you here as a long-lost family member or are you here to talk about Seaborn?"

She nodded. "A little of both, but mostly I want to hire you to defend my husband. His trial finally comes up in a couple of months. I have a little money saved, but when my husband gets out of jail he'll be able to pay you in full."

"I wish you had come to me sooner. It won't be easy after three years to find all the witnesses and . . ." He wanted to help but felt there wasn't much he could do.

"I know. But things have been difficult." She was determined not to let him see any tears. "Just finding enough money to live on has been hard. Everything had to be signed over to his brother Addison and Addy plans to keep everything. Seb knew his brother was a donkey's behind but he just didn't know how big a one he was."

"Liddy Mae, I've heard and read about the case against Seaborn and it looks pretty cut and dried to me."

"King Porter, you just listen to me." Her grief quickly turned to anger. "Seb didn't kill nobody. When everyone else goes deer or quail hunting, he stays home. Addy and his gang makes fun of him but he doesn't let them get him down. Seaborn shot a rabbit once and was sick for a week. He still dreams about it. There's no way he could have shot a human being and if he did he'd be so sick he'd have to go to the hospital, I swear."

"But it was his car and several witnesses swore it was him doing the shooting."

"It was his car but he wasn't in it. Addy borrowed the car that day. Said he had to drive over to Texas City on some business. I don't like to point fingers but if you ask me it was Addy."

"But the brothers don't look anything alike. Aren't they half-brothers or something?"

She nodded. "They don't look alike when you see them together, but some people get mixed up when only one of them is around. I think that's what happened. When the newspapers said that car had been identified as belonging to Seaborn, then the witnesses said it was Seaborn who did the shooting."

"What proof can you offer that it wasn't Seaborn?"

"I was hoping we could get that little girl to testify. Once, when I asked her point-blank if she saw Seaborn shoot that man, she shook her head no."

"The judge isn't going to believe this child, Liddy."

"She's not a child anymore. She's already a young woman, nearly fourteen."

"But she doesn't talk—hasn't talked since that day."

"I know, but I was hoping we could come up with some doctor who could help her." Liddy, despite her good intensions, burst into tears. "I just don't know what to do or where to turn, King. You're my last hope." She cried harder.

Porter handed her his handkerchief and, when she had gotten herself back into control, he said, "I don't know any doctor . . ."

Liddy snuffled a bit, "I read about this doctor in Chicago who uses hypnosis . . ."

"Let me talk to Seaborn." Both had tried to speak at once.

"If he can convince me he's innocent," said King, "I'll search for a doctor. If there's one to be found and he agrees to come here and if Mattie Gillingwater agrees to the treatment we might have a slim chance. You understand how many ifs are involved?"

Liddy Mae said that she did.

King drove his Model-T Ford over to the county jail. It was a pleasant October day and when he signed his name, handed over his briefcase, and even when he emptied his pockets, he didn't complain. He hated being searched but he was in such a good mood he was determined to let nothing spoil the day.

When his briefcase had been searched, the jailer brought it to him.

"You're here to see that mob guy?" the jailer asked.

"I am here to see Mr. Barnito. To my knowledge he is not mob-connected."

The jailer stared hard at the young man but Porter returned the stare and the jailer dropped his eyes first. The man walked out of the room slamming the door behind him.

"Mr. Porter?" The inmate was escorted into the room. "I'm Seaborn Barnito." He held out his hand. "You my attorney?"

Porter took the hand, pleased to see a clear directness in the other's eyes. "That's what we're here to discuss. I want you to tell me what happened."

"Liddy Mae sent you? You're her cousin?"

"Yes to both questions. Now why don't you tell me what happened on the evening of June 28, 1936."

Seaborn recited the story which sounded much the same as the one Liddy Mae had told him. How his brother Addy had borrowed his Pierce-Arrow about noon on the day in question. Addy said he had to go over to Texas City on important business that couldn't wait, and how Addy's Buick LaSalle was in the shop. The car wasn't returned to Seaborn until the early the next morning.

Seaborn usually went home for dinner every evening and that day without a car he had walked. He saw no one nor spoke to no one. Liddy Mae wasn't home when he arrived. She'd gone to a neighbor's house for a bridge party.

"So you have no alibi. No one who will say you were at home at the time of the shooting?"

"That's right."

"What about Levi Clardy?"

"I knew him, but we weren't friends or anything."

"There's been some talk that you were involved with his wife, Elizabeth."

"That's simply not true. I knew her but only to speak to and

certainly never thought about her in that way. I'm in love with
Liddy Mae."

"Do you think your brother could be the shooter?"

"Yes."

"But why? What motive would he have?"

"Greed mostly. Oh, I don't know. We've never gotten along
all that well. He's actually my half-brother—we had different
mothers. He got into trouble constantly because he felt ne-
glected, I guess. Our dad used to whale on Addy a lot. I didn't
think he was the shooter at first, but in light of things that
have happened since, I'd be stupid if I kept proclaiming his
innocence."

"What things?"

"I had to sign the nightclub over to him. I wanted to put it
in Liddy Mae's name but her father and mine both had a fit.
Said it wasn't fit for a genteel woman to be involved in such as
nightclubs and gaming halls. Now Addy has control of my
business and is trying to gain control of all my assets. Liddy
managed to let me know of his plans before he could get everything and she got a friend at the bank to help her put some of
my money in my safety-deposit box."

"What reason would Addy have to kill Levi Clardy?"

"He was the one having an affair with Clardy's wife, and I
wouldn't be a bit surprised if she didn't put him up to the
whole thing. Thing is, Elizabeth Clardy disappeared. Right after
the funeral. I first thought she was just laying low, but she must
be long gone because no one has seen her since."

King got up and paced the small room for a few minutes.
When he sat back down, he took some paper from his brief-
case, took out his fountain pen and unscrewed the cap. He
began writing but a big blob of ink puddled out on the paper.
Some days he hated ink pens. He put it and the paper away.
"Everything sure points in your direction."

"I know. But I think if you could find Elizabeth Clardy and
find some evidence Addy was seeing Elizabeth—maybe that'd

throw suspicion on Addy. He sure had the motive and the means." Pain showed in Seaborn's eyes as he spoke.

Can't be easy to accuse your own brother, thought King, but sometimes family is your worst enemy.

"The obvious thing to clear you would be Mattie Gillingwater."

"Liddy Mae has some ideas on that. Some newfangled technique she read about," said Seaborn. "This hypnosis expert in Chicago."

"She mentioned that," said King. "Hypnosis isn't new but using it to get through to someone traumatized this way is one of the newest tools it's being used for—well, that's what Liddy Mae told me anyway." He looked hard at his client-to-be. "Things like experts and private investigators cost money, you know."

"If I can get out of here . . ."

"You can sign a paper to give me the authority to conduct business for you. Pay your bills, such as that?"

"Sounds like you've decided to represent me?"

"Let me check a couple of things and I'll get back to you."

"Can you help Liddy Mae by getting her some of my money?"

"No problem. I'll draw up the necessary papers and bring them by tomorrow morning." Porter stood and the two men shook hands.

The jailer gave King another hard look as he unlocked the door but King ignored him. No sense letting the man see how unsure he was about this case.

KING HIRED a private investigator who'd worked for him before to try and locate Elizabeth Clardy. It was as if she'd dropped off the face of the earth.

In the meantime, the doctor from Chicago came to Galveston, financed by funds taken from Seaborn's bank-deposit box.

The child hesitated at first, but finally agreed to be hypnotized. Seaborn's trial began but nothing worked right for Porter.

He found no one to substantiate his client's whereabouts on the night in question. The witnesses to the shooting said they had not seen the actual shooter and wouldn't pick anyone out from a lineup. The one thing they were all sure about was that car. This didn't especially hurt his client but it didn't help either.

King planned for Seaborn to testify in his own behalf and they worked long hours on strategy.

When Liddy Mae and Seaborn had about given up hope, Elizabeth Clardy came to see King.

Dressed in a fashionable navy-blue shirtwaist dress with a lace collar and cuffs, she had drawn her dark brown hair into a matronly bun which did nothing to hide her attractiveness. She wore navy gloves and a small hat with a veil covering her startling green eyes.

"Mr. Porter, I have been a foolish woman. I honestly believed Addy Barnito when he said he loved me. All he actually wanted was to bed me." She blushed at speaking so boldly.

"Did he kill your husband?" King asked, his tone abrupt.

She burst into tears. When she had cried herself out, she took out a hanky and blew her nose. "I'm sure he did. Poor Levi. He never hurt anyone. He was a good man but he was so boring. Addy was all flash and dash. He turned a girl's head quicker than you could spin a slot machine."

"But you didn't actually see him kill Levi?"

"No. Of course not. I wasn't with him when it happened but later he bragged how he had fixed his brother and fixed him good. It wasn't until afterwards I heard that Seaborn was the major suspect. I really, really hoped the police would discover Addy's involvement, charge him, and cart him off to jail." She shivered. "I left and moved to Florida, but friends here let me know the trial wasn't going well. I couldn't let an innocent man be convicted. My sleep at night is dismal enough without adding more to it. So, here I am."

King knew Elizabeth Clardy couldn't testify to a killing she did not witness. Everything she told him would be construed as hearsay. But she gave him the names of people who had seen them together and she could swear that she never had been involved with Seaborn, thereby eliminating his motive.

After Mrs. Clardy left, King opened his touch-control Royal portable typewriter and typed out a list of names and addresses that she had given him. People who she thought might have information of an affair between Addy and herself. He then copied the list on his new Mimeograph Stencil Sheet copier, placing one copy in a file folder and two copies in his briefcase. He wanted his investigator to begin checking Mrs. Clardy's story first thing in the morning. He took the list by the man's house and left a copy with him.

The weather had turned balmy again. Typical Galveston weather for fall. He passed the seawall on his way home, pulled over and walked out on one of the fishing piers. Puffy white clouds with black bottoms dotted the blue sky and a fresh breeze cleansed the air of its usual fishy smell.

The Gulf was a dark greeny-blue today and, with the clouds and wind, King knew a rainstorm would move on shore in a few hours. He watched the waves come in, decorate the sand with foam and rush back out. The lights came on over at the Balinese Room—the dinner club and casino owned by the Maceo brothers, and he wondered if the state would close down all the gaming clubs like some of the new politicians up in Austin had bragged about doing. "You can't legislate people's morals," he said to the sea gulls. The gulls paid him no attention, they only squawked and kept swooping down to the boards looking for things to eat. "The government tried once to run people's morals back during Prohibition and look where that got them," he said aloud.

Maybe the casinos wouldn't matter, he thought. Rumors of

war persistently rumbled around Europe and some of his fellow attorneys predicted that funny-looking German egomaniac would be trouble. If war broke out, people would need the diversion that gambling could provide. He turned and walked back to his car.

That evening when Liddy Mae came to King's house, Mattie Gillingwater skipped up the walkway in front on her. "Mattie's been staying with me some. Dr. Schneider thought it might help if she knew me better."

"The doctor's gone back to Chicago," said King. "He finished testifying today and I put him on his train. He said he thought Mattie was too young for his treatment but he would be willing to try again in a few months."

"I take it he wasn't much help?"

"Well, he made a good witness, unfortunately he could only testify to his opinion of Mattie's condition. Nothing about Seb's guilt or innocence."

"So that was a lost cause?" asked Liddy Mae.

"Not totally. He gave more credibility to our case, and all that helps. I just hope it will be enough."

Liddy shook her head. "Nothing is going to help."

Beau walked up on the front porch and scratched at the door, meowing to be let inside.

"Mattie, will you let Beau in?"

The girl smiled happily, ran to the door and let the cat in. She helped King feed Beau and then sat and stroked him. Mattie and Beau chased each other around the house until the noise level got so high Liddy Mae had trouble thinking and asked them to stop. The cat and the girl settled down on the floor, nearly nose to nose as if engrossed in some deep communication.

"Things don't look so good, do they?" Liddy Mae asked King.

"Not right now, no. But we won't give up. You'll never ever see me giving up."

"I remember. Even as a little kid you were tenacious. Rather like a bulldog worrying a bone." Liddy Mae smiled but only with her mouth, unable to hide the worry in her eyes. "What's your new plan of action?"

"The trial's getting ready to close and we need something . . . anything to create strong doubts. I'll keep trying to find witnesses who saw Addy and Elizabeth Clardy together," King said.

"Even if you find someone they might not want to talk."

"Then I'll subpoena them."

"People don't like to talk about Addy Barnito or what he's been doing. They're a little afraid of a mob connection."

"There is no mob connection," Porter said. "Addy and Seaborn are not connected to any of the families in Chicago or Detroit. Addy would like to be, but the made guys aren't interested in a little small-time Texas hustler."

"It won't be easy convincing them of that."

"If I could just find one person who saw something, and convince them to come forward."

"What would I have to say?" asked a small voice.

King and Liddy Mae turned to Mattie who was still face to face with Beau.

"What the . . ." said King.

"Mattie, was that you?" asked Liddy Mae.

"I guess so," said Mattie. "I'm ready to tell Mr. Porter what I saw."

Mattie Gillingwater said in all sincerity that Seaborn was not the man she saw with a gun who killed Mr. Clardy. Her description did fit Addison Barnito, however. Jubilation ruled the defense's camp when the judge ordered Seaborn freed.

Addy was placed into custody after trying to flee the island. Seaborn went to visit Addy in jail but his brother refused to see him.

"Don't you think that hypnosis helped Mattie?" asked Seaborn. "Maybe she had sort of a delayed reaction to that doctor's treatment."

Liddy Mae and Seaborn had invited King for a celebration dinner.

"No," said King. "I think we made her understand the only way she'd ever be free and safe was to talk."

"Neither of you are right," said Liddy Mae. "It was Beau."

"My cat? What did my cat have to do with anything?"

"I don't know. Except somehow Beau got through her wall of silence and broke it down. He showed her she didn't have to be afraid. That talking was the right thing to do." She stopped talking for a moment, her head tilted as if listening to someone that only she could hear. "Beau's a Halloween cat, you know. Something magical about black cats."

"And you think Beau did all that?" asked King. "Communicated with Mattie?"

"Yes. I really think so," said Mattie.

"If Mattie says it," said Seaborn, "it's true. And you, Mr. King Porter. I'm going to call you Bulldog from now on because you keep after something until you get it right."

Bulldog Porter's nickname stuck.

When Liddy Mae's and Seaborn's first child was born they named her Mattie. When their second child was born, he was named King Barnito, but everyone called him Beau.

"DON'T YOU still have a black cat named Beau?" asked C.J.

"Sure do. I forget which number he is, but he's descended from the original."

"Are you sure he's not the original?" I asked with a teasing tone. "I been told how cats have nine lives. And isn't his birthday the same as yours?"

"It's not really. Only say that's his birthday so I won't forget it. Always say it's the same as mine cause I know when mine is—just do it to make things easier." His voice took on a strange tone as he offered his explanations.

"Yes," said. C.J. "That's got to be one magical cat—lives forever and communicates with—"

"And of course, he's not the original," Bulldog interrupted. "But I will say Beau's spirit lives on, I am very sure about that."

"Rather like his tenacious master—Mr. Bulldog Porter," said Larry.

We all agreed with laughs and smiles, and went out to finish celebrating our pal's eighty years of life.

Cat on an Old School Roof

Peter Crowther

Nations are gathered out of nurseries.
　　　　—From a review of Samuel Smiles's 'Self-Help' (1859)

*If a composite history of all the public
schools is ever written it will be, in reality,
the history of England.*
　　　　—Anon

RICHARD LATCHPOLE LOVED to climb the steep slope of
Biggins Hill on a Sunday afternoon.

At the top, where the land flattened out into fields and
hedgerows which rolled all the way to Skipton and Otley, he
would sit cross-legged and stare into the valley below, making
believe the panoply of streets and houses which stretched before him was a gameboard, and that he was back at home in
Wiltshire, amidst the security of his own family and his own
belongings.

It was a clear afternoon simply because it was a Sunday,
when the mills and factories overlooked by the blackened
facade and the clocktower of Derwent School For Boys were

empty, still and deathly silent, the monolithic chimneystacks holding their sooty breath for the day.

From the grassy banks of Biggins Hill, even the cobbled streets appeared empty, though Richard knew that people were walking down there. He knew that there would be a buzz of conversation between neighbors and the sound of children playing, running with hoops and sticks, skipping-ropes slapping the ground to boisterous rhymes and, from the numerous Inns on the street corners, the occasional clink of glasses and the heady music of laughter.

The weekend was Richard's favorite time. In fact, it was all the boys' favorite time. It wasn't because there was no work to do, for even though classes were only Monday through Saturday, Sunday was still considered to be a day for prayer, reflection, and private study. It was because the weekend made home seem nearer.

"Idle hands and minds make up the Devil's time," Reverend Beckett delighted in telling the boys every Sunday at the close of the early morning service, as they filed out of Derwent's Chapel to assemble in the quadrangle for official dismissal.

"I trust that you will find sensible and productive pastimes for yourselves in the hours ahead," he would say, his voice booming above the sound of shuffling feet echoing around the Chapel's cavernous walls and bouncing off the labyrinthine maze of pews and crosswalks, their wooden surfaces polished by generations of backsides and school shoes. Then the Reverend would add, as a final resort, his eyes twinkling malevolently, "but should any of you feel that additional work would be helpful, you should see either your Home Form Tutor or one of the Senior Prefects."

Thinking of such a suggested course of action now, engrossed in the heinous crime of idly peeling the protective carapace leaf from a long stalk of grass, Richard smiled to himself.

It had happened only once, shortly after Richard's arrival at the school at the start of September 1852, some three years ago. A young boy named James Wheeler, a second yearer who should have known better, had boldly strode across the Quad to Montague Dearlove, one of the Senior Prefects (and, coincidentally, one of the most hated and feared members of Derwent outside the Masters' Common Room—a particularly troublesome situation in view of the fact that Dearlove's younger brother, Nigel, was in Richard's form), brazenly proclaiming that he feared he had insufficient prep to engage his mind fully until lessons recommenced the following day at 8:00 A.M. sharp.

Perhaps, Wheeler had opined, adjusting his spectacles on the bridge of his nose, Dearlove might be able to suggest some sensible activity in which he could productively engage himself during the coming afternoon.

Amidst sniggers from the other Prefects surrounding him, and swirling his black gown around himself, Dearlove clasped his hands behind his back and craned his neck towards the hapless youth until his pointed chin almost touched the boy's forehead.

Even from where he was standing, on the Refectory steps with Willishaw and Wooton, and some way from the incident, Richard heard one of the other Prefects mutter, "Impudent young bugger," and yet another say, "Blighter needs something else upon which his threadbare brain can concentrate, Monty."

Dearlove reached out and grabbed hold of a tuft of Wheeler's hair and, swiftly turning around, stalked away to the Prefects' House with the lad in tow. They did not see Wheeler again that day but the next morning, the Monday, he did not appear for his lessons. Word spread that the Prefects had held a Trial and that Wheeler had been found Guilty Of Conduct Unbecoming Of A Young Man. His sentence had been a half dozen strokes of the cane—administered by Dearlove himself—and to spend the night tied to one of the boilers in the cellars beneath the Refectory.

The boy's back had been extensively damaged, skin burned and blistered, and the base of his spine had been so bruised by Dearlove's "careless" strokes of the cane that he was unable to sit with any degree of comfort for several weeks.

Though everyone knew what had happened, Wheeler was obliged to attribute his sorry condition to a reckless climbing escapade across the wooden trestle that spanned the boiler, an expedition during which, his footing momentarily lost, he had tumbled down between the boiler and the wall to become jammed, there to spend the night until the caretaker carried out his morning inspection. A further punishment of a formal letter to Wheeler's father—which undoubtedly resulted in considerable losses of home privileges when term ended— quickly ensued.

The first few days following the first of these punishments, Wheeler spent in the School Hospital. When he was considered well enough to resume his studies, he did so with one month of Evening Detentions, during which he was expected to catch up with work he had missed. Quite whether the detentions had been prescribed to enable Wheeler to do that or simply to serve as a further example to other students that they should plan their travails so that their supposedly free time was more adequately filled, Richard Latchpole was never sure.

What it did teach him, however, was to keep his own council and make friends only when he was sure that his proposed new comrades could be trusted. Thus Jeremy Willishaw and Bertram Wooton were the only ones with whom Richard spent any appreciable or even measurable time. Plus one other, his greatest friend in the entire school: Denbeigh.

Denbeigh's name was almost certainly not Denbeigh, nor was he a student at Derwent. He was a cat, a brown and white tom with jagged markings on his back legs, the longest face-whiskers Richard had ever seen, and a particular fondness for scraps from the Refectory. Indeed, Richard, Jem and Bert believed that Denbeigh was in all probability the Derwent occupant most appreciative of the School's meals . . . though exactly where he lived when he was not spending time with Richard in the Dormitory was something of a mystery. Most days the cat would arrive in the early hours, when the dorm was awash with the sound of smacking lips and the groans of boys drawn from their sleep by the insistent banging of one of the House Monitors.

Richard had little time for Denbeigh in the morning, his attention restricted to an appreciative ruffle of the cat's collar before he scurried along to the bathrooms for a full body wash in the invariably tepid water. And each day when he returned, somewhat more awake, his skin buffed like an apple's peel and his hair plastered down, Richard would look for Denbeigh without success.

Then, in the evenings, Denbeigh would mysteriously appear once more, drifting into the dorm like a small, black ghost, creeping stealthily along the polished wooden-floored corridors of the third floor of the Dormitory Block, and then he would spend the next hour or so after Lights-Out daintily eating whatever tidbit Richard had rescued for him from the Refectory—a practice that Richard saw fit to keep to himself, even from Bert and Jem.

The cat was certainly appreciative, in his own small, feline way.

On more than one occasion, usually before dinner, Richard would discover small presents, presumably "rescued" from the mysterious depths and shadowy recesses of the old buildings, half-buried beneath his pillow, in the flap of his sheets or beneath his bed, alongside (or even in) his slippers.

Sometimes these gifts would be nothing more exotic than a rusty nail or a piece of wood, its surface dusty and forgotten by whoever abandoned it. On other occasions, Richard had returned from a hard day's labor declining Latin verbs or discuss-

ing the "sheer stupidity" of the working classes which so steadfastly refused to move where the work was abundant, to find
the still body of a mouse or a small bird, their fur and feathers
gloriously intact, their faces so peaceful in their appearance
that they might just as well have been napping.

Such discoveries made Richard shudder and mentally promise to himself that he would scold Denbeigh when the cat next
put in an appearance. But then, when Denbeigh did appear
later that evening, his face a mask of pride and anticipation,
Richard had not the heart to chastise. And, instead, the cat
would receive his "reward" as a token of appreciation for such
fine gifts . . . despite the fact that, like all of the other bric-a-
brac brought by Denbeigh, such treasures had already been
consigned to the huge steel dustbins behind the Refectory.

The sudden sound of the School's bells pealing across the
valley interrupted Richard's thoughts and he turned in their
direction, staring down the well-trodden path that descended
Biggins Hill all the way to the gates of Derwent.

There was an urgency in their cacophonous tone—something that suggested all was not as it should be, for the bells
usually rang only to announce the morning service or Sunday
evening prayers. Without further thought, he tossed the piece
of grass into the air and got to his feet. Seconds later he was
making his way back down Biggins Hill towards the school.

OUTSIDE THE gates, Richard met up with Jem and Bert who
were standing waiting for him.

"Where have you been?" Bertram Wooton inquired, wiping
a long strand of blond hair from his forehead as Richard approached.

"Biggins Hill," Richard replied. "What's the matter? Why
are the bells ringing?"

Jem Willishaw shrugged and straightened his cravat, blink-
ing. "How do I look?" he asked the other two, stifling a yawn.

"I was taking a nap when they started," he said, his gentle lisp turning the word "was" into "wath."

"Fine," Bert said. "Come on, they're assembling everyone in the Library."

As they started to walk, Bert said, "You recall my mentioning my asthma the other day? And you mentioned that you would be prepared to swap beds so that I could be nearer the fresh air afforded by a greater proximity to the door?"

Richard said that he did.

"Well," Bert announced with a big smile, "I took you at your word. Jem and I moved my bed across to where yours was and moved yours over to where mine was."

Richard shrugged. "I hope it does the trick."

"Now you can thee why I wath tho tired," Jem lisped, and they all laughed.

As they moved past the school gates they saw, across the Quad, the unmistakable dashing figure of Montague Dearlove slip through the Prefects' entrance and close the door behind him. Dearlove stood for a few seconds watching what was going on. Then a younger boy broke from the ranks and ran up to him.

"What collective noun doeth one uthe for Dearloveth?" Jem whispered, nodding towards the Dearlove brothers.

Richard sniggered.

"If one were being alliterative," Bert observed, "one might say 'a den.' "

Richard nodded. "Or 'a dearth.' "

" 'A despot'?" added Jem, pronouncing it "dethpot."

" 'A dank'?" said Richard. "Or 'a dire'?"

They all laughed.

"He must have run all the way from town," a voice behind them whispered.

Richard turned around, frowning, and looked straight into the eyes of David Littlewood, a rotund second-former with a pince-nez attached to a length of what appeared to be pajama cord fastened to his lapel. "Who?" he asked.

Littlewood nodded toward Montague Dearlove. "He was down in town ages ago . . ." He glanced myopically to either side through his spectacles as he leaned forward, adding with a whisper, "drinking. That was ages ago. I saw him across the street as I was heading back to school, and it's taken me a half an hour . . . and I wasn't dawdling."

Bert Wooton asked where Littlewood had seen him.

"The Dog and Duck on the corner of Derwentwater Road."

"Who wath he with?" asked Jem.

Littlewood shook his head and shrugged. "Nobody from school. He was talking to two rather rough types," he added, adjusting the spectacles. "I made sure he didn't see me." Littlewood then moved off to join the rest of his form.

As they waited for the mass of boys to form into lines, Bert, Jem, and Richard watched Montague Dearlove move his young brother over to the wall. They seemed to be locked in deep conversation, arms waving around . . . with Montague leaning forward and talking right into Nigel Dearlove's face.

"What do you suppothe they're talking about?"

Bert shrugged. Then Nigel Dearlove walked quickly back into the main body of boys and, after reaching into his pocket and slipping something into his mouth—undoubtedly a mint, employed to hide or at least disguise the smell of beer—Montague walked up toward the main building, pushing or thumping an occasional boy into line.

Up ahead, the entire school was filing into the austere entrance to the Library wing of the main building, a crocodile line of dark blue long-tailed blazer jackets and gray flannel trousers gathered below the knees where long black socks stretched down to polished shoes, all moving slowly and silently between the huge oak doors. At either side of the line, his back to the doors, a prefect stood watching, his eyes alighting on each of the boys as they passed by with heads invariably hung low. While nobody had any idea what had caused this unusual gathering, they feared the worst.

Richard, Jem, and Bert slowed their trot as they reached the end of the line and fell into place. "I say," Bert said, a note of mystery in his voice, "I wonder where all the other prefects are."

He had a point. Usually, the entire prefects' common room was present at such events as speech days and award presentations but here there were only the two prefects guarding the doors, presumably to dissuade boys from talking and jostling. The prefects' faces showed no warmth. In fact, quite the opposite. They were studying each boy—or, more accurately, the top of each head—as he passed them, scowling in disdain or outright disgust—as though the shuffling column comprised nothing more than animals muddied by a life spent in the blissful ignorance of the fields, wandering inside the abattoir to be slaughtered.

The thought made Richard shudder.

"What'th the matter?" Jem's voice lisped from behind Richard, the low volume making the impediment even more sibilant than usual.

"Someone walked over my grave I suppose," Richard whispered over his right shoulder.

"No talking!" a gruff voice barked from somewhere up the line. It was unlikely that the comment had been intended for them, as there was still some way to go before they reached the doors, but the harshness of the words and their delivery added to the three boys' sense of impending doom.

Once they were inside the corridor, the two prefects—Burgess and Helliwell—stepped forward and pushed the doors closed with an ominous crash. The corridor itself was full to capacity, the boys at the front—standing immediately before the main doors into the library—spilling slowly through the bottleneck and into the book-lined room, all shuffling silently,

their shoulders bobbing side to side as they moved into standing rows facing the front.

As Richard took his place, and Burgess and Helliwell closed
the Library doors, he saw that all of the Masters were assembled in a line facing them, their faces gray and drawn. At the
front of the gathering stood Reverend Beckett and, his eyes
scanning the faces before him, the Headmaster, Clement
Jameson Stewart.

Helliwell placed his hands behind his back and stood legs
astride in front of the doors. Burgess walked purposefully to the
front of the room and nodded curtly to the Headmaster.

"Boys, you are gathered here today," Stewart began, his tone
sepulchral and cold, "because something has happened that we
are in urgent need to address."

Richard glanced to his right to look at Bert Willishaw but
instead caught the eyes of Helliwell. The eyes opened wide for
a moment, glaring, and Richard looked away.

"It has been brought to my attention that there is a thief
amongst us."

Although no actual words could be heard from the assem-
bly, there was the vacuuming sound of a rush of air being
suddenly breathed in.

"Several items have been lost or misplaced," Stewart continued, "their disappearances reported to Mister Grainger over
the past few days."

In the massed ranks behind the Headmaster, Kenneth
"Twitchy" Grainger flicked his head and his left shoulder, his
eyes scanning the ranks of adolescents before him. It was his
way, a nervous tic.

"Now, we all understand and accept such occasional mis-
placements," Stewart droned on, his voice momentarily soft-
ening. Then the bushy eyebrows furrowed and the eyes became
hooded. "But the sheer volume of these reports in so relatively
short a time has given cause for concern." Stewart turned
around. "Is that correct, Mister Grainger?"

A flick. "That is correct, Headmaster." Another flick and a twitch, and the vaguest hint of a thin-lipped smile as the eyes went on about their business of scanning.

"Thus," the Headmaster explained, "it was brought to my attention. And I have initiated a search of the dormitories and the workroom desks."

Jem Wooton leaned against Richard. "So that's where the Prefects are," he whispered. Richard shook his head and grimaced, hardly daring to look in the direction of Helliwell. Jem moved away carefully.

"We are all to stay here until such time as the Prefects have reported back," Stewart said. He raised his arms and stretched them out in front of him, then lowered them slowly. "You may sit. Quietly!" he added as the boys took the instruction as an opportunity to comment amongst themselves on the afternoon's developments.

Everyone sat and crossed their legs.

"Now," Mister Stewart said, walking to the side of the room. "Does anyone have anything to say to me about this matter?"

He waited, watching the faces.

Richard, Jem, and Bert sat as erect as they could, craning their necks to see if any hand rose waveringly from the mass of boys in front of them. But there was nothing.

"Does anyone have any questions?"

Now a hand shot up. The Headmaster looked to the Masters. Professor Rushton stepped forward and whispered something to Mister Stewart.

Turning back, Stewart said, "Yes, Griffin."

"Sir, I wonder—"

"Stand up, lad!" Professor Rushton barked gruffly.

Griffin rose unsteadily and clasped his hands behind his back. "Sir, I wonder if you might inform us as to the nature of the missing items?"

Mister Stewart wafted his gown around him like a voluminous cloak and clasped his hands behind his back. "I fail to see the relevance of your question, Griffith," the Headmaster began.

"Griffin, sir," Griffin shouted.

Muted sniggers sounded from around the library. Professor Rushton glared into the assembled ranks, as did Mister Grainger, his head and right shoulder twitching madly.

"Pardon me, lad?" the Headmaster inquired.

"I'm Griffin, sir." Griffin looked around the faces of the boys in front of him and raised an arm. "That's Griffith, sir." He pointed to a dark-haired boy with bushy eyebrows sitting a few rows from the front of the room.

"Quite," Mister Stewart said, glancing down at the other boy who had raised a reluctant hand. "Well, Griffin, I fail to see the relevance. Suffice to say that the owners of these items—which, for your information, comprise various timepieces, cuff links, collar studs and the like—know exactly what they look like. And anyone who is not the owner is expected to know that such items are not their own property."

"I think what the Headmaster is saying," Professor Rushton said, his voice booming out so loudly that even Mister Stewart seemed to cringe momentarily, "is that it doesn't matter what the missing items are. Boys are expected to report seeing or finding anything that does not belong to them." He turned to the Headmaster and raised his eyebrows.

Mister Stewart nodded and turned back to face the room. "Quite," he said. "I thought I had already said that but I am, of course, grateful to Professor Rushton for his clarification if, indeed, such clarification were necessary. Now, are there any further questions or—"

The door behind the teachers opened and two prefects sidled in.

Mister Jones, the English master, moved across and whispered to the new arrivals. One of the prefects, Hick, was showing something in his hand and whispering to Mister Jones. The

English master nodded, accepted the item and walked across to the waiting Headmaster.

More whispering ensued, both amongst the masters and in the body of the audience. As he looked around the faces, Richard saw Nigel Dearlove mouthing something to his brother, who was standing over between two bookcases. Montague Dearlove was glaring, eyes wide, and shaking his head. Richard frowned and glanced back at Nigel, attempting to read what he was mouthing, when the Headmaster gave a loud cough and held something up for all to see. It was a watch of some kind, hanging by a chain and swinging gently from side to side.

"This watch belongs to Cedric Hardacre." He took the watch in both hands and studied it. "His name is engraved on the casement," he announced. "However, I would like Hardacre to stay behind to verify that it is the watch he reported missing last week. And I would also like to see . . ." The Headmaster turned to Mister Jones, frowning. The English master lifted a hand to his mouth and whispered something. Mister Stewart nodded.

"And I would also like to see," he continued, turning back to face the audience, "Bertram Wooton."

The gasp from the assembled boys was almost palpable, with heads turning and craning towards the ranks of the fourth years, one of whom, Bert himself, sitting between Richard and Jem, had turned a bright shade of red.

"Bert?" said Richard. "You didn't—"

"I didn't do anything," Bert protested.

Boys were already standing and starting to file out of the large doors at the front of the library, while Montague Dearlove and Adrian Helliwell were busy threading their way from the side of the library, through the mingling bodies, in a direct line toward Bert, Jem, and Richard. As he watched them, Richard thought he saw a look of confusion on

Dearlove's face and, when he glanced beyond the advancing prefect, he saw a similar expression on the face of Dearlove's unctuous brother.

Now on his feet, Bert was backing slowly away from the prefects.

"Don't you move, lad," Helliwell shouted. He cuffed one boy about the ear who had accidentally got in his way and barked, "Orderly line, lad. Make an orderly line."

Richard turned around. "Did you take any of these things, Bert? Really. You must say if you did."

"I didn't. I didn't take anything." Bert looked at Jem Willishaw's face. "You believe me, don't you?"

Montague Dearlove's thick hand reached out and grasped hold of Bert's shoulder. "Come on, you little thief," Dearlove said. "Headmaster wants to have a few words with you."

As he was being pulled away, Bert said, "I want him to come with me." He nodded towards Richard. "I haven't done anything and I want him to come and hear exactly what I'm being accused of."

Richard raised his eyebrows in surprise and looked at Jem. Jem shrugged. "Go with him, Richard. It'th hith right to athk." Which was true. The School's rules included a reference to boys being accused of something having the right to appoint a witness to hear the charges. Of course, it could only be carried out with the witness's consent.

"Well, lad," Helliwell snapped as he grabbed Bert's wrist. His face broke into a broad smile that was completely without humor. "Are you coming to see your friend sent down?"

Richard glanced at Bert and saw his friend mouth the word "please." "Yes, I will come to hear the charges," Richard said. As they moved off towards the front of the now emptying library—where the assembled might of the teaching staff remained silently waiting and watching, hands behind backs like black-winged rooftop gargoyles, stern expressions on their faces—Richard turned around and shouted to Jem. "I'll see you when I return."

Then he marched off with Bert and the two prefects.

WHEN RICHARD returned to the dormitory there was just one person there. Everyone else was down in the Refectory or out in the quad, enjoying the late afternoon sunshine and discussing the revelation of the events in the library. The one person, Jem, looked up from the floor.

"What happened?" he inquired, carefully placing a threaded tassel between the open pages of his Latin reader. He sat up, crossing his legs.

Richard removed his jacket and threw it across the bed. "It's bad," he said as he plopped down beside the jacket. "Bert is to be expelled. They found the watch in Bert's bed."

"Oh, no. Poor Bert. When doth he leave?" Jem lisped.

Richard did not respond. "Somebody must have put it there," he said, more to himself than to his friend. "But who? Who could have done it? And why?" Richard scratched his head. "Nobody could possibly have expected a dormitory check this afternoon."

Jem fought against voicing the thought that perhaps Bertram Wooton was a common thief. "Maybe it wath one of the prefects . . . Hick?" he ventured, frowning. "It had to be either him or—"

"Hold' on," said Richard.

Jem looked across and saw Richard staring at a small, hand-painted vase on the cupboard beside the bed.

Richard sat up and peered over the side of the bed. He reached down and lifted up a pair of black shoes, their surfaces so polished that, for a second, they caught the fading light shining through the windows and reflected it like a sunflash.

"What ith it?"

"Oh, no," Richard said, dropping the shoes and leaping from the bed. "This is Bert's bed. He changed it."

Jem shook his head and got to his feet. One of his legs had gone into cramp and he bent down and rubbed the back of it furiously. "You knew that. He told you when we were going into the library, remember?"

Richard looked across the room at the familiar sight of his own bedside cupboard and the old glass his grandmother had given him. There, beneath the bed, partly obscured by the trailing topsheet, were his slippers and the chipped enamel bedpan. "There is my bed," he said.

Jem followed his friend's eye and nodded. "But you knew—"

"It was Denbeigh," he said.

"What did Denbeigh do?"

"He brought the watch."

"Denbeigh? The cat?" Jem shook the last vestiges of cramp from his leg and sat down on Bert's bed. "Why would a cat bring Bert a watch?"

"He didn't bring it to Bert," Richard said, checking the door to make sure they were not being overheard. "He brought it to me!"

Richard told his amazed friend all about Denbeigh's visits for scraps from the Refectory and about the cat's curious sense of paying for all services rendered. "A dead mouth," Jem hissed, his face screwed up as though he was recovering from a hastily administered medicine of particularly unpleasant flavor. "Not a prethent of my own choothing," he sprayed.

"Nor mine," Richard agreed. He walked across to his own bed and tested the mattress. "And all of this means that Denbeigh has found where the stolen property has been stored."

"Tho, what do we do now?"

Richard shrugged. "There's nothing we can do. We simply have to wait until later tonight and hope that Denbeigh comes as usual."

"With a prethent?"

"With a present. Then we have to try to follow him, find out where he goes, and . . ." He let his voice trail.

"And then what?"

Richard didn't say anything. The whole thing seemed ridiculously optimistic and doomed to failure. Even if Denbeigh did come, there was no guarantee that the cat would take them to the stolen property. And what if Denbeigh had simply found the watch by itself? It could be that Hardacre had simply dropped it somewhere. And even if they did find the property, what then? If they went to the Headmaster with such a cock and bull story it could end up with all three of them being expelled. He glanced across at Jem and saw similar concerns in his friend's eyes.

With the sheer hopelessness of the situation weighing heavily on their minds, Richard and Jem left the dormitory and went down to the Refectory. Perhaps a cup of tea would help. . . .

IT WAS after lights out that Denbeigh appeared that evening.

The dormitory was silent, save for an occasional creak of bedsprings and Conway's dronelike snoring from the end of the room.

In the moonlight spilling through the corridor windows and into the dormitory itself Denbeigh's shadow crept before him, momentarily elongated and shifting mysteriously, moving stealthily as though it were investigating the ground before its master came along, albeit mere inches behind and, of course, inextricably attached.

Richard saw immediately that the cat held something in its mouth.

He had switched beds again and was in his usual position just in front of the door. Denbeigh stopped for a second and looked along the walkway between the bed-ends: Richard could see his eyes and he wondered what, if anything, the cat was considering. Then, just as he feared it was about to turn around and flee, the cat turned back to face him and padded noiselessly the final few feet to Richard's bedside. It stopped, shrank back onto its hind legs, and jumped onto the eiderdown.

Richard leant forward and tousled Denbeigh's back, feeling the ever-present soft and rhythmic purring emanating from deep within the animal. "Now then, my feline friend," he whispered, "what's this you have brought for me, hmm?"

The cat released the object into Richard's hand and immediately set to cleaning itself while Richard considered his "present."

It was a tie clasp, gold by the weight of it, with a small tightly linked chain extending from a small stone set in a tiny clasp at the front which connected by a spring clip to the restrainer at the rear. Although the dim light did not allow him to make out the detail, Richard was in no doubt that the item was extremely valuable in pure financial terms, and probably of sentimental value to its owner as well.

Checking along the room to ensure that his visitor had not been observed, Richard tucked the tie clasp beneath his pillow and turned to Denbeigh. The cat had completed its wash and was waiting patiently, watching Richard's hands carefully to see if they would suddenly reveal a morsel or two. Richard fought a snigger. "I can't tease you," he whispered. "It isn't fair."

He reached across to his bedside cupboard and pulled a handkerchief ball from behind his glass of water. Denbeigh watched, craning his head and sniffing as the handkerchief passed mere inches above his nose. Then the cat shuffled closer to Richard and waited as he pulled back the corners of the handkerchief and revealed a thick chunk of haddock and two small boiled potatoes.

"What' about that, then," Richard said quietly as Denbeigh settled down on the eiderdown and chewed the first morsel of fish.

Richard did not see the approaching shadowy figure until it had almost reached his bed and he jumped so violently that, for a moment, he was afraid that Denbeigh would run off.

"He came!" Jem hissed, his smile wide and friendly. He reached over and stroked the cat's head while Denbeigh shuffled closer to the handkerchief for another handout.

Richard closed the handkerchief and leaned his head close to the cat. "I will give you some more," he whispered, "but first I want you to take us to where you got this." He reached under the pillow and waved the tie clasp.

"Gosh!" Jem ventured. He thrust his hands into his dressing gown pockets. He felt a mixture of excitement and trepidation, unsure which of these sensations was going to get the upper hand.

Denbeigh sniffed at the clasp and its dangling chain and pulled his head back. What were they thinking of, these stupid boys: why, this was the very thing that he had brought to them . . . and it was certainly not edible.

Richard returned the object to the safety of his pillow and, pulling back the eiderdown—taking care not to disturb his visitor too much—he swung his feet out of bed and down into his slippers. Then he pulled on his dressing gown over his pajamas and tied the cord around his waist.

The two boys tiptoed to the door where Richard rubbed his nose in the handkerchief? "Mmm," he whispered. In actual fact the thing smelled foul.

"Come on, then," Jem hissed.

Denbeigh watched from the eiderdown, his head clicking first to one side and then to the other as he considered the pair of them.

Richard waved an arm up the corridor outside the dormitory. "Show us," he whispered. "Show us where you got it."

"If we're not careful, someone'th going to wake up," Jem confided in his friend as they watched the cat.

"We don't have any choice," Richard said.

He waved along the corridor again and Denbeigh stood up on the bed.

The boys stopped moving and waited.

Denbeigh lifted his feet awkwardly, the claws catching on the threads, and approached the side of the bed with great caution. Then, in one beautifully fluid movement, he pounced gracefully to the floor with a soft thud.

Jem looked down the dormitory.

At the far end, Lawrence Conway shifted in his bed, a mound of whiteness turning like a whale and making a noise like a duck. Miraculously, Conway woke neither himself nor anyone else and, presently, the normal breath-filled silence was restored.

They looked at each other and then down at the cat. Denbeigh was standing next to Richard's bed, his tail slowly twisting around over his back.

Richard hunkered down between Denbeigh and the open door leading to the corridor. "Come on then, old boy," he said softly. "Take us to your special place."

The cat gave a final swish of its tail, walked calmly around Richard and out of the door.

With only a cursory glance back along the two rows of beds—his eyes stopping briefly on Bert's unmade bed, and then on his own and Jem's—Richard nodded to Jem and they followed the cat out into the corridor. A more detailed examination of the dormitory would have revealed that not three, but four of the dormitory beds were unoccupied.

THE CORRIDOR stretched ahead of them, moonlight dappling the polished wooden flooring with a mixture of shadow and light. The fact that it was windy outside and clouds were constantly scudding across the moon gave the scene in front of them an almost living texture, the shadows of the crisscrossed window-leading and the wooden casements swaying first one

way and then the other . . . almost as though Richard and
Jem were making their way along the deck of a ship.

At the end of the corridor the windows gave way to a blank
wall on either side before turning left to the main staircase.
Here it was dark and the two boys had to guide themselves
along by trailing their hands against the wall.

"Can you thee him?" Jem's voice hissed urgently.

"Shh!"

The truth of the matter was that Richard's eyesight was only
now enabling him to see anything, and he dreaded that they
might be walking straight into the arms of one of the masters.
They simply had to trust to luck and hope that Denbeigh was
just ahead of them. Though where the cat was leading them
was another matter entirely.

Presently, they came to the stairs and the light improved.

A huge domed window above the staircase bathed the entire
landing and the first two flights in a serene glow.

Across the head of the stairs, the corridor continued around
to the right and led to three more dormitories. Richard waited
and looked around to see if Jem was following. Once he could
see his friend's familiar figure he turned back and tried to per-
suade his heart to slow down.

Directly in front of them, Denbeigh was standing beside the
banisters. He was watching them.

"I think we should go—"

"Shh!" Richard pulled Jem close. "Don't talk."

Jem nodded reluctantly.

The two boys crept forward until they were towering above
the cat. Richard bent down and stroked Denbeigh's back.
"Where do we go now, old boy?" he whispered calmly. "Go
show us . . . go show." He waved the handkerchief parcel
enticingly and pointed indistinctly with his other arm, hoping
that the cat would take it as a general instruction for him to
lead them to his secret place and not simply to proceed in a
specific direction.

Suddenly, the cat sprang up onto the banister.

For a second, Jem thought it was going to fall off and plummet to the floors below—he had no head at all for heights—but the cat seemed supremely confident. Denbeigh took two steps further along, to a point where the banister turned up to the next floor, which, as it led only to some storerooms and out onto the roof, was out of bounds to the boys of Derwent. The cat jumped effortlessly across to the wide wooden shelving that ran along the side of the wall. It was a superb achievement—some six feet or more, and all uphill.

"Crikey!" Jem hissed. "Look!"

Richard looked along the shelving and could see what Jem was so concerned about. A series of porcelain plates were propped against the wall and secured from falling by a wooden lip at the edge of the shelf. They were perfectly secure as long as they were not moved. But that seemed unlikely. Denbeigh was already creeping along to the first plate.

Richard thrust the handkerchief parcel into his pocket and trotted to the stairs, climbing the first couple to try to get his hand up onto the shelf. But it was too high for him to reach. He waved for Jem to join him.

Jeremy Willishaw moved nervously to his friend. He had a bad feeling about all of this. Perhaps Bert was guilty after all, and they were just going to get into a whole mess of trouble. But he didn't have time to consider the full consequences. As soon as Jem reached him, Richard spun him around and made him bend over. There was a little shuffling, with Richard *shhh*-ing loudly, until Jem complied. Richard immediately stepped onto his friend's back and, flattened against the wall, edged his way to a position where he could reach his arm along to Denbeigh.

All of this time, the cat was standing patiently watching them.

"Jem!" Richard's voice echoed in the stillness, and he repeated his friend's name as a whisper. "Jem, there's a hole in the wall along here."

"Hole in the wall? Where?"

"On the shelf."

As Richard passed this information, Denbeigh casually moved forward a few inches and disappeared into the hole.

"Drat!"

"What ith it?"

"He's gone."

"Into the hole?"

"Yes." Richard stepped down from his friend's shoulders onto the stairs. Then he climbed a few more steps, trying to keep an eye on where the shelf level might be, and suddenly found himself looking out of a window.

Outside, the trees blew and the moon shone and the whole world was asleep. He moved two more steps, leaning against the protective rail which prevented anyone stepping accidentally onto the windowsill, and leaned forward, pressing his face against the glass.

There was a sudden movement in the roof to his left and a shape fluttered out of hiding amidst the stonework and wainscoting, whirling into the night, the moonlight catching its wings momentarily before it wheeled around the far side of the roof.

"He's got into the roof somehow," Richard hissed. "Just disturbed a pigeon."

"The roof!" Jem groaned. "That thounds high."

Richard stepped back, frowned, and then returned his face to the glass. He looked back at the spot where the pigeon had flown from and then looked in the other direction. Then he looked down. "Ah, there's a ledge out here. It runs across from this window to a smaller window above where the pigeon was disturbed." There was a pause and then he pulled back. "Jem, I'm going out."

"No," Jem said, waving his arms. "You can't go out there. You'll be—"

"I'm going out and that's all there is to it." Richard stepped over the protective rail and onto the windowsill. Seconds later, he had unfastened the window catch.

The night air felt cold around his bare ankles.

"You're not going out there," Jem hissed. "Pleathe don't go out there."

Richard slid around the open window and placed his left foot tentatively on the stone ledge outside the window, the wind whipping his pajama legs like tent awnings. Somewhere out in front of him, way across the playing fields and in the woods at the foot of Biggins Hill, a fox barked.

Go back, a voice said in Richard's ear. For a moment, he thought he would do just that . . . and then the image of Bert's face came to him. *It's really your fault that he's in this mess*, said another, more benevolent, voice. *The cat thought it was your bed.*

He looked to his side along the wall and saw that the ledge he was standing on was quite wide and it certainly seemed to be in a good state of repair. Turning carefully around so that he was facing the wall, Richard inched his right arm out until it was stretched against the stonework, his fingers feeling for small purchases in the porous stone and the cement pointing. Then he started to move, shuffling his right foot out, investigatively, and then bringing his left foot up to join it. Soon, the window through which he had just come was behind him. Now only the night and the wind were with him.

He was almost at the corner when he heard voices below him.

Richard stopped and closed his eyes.

He could feel his heart beating in his throat. Suddenly he felt a strange feeling of lightness, of wanting simply to lean back and lie down and float away . . . away from the ledge and the voices and the whole business of Denbeigh and the stolen property.

Then he tucked his head down into the collar of his dressing gown and slowly opened his eyes. The small window was just ahead, about six feet to the right of the corner he was approaching. He took another step, perhaps a little too adventurously, and slipped forward. His right hand thudded against the adjoining wall and for a few seconds, Richard could feel his bottom and lower back buckling outwards. He straightened himself and shuffled into the corner, securing himself with his right hand, which was stuck out slightly behind him against the wall that ran a right angle to the one against which he was pressing himself.

He ventured a slow look beneath him, momentarily feeling the vertiginous pull of the ground far below . . . seemingly reaching up for him almost hungrily. He could make out the shadowy figures of three men talking, apparently heatedly, though he could not hear what they were saying. The main thing was that the voices did not seem to have been anything to do with him.

He waited.

Presently, amidst more muffled discussion, the three men disappeared into the building and a door slammed.

Richard lifted his head, took a deep breath, and continued along the facing wall. It seemed only a minute or so later that his face was in front of the window. Pressing his face against it, Richard tried to see what was beyond but the window was so dirty it was almost black and he could see nothing. He held his breath and attempted to prize open the wooden frame—it was open.

The breath came back out in a flood of relief.

He crouched down beneath the window and pulled it out and up, straightening as he did so that the wooden-cased pane rested against his head. Then he reached inside with both hands and started pulling himself up.

Soon, he had got his entire body through the window.

He was in the roof of the main building, a series of overhead roof windows flooding the entire area with moonlight. Ahead stretched a series of raised wooden beams, dusty plasterboard lying between them.

The entire roof was littered with boxes and tea chests, all dusty and many of them covered with pigeon droppings. Richard could see two of the birds lying crumpled against a tea chest with faded writing on its side.

Denbeigh, he thought. This was Denbeigh's secret lair.

He grasped hold of a piece of pipe that ran down the side of the window and pulled himself the final few feet so that he could get his right foot into the window casement. Then, crumpled into a fetal position in the window, he carefully stretched out his legs and dropped to the floor. He made hardly any noise landing—though his ankle twisted awkwardly and he slumped prone to the floor—but the window slammed behind him like a crack of thunder.

A shadowy figure rose up behind a clutter of boxes in front of him. Then another joined it, this second one not as tall as the first.

"Ah," said Montague Dearlove, "a visitor. Capital!"

The prefect stepped forward around the boxes, moving carefully so that he trod only on the beams, and approached Richard's crumpled figure.

Richard pulled back from Dearlove's outstretched hands, but there was nowhere to go. The fingers grasped his dressing gown collar and he was pulled to his feet. He winced at the pain in his ankle.

Dearlove looked down and smiled. "Hurt ourselves have we, hmm?" He kicked the side of Richard's ankle and the boy slumped sideways against the wall. "Looks painful," Dearlove said.

The other figure scurried across the beams.

"It's Latchpole!" Nigel Dearlove said. "What are you doing here?"

Richard didn't say anything.

Then, somewhere off in the distance, but inside the building, a whistle sounded and then another.

"What was that?" Dearlove inquired, his voice calm. He cocked his head to one side and smiled at Richard.

"A whistle," Dearlove's brother whispered.

Without moving his eyes from Richard, Dearlove lashed out with his right hand and slapped his brother across the face. "I know it's a whistle, brother mine. I want to know why it's there."

Richard shrugged.

Dearlove nodded. "Perhaps someone saw you coming here, hmm?"

"I . . . I don't think so," Richard stuttered.

Dearlove frowned. "No matter," he said, clapping his hands. "We'll have this matter resolved nicely now."

"What do you—"

Dearlove interrupted his brother and barked, "Get the loot."

"Wha—"

He slapped the younger boy again and grabbed his blazer collar—only now did Richard notice that both boys were wearing their usual day clothes. "I said, get the loot." He pushed him away and Nigel almost lost his footing across the beams. "Bring it to me."

Dearlove turned to Richard and smiled. He kicked the ankle again. "How's the foot feeling? Strong enough to walk, hmm?"

Richard could feel tears in his eyes. "I . . . I don't think so," he said.

"Capital," said Dearlove.

Nigel stumbled back across the beams holding a rugby shirt in both hands. The shirt was stuffed with watches, tie clasps, cuff links, pens, some wallets, and various other items. He laid the shirt at his brother's feet and stepped back. Another whistle sounded below them and they could hear voices shouting in the distance.

Dearlove stooped down to the shirt and rummaged through the stolen property. "Now then," he said, "I think we'll hold onto that." He lifted a shiny watch and dropped it into his jacket pocket. "And . . . those." A pair of cuff links shaped like an animal's head—Richard couldn't make out what the animal was supposed to be: a lion, perhaps, or a tiger.

Dearlove lifted a few more items, all of which went into his pockets, and then he lifted the shirt and stood up. "The rest," he said, sounding quite regretful, "is yours." He smiled at Richard.

Was he trying to bribe him? Richard shook his head. "I don't want them," he said.

"Ah," said Dearlove, "I fear you have no say in the matter." He turned to his brother and snapped, "Put it all in his pockets."

Nigel Dearlove looked amazed. "Why? They're ours."

"And now they're his," Dearlove said, sounding almost kind. "Now do as I say and put them in his pockets!"

Richard started to protest and back away but Dearlove kicked his ankle again and this time the tears came.

"Ah, look . . . the cove's crying." Dearlove smiled as his brother transferred all the items from the shirt into Richard's dressing gown pockets. "I like that. A crying cove—nicely alliterative."

His task completed, Nigel threw the shirt to the floor and stepped back.

"Capital!" Dearlove said, smirking. He clapped his hands and pointed to the window. "Now, off you go, back the way you came, there's a good chap. Thanks for dropping by."

Richard looked up at the window. "I . . . I can't go back out there," he said. "I can hardly stand, let alone walk. I'll fall."

Dearlove clapped his hands and laughed. "I do believe you're right," he said, "but let us just make sure, shall we?" He kicked Richard's ankle again. "There, that should do it. Now, let me give you a leg up."

Dearlove stepped forward and lifted the hapless Richard up and pushed him through the window. Before he knew what was happening, Richard was half out, staring down at the ground far below, with Dearlove pushing him by the feet.

He jammed his hands into the window casement and turned his head so that he was looking back into the roof under his right armpit.

What happened next happened quickly.

From nowhere, a shadowy shape appeared. It seemed for all the world as though it had been thrown, suddenly coming into view from somewhere over to the left of the two boys and landing against Montague Dearlove's chest, howling and spitting ferociously.

"What the—"

Dearlove staggered backwards, missing the raised wooden beams and landing heavily on one of the wide plasterboard gaps between them. There was a loud crack.

For a second, Dearlove stood there, his arms pinwheeling behind him. His face still looked calm and Richard thought he could still see the trace of Dearlove's malevolent smile.

Then there was another crack and a flurry of dust as the ancient plasterboard ceiling reacted to the prefect's weight and splintered. Just before he disappeared, Dearlove's eyes fixed on Richard's and they narrowed menacingly. And then he was gone.

There was a distant thud.

As he pulled himself back through the window, Richard saw Nigel Dearlove rush across to the wide hole in the plasterboard and look down.

"Monty," he shouted. "Are you all right?"

There was only a deep groan in response. Then another

whistle and the sound of running feet. And then voices, one of which shouted, "Stay where you are up there!" There was no hint of ambiguity in that instruction.

A CARRIAGE was called to take Montague Dearlove to hospital.

The prefect had broken both legs and the policeman who discovered him suspected that the boy's back may also have been damaged. Only time would tell, he informed Mister Stewart, Mister Grainger, other masters, Reverend Beckett, a depressed-looking Nigel Dearlove, and, of course, Richard, Jem . . . and Bertram Wooton. "Certainly," the policeman said, with a solemn shake of his head, "it's doubtful that 'e'll walk proper again."

Sitting in the tall-backed leather chair, Richard rubbed his swollen ankle and tried not to feel smug.

They were all assembled in the Headmaster's study. The clock in the corner struck four times. Outside the windows, the first signs of a new dawn were glinting behind Biggins Hill.

They had heard how a man had been apprehended in town while trying to burgle a house and he had been discovered to have several items belonging to various boys up at Derwent school—the Headmaster having already informed the local constabulary of the missing possessions. The man had needed little persuasion to explain that he had bought these items in all good faith from a young gentleman who himself was a Prefect at the school. Thus it had been that, fortuitously, as it turned out, the policeman had been on the premises when Dearlove fell through the ceiling.

Mister Stewart turned his attention to Richard. "That was a foolish thing you did, Latchpole," he said, though his voice was not stern. "As it turned out, you were fortunate to come out of it with your life."

Richard nodded. "I know, Sir," he said.

Standing by the Headmaster's side, Mister Grainger

twitched his head twice and smiled. "But a damned fine show, boy," he said.

The Headmaster glanced at his colleague and seemed to wince a little. Then he said, "Quite, Kenneth," quietly.

The policeman switched his helmet into his left hand and reached out his right to tousle Richard's hair. "Looks to me like 'e'll make a good detective when 'e's a bit older." He winked at Richard but when Richard tried to wink back, he closed both eyes. Winking, along with several other things, was something he never seemed able to do.

"And the real hero of the piece?" the Headmaster said. "Where is he?"

Richard looked up. "Denbeigh?"

The Headmaster nodded.

"Seems like we all owe that cat a great deal," Mister Stewart said. "From now on, he has the run of the school."

The policeman sniggered. "With all due respect, 'eadmaster, it strikes me 'as 'ow 'e already 'as!"

THE MUMMY CASE:
A MIDNIGHT LOUIE PAST LIFE
ADVENTURE

Carole Nelson Douglas

"OUT OF MY way, Worthless One!" With these welcoming words, Irinefer the Scribe's sandal scuffs a cloud of desert dust into my delicate nostrils.

I sneeze, elude the kick that follows the scuff and duck into the nearest doorway.

I may be Worthless, but I would think one of the Sacred Breed would get a little more respect in this Necropolis.

But when a Pharaoh dies, two things are certain: the eternal embellishment of his royal tomb will finally end, and the endless plotting by grave robbers to sack his tomb will begin.

Here on the shores of the river Nile, "eternal" and "endless" are pretty flexible concepts. I am lucky that we of the Sacred Breed are accounted to possess nine lives. Frankly, with such a heritage, there is little need for us to partake in stripping down to our remaining *Ka*s and crossing the River of Death with our human master.

Even a Pharaoh is only accorded one *Ka*, or material soul. You would think these one-*Ka* wonders would not be so hasty to rip we of the Sacred-Breed-of-Nine-*Ka*s from our earthly hides before our appointed times. But those unfortunate enough to have attended Nomenophis I, who decreed that his household servitors should be present in his tomb in more than pictorial fashion, had no choice. So came the ceremonial gutting, the claustrophobic swathing in a length of linen as long, narrow, and winding as the river Nile, and even the household cat ends up with its empty hide preserved in its original shape and its innards in a jar more suitable for a potent attar of lotus. So much for being a Sacred Breed.

Yet some, especially the humans under discussion, consider Egypt the height of civilized society in these times and climes.

Perhaps I am a bit jaded. I have recently lost my own mother to the prevailing customs.

Our recently designed family cartouche bears the Eye of Horus, a symbol of theft and restitution. In one of those gory tales religion the world over seems to favor, the Egyptian god Horus's eye was stolen by his jealous brother Seth, but was restored by order of a court of gods. Perhaps this is where the "eye for an eye" adage I have heard in my travels came from. Or perhaps this is where the expression, also heard in my travels, "gypped" came from.

Since my mother and I were apparent imports to this land, being as black as a ceremonial wig rather than the usual burnt-cinnabar shade of both the people and felines who inhabit the Nile valley, we occupied an unusual place here.

The Egyptians called us by unpronounceable syllables we ignored whenever possible, but my moniker translates to "Heart of Night."

I suppose the title is a comment on our family's ebony good looks. My mother was known as Eye of Night, since it was her job to keep a vigilant watch on the persons and events surrounding Pharaoh, and to warn him of any untoward acts, such as attempted assassination.

It was obviously in her personal interest to keep our Pharaoh alive as long as possible.

Unfortunately, he died of indigestion, an internal affair my mother could have done nothing to prevent.

So passed his servants, including my esteemed maternal parent, in a paroxysm of the embalming arts that left the linen supply of Thebes in a severe shortage.

Not being a member of the Pharaoh's household, I escaped the general weeping and winding to live to mourn my mother's passing.

Unfortunately, I have lost not only a mother, but also my sole connection to the palace, where once I had visiting privileges as the offspring of a member of Pharaoh's bodyguard.

This has meant I must make my way in the City of Cats near the Necropolis. This is not the fabled Bubastis where Bastet Herself, mother of all cats, reigns, but a feline colony that forages in the shadow of the Pyramids, catching vermin unhoused by the constant construction and begging food from the artisans and slaves always laboring on the massive tombs, which give the term "work in progress" an entirely new dimension.

Since I am suspected of being a foreigner, and am now also an orphan bereft of parental protection, life after mother's death has not been easy.

The resident feline in the rooms beyond my doorway shelter swats me on the posterior.

"Out of my house, familyless foreigner. Positionless beggar!"

Like ill-tempered master, like servant, I think. I ebb before a paw gloved in sphinx-colored fur, a lean Abyssinian with a revolting kinship to the metalwork feline statues scattered about the royal city. Even the commonest felines here, being considered Sacred, think that they are to the linen and bronze born.

I slink away, contemplating another tasty repast of locusts and cactus-cider.

If only I could demonstrate that I possess some of my mother's peerless hunting instincts, I could win a place in the palace and sleep on an ebony-and-ivory inlaid chair with a zebra-hide pillow.

I would look very good against zebra-hide.

A hiss erupts from behind the mud-daub wall of another house.

I arch my back, preparing for defense.

But this sound is a *psst* for attention rather than the usual *ssst!* of hostility.

An aged Abyssinian who wears a palace collar is escorted by a pair of husky Necropolis cats, commoners, but uncommonly large.

"Heart of Night, I wish a word," says the old one.

"You are Ampheris, Counter of the Royal Vermin."

As an "outside" cat, Ampheris was not considered part of the royal household and thus escaped the recent bagging, binding, and burying.

"True. A pity that your revered mother has passed to the Underworld. She was a peerless hunter. Have you any talent along that line?"

I edge into the shade they occupy as if they owned it.

Ampheris nods at his bodyguard. They push a shallow bowl of sour goat's milk toward me. I lap delicately inside the scummy outer ring and consider. This is a serious matter if I am being offered drink. My whiskers twitch more at the scent of opportunity than at that of rancid milk.

We all crouch on our haunches.

"What is up?" I ask.

One bodyguard growls, as if I had made a jest.

The old man answers. I doubt his henchmen can talk. "It is what is up . . . and walking . . . that is the question, Son of She Who Sat Beside Pharaoh's Sandal." The royal grounds-keeper is so old that his whiskers never stop trembling.

"Something walks here, in the Valley of the Kings? Or in the palace within the city?"

"Here," Ampheris hisses, his whiskers quivering anew. "Have you not heard?"

"I am not exactly *persona grata* in this Necropolis."

"I see why you are held apart. Perhaps it is the foreign words you employ, such as this '*persona grata.*' What language is that? Manx? Mesopotamian?"

"No, nothing edible. Something I picked up on my travels among the uncivilized tribes in the lands across from where the Nile empties into the sea."

"There is nothing solid beyond where the river Nile empties into the sea. But there is something . . . semisolid . . . here on the Necropolis under the shadow of the Pyramids."

I keep mum; that is the best way to learn things in the Eye of Horus game. My mama told me that much.

"I have seen it," one bodyguard growls, sounding ashamed. "In all my seven lives I have never seen anything so terrifying. A mummy that walks."

I nod to gain time. How can a mummy walk? The first thing the embalmers do is wrap every limb up tighter than the Pharaoh's treasure. Even a dead mummy cannot crawl. And they are all decidedly dead. I tell these Sacred ninnies so.

The old guy nods. "Yet this apparition has been seen by others of our kind here. It walks . . . upright. It . . . gleams linen-white in the moonlight."

"Has anyone attempted to question this restless mummy?"

One bodyguard catches my ruff tight in nail-studded paws. "Listen, stranger, you would not be so glib if you encountered this abomination. You would draw back and slink away and count yourself lucky to do so."

I shrug off his big mitts. "Maybe I would. And maybe I would not. Especially if there were something in it for me."

Their six amber eyes exchange glances before returning to confront my green ones.

"Should you banish this restless spirit," Ampheris says slowly, "the Sacred Breed of the Necropolis would deign to accept your unworthy presence. We would allow you to live and hunt among us."

"As if I would want to! No, I seek a more fitting reward. My mother's old position at the palace."

"Impossible! That is awarded at the discretion of Pharaoh."

"Perhaps you could trot indoors and put in a good word for me with Nomenophis II."

"For what?" snorts one of the bodyguard.

Ampheris nods and trembles. "Put this unnatural mummy to rest and we will see."

"It might be Nomenophis I, has anyone considered that? He is the most recently dead human of note."

Ampheris wrinkles his already creased forehead fur into a semblance of sand dunes. "But the mummy that has been glimpsed is not human."

"Of course it is not human if it is mummified, yet walking. It may be a demon, or a god. One never knows."

"Idiot foreigner!" scoffs a bodyguard. "This mummy is of our own breed."

"You mean that a mummified *cat* stalks the Necropolis?"

"Exactly," Ampheris says. "I fear that Pharaoh would not be sufficiently grateful for your laying such a thing to rest, as it is not his royal sire. The most reward you can hope for is a better toleration of your presence among the Sacred Breed."

I shrug. Any improvement in my status is a step up, and I come from a long line of high-steppers.

BY THE time the Sun God's boat is sinking slowly in the West, I have accosted and interrogated most of the individuals whose names were given to me.

It has not been easy. I have had sand kicked in my face and tail, and have been spit at and hit. I have even had to resort to pinning my witnesses against a wall until they burp up their stories like so many hair-balls.

My last victim . . . I mean, witness, is Kemfer the jeweler's companion. He is a wiry but cowering sort who wishes only to be off the streets before night falls and "it walks" again.

"How tall?" I ask.

"T-two tail-lengths. Let me go please. My master is calling me home for supper."

I do indeed hear a human repeating "mau, mau," the Egyptian word for cat. "You say it walks upright on two legs, like a human? Then why do you think it is a cat?"

"The upright ears, you imbecile! Oh, sorry, I did not mean to call Your Honorableness names. Please let me go. It darkens."

"But you saw it by night?"

"Yes, and I will go forth by night no more."

"Are you sure you did not see the ears of Anubis?"

Now the creature trembles like old Ampheris. "The jackal-headed embalming god? Say not so, for then we are all doomed!"

"Well, I could use the company," I reply sourly. At least this sorry specimen of the Sacred Breed has a home to go to by night.

I relax my grip. The creature whines and kicks up a dust devil of sand as he streaks away.

I shake my head, only partly to dislodge the stray grains from my ears. My dear departed mama, foreign-born or not, was worth twenty of these craven Necropolis cats.

I see my only option is to hunt this apparition myself. And since pale funereal wrappings are its hallmark, I shall have to do so by night. At least it will not see me first.

I head down the mean streets that twist and turn past houses warmed by window-squares of lamplight toward the deserted valley where only the dead keep each other company.

I do not believe in risen spirits, mummified or not, but I have heard ample testimony that something unnatural prowls the Valley of the Kings.

I call upon the protection of Bastet as I move alone toward the artificial mountain range of tombs glowing softly gold in the last rays of the departing Sun God.

The hot sands are already cooling beneath my pads and

night's sudden cloak blends into my despised dark fur. I am unseen but not sightless, silent but not mute, uncertain but not fearful.

Once human habitation has been left behind, only sand and stone stretch around me. I pause to listen to the skitter of the night, the scratch of verminous claws, the sinister hiss of scales slithering over sand, the distant call of a jackal.

I hear a sudden scramble behind a broken pyramid stone left to mark its own grave in the desert. This may be some nocturnal drama of stalk and kill, dueling beetles, anything normal to the night, but I hasten over, leap atop the cut stone and peer beyond.

My keen night vision sees sands swirling up, a mouse in their midst, eyes gleaming red, and a stiff, plunging, ghostly white figure lurching after it.

The hair lifts along my spine and tail.

For this creature indeed walks upright on two legs, yet its head has a distinctly catlike profile. Were it more than two tail-lengths tall, I would take it for the mummified form of Bastet herself, She of the Human Female Body and the Feline Head.

But all statues I have seen of Bastet cast her in a gigantic mold, three human-heights high. Even if the sculptors exaggerate in the way of men personifying gods, Bastet must be at least of human height.

Whatever this monster's composition or identity, I must challenge it, or fail.

I dive into the fray below, my arrival freeing the desert mouse to retreat into a crack in the stone block.

I am left facing a furious monster, a growling, spinning, spitting dervish of aggravated linen. Funereal wrappings whip around the figure like human hair. I snag one with a claw and begin pulling. Perhaps the apparition is disembodied beneath the wrappings. Perhaps I will free a trapped spirit. . . .

I am hit by a dust-spout of linen and knocked onto my back.

The weight crushes me to the desert floor until my spine is cradled by sand. My claws keep churning, snagging in linen and pulling, cutting, until loosened wrappings fall over my face, smothering me.

I fight the toils of the funereal art, digging my own grave deep into the sand, providing my own shredded cerements. My strength ebbs, and the monster atop me has grown no less heavy with the loss of its linens.

Yet it tires too. I finally open my grit-caked eyes to discover we have both ground ourselves into a sand-trap, our contending bodies frozen from further motion by the sand our fight has kicked up.

I feel matted fur sprouting like grass between the rows of savaged linen. Only the creature's face remains shrouded. Faint, eerie and still-angry moans emit from it.

I heave upright, dislodging drifts of sand over my foe. After moments of furious kicking, I am upright and my exhausted opponent is encased in sand from neck to foot. Talk about a mummy case.

It now is high time to solve the mystery of the resurrected mummy. I start pawing delicately at the facial wrappings, loose but still intact.

I am beginning to suspect exactly *what* the mummy is.

A few dreadfully crumpled whiskers spring out from the unwinding linen. Then a spray of sand from a choked mouth. Finally I unveil an eye, which reflects gold in the moonlight, and I now know *who* it is.

The eye is green.

"Mummy!"

A hiss and spit are my only reward.

I unwind further, at last revealing the sadly abused fur and face of my supposedly former mother, Eye of Night.

"But you are three days dead!"

"Close," she agrees, struggling upright.

Her once-sleek black fur is mottled into curls by the linen's long press. Her poor tail has been bound to her body like a broken limb. Her mouth is dry with sand.

She pants. "And three days starved. See what you can get me."

I turn to the crack.

LATER, AFTER a desert buffet of fare far below the palace menu, my mother sits licking her lackluster fur in the moonlight, and tells me her story in a voice hoarse and shaking with anger.

"First," she says, "I have been prevented from joining my master in the afterlife. I will not sit beside his royal sandal on guard for eternity. Whoever has done this shall pay."

"Still, I am glad to see you alive."

"I will not be able to enjoy my additional life unless I find the person who has done this."

"Then the one behind your resurrection was human?"

"In word and deed. I was taken to the embalmer, where I was . . . hit upon the head. I naturally assumed the blow would be fatal to my earthly body and that I would awake in the underworld in the court of Pharaoh, in my rightful place of Pharaoh's Footstool."

I nod.

"But when I awoke, I was . . . alone. Wrapped in linen, it is true, but with my insides intact. I was neither here nor there, but in some blasphemous in-between state, that I knew immediately. But though I could see that, I could not see past these blinding bindings that you have removed." She pawed the piled linen strips.

"Why? Why was I not permitted the ritual death and resurrection in the underworld? Was this some way to harm my master after death? It is a great puzzle."

"The great puzzle is that you are still alive, honored parent. You were abandoned in bindings in the waste between the Valley of the Kings and the Necropolis. You should have died of hunger, heat or thirst, or been easy prey for some jackal. Yet you fought to free yourself from the bindings, and your struggles were seen by the Necropolis cats, who feared you as a demon."

"I was hungry. Hungry! As if I were alive. I could barely move at first, but finally my writhings loosened the linen and I could flail along like a fish spit out of the Nile to the shore."

"No doubt you bewailed your lot."

"I screamed to high heaven."

"No wonder they took you for a monster." I stood up and began to dig in the sand.

"Excuse me, lad, but I do not think now is the time for a bathroom break, not when we face a conspiracy of great umbrage and import to all of Egypt. Pharaoh must not be cheated of his attendants in the afterlife. It is sacrilege."

"Perhaps," I say, still kicking sand, "but I think it is also something else far more common to this world than the next."

She sees that I have contrived to bury her wrappings under a mound of sand.

"You conceal the evidence of this outrage?"

"You must take on a new identity. You are not known in the Necropolis except by name and position. I can introduce you as my aunt from . . . Sumeria."

She rises weakly to her feet and stamps one. "Can you not understand, Heart of Night? My duty to Pharaoh is not over, so long as whoever has separated us for eternity lives."

"Oh, I see that perfectly well, Auntie . . . Jezabel. That is why we must keep you dead and buried until we can expose the criminal."

"How?" she wails in a fit of maternal exasperation.

"First," I say, "we must discover what and why. Only then will come 'who.' "

MY MAMA is no shrinking lotus, but even she pauses when she realizes what our next step must be.

"You wish us to disturb the dead? To break into the tomb and desecrate the royal resting place?"

I have led her into the base of the Necropolis for a long drink from the potter's jar where he keeps water to moisten his wheel. Not a soul, human or feline, has stirred. Ordinarily the Sacred Breed overruns the Necropolis night and day, but the mummy sightings have driven them indoors.

"It is necessary. There is something I must see for myself in Pharaoh's tomb."

"I suppose," she says glumly, trying vainly to uncurl her whiskers by wetting them in the jar, "that is the place that I was meant to be."

"Exactly. Taking me there only fulfills your disrupted destiny. Besides, I know little of tomb construction, and I imagine you must have heard the plans discussed in the palace."

"Endlessly," she says tartly, rising off her haunches. "Then let us be off. I need to stretch my limbs."

I follow her lead, not caring to mention that her tail bends crookedly to the left. My mama has much in common with Bastet, in that she can be a benign godlike force and also one Hatshepsut of a demon-raiser when riled. Especially when raised from the dead.

The walk is long and the moon has only sailed halfway through the sky-bowl when we pause in the awesome shadow of the pyramid. This man-made mountain, smooth as sandalwood and as precisely pointed as an arrowhead made for a behemoth, seems like a monument worthy of its mighty occupant, Death.

My mama has finished lamenting her impious fate, though, and is all business.

"There are secret ways into every pyramid. Stones that balance upon the weight of a hair to spring open. Sniff for air."

So I come to scraping my nose raw along stone seams so narrow the advertised hair could hardly slip into them.

Suddenly my mama stretches up her front feet. Just as suddenly they plunge forward back to the level, taking her with them. I find the stone has swung open wide enough to admit a mouse. Apparently my food-starved mama fell right through. I must grunt and groan my way past, much compressing my innards. Maybe hers were removed after all. . . .

"Hush!" she warns from within.

I sense a draft of air and we soon are following it up a long stone-paved ramp.

"I have seen the plans," she hisses in the dark. "No one expects a cat, no matter how sacred, to understand the science of humans. But living in the palace taught me the value of learning the humans' labyrinthine ways."

Whatever, I just hope she can lead us out of this maze.

Then I see the light. My mama is a haloed silhouette ahead of me. She stops.

"This is wrong, Heart of Night. No one should be in the pyramid now."

"Not even some artisan finishing up a frieze?"

"No one."

Mama pads grimly forward, and I follow.

The passage opens into another, then finally into a large chamber lit by the flicker of an oil lamp. I brush by my mother to reconnoiter. She may know her pyramids, but I know the perfidy of humans from my time in the Necropolis.

But no humans are present, just the flickering lamp scenting the air with a rancid odor. Or, rather, the only humans present are a painted parade upon the walls. Several Eyes of Horus gaze down on me, as well as a number of insect- and animal-headed gods. I do not spot the Divine Bastet.

I do spot the massive stone sarcophagus that occupies the center of the room.

Mama jumps atop this with an impressive leap for one in her recent condition.

"It is untampered with," she reports with satisfaction. "In fact, from up here, I see no signs of disruption."

"There must be something. Why else the lamp?"

I take advantage of its erratic illumination to study the paintings. The figures, so stiff in their ceremonial headdresses, seem to move in the uncertain light. I see Nomenophis ministered to by serving girls. Offering something to wing-armed Isis. I see sacrificial geese and bulls. I see the noble cat in several representations, all sitting, all in formal profile, like the people. Like the people, the cats are all a burnt-sand color, ruddy-brown.

All except one.

The painting depicts Nomenophis in his throne room. Officials and gods gather 'round. At his feet crouches, not sits, a single cat. She is black.

"Look, Mama! You are in one of the paintings!"

"Hush, boy. Of course I am. As I should be here in my mummified form, with a canopic jar of my vitals nearby. Instead I am robbed. Robbed of my immortality. The painting is a lie! I am no longer Pharaoh's Footstool! . . ."

Her voice has risen to echo off the stone walls.

"Hush," I tell her in a reversal of roles. "Whoever has lit this lamp may still be within hearing."

I leap up beside her and survey the room in all its glory. I know Nomenophis inhabits a richly painted and inlaid mummy case beneath this stone sarcophagus. I know that beneath that his linen-wrapped mummy wears jeweled gold headpiece and collar.

But the tomb itself has not been breached.

I look around, until my eyes rest upon something that should not be here, but is.

My mother ceases her mourning long enough to notice and follow my fixed gaze.

"My mummy! It is here."

Indeed, a wrapped white figure of a cat sits upon a costly

throne (quite appropriate placement for one of the Sacred Breed).

"Who has usurped my place?" my mama demands, assuming the very same combative crouch in which she is depicted so handsomely on the tomb wall.

"I am not sure that anyone has."

"And what does that mean?"

I am too busy casting my particular Eye of Horus, representing theft and restitution, about the premises. I spy a pile of linen windings near the oil lamp on the floor. The inspiration of Bastet floods my brain.

"I apologize for urging you to er, shut up earlier, Mama. I think you should resume your caterwauling, but first . . ."

In a few minutes my mama's finest notes are bouncing off the sober faces of Isis, Osiris, Selkis and Neith on all four walls.

I join her, and quite an impressive chorus we concoct in the silence of a deserted tomb.

I soon hear running sandals slapping stones down the long, dark corridor leading toward us. I also hear the sweet sound of curses.

A moment later two kilt-swathed men burst into the lamp-light.

That is when Mama and I proceed to dance atop Nomenophis's sarcophagus.

We are not particularly good dancers, but manage to totter on our hind feet and bat our flailing front feet enough to provide an artistic flurry among the mummy-wrappings that drape our assorted limbs.

"The fury of Bastet," howls one man, falling to his knees and pressing his forehead to the cold stone.

"We have offended the goddess!" screeches the other, doing likewise. "I told you we should not tamper with the mummy of the Sacred One."

At this, two of the Sacred Ones leap off the sarcophagus on

to the temptingly revealed naked backs of the prostrate worshipers of Bastet.

Claws dig deep and often. The wretches's howls mingle with our own. They rise to evade our rear harrying, and find their faces being inscribed with the sacred sign of Bastet: four long parallel tracks repeated to infinity.

Soon we are alone in the tomb, listening to the eerie echoes of tormented escapees.

I leap off the royal masonry to meet the mummy who has replaced my mama.

"Heart of Night," she calls after me. "You have seen the Revenge of Bastet. Touch not the cat."

"I do not touch the cat . . .

" . . I level it." With one paw-blow I knock the mummy over and begin unraveling the wrappings. I am getting good at this.

While my mama howls her horror (receiving fresh echoes down the corridor with every bleat), I turn the mummy into shredded wheat.

Lo, this mummy's innards have been left inside too, only they gleam hard and gold in the lamplight.

"Those are the royal artifacts of Pharaoh," my mama says from her perch, stunned.

I nod. "That is why you were shuffled into some spare wrappings and thrown into the desert to die. Your false image here hid the items the servants filched during the funeral. Even as Pharaoh in all his richness was lowered into his sarcophagus, those vermin were wrapping priceless trinkets into a feline-shaped treasure chest. No wonder they fled just now as if the breath of Bastet were smoking their heels behind them."

"But they escaped."

"Marked by the tracks of Bastet? People will comment on their condition, and in their current state they will not have the wits to conceal anything. Also, the stone is askew that opens the secret passage we used. Someone will soon notice.

We must guard the mummy treasure until the authorities arrive."

"But that may take hours, even days."

"Shall I go out and hunt food first, or you?"

SO IT is written that when Pharaoh's guard came to his father's tomb two days later, after the thieves had been found and confessed, a fierce black cat was found crouched over the spilled booty from the mummified cat wrappings.

The mummy of the former Pharaoh's cat, the valiant Eye of Night, was missing and presumed to have been assumed into the underworld by Bastet Herself, whose Terrible Tracks still marked the backs and faces of the would-be thieves.

And so it is now inscribed on the tomb walls of Nomenophis II, who will in his own day go into that underworld that all Egyptians long for, that the position of Pharaoh's Footstool is once again occupied, by Heart of Night, son of Eye of Night, who will live in human memory for two thousand years . . . or possibly more, so long as Bastet and the Sacred Breed are revered to the ends of the earth.

The Eye of Horus, representing theft and restitution, never sleeps. Evil-doers, read Heart of Night's cartouche and weep.

M   99000134
Cat crimes through time

OLD CHARLES TOWN LIBRARY
CHARLES TOWN, WV 25414

(304) 725-2208